Moonlight Kin Vol. 1

Moonlight Kin 1: A Wolf's Tale

Moonlight Kin 2: Aidan's Mate

Moonlight Kin 1: A Wolf's Tale

1

Damon Phelan Laroche scented his prey as she walked alone down the frost-covered cobblestone street. She smelled of fresh dandelions on a dewy spring morning. Brightness and light. Feminine heat.

Too bad she had to die.

The Lycanian Elders had spoken. The only way to end centuries of violence was to kill the woman, Madeleine Lucine Valois, known to all Lycans as *The Hunter*.

Damon crumpled the photo he carried. He no longer needed it. Now that he had Madeleine's scent, he could find her anywhere, anytime.

The cool New England breeze brought him more tantalizing information about the doomed woman. Damon shook his head and his brow furrowed. No, that couldn't be right. He inhaled deeply, convinced that his acute senses had somehow made a mistake.

They hadn't.

Damon's heart began to pound, raging in his ears as he struggled with the astonishing truth.

Blood did not taint her delicate hands.

How could this be?

The answer was it could not.

Werewolf blood may visibly wash off after a kill, but the scent took several *months* to wear off. Even the slightest drop would be evident to a Lycan. Yet there was no denying what his senses relayed.

Damon froze.

He knew Madeleine was the latest werewolf hunter. As the only child in her family, it was her duty to hunt and bear the next generation. She'd inherited the dubious title of Hunter from her aged father, the despised Gaston Valois, who'd inherited it from his father before him and his father before him.

So how had she remained unaffected?

Once again, Damon's nose sifted the cool night air, sharing intimate details with the natural predator within. Details he wished he wouldn't have learned.

Madeleine Valois, The Hunter, was *untouched*.

Damon's mind reeled at the news, while the visceral impact tightened his groin. As Alpha, the pack depended on him to defend and protect them. His seed would bring the next generation into being. As a man, he could not ignore the urge to taste—to conquer, the *forbidden*.

How could she have reached this age and remain untried? Unclaimed? He had to be mistaken.

Damon took a step back into the darkened alley. Humans made no sense at all. Werewolves never left females unprotected. If the women were attacked, injured or worse, there would be no way of ensuring pure bloodlines and the continuation of the species.

He shook his head. *Stupid humans*, he thought with a mixture of pity and sorrow. *When will they ever learn?*

Turning, Damon allowed the comfort of night to embrace him. His eyes were as accustomed to the dark as they were to daylight. He made his way down the narrow alley, past the putrid garbage cans, until he reached the back wall of the New Salford post office.

His muscles bunched beneath his skin as he crouched and then leapt to the roof effortlessly, landing silently on the shingles. His human form was no hindrance to his wolf-enhanced athletic abilities.

Bones popped in his neck, as Damon rolled his head to relieve the tension. It had been a long time since he'd hunted a human. And he'd *never* hunted a woman. Like hogs, sheep, or cattle, he found no sport in the kill.

This was no ordinary woman, he reminded himself.

She was the Hunter and her family was the keeper of the Book of Lycan. The thought of the information that book held diminished any temptation he might've felt, along with any mercy. Somewhere in that weathered tome was a record of his brother Jacque's death and Damon intended to find it, even if it meant using the woman to do so. Once he had the book in his hands, then he'd carry out Madeleine's death sentence.

Waves from the cold Atlantic crashed with ferocious fervor against the rocky shore in the distance, echoing off the brick walls of the historic New England buildings. Madeleine's journey home would take her right past him.

Low clouds hung ghost-like from the night sky, their figures haunting, menacing, and changing with each blast of cool spring air. A foghorn up the coast moaned deep, its lonesome bellow calling out to tiny boats unfortunate enough to be upon the turbulent sea.

Damon's emotions mirrored the water, swirling dangerously close to the surface like an eddy.

Madeleine paused at the entrance to the alley, tilting her head from side to side, listening. He knew she couldn't see him from his rooftop vantage point, but Damon had a clear view of her.

Untamed hair cascaded past her shoulders in a silken blanket of gold so pale that it appeared white under the half-moon. Her delicate oval face glowed, illuminating the darkness. Full red lips, the color of ripe apples in fall, practically begged him to kiss them. Her vibrant blue eyes sparkled with intelligence…and uncertainty.

Damon swallowed hard, fighting the unexpected lust that racked his body. He'd been too long without a woman. That was all. It wasn't her nearness that affected him. The signals of anger and arousal were similar enough to be easily confused. The wires in his body had simply gotten crossed. Damon continued to watch from the safety of the roof.

Madeleine wore oversized clothing, which seemed to swallow her in the darkness. An ill-fitting shawl with bits of scraggly yarn poking out like fuzzy barbed wire cloaked her slender shoulders.

He continued to stare. Trying to see past the image she projected. To Damon's unfettered eyes, Madeleine's attempt to hide her form failed miserably. Without thought, he inhaled, breathing in her musky richness. In another week, she'd be in heat.

Need assailed him. Restless and angry, it reached inside and pulled at the very core of his existence. Unaccustomed to the loss of control, Damon growled, annoyed that he had to rein in his baser instincts.

If it weren't for the book, he'd kill her now and be done with it. But his people were counting on him to get to the truth. The Elders might not care about the Book of Lycan, but the local pack did. They'd lost too many members to just let it go.

Madeleine shuddered at the sound of his warning growl, her eyes growing wide as she stared into the darkness, searching for its source.

Come to me, Damon willed in an attempt to enthrall her.

The wind gusted, sifting through his hair, before taking tiny bites out of his exposed flesh. Yet Damon barely felt the cold as he basked in the glow of her ethereal beauty.

Madeleine's eyes glazed and she stepped into the alley. Her footfalls tolled heavy on the cobblestones as she dragged her feet forward. Damon could see the struggle from within taking place as he forced her to move toward him. Her will was strong, but his was stronger. A second later Madeleine's face pinched with pain and a small cry escaped her throat.

The mournful sound shattered Damon's concentration. His chest seized as her pain lashed out at him.

She blinked twice and shook her head to clear it. Free from his thrall, Madeleine whirled around and hurried down the street, without so much as a backwards glance.

Shocked, surprised, and more than a little intrigued, Damon stared at her retreating form. No one had ever broken from his hypnotic thrall. It was strong and especially effective on women.

But not on Madeleine.

Was it her Hunter instincts that made her so strong or something else?

Damon threw his head back, releasing a wailing howl, which pierced the relative tranquility of the spring night. He heard doors slamming, windows clattering shut, and locks fastening, along with the rapid beat of a fluttering heart.

Madeleine. Her name was a curse and a dream that remained mired in his churning emotions.

He howled once more, for all to hear, claiming his pack, his territory—*the woman...*to do with as he willed. A smile curved Damon's mouth before he melted into the shadows.

Soon, he thought.

Madie pulled the corners of her gray woolen shawl together, her fingers numb from the cold. Shivers racked her body as the bone-shattering howl shook her to the core. Her boots clip-clopped on the cobblestone as she picked up her pace.

The fog closed in, swirling around her, so dense that the air seemed to squeeze from her lungs. She didn't know why she'd had the overwhelming urge to enter the darkened alley. Commonsense told her it was foolish, yet she'd gone anyway, compelled by an unknown force. Her heart skittered in her chest while her stomach coiled in fear.

Madie hurried along the uneven bricks, stumbling when her boot heels caught in the cobble cracks. She righted herself quickly and continued. The muscles in her legs burned and her lungs ached.

Standing sentry, like gravestones in a cemetery, a few parked cars dotted the sides of the street. Their daytime occupants now tucked safely into bed. Where she should've been hours ago. Long threatening shadows spread out from every storefront. Welcoming in the daylight, the historic Massachusetts's buildings appeared menacing in the darkness. She rushed on.

The howl pierced the cloudy sky again, its mournful sound speaking to something deep within her. Madie's steps faltered as she fought the urge to answer.

Answer?

How was she supposed to do that? Throw her head back and howl?

The thought was ridiculous and a nervous giggle escaped before she could stop it.

It's just a dog. Keep going. It probably wants inside.

The hair on her nape stood on end and her skin prickled. A tingle started at her toes and worked its way up her body. Papa had described that sensation many times when he hunted. Madie glanced over her shoulder, bracing for an attack.

It never came.

Nothing was there.

"Told you it was a dog," she mumbled to herself.

She forced down the anxiety that threatened to lock her muscles and hurried along the frost slick road. The exertion caused puffs of breath to form eerie circles in the cool night air. Her feet and her hands ached from the numbness.

One more block to go.

Something that sounded suspiciously like claws raking stone came from her left. Fear quickly turned to terror. Why had she gone to the midnight horror show? She wished now that she had sided with the town council when they'd suggested more lights on this end of Milford Street. Why hadn't she driven to the movies? The cold punched at her lungs, snatching her breath away.

The bright yellow door to her apartment shone like a beacon up ahead. Unconcerned with how it might look to anyone watching, Madie sprinted toward home. She grabbed her purse off her shoulder and plunged her frozen hand inside, ignoring the pain in her fingertips as she searched desperately for her keys. Her hand closed around the familiar heart-shaped keychain. Triumphant, she snatched the keys, then promptly dropped them onto her stoop.

Her actions mirrored every slasher movie she'd ever seen, including the ones tonight. Desperation clawed at Madie as she bent down to pick her keys up. Whatever was in the alleyway felt *closer*.

"Open, open, open," she commanded. Her fingers trembled as she shoved the key into the lock and turned it. With a soft click, the door opened.

"Thank goodness," she muttered as she rushed inside.

The interior of her apartment was dark. Darker than it had been outside. Madie's heart thudded in her chest, beating double time against her ribcage. She listened for anything out of place. Silence met her.

Did that mean she was alone?

The scrape of stone came again. Madie slammed and locked the door behind her, then threw her back against the wooden structure for good measure. She'd take her chances.

Despite the deadbolt, Madie knew in her bones that whatever was outside could get in if it truly wanted to. She rubbed her hands along her arms, fighting a shiver that had nothing to do with the cold.

She pushed away from the door and flipped on all the lights. Madie checked all the prime monster-hiding areas, behind her yellow throw-covered couch, in the closet, the shower, and under the bed. Grateful for once that her apartment wasn't spacious.

Handpicked for its coziness, this dwelling stood for so much—college, future dreams, and true freedom. It might be small, but it was home...at least until she graduated.

Madie walked across her modest parlor into the kitchenette. A cup of green tea would banish the last of the cold and steady her frayed nerves.

Holding the mug with both hands, she blew on the surface of the hot liquid, inhaling the pungent musty odor as she debated whether to phone her father. They'd been close at one time. Well as close as a father, who'd wanted a son, could be to his only child. But those days were long gone. They'd died the same day her mother passed.

The warmth of the mug chased the last of the chill from her hands, but couldn't penetrate the bone-deep fear. The howl kept forcing its way into her thoughts. She remembered childhood stories passed down by Papa about two-legged wolves that walked upright. Said to look human, the creatures could stand beside you, enthrall with a single thought, and you wouldn't know the truth until they ripped your heart out.

At the time, Madie had dismissed the stories as nonsense, thinking Papa had obviously read one too many fairytales. Yet, there was no mistaking the howl. It *had* been a wolf. Hadn't it? She knew wolves didn't come near the city. In fact, other than Wolf Hollow in nearby Ipswich, they were extinct to the area.

Something else lurked in the darkness tonight.

A shiver tickled her spine and traveled all the way to her toes. Madie took a sip of tea, praying the warm elixir would ease some of her tension. "You've just watched one too many movies. Let it go."

She shook her head and finished the contents of the cup. She wouldn't call. There was no sense feeding Papa's delusions. They were already bad enough and were growing worse by the day.

Madie put the cup in the sink, then headed upstairs to bed. "No more midnight horror movies for you. Next you'll start believing that werewolves are real and the grotesques on the courthouse come to life."

Even as she said the words, Madie walked unerringly to the corner of her bedroom and picked up her baseball bat. The weight of the heavy wooden club in her hand calmed her instantly.

Better safe than dead.

2

Damon arrived home agitated by his response to Madeleine Valois and the information he'd obtained.

Untainted—untouched.

Impossible!

He slammed his fist onto the thick antique table, shattering the wood, and sending splinters flying through the air. *Damn, that was a new purchase.* His hand stung where the small iron spike bit into his palm. Blood oozed from the cut, but in a matter of hours, the injury would disappear as if no wound ever existed.

Such was the blood of the wolf.

The fire in the hearth blazed as he tossed the remnants of the furniture into the hungry flames. The maple wood gave off a sweet odor as the smoke rose up the chimney. As if sensing his torment, the wind outside his colonial home moaned.

Damon growled, catching his wild reflection in the mirror above the mantle. He looked tired. Dark circles hung like crescent moons beneath his bloodshot eyes. His unruly sable hair stood on end, giving him a maniacal appearance.

He was running out of time. The full moon would arrive in two weeks. Already he could feel its pull by the ache in his bones as they shifted and thickened beneath his skin. Despite the tired redness, his hazel eyes had already begun to lighten. By the time the moon ripened, they'd be amber gold.

Damon decided to abide by the Lycanian Elder's ruling, but in his own time. Finding the book came first. As far as he was concerned, the Valois's had violated the peace treaty the second they took his brother, Jacque's life. The act of killing left them open to Lycan law and werewolves weren't known for their forgiveness. In the end, someone would pay for the pack's loss—*for his loss.*

Turning away from the mirror, Damon retrieved the file on Madeleine Valois from a nearby table. Her pale beauty flashed before his eyes, causing a visceral reaction that made his attraction to her difficult to ignore. He longed to touch what his senses had observed.

She was human, he reminded himself again. He didn't *do* humans... anymore.

Damon fisted his hands in frustration, ignoring the stab of pain as his fingernails dug into his tender palm. He raised the wound to his face and leisurely licked away the blood, groaning as the sticky substance washed down his parched throat like a crimson cocktail. The taste was intoxicatingly arousing and enough to make his cock hard. He smiled.

Vampires weren't the only creatures aroused by blood. Of course, they didn't exist. The bad behavior of a few Lycans centuries ago had given rise to the undead myth. Storytellers and fiction writers filled in the rest.

Damon paced back and forth in front of his gray marble fireplace, his footfalls echoing on the hardwood in the still of the house. He picked up the photo on the mantel and studied the smiling faces. He'd been ten at the time the picture was taken. Jacque had been twelve. They'd just gotten new bikes from their dad. It was a big day, a happy day. One he'd remember forever. Damon ran his thumb over the photo. So many great memories cut short thanks to the Hunters. He set the picture back on the mantel and swallowed his grief.

Madeleine wasn't his brother's killer. His senses hadn't lied—at least not about that. He was sure of it. There was no way she could've killed Jacque without getting a drop of blood on her. Even if she wore gloves, the blood would've hit her somewhere. That didn't mean she wasn't somehow involved. She could've very well been an accomplice.

Nevertheless, Damon would follow orders. Carry out the decree. Kill her. Innocent or not.

Soul be damned.

Jacque deserved to be avenged. Blood was blood, he reminded himself.

Damon hesitated. Therein lay his conundrum. Werewolf blood *was* different. No amount of scouring could remove the scent. His keen canine senses would have detected its sharp tang instantly. Yet, Madeleine had smelled of fragrant flowers, feminine musk, and the onset of her monthly heat.

So if the latest Hunter hadn't done the job, then who had killed his bother?

His mind searched back to that painful moment in time. The pack had enjoyed years of uneasy peace with the Hunter until that fateful night two months ago when several Lycans found Jacque dead.

Damon remembered the evening Luc, his Beta conveyed the news in vivid detail. Overcome by grief and rage, the beast inside Damon slipped out and nearly destroyed everything in his own living room.

He shook his head as he ran his palm over the smooth arm of the new brown leather furniture that he'd purchased to replace what he'd ruined. Even now the pain of loss sliced deep.

By the time Damon had calmed down enough to go to the scene of the crime, Jacque's body had vanished, leaving no blood trail to follow.

A cry of anguish ripped from deep inside him as the memory burst forth, shattering his heart again. He couldn't bear to think about what the Hunter had done with Jacque's remains.

Damon imagined all sorts of horrific possibilities, including his brother's wolfen head stuffed and hanging over a mantle at the Valois family estate. Since Jacque's disappearance, four more pack members had gone missing and were presumed dead.

Blood or no blood, the Valoises that claimed this territory had committed the murders. They'd made sure to let the Lycans know by leaving behind their usual calling card, a silver coin with the east coast family's crest on one side. For centuries, the coins had been the way of identifying which branch of the family made the kills. Each Valois family had their own crest and their own coin.

There was no mistaking who was behind the murder. They'd practically signed their name to the heinous deed.

Damon reached into his pocket and pulled out the coin. He rubbed the crest with his thumb, then slipped the coin back into his jeans. He carried the reminder of their treachery with him and would continue to do so until his mission ended.

The family of Hunters left behind a bitter pill to swallow. Madeleine *may* be innocent—for now—but it was only a matter of time before she followed in her family's bloody footsteps. The Valois curse would take care of it, whether she chose to or not.

There was no escaping fate for either of them. Beauty or no beauty, the killings would not happen again, as long as Damon was alive and still Alpha.

His muscles rippled beneath his shirt, straining with each inhalation. Frustrated, Damon calmed his breathing. Nothing made sense. Madeleine was the Hunter, yet she did not hunt. Was Gaston back to his old ways? Given his fragile state of health, it seemed unlikely he'd be able to take down a Lycan in his prime much less the four that had followed since his brother's death.

Blood never lied.

It was obvious Damon needed to do more investigating before he took his suspicions to the Elders. He must be certain. The Elders did not appreciate hunches or innuendos, only facts.

All werewolves knew humans were sniveling creatures, who could not be trusted. Yet in truth, very little was known about the Hunters. Like Lycans, they'd spread out around the world and kept a low profile to avoid discovery. The Elders foolhardily offered a peace treaty with scarce information to go on. The document was intended to prevent any more needless deaths. What it did instead was bind Lycan hands, preventing them from retaliating without permission of the Elders.

Moreover, Gaston Valois complied quickly—too quickly, which should have raised a red flag. Instead, the Elders rushed in, drafting the treaty in haste, before thoroughly investigating Valois's motives for compliance.

The pack now paid the price for their folly.

Damon opened the file the Elders had put together on Madeleine. Scanning the pages briefly, his eyes settled on her class schedule. Mrs. Raven Montgomery jumped off the page. Next to the name was a phone number. So Raven was her professor. Damon smiled, his next move becoming clear. He dialed the professor, pleased when a woman's voice answered the phone.

This will be easy.

Within seconds, the professor was agreeing with everything he said, unable to resist the compulsion in Damon's voice. Soon all would be arranged. The bloodline would be severed and the killer punished.

For the sake of werewolf survival, Madeleine Lucine Valois would die.

3

Madie rushed through the door leading into the art department—late again. Despite it being a Saturday, people milled in the hallway. A sure indication that the class was already full. Students buzzed, clamoring to be heard, their voices rising in excited chatter. The heat and nervous energy was palpable.

Today marked the end of their final art project before graduation. The professor had chosen to hire a live model to close out the class. Failure at this stage wouldn't keep Madie from graduating, but it would lower her overall grade point average.

She paused a moment to catch her breath and tighten her severe ponytail. Sunlight filtered through the windows, causing dust particles to swirl and bob in the bright rays.

Brown wooden stools perched in front of empty easels were arranged in a semi-circular pattern around a center platform. Dr. Montgomery's oak desk had been positioned against the wall in what would normally be the front of the class. Coats and jackets hung from old-fashioned wooden pegs at the back of the room.

Madie removed her coat in a flurry, almost knocking over one of the nearby easels in the process. She steadied the stand, then hung her coat beside the others. She scanned the room for her friend, while wiping her sweaty palms on her oversized sweater. Madie crossed her fingers, hoping against hope that Sarah arrived early enough to save them a good spot.

A hand waving frantically back and forth caught her attention. Madie released a tense breath as relief flooded her. Sarah had scored places over by the windows, right in front of the model's platform.

Madie smiled and gave a quick wave back. She ignored her classmates' curious glances and hushed whispers as she threaded her way through the crowd. She should be used to the gossip about curses and werewolf hunters by now, but the chatter still hurt. When Madie made it to her seat, she opened her case and put her drawing pad onto the easel, then hugged Sarah, who'd jumped up to greet her.

Though close friends, they were as different as Spam was to filet mignon. Sarah was the type of woman who grasped life with both hands, tasting and experiencing whatever her heart fancied.

She had dark luxurious hair, sun-kissed skin, and a bawdy personality, while Madie's white blonde hair clashed with her dark, guarded demeanor. She was the first to admit that she had trust issues. When you grew up cloistered in the Valois family, it was mandatory.

Sarah may not realize it, but Madie lived vicariously through her, since her own personal experiences didn't extend beyond the pages of a book—thanks to years of private tutors, personal bodyguards, and homeschooling.

To grasp life by the horns would require interacting with other people, trusting them. Madie had neither the social skills nor the inclination to do so. She was just happy that she'd managed to find one person to call friend. Madie glanced over at a couple of students who snickered at her, then turned away.

There were worse things in life than only having one good friend. Like having no friends at all.

Sarah held a green pouch in her palm. "Look what you forgot."

Madie took the pouch. "Saved me again. What would I do without you?"

"Forget your head." Sarah laughed and then plopped down on the stool next to her.

"No doubt. Speaking of losing my head, I nearly lost it last night after the movies. By the time I made it home, I'd managed to scare myself silly. Next time, we're watching creature features in the afternoon."

"Wimp." Sarah chuckled.

Madie clucked like a chicken, which made Sarah laugh harder, then she untied the ends and rolled the pouch open to reveal the various pencils inside. Double-checking their sharpness with the pad of her index finger, Madie laid the pencils out in front of her blank canvas and absently arranged them into a straight row.

"The model should be here any minute," Sarah blurted with barely restrained excitement in her voice.

"Sarah Ann, you act like you've never seen a naked man before."

"I've seen plenty of naked men. You're the one who hasn't." Sarah arched a brow in challenge, daring Madie to deny her claim.

Blood rushed to Madie's cheeks. Blushing easily was an unfortunate trait she'd inherited from her mother. "I've seen a naked man before," she muttered.

"Walking in on Jerrod, Tom, Steven, or Michael coming out of the shower doesn't count. They're my brothers." Sarah gave a mock shudder. "Let me just say for the record, 'Ew'. Just thinking about it might send me to therapy."

"Did Steven say that I did it on purpose? It was an accident. I swear." Madie pulled at the collar of her sweater, trying to cool her heated skin. It wasn't her fault Sarah's brothers made a habit out of leaving the bathroom door unlocked while they showered in the morning.

When it came to men, Madie knew she could talk a good game, but in the end that's all it was—talk—she didn't have any firsthand experience. And it wasn't due to lack of trying on her part.

Between homeschooling and her family's kooky reputation, Madie hadn't experienced much of anything, which was just the way her father liked it. From as early as she could remember, he'd drilled it into her head that she had to remain pure of heart, mind, and body. Thanks to his overprotectiveness, she'd become a social pariah.

Sarah, on the other hand, was known to her friends as being a big flirt. Strangers preferred harsher terms like slut or whore. Her friend wasn't a whore, but women can be cruel when it comes to judging other women, especially if those women are prettier than they are and catch the attention of their boyfriends. Sarah loved sex and refused to be ashamed by that fact.

Like Madie, Sarah had started college late and her reputation kept her from making a ton of girlfriends. In each other, they saw a chance to have what they'd desperately needed in their lives. That had been over two years ago and their friendship was still going strong.

Sarah had celebrated her twenty-fourth birthday the week before. Madie's head still ached at the thought of *that* overindulgence. She refused to think about the fact that her own birthday was closing fast and would be upon her in two weeks. Once she hit twenty-five, her fate was sealed—or so her father claimed. Madie didn't believe in curses or fate.

Stop being so melodramatic. Try to enjoy the time that you have left.

Curse or no curse, Madie was stuck with going through with Papa's silly initiation. He was determined to bring her into the *fold*. The only reason he'd allowed her to go to college was because he'd promised her mother before she'd died that Madie could have two years of freedom.

That freedom had cost Madie her inheritance. Gaston had put a freeze on her account that wouldn't be lifted until after her birthday, and even then, it wouldn't happen unless she returned.

"Are you still planning to go home the week after graduation?" Sarah asked.

Madie nodded.

"Are you really going to let your father put you through that silly woo woo stuff?" Sarah voiced Madie's unspoken concerns.

"I don't have a choice. I promised," Madie said. Not that she needed a reminder. It was the only thing on her mind next to graduating. "We need that money to open up the art gallery, remember?"

"I remember," Sarah said. "But everyone has a choice."

If she had any other choice, she would've already made it. "Not me."

None of this would have occurred if her mother were still around. Papa hadn't been the same since her death. Instead of grieving, Gaston had turned his attention on her. Madie couldn't seem to do anything right.

Gaston had always been gruff, but lately he'd become domineering. He wanted to know where she was and who she was hanging out with at all times. He questioned her appearance, especially her hair color. Like it was her fault that she'd been born with blonde hair, not red.

He'd even gone so far as to hire a man to follow her and keep tabs on her movements. When one brave guy got the courage up to ask her out, Gaston paid him to go away, then suggested an arranged marriage instead. Fatherly devotion was quickly becoming obsession.

For the first time in her life, Madie *feared* her father and what he might do.

But she'd vowed to her mother that she'd follow her dreams no matter what. If that meant pacifying Gaston and going through with some ridiculous initiation, then so be it. She'd look after the old musty books and pretend to be the next great white hunter. He'd just have to get over the fact that she wasn't going to kill anything on her watch.

"What about a loan?" Sarah asked.

"You know I can't get one without my father co-signing."

"You're almost twenty-five years old."

"I'm aware of that. I am also painfully aware that I have no real credit. Banks frown on that sort of thing." She grinned. "Besides, Gaston has Mom's fortune, my inheritance, spread out in all the banks in the area. No banker in his right mind would risk losing the Valois's business to appease a broke college student."

"What about out of the area?" Sarah asked.

"I barely make enough to cover rent and expenses. I wouldn't even qualify for a cheap car loan," Madie said.

Sarah's expression grew serious. "So where does that leave you?"

"Up a creek, paddling with a teaspoon." She shrugged. "I'll have to go through the motions. Pretend to become 'Madie the Mad Slayer', then the money will be mine."

Sarah laughed and rolled her eyes. "Sounds easy."

"Yeah, easy," Madie murmured, hoping against hope it would turn out to be.

Her final year of school was almost up and things hadn't worked out the way that she'd planned. Graduation was next Saturday and she was no closer to realizing her dream of owning an art gallery. Before she could get too depressed about it, the door flew open and banged against the wall.

Everyone jumped. All eyes turned, riveted on the man who'd walked into the room.

Madie's breath seized in her lungs.

"Whoa! Talk about making an entrance. I'm in lust. I think I just met my future ex-boyfriend." Sarah kept her voice low, so only Madie could hear her.

She glanced at Sarah. "You're so bad."

"You love me and you know it." She winked. "I better double check my supplies, because I'm not about to miss an inch of him." Sarah's gaze scrolled down the length of the man before reversing direction.

Madie's eyes were drawn to the statuesque man lounging just inside the doorway. He wore a white towel around his trim waist and from the looks of it, nothing more.

Sable-colored hair flowed wildly from his head as if someone had been running their fingers threw it all night. Maybe some lucky woman had. Madie tackled her thoughts before they went any further.

Sinewy muscles rippled beneath tanned skin to form his exquisite chest. Dark hair arrowed south down the hard slab of his abdomen, ending in a perfect 'V' at the white towel snugged around his waist.

No stranger to the gym or a hard day's work, his well-developed arms were lined with veins and flexed with the littlest of movements. The muscles in his long legs rippled with silent power as he shifted his weight. Yet the man wasn't bulky. He looked built for speed, agility, and most of all, *sex*.

Lots and lots of sex.

His relaxed stance screamed confidence. It was the kind of confidence that made his nakedness seem as natural to him as breathing. The kind of confidence that Madie would *never* have in this lifetime. Yet her palms itched to touch him.

His hazel eyes assessed the room slowly, before coming to rest upon her. First *contact* felt like a visceral punch to the gut. Madie stared unblinking—captured by his gaze as he studied her with a curious intensity.

Voices faded. The room seemed to shrink around her, closing in until only the two of them existed. Madie fell into those deep gold-flecked pools, trapped by the liquid honey promises she saw there.

The heat of attraction crackled in the air, sending shivering sparks over her skin. Her heart thundered. Torn between the need to flee and the urge to jump into his arms, Madie clutched her easel.

His unwavering gaze continued to bore holes through her, probing, searching, and studying. But that wasn't what freaked Madie out. It was the hunger she saw, lurking just below the surface. She'd never seen anything like it, nor had that kind of hunger ever been directed toward her.

She attempted to steady herself, her mind a mixture of fear and desire... yet still he held her, refusing to let go.

Dr. Montgomery cleared her throat.

Blinking, the model broke eye contact. Madie felt her energy drain and she dropped back onto her stool, unaware until that moment that she'd even risen. Her nerves tingled like a thousand tiny needles prickling her skin. She took a shuddering breath and slowly released the easel, pretending to smooth the blank paper.

What in the world just happened, she wondered. Her body ached from the loss of contact.

Yet he hadn't *physically* touched her.

"Are you okay?" Sarah's question penetrated her dizzying thoughts.

Madie's lids shot open. "I-I'm fine, why?" She swallowed hard and squared her shoulders, forcing herself to sit up straight.

"It seemed like you were about to run across the room and jump his bones. Not that I blame you, but that's more my style, not yours." Sarah's green eyes narrowed as she searched Madie's face. "Are you sure you're feeling okay?"

She took a deep breath and slowly released it. "Y-Yeah, why wouldn't I be?" Madie gave Sarah a reassuring smile, even though she was shaken from the incident. "I had a head rush, probably from not eating."

"Head rush?" Sarah laughed. "Is that what they're calling lust these days?"

"Sarah!" Madie gasped.

"Oh please, you know it's true. He's yummy." Sarah glanced at the man once more. "Do you know him?"

"No!" Madie said with a little too much force, as she gazed at the model. It took effort, but she finally drew her eyes away from his perfect form. "No," she repeated calmly, sure beyond a doubt that she'd never met him before. Madie ignored the little voice in the back of her mind that said she'd like to. "Why do you ask?"

Sarah snorted. "Because he sure looks like he knows you. Or wants to."

"Don't be silly." Madie's voice cracked, coming out in a high-pitched squeak. "He was probably looking at something out the window."

"I doubt he finds the parking lot fascinating." Sarah grinned. "I'm telling you, Madie, he looked at you like a starving man looks at a turkey sandwich with a side of gravy fries."

Madie glanced back at the model. "Well, he's not looking at me now," she said, unable to hide her disappointment. She'd spent her whole life dreaming of storybook moments and not once had they happened… until now.

The model spoke softly to their professor in a deep rumbling baritone. His bronzed shoulders blocked much of the conversation from the class. Whatever he was saying must've been good because Dr. Montgomery practically purred in response. She'd obviously forgotten she was married.

Madie curled her fingers into fists. The professor's not so innocent reaction tore at her insides and it only got worse when the woman leaned into the man's bulk, lightly placing her fingertips on his thick biceps. He flexed under her touch, and then flashed the instructor a devilish smile that showcased his dimples.

Could he get any hotter?

Madie wanted to scream at her professor to get away from him. She wanted that smile for herself. Strike that—she needed it. The possessive feelings frightened her because they were so utterly foreign. The truth hit Madie a second later—she was *jealous*.

No way!

She couldn't be jealous. It must be the stress of graduation and Papa coming to get her. That had to be it. What else could it be? She didn't even know the guy. Disgusted by her uncharacteristic behavior, Madie looked away. It only took a moment for her traitorous gaze to seek him out once more. Pathetic.

The model turned from the class for a moment. His back rippled as he adjusted the towel, then he faced the group again.

Madie's mouth practically watered in anticipation. Butterflies wreaked havoc in her stomach. She knew that she'd never met him before, but still...

There was something *familiar* about him.

The professor held up her hands to quiet the room.

"Everyone, I'd like to introduce our model. This is Damon Laroche. Our scheduled model cancelled at the last minute. Damon was kind enough to volunteer to fill in and pose for us today. Please give him a warm welcome."

The class exploded in applause, especially the women, many of whom let out inappropriate catcalls.

Once again, those gold-flecked eyes captured Madie's gaze. With an arch of his brow, he issued a subtle invitation. Tightly leashed desire burned from within him, along with some other emotion Madie didn't recognize or understand.

Everything about the man looked feral...and hungry.

Unable to break his pointed gaze, Madie flushed with a sudden rush of heat. Something untamed from deep inside her longed to answer his unspoken invitation.

She imagined their sweat-covered bodies writhing on soft sheets as they came together in a fierce coupling. Her body shuddered and perspiration dotted her brow. His eyes shifted subtly and her nipples tightened painfully beneath the lace cups of her bra.

His knowing gaze roamed from her face to her sensible shoes, taking in her obscured figure. He paused once more on her aching breasts, as if he could see right through her sweater. Need tortured Madie with its invisible hands, plucking at her engorged nipples. Damon's firm lips twitched ever so slightly as if he knew exactly what he was doing to her.

Madie sat breathless, her body quivering with untapped desire.

Unmistakable hunger clouded Damon's eyes turning them nearly molten gold. His body practically hummed with leashed power. The energy emanating from him could have illuminated the entire town of New Salford, Massachusetts for a month. He licked his lips, the movement casual, as if remembering the taste of something decadent.

Madie melted inside. She imagined that tongue tasting her skin and almost spontaneously combusted on her stool. Moisture pooled between her thighs. She squeezed her legs together to stave off the growing need.

A confident slash of a smile teased the corners of his sensuous mouth, and then spread across his handsome face. If it were possible, that wicked grin made him even more devastating.

Entranced, Madie waited in anticipation. Like an expert artisan, her gaze caressed his high cheekbones, playing at his lips, then moved down to his firm chin. She lingered there, cataloguing subtle details that would eventually go into her sketch, before admiring the corded muscles of his neck and wide expanse of his shoulders. Methodically, she retraced her path, returning to his face. She refused to look any lower for fear of what she'd find.

Without preamble, Damon winked and dropped his towel. Several students gasped. Those mesmerizing eyes dared Madie to look. She did, and all remaining logical thought slipped from her mind.

4

Gaston Valois sat at his kitchen table nursing his morning whiskey. He swirled the amber liquid around the tumbler, while he stared at his daughter's picture. She was so like her mother, beautiful...*and weak*. Nothing at all like him. That fact burrowed into his flesh like a tick, slowly sucking away his sanity. He should never have allowed her to go to art school. The two years of freedom had gone to her head.

Not that she'd been totally alone. For the first year, Gaston had hired a bodyguard to watch over her. The man had made sure to keep the young men at her school from sniffing around her. She was born for greatness. The only way to achieve that was by maintaining her purity.

Gaston wasn't about to let her destroy her future by getting herself knocked up by some idiot, who didn't know the first thing about the *real* world. It was only in the last year that he'd allowed her some space by pulling back the protection detail. And look where that got him.

Madeleine was now full of crazy ideas. She wanted so desperately to open an art gallery that she was willing to shirk off her responsibilities to the family. He balked. It wasn't going to happen. Hunters didn't own galleries. Hunters were put on this earth for one thing and one thing only—to kill rogue werewolves.

If a few other wolves were killed by accident in the process, then that was acceptable collateral damage. He wouldn't lose sleep over it.

Her weakness and selfishness was why he'd had to resort to threats and drastic measures. Gaston didn't like the idea of forcing Madie into compliance, but she'd given him little choice in the matter. Without the ritual binding her into the position of Hunter, she'd never fully come into her powers. And she'd need all the help she could get, if she was going to hunt the most dangerous animal on the planet.

A knock sounded on the door, interrupting his thoughts. Gaston glanced at the clock across the room. His guest was right on time.

"Enter." Gaston knew who it would be before the door opened. He'd summoned the man, who he'd one day call son-in-law, to flesh out the next steps in winning his daughter's hand in marriage.

Like any good father, Gaston had done his homework. The man had come from Minnesota after losing his family and his legacy to a feral werewolf pack. Gaston had found the obituaries online and read the headlines in the papers. The deaths had been attributed to animal attacks. He knew better.

The young man's need for revenge resonated with Gaston for he, too had lost loved ones to the werewolves over the years. He had no intention of losing his only daughter, the last of his line, before she had a chance to bear the next generation of Hunter. If that meant coercing her into marriage, then so be it. Fortunately for him, she needed her inheritance desperately enough to agree to just about anything.

Jack Hanson stepped through the doorway and stopped. He was a handsome man with dark hair and gray stormy eyes. Tall and well built, he reminded Gaston of himself in his younger years, except he'd never had dark hair.

"You wanted to speak with me, sir?" Jack asked.

"Yes." Gaston tossed back the contents of his glass. The warm burn of the whiskey shot fire down his throat. "Shut the door behind you and take a seat."

Jack complied.

"Did you bring the proof that I asked for?" Gaston asked.

He nodded and pulled a folder out of his jacket, then dropped it onto the table. "It's all there," Jack said.

Gaston reached for the folder and flipped it open. Inside, the photos of four different people who'd been ripped apart were displayed in gruesome detail. He studied each photo carefully, before closing the file. "And you're sure they're all human?"

Jack nodded. "I checked each one myself. We have to do something. We cannot let the Moonlight Kin pack get away with these murders."

"We won't." Gaston indicated to the seat across from him, then grabbed another glass and filled it. He pushed the tumbler across the table. Jack picked it up as he sat, but didn't take a drink. Gaston refilled his glass, then set the bottle aside.

"What are we drinking to this morning?" Jack's brow furrowed.

"Your future. My daughter's future. Your upcoming wedding. Take your pick." Gaston clinked glasses with the young man, then tossed the shot back.

Jack straightened in his chair. "And what if she's not interested?" He set his glass down onto the table without drinking to the toast.

Gaston's eyes narrowed. "I'm sure you can figure out some way to make her interested. You're a handsome guy. I doubt that you have any problems with the ladies. My daughter is naïve. I've made sure of it. That makes her gullible and ripe for the picking so to speak."

Jack ran a hand through his hair. "What if I'm not her type?"

"Her type? What does being her type have to do with it? I'll make sure that she agrees to go out with you," Gaston said. "All you have to do is close the deal. Since I won't be around forever, I don't really care how you do it. You know what we're up against." He indicated to the folder. "I need someone strong to run this territory. Someone willing to do what it takes to keep these beasts in their place. I haven't worked this hard and this long to lose the eastern territory to the local Lycan pack now."

A tic emerged in Jack's shadowed jaw. "I won't let that happen," he said.

"That's what I'm counting on," Gaston said.

"What about the other territories?" Jack finally took a sip of his drink. His nose wrinkled and he set the glass down.

Gaston poured himself another glass of whiskey. "My brother's sons will take care of those. They're lucky. Their wives bore them many children—all boys. None of my brothers were cursed with a daughter. Their spouses weren't weak like mine." *Or unfaithful.*

"Some people consider a daughter a blessing," Jack said carefully, as he stared at his drink.

"Only fools who don't hunt werewolves." Gaston slammed his tumbler onto the table.

Jack didn't even flinch.

It was one of the many things about the man that Gaston admired. Nothing seemed to scare him or rattle him. He may not have started his life out as a Hunter, but he was a *natural*.

Calm, cold and calculated, Jack considered every move before making it. His sense of self was unprecedented in a man of twenty-eight. It had taken Gaston years to achieve that level of detached ruthlessness.

"So what's the plan?" Jack asked.

"My daughter graduates from art school in a week. Her twenty-fifth birthday falls on the following Saturday and coincides with the full moon. While her defenses are down, I want you to get to know her. Use the charm you hide so well to sweep her off her feet. Once you plant your seed inside her, I'll demand that you marry. Madie is a traditionalist. She won't want to bring a baby into the world without it having a father. Trust me. I raised her right." Gaston's head became fuzzy as the whiskey worked its way through his system.

"I'll do my best, sir." Jack rose from the table.

"You'd better do more than that," Gaston said. "The future of mankind is depending on you."

Jack paused at the door. "What about the Moonlight Kin pack?"

"Once Madeleine has completed the initiation ceremony, we'll hunt them down and kill them all. We'll sort out who the guilty party is after we skin 'em."

Jack waited until he'd left the room to smile. His plan was working better than he'd ever imagined it would. He'd expected it to take a while to garner Gaston's trust, but it had only taken a couple of months.

Initially Jack had been shocked that Gaston didn't keep records of current pack members, other than the dead ones, but his oversight had worked in his favor. The old man had listened to his sob story, then done a cursory look at his history. Afterwards, he'd welcomed him with open arms.

The move spoke volumes about his deteriorating health and his desperation.

It was that same desperation that Jack had easily exploited. It's how he found himself in his current position. The folder with the photos of the corpses helped him put the finishing touches on his story.

No one, including the old man, suspected that he was behind the deaths and that all the bodies had been wolves. By the time they found out, it would be too late. They'd have already made a fatal blow against their mutual enemy, the Lycans. Damon and the others wouldn't know what hit them.

Until then, Jack would bide his time and go along with Gaston's plan. He didn't think seducing Madeleine would be as easy as the old man envisioned, but Jack had no doubt he was up for the job. He'd seen her photo. She wasn't *unattractive*. Though she wasn't his type. He'd never been into wallflowers. He preferred his women to have a little fire in their blood.

The fact that Gaston wanted Jack to impregnate his daughter had been a surprise, especially since the old man didn't seem to care how he went about it. Despite his claims otherwise, there was no love loss between father and daughter. She was a vessel, nothing more, nothing less.

Any other time, Jack might actually feel sorry for her, but Madeleine was his means to an end. Jack knew if he somehow succeeded in knocking her up, which was unlikely, he would gain the ultimate coup against the werewolf pack...and Gaston Valois.

How did that proverb go? *The enemy of my enemy is my friend.*

It was true—at least for now.

He grinned wider.

Gaston Valois had just given him the opportunity of a lifetime. No way would he pass up the chance to take them both down.

5

Madie stood behind the counter at Berta's 50's-style diner, staring at the old-fashioned cash register as if it were a foreign object. She'd worked part-time at Berta's for the past two years. The diner was steady employment for a full-time student.

She gazed unfocused at the cash in her hand. The recollection of Damon's perfect anatomy flashed before her. Madie decided he was *anything* but average, at least according to her Life Drawing classes.

Damon was unblemished perfection—smooth, powerful, and erotically male. His shaft was long and thick with an intimidating plum-sized head. Instead of being a pale pink, like she'd expected, his sex was tan like the rest of him. The man obviously spent a lot of time naked.

Madie gulped, as the ache that began the second he'd dropped the towel in class returned with a vengeance.

The bell on the Berta's door clanged, startling her from her carnal thoughts. Heat rose to her face as she looked up and saw Sarah enter. Madie quickly punched a button on the register and the drawer opened. She shoved the money inside, before bumping the drawer closed with her hip.

Sarah shut the diner door, banging the bell even louder. She turned to Madie with a sheepish grin on her face.

"Sorry, I forgot." She laughed, making an exaggerated frown with her lips. "My bad?"

Madie placed her hand on her hip and gave her a mock scolding look. "You always forget the loose spring when you open that door. I'm surprised the bell hasn't shattered the glass."

"I said I was sorry, m-o-m." Sarah planted a fist on her slim hip, mirroring Madie. "Now let's get out of here and go for a pint."

"Sarah..."

She batted her eyes innocently. "Hey, I can't help it if you look like you could use one."

"What's that supposed to mean?" Madie asked, affronted. "Actually, forget I asked. I can't go tonight. I barely made it out of bed this morning."

"Oh, come on. You need to do something to wipe that silly expression off your face," Sarah begged, a playful lilt to her voice.

"I'm not twenty-one anymore and furthermore," Madie's eyes narrowed, "I don't have a silly expression on my face."

"Keep telling yourself that." Sarah dragged out each word as if Madie were dim.

Madie straightened a few ketchup bottles. "I don't know what you're talking about."

"Playing dumb won't save you. I'm onto you now," Sarah said. "You may not be twenty-one, but you don't have to act like you're a hundred."

"Sometimes I feel a hundred." Madie reached under the counter for a clean rag.

Sarah rolled her eyes. "Oh, please, we're only a year apart."

"But I *feel* so much older."

Sarah huffed. "Stop being a drama queen."

"Hey, I resemble that fact." Madie snorted. "And anyway, I'm almost twenty-five." She scrunched her face and hunched over, attempting to do her best impression of a crone. They both burst into giggles.

"You keep saying that like it should mean something." Sarah tilted her head and smiled. "I know what your problem is."

"I don't suppose I can prevent you from telling me?" Madie asked.

Sarah shook her head. "Nope."

Madie wiped at a nonexistent smudge. "Get it over with then."

"I think you've got a crush on a certain art class model." She waggled her eyebrows.

"Get real. First of all, I don't know Damon. Secondly, I don't get crushes. I'm too old, remember?" Madie laughed again, hoping that Sarah didn't notice the renewed flush creeping over her cheeks.

"So not buying it," Sarah said. "Since you're obviously not too old to blush." She pointed at Madie's face. "Get any redder, and you'll match that Dr. Pepper can behind you."

Madie stuck out her tongue, blatantly ignoring Sarah's last comment. Maybe a beer, or better yet a cup of hot chocolate, would do her good.

Anything to get her mind off Damon Laroche.

She'd felt hot and antsy all day. It shouldn't come as a surprise that her best friend noticed and called her on it. Not much escaped Sarah. When a reaction was this obvious, a person would have to be blind to miss it.

Madie wiped down the counter and closed out the register. She took off her apron and went into the backroom to say goodbye to Berta, who was finishing up the books.

Sarah and Madie strolled arm-in-arm out the door and up the cobblestone street toward a nearby local pub called The Pork and Whistle. The owners, Ewan and Janet MacLeod, were a couple of ex-pats from Scotland who'd settled in New England twenty-five years ago, though you'd never know it from the thickness of their Glaswegian accents.

The pub's familiar wooden doors framed ornate stained-glass windows. Violets twisted and curved around wolfsbane, blending into a hybrid plant that bled from its petals, as if mourning the loss of a loved one. The scene was sad, but strangely soothing at the same time. The unusual design always mesmerized Madie and kept her wondering about its true meaning.

Sarah opened the door to the pub and stepped inside. Madie followed on her heels. Cigar smoke rose in a thick smog over the room, since the door to the cigar room inside the pub was rarely closed. Madie's nose burned and her eyes watered, while attempting to adjust to the pub's usual climate.

She really didn't like drinking establishments, but was determined to enjoy the time remaining, before responsibility took over her life.

Madie cringed at the thought. During their last chat, Papa, or Gaston as she'd taken to calling him, had been adamant. *Go through with the ceremony or be disinherited.* His mood swings and paranoia grew worse with each passing year. He reminded her daily that she was his only child and therefore responsible for carrying on the family tradition. The guilt ate at her conscience.

With a sigh, Madie followed Sarah through a maze of tables and barstools. The crowd swelled, busting at the seams. Several men stared with open appreciation at her friend's petite form, their gazes lingering on Sarah's heart-shaped butt.

Madie envied that bottom. Her butt hadn't been that size since she was twelve.

Not an eye flicked in Madie's direction. When Sarah was around, she might as well be invisible. Madie reminded herself again that she didn't care, didn't want to attract attention, and didn't want men's interest. That's why she dressed the way she did. And she'd never regretted it until today.

That hadn't stopped Damon from looking. The thought burst forth before Madie could censor it.

The women walked toward the back of the mahogany paneled room, to one of the few empty red leather booths available. Before they could remove their coats and sit down, the waitress approached, pad in hand. Sarah ordered a pint of ale while Madie asked for a cup of hot cocoa.

Sarah's eyes narrowed on Madie, but she said nothing.

When the waitress left, Madie lowered her voice so they wouldn't be overheard. "Does it ever bother you?"

"What?" Sarah asked.

Madie indicated to the room. "All the men ogling you."

Sarah shrugged and said, "I hadn't noticed."

Madie knew it was the truth. She might be a big flirt, but a man had to catch Sarah's attention before she noticed that he was alive. Otherwise he became part of the scenery like plants or trees.

A lumberjack-looking guy with sandy colored hair and snug blue jeans gripping his firm thighs ambled over to their booth. A plaid shirt covered his barrel-shaped chest. His features were appealing in a paper-towel spokesman kind of way.

"Can I buy you a drink, darlin'?" he asked, his soft southern drawl and aw-shucks charm aimed squarely at Sarah.

She smiled sweetly and batted her lashes, in true Southern Belle fashion. "My, but aren't you a long way from home, sugar?" she replied in a honeyed accent.

Encouraged, he grinned and nodded. "That I am."

Sarah shot Madie a bored look that told her without words she'd already dismissed him. Sarah turned her attention back to the man. "I appreciate the offer, Rhett honey, but I don't think your wife would like it much." She flicked her dainty fingers, shooing him away.

Surprise and disappointment washed over his features as he glanced down at the impression his missing ring had left on his finger. His shoulders drooped and the man walked back to his table. His friends shouted and pointed at him, their loud guffaws echoing off the beamed ceiling.

Madie snorted. "Why, I do believe that southern boy was sweet on you."

"He's a jerk." She snorted. "Speaking of crushes." Sarah dropped the fake accent. "What about you and model boy?" She gripped the edge of the table and leaned forward. "You're not going to convince me that you don't have it bad for him. The Jaws of Life couldn't have cut through the sexual tension arcing between you two in class today."

Madie chewed on her lower lip. She wished Sarah would keep her voice down. She had the distinct impression someone was eavesdropping. She casually glanced around the pub, but no one seemed to pay any attention to them. A few men gathered by the dartboard, debating a throw. The barstools were full of locals, catching up on the day's fishing results. Everything looked blissfully normal.

"I've never seen a man that big, have you?" Sarah continued, her eyes glowing with interest.

Madie glared at her. "Shh, someone's going to hear you."

"I don't care. Damon was perfect." She drew out the last word for emphasis. "Heck, I'd butter my own butt and call myself a biscuit, if I thought there was a chance he'd nibble. Know what I mean?"

It would take a simpleton not to know what Sarah was talking about. Madie might be a bit naïve, but she wasn't stupid.

Sarah shook her head. "Of course you don't, you haven't been with a man yet."

The temperature in the room suddenly shot up or at least it felt like it. "H-How do you know that I haven't?" Madie's frustration seeped out, undisguised.

"You told me at my party, remember?"

"Ah, no." Madie frowned. "I do recall lots of wine." As her foggy memory began to return, Madie cringed at what she'd shared with Sarah...and unfortunately the rest of their class.

Sarah stared at her moment and then laughed. "You were talking about werewolves and initiations."

Madie did recall that part of the conversation, but decided to deny it anyway. She shook her head and mentally vowed she was never going to drink again. She'd humiliated herself the night of Sarah's party. It probably wouldn't have happened had she not received a phone call from her dad reminding her that he'd be up to get her soon.

She'd woken with what tasted like a mouthful of bitter cotton and a full-blown orchestra pounding out a never-ending version of 'Small World' in her head.

As her stomach emptied its contents every hour on the hour, Madie had prayed for death, but hadn't been so lucky. Art school wasn't exactly like a frat house, but no one would've known it from her behavior that night.

Worse still, she talked about her father's obsession with werewolves.

What had she been thinking?

Truth was she hadn't. Never in all of her twenty-four years had she kicked up her heels, until that night. Madie decided that regretful evening was the first and last night she'd do anything so impetuous.

Madie scanned the room again, her discomfort growing. The spot between her shoulder blades itched. With some reluctance, she turned back to Sarah, who stared at her expectantly.

"I'm saving myself," Madie said.

"For what?" Sarah asked. "Do you have an expiration date that I don't know about?"

"No," she said with a laugh. "I'm saving myself for the right man."

Sarah broke into uncontrollable giggles. "Take my word for it, there's no such creature." There was a wistful note to her voice that hadn't been there before, almost as if she wished that she was wrong.

Madie decided not to comment.

The waitress brought over a glass of champagne and placed the bubbly in front of Sarah.

"We didn't—" Madie said, before the waitress cut her off.

"This is from the gentleman." The waitress gave a quick nod over her shoulder, and then winked at Sarah. "Lucky girl."

Sarah frowned and looked at Madie. "Some guys won't take a hint."

They swiveled in unison to where the lumberjack had been seated. He was gone. In his place, sat a man with broad shoulders and long pale blond hair that almost looked snow white under the low lighting. He was similar to Madie in coloring, but a hundred times more striking.

The beauty of his fallen angel face was almost painful to look upon. High-sculpted cheekbones led to a sinfully full lower lip. His sharp blade of a nose rose ever so slightly as he lifted his head in acknowledgement. His flawless looks couldn't diminish the power emanating from every pore. He dwarfed the table he sat at and the men standing nearby.

Both women stared, transfixed.

His hard gray eyes turned to Madie, their emotionless depth slicing deep, leaving her cold. She rubbed her arms to ward away the sudden chill. The instant those same icy eyes returned to Sarah, they became heated, capturing her gaze, holding her spellbound under his long perusal.

He inclined his head and raised a matching glass of champagne to his lips, swiping the excess liquid from his mouth with the tip of his tongue. Out of her peripheral, Madie saw Sarah mirror his actions.

The room practically sizzled as the man rose from the table. A sensual smile flitted across his perfect face. His gaze held a promise, a vow to Sarah left unspoken. Instead of coming over to introduce himself, the man exited the bar. Madie turned in time to see Sarah's color go from tanned to bright pink.

"Where's he going?" she asked.

Snapping her fingers in front of friend's face, Madie asked, "Now who's crushing?"

Flustered, Sarah croaked, "You, of course." Her tone was hoity, but her fingers trembled as she placed the glass of champagne back on the table. "That m-man was nothing special." Her chin firmed.

"Riiiight." Madie hid her mirth. She'd never seen her friend act this way around *any* man. Sarah flirted, and she certainly slept with her fair share, but she'd never lost her self-awareness until now. It was amusing to see her friend go from discombobulated and back to her old fiery self in a matter of seconds.

The pale blond man was gorgeous, no doubt, but something about him gave Madie the creeps. She decided that Mr. Laroche was a much more enjoyable subject and far safer. "I might have had a little crush on Damon in class," she begrudgingly admitted.

"A little crush?" Sarah's eyes crossed. "Girl, that man was a god! Talk about impressive equipment. I could just imagine him going wild, his blond hair falling over his shoulders as he ripped my clothes off, and ravished me on his king-sized bed." Sarah's voice rose with unchecked excitement. She practically yelled the last part to compete with the other patrons.

Madie glanced around. People were beginning to stare. "Sarah

Ann, you've been reading too many romance novels," she admonished. "Besides, Damon's hair isn't *blond*."

"I meant dark brown." Sarah frowned. "Besides, what's wrong with romance novels?" A hint of indignation colored her voice as she pointedly ignored the slip up.

"Nothing..." Madie sighed. "Romances are great, as long as you don't let them replace r-e-a-l-i-t-y."

"Oh please, only a politician or an idiot journalist would confuse fiction with real life. True romance readers don't have that problem." Sarah rolled her eyes. "Admit it, Madie. You would like nothing more than for your hero to come through that door, sweep you off your proverbial feet, and carry you away from your family obligations."

Madie shifted in her seat. Where was their waitress? What was taking their drinks so long to get here?

She didn't want to discuss make-believe heroes or her attraction to Damon anymore. One made her realize all too well what she wasn't going to get. And the other simply made her uncomfortable.

No man had *ever* affected her that way.

If she were being honest, she'd admit that her toes were still curled. Madie balked. Fat chance of that happening. "What are you planning after graduation?" she asked, already knowing Sarah's answer, but desperate for a change of subject.

Sarah fidgeted with the champagne glass. "You mean after the family cruise to the Bahamas?"

Madie nodded, trying to keep her expression neutral. Just once, she wished her family had done something, anything beyond hunt in the name of togetherness.

"Well I was going to work for you." Sarah paused. "But since you won't have the art gallery up and running in time, I figured I'd work for one of the other galleries in town. One of us has to make connections." She winked.

"Good plan." Madie grasped Sarah's hand on top of the table, giving her fingers a firm squeeze before releasing her.

Sarah smiled. "You will get that gallery someday. I know you will."

"Thanks for the vote of confidence. Now if I could just get Papa to stop pushing me to marry, I'd be set." Madie frowned, sinking deeper into the booth to make herself less visible.

"I thought he quit that last year," Sarah said.

"I wish," Madie said. "Gaston hates the fact that he and Mom married so late. He has another blind date lined up for me next week. He swears this one will be different." *Yeah right...*

Sarah's face skewered. "Has he lost his mind? This is America, not the Middle East or India."

"He might have," Madie mumbled, sick to death of the pompous show dogs with good breeding her father paraded in front of her. Marriage was difficult enough without adding complete strangers and low expectations into the mix.

"Who's this latest loser?" Sarah asked, crossing her arms over her chest.

Madie loved that her friend was indignant on her behalf. "Not sure. Papa says he's one of his hunting buddies and shows real promise. He hasn't given me a name yet." She laughed. "I think he figures if he does I'll call the guy and cancel."

"Hunting buddy?" Sarah pretended to stick her finger down her throat and gag. "You're not going to go out with him, are you?"

Madie shuddered at the thought of dating a man who was friends with Gaston. "No way."

She frowned as she recalled all the nights as a child she'd spent hunting with her father in the woods around their estate. He'd insisted she attend the excursions.

More like executions.

Decades' worth of wolf pelts lined the walls of the estate, not that Madie ever shot any of the creatures who'd been brought in specifically for the hunt. She winced every time she laid eyes on those furs. To this day, Gaston insisted that the pelts belonged to werewolves. In his mind, that excuse justified the kills.

Twice Madie came upon fresh wolf tracks in the snow, only to brush them away with her heavy winter boots before her father could descend upon her. At least on those nights, the poor defenseless animals they'd been tracking had escaped death. Madie cherished those rare victories.

Sadly, there were no wolves left now.

Sarah nudged her. "Maybe he'd stop trying to set you up, if you met someone and told him that you were serious. Someone like Damon Laroche," she said.

"Doubtful," Madie said. "Gaston is pretty insistent." It took her a moment to realize that Sarah was staring at something behind her.

An ominous hush fell over the tavern. Madie followed Sarah's gaze.

In the doorway stood Damon Laroche.

And he was staring right at her.

6

"Speak of the devil. If you don't want him, I'll be more than happy to take Damon off your hands." Sarah smoothed her long, dark locks and applied a fresh layer of red lipstick.

Madie leaned back into the shadows, her heart slamming against her ribs. What was he doing here? It made her angry that Damon had such an affect on her. She didn't need any complications while she tried to figure a way to out-maneuver Gaston. Damon Laroche might as well have *complicated* tattooed on his forehead.

Act upon your urges. The little voice inside her head taunted. *What's the worst that could happen?*

"A lot!" she said, knowing it was the truth.

"Did you say something?" Sarah glanced her way, then back at the throng, not waiting for an answer. Her elfin-like face twisted into a scowl. "I've lost Damon in the crowd. No wait, there he is."

Was it too much to hope that he was here to meet someone and would leave them alone?

Sarah straightened in her seat. "I think I'm going to ask him out... unless *you* want him."

Want him? "What? I don't want Damon Laroche. Why would you say that?" Madie's voice quivered as she lied and her stomach churned. If Sarah asked Damon out, there was no doubt that he'd say yes. Men didn't turn Sarah down. Ever.

"Wild guess," Sarah teased, holding a note of challenge in her voice.

Madie said nothing. Instead, she seethed inside. She clutched her hands together under the table as she fought the urge to reach over and strangle her best friend.

"Last chance," Sarah said. "Just admit that you like him."

"Sarah, this is crazy," Madie said. "I don't even know him."

"If wanting Damon Laroche is crazy, then call me crazy with a capital 'C'." Sarah made the symbol of a 'C' with her fingers for added drama.

If Sarah went out with Damon, it would be only once—like all the other men Sarah dated. Just long enough to...Madie sighed. She didn't want to think about what they'd do once they were alone.

Her stomach continued to gnaw at her insides until she felt physically ill. Madie realized once again that she was jealous.

"I knew it!" Sarah exclaimed. "You do have a crush on him. I can tell by the grimace on your face. You look like you sucked on a lemon."

"Do not," Madie said defensively.

Damon knew he'd find Madeleine here. He'd parked his SUV near her home and followed her sweet scent past the coffee shop, all the way to the old pub door. He'd been so wrapped up in her aroma that he almost missed the faint odor of werewolf lingering in the air.

He fought hard to identify the wolf, but he was too late. Whoever had been there was long gone now. The mixture of cloying perfume, cigar smoke, and stale beer had effectively diluted the scent.

Had to be one of the pack, since strays had to come to him to enter their territory.

Since there were no laws against Moonlight Kin hanging out in pubs, Damon dismissed the appearance as unimportant. The door burned his hand, thanks to the wolfbane in the stained glass.

Everyone stopped talking the second he stepped inside. The hair on the scruff of his neck rose as his wolf sensed the danger. On the outside, he remained calm, but in a glance he managed to take in the whole room.

One of the women he sought was seated toward the back in a booth.

He didn't immediately spot Madeleine, but he knew she had to be nearby, perhaps hiding in the shadows. Damon couldn't decide if she was behaving more like a hunter or like prey.

He ignored the curious glances darting his way and moved farther into the pub. Rumors of dark *magik* and monsters had surrounded the pack ever since they'd settled in the area a few hundred years ago. Damon was amused by the superstition given New England's history with witches. Of course none of the rumors were true.

The Moonlight Kin weren't monsters. They were a separate species. Fortunately, they appeared human enough to blend in…most of the time. As for dark magik, the pack wouldn't know the first thing about spells, other than to leave them alone.

The dark-haired woman he'd seen talking to Madeleine in class continued to stare at him. Damon had seen that look on women's faces many times. In his younger years, he would've taken her up on the unspoken offer, but not anymore. Fortunately, the look did give him one thing—an open invitation. All he had to do was smile and he'd be welcome at their table.

Humans truly had no sense of self-preservation.

Werewomen knew better than to blatantly flirt with him like the brunette was doing. The women in his pack accepted him for what he was: aggressive, sexual, dominant—Alpha. They wouldn't dare tease him, knowing that such a deliberate act could challenge the wolf inside him to come out and mount them.

Damon looked at the brunette and grinned, then slowly made his way across the crowded room.

Sarah started to rise to go find Damon, but stopped midway.

Madie watched Sarah's expression abruptly change to one of surprise. "What's wrong?"

She straightened out her clothes. "Do I look okay?"

"Why?" Madie asked.

"Because I think he's coming over here." Sarah looked at her and winked. "May the right woman win."

They both knew who that would be. Madie slumped, wishing the cushions in the booth would open their stuffing-filled mouths and devour her.

She peered into the crowd. Sure enough, Damon made his way toward them. Madie's stomach somersaulted as she tried to think rationally. Was it too late to run? She could always tell them she needed to use the restroom and then slip out the back door. Madie dismissed the idea as quickly it surfaced. She may be a lot of things, but she wasn't a coward.

Sarah hummed 'The Wedding March' loud enough for the surrounding tables to hear. A few men raised their eyebrows and smiled encouragingly, hoping to catch her attention, but it was too late. She already had her eye on her next conquest. Madie doubted it would take long before Damon was groveling at Sarah's feet like a dog wanting treats.

Not that it mattered. Not that she cared.

And she'd keep telling herself that until she believed it.

Damon knew Madeleine registered his presence, but she feigned indifference. When he stopped in front of their booth, he could hear her heart jump. She continued to stare at the scratched up table as if she'd never seen one before. Madeleine wasn't going to make this introduction easy, which was fine with Damon. He loved a good chase.

Unduly pleased with himself, it took a moment for the treacherous thought to register. When it did, Damon stilled. What was he thinking? This wasn't about a sexual chase.

She was a human female, far inferior to her wolf counterpart. He was here to get information and gain her trust, nothing more—nothing less.

"You were in class today, weren't you?" he asked the dark-haired woman, while applying just the right amount of shyness, a tactic he knew from experience made human females fawn.

"Yes," she gushed, obviously pleased that he remembered.

"I'm Damon Laroche." He stuck out his hand to shake hers.

"My name is Sarah Ann Gilbert," she said coyly, then quickly shook his hand. She flipped her long raven hair over her shoulder and batted her eyelashes. The move looked practiced and well used. "And this is Madie Valois." Sarah waved a delicate hand toward his prey.

"A pleasure to meet you." Damon smiled at Sarah. He only spared Madeleine a quick glance. He didn't want her to know that he recognized her last name. For now, it was better that she thought he was interested in her friend. "Mind if I join you?"

"Not at all." Sarah made a big show of scooting over.

Madeleine made no effort to move.

Damon sat down beside Madeleine, almost landing in her lap. She let out a surprised yelp as he scooted into the booth, forcing her over. He settled his hard thigh against her leg, before dropping his jacket next to Sarah.

Madeleine shot him a frosty look, then slid farther away until she was pinned against the wall. She rubbed her leg where he'd *accidentally* touched as if that could somehow wipe him off her clothing. Her fingers continued to worry the spot, but he pretended not to notice.

Her general disregard of his charms certainly gave her the appearance of an Alpha female, but not her other behavior. Alphas never cowered. And they definitely didn't back down when challenged in any way.

None of this made sense.

"Were you in the art class today, too?" he asked.

From her stunned expression it was obvious that the question had shocked her. "You looked right at me," Madeleine said in a strangled voice.

"Really?" He shrugged. "Hmm, I don't remember seeing you."

For a second, Madeleine allowed the surprise and disappointment to show on her face. She shot Sarah a quick look of disbelief, before carefully blanking her expression. A rich shade of pink rose up her neck and her jaw firmed. As he watched, Madeleine's shoulders drooped and she caved in upon herself, diminishing her size and her presence.

Damon had hoped his question would rattle her. Tweak her temper. Instead, she'd deflated before his eyes. He hadn't expected her to react so...out of character. She was the Hunter. Confident. Strong. Fearless.

What was going on? He inhaled. The sweet scent of excitement that had been there only moments before had soured into defeat.

For some reason her reaction disturbed him deeply. He wanted the fire back that he'd sensed in class, not the false serenity and retreat. Damon gave Madeleine his best wolfish smile, one guaranteed to melt hearts and loosen inhibitions.

Her brow furrowed and she looked away, studying the table once more.

Maybe he wasn't as charming as he'd thought.

7

The waitress paused at their table, delivering a pint of beer to Sarah and a mug of cocoa to Madie, who wondered if she'd left town to get their drinks given the time it had taken her.

The woman leered over Damon for a few minutes, doing everything to catch his eye. When it became obvious that he wasn't interested, the waitress took his wine order and walked away.

"Hope you're not thirsty," Madie muttered.

Damon laughed.

"So, how long have you been a model?" Sarah lifted her pint and sipped the foam off the top of the drink.

"Not long," he said. "Modeling is only one of my many interests. How long have you ladies studied art?"

Sarah swallowed the beer and delicately patted the side of her mouth with a paper napkin. "A couple of years. We graduate next Saturday, then it's back to the real world. Right, Madie?"

"Right." Madie brushed a loose strand of hair from her face, trying to keep her discomfort from showing as she attempted to ignore the fact that Damon's strong thigh continued to touch hers. The warmth was so distracting she barely kept track of the conversation. "I'm sure Mr. Laroche isn't interested in our big plans for the future."

He inclined his head. "On the contrary, I'd love to hear more. I have a strong interest in art," he paused, his voice lowering an octave, "among other things." His eyes flicked to hers.

An odd tingle skittered through Madie's belly and she gripped her mug of cocoa tight. Damon was playing with her. She didn't understand why, since he'd made it blatantly clear that he was interested in Sarah. Maybe he wanted to make her friend jealous or maybe he had dreams of a ménage. Either way, he needn't have bothered.

Sarah tucked one leg under her. "So tell us about your other interests."

Damon's heated gaze shot to Sarah's face. Her eyes widened. For a moment, she appeared rattled, then Sarah gave him a secretive smile that Madie could've done without seeing.

The waitress delivered Damon's glass of wine in record time. Figures. He lifted the glass to Madie and Sarah in mock salute before taking a sip. He swallowed the wine and set his drink on the table. "As I mentioned, I have many interests, but mainly I deal in priceless art."

"You're an art dealer?" Madie asked, incredulity filling her voice. She couldn't help it. She hadn't expected him to say that.

"Collector and dealer, yes."

"That's wonderful," Sarah said. "Isn't it, Madie?" She kicked her under the table.

Madie rubbed her shin. He had to be lying. No way was Damon Laroche an art collector. She'd have heard of him before. Madie had made a point of researching all the serious dealers and collectors in the area. "You don't have a gallery in New Salford, so where do you keep your pieces?"

Damon cocked an eyebrow.

Madie back peddled. "If it's not too personal a question."

"Mainly in my home." He gave her a sexy smile that would've made any woman's panties wet. "Would you be interested in seeing them?"

"Me?" Madie pointed to herself to make sure she understood him correctly. She would give anything to see his private collection, but knew that going to Damon's home was a bad idea…for many reasons. Not that she could think of any right now, but those reasons would come to her eventually.

His earlier nakedness flitted through her mind. They were discussing art, not sex. Madie grimaced, shaking her head. She couldn't even handle sitting next to him, much less spending time alone with him. Of course, he hadn't said that they'd *be* alone. Maybe he was referring to them both? Asking for clarification would only emphasize her lack of sophistication. When in doubt, decline.

"Sorry, I can't," Madie said. "Thanks for the offer though."

Damon shrugged. "Suit yourself."

"I'd love to see your collection," Sarah said.

It was Madie's turn to kick Sarah under the table. Her friend yelped, then scowled at her.

"Drop by anytime." Damon pulled out a business card and handed it to Sarah.

"Oh my god!" Sarah's eyes goggled. "You own the Mathis Collection?"

"Yes," he said modestly.

Madie's eyes widened in shock. Like all serious art students, she'd seen the Mathis Collection in books. It was famous because it contained all five paintings by Zachariah Colbert Harley Mathis, a nineteenth century impressionist, who'd been inspired by Monet's works. The collection never toured and had only been glimpsed by a select group of art historians. To get invited for a private viewing was tantamount to receiving an invitation to visit the President of the United States.

"He's Madie's favorite artist," Sarah said. "Isn't he, Madie?"

"I wouldn't call Zachariah Mathis my *favorite*, but his work is very nice." Okay, so he was her favorite. Had been for years. Madie had no idea that the collection was housed in New Salford. Until a minute ago, the town's biggest attraction and claim to fame had been a giant clamshell.

Madie mentally kicked herself. She should've said yes, when Damon offered to let her see his art. Now she was going to miss out on being one of the few people in the world privileged enough to view the collection.

She tried not to sulk over the fact that Sarah was going to get to see it without her. *You're the one who told him no,* the little voice inside her taunted. *It was probably for the best*, she told herself.

Damon was out of her depth both personally and *professionally*. She'd had her doubts when he posed nude in class, but his announcement about the collection alleviated them all. She was a newbie to the world of art and in life, eventually he'd figure that out and not want anything to do with her.

Despite his down to earth persona, Damon was cultured, wealthy, and sophisticated. He was the type of man who'd eventually expect *things*. Perhaps not as a condition for seeing his collection, but definitely later. Things that Sarah was well versed in and that Madie only knew in theory. As long as she stepped back now, there was a chance she'd save face.

There was no mistaking the longing in Madie's eyes, when Sarah mentioned his collection. Damon had seen in clearly. Had he been in doubt at all, it was confirmed when he caught whiff of her scent. Madie brimmed with the sharply citrus aroma of excitement. The Mathis Collection was her favorite. She wanted to see the art, but pride prevented her from saying so.

He considered inviting her again, but decided against it. Damon didn't think it would take much to change her mind, but it was too soon to push the idea. He'd give Madie time to come around. Perhaps he'd drop into Berta's Diner tomorrow. It would give her a night to think about it. Dwell on the fact.

If that didn't work, he could always plant the idea in Sarah's mind. It was so open and pliable that it would take nothing to manipulate her thoughts. It didn't hurt that she was willing to do just about anything to please him.

He and Sarah talked personally for the next hour, exchanging bits of information about themselves. Madie added a few words here and there, but severely limited what she shared. Given her history, he wasn't surprised.

By the time Sarah finished chatting, Damon knew all about the gallery that Madie planned to someday open. The news surprised him, even with what he knew about her family. Had Gaston Valois changed that much over the years? He thought about his brother, Jacque. Not a chance. Madie was dreaming if she thought she could escape her destiny that easily.

Madie yawned dramatically and pushed back her third cup of cocoa. "I better get going." She glanced at her watch, and then at Sarah. "Are you coming?"

Sarah looked at Damon. "No, I think I'll stay here."

Madie snatched her purse off the bench seat with unchecked fervor. "If you'll excuse me," she said, not making eye contact with him.

"I'd better go, too. It's getting late and I have an early start tomorrow." Damon slid out of the booth and stood, his body blocking her exit. If she wanted to go by, she'd have to touch him to do so.

His gaze caressed her as she tried to slip past him. Though she'd done her best to keep the connection to a minimum, Madie's breath caught on contact and her body heated.

Why did she have to smell so yummy? Vanilla and spice mixed with a swirl of something feminine and musky. Even breathing through his mouth didn't help. Damon's body tightened and his hands fisted to keep from reaching out to feel her softness.

If she weren't human and the Hunter, Madeleine would be his ideal Moonlight Kin bondmate. Damon scoffed at the ridiculousness of the thought. The chances of a human female bearing him a child and turning into a werewolf were about as good as him sprouting wings and becoming a fruit bat. It just didn't happen, not without wolf blood being somewhere in the family tree.

Still, her ghostly beauty and ample curves embodied his dream of an Alpha female.

Not that it mattered, since dreams and preferences wouldn't even come into play when it came time to choose a bondmate. A werewolf's *body* decided who the wolf would bond with. No amount of thinking or dreaming could change that fact.

Shocked again by the sudden direction his thoughts had taken,

Damon paused to collect himself. Madeleine was the enemy. Sure she was naïve, innocent, and insecure, too, but he couldn't allow himself to be distracted by her soft features and lushness.

His sex stirred of its own volition. Images of Madeleine naked, on her hands and knees, her moist flesh quivering in anticipation flashed through his mind in quick succession. Damon saw himself moving behind her. He watched as he sank his cock in deep, his hips cradled by her round bottom.

With each thrust, he claimed and retreated, hurtling them both toward the ultimate release. The scene quickly morphed to something far more raw and heated. Damon's rising need devoured his sense of self until only the primal part of his mind remained.

He shook his head to disburse the fantasy and shoved his hands in his pockets to hide the obvious bulge.

Damon wasn't sure exactly when he'd decided to have Madeleine, perhaps last night in the alley or maybe when he'd first received her photo, but tonight had eliminated any lingering doubts. He wanted to fuck her so bad that he could taste it. The need to do so was nearly overwhelming. He'd never wanted a woman this much. *Ever.*

Too bad the sexual interlude would end with him taking her life.

"May I escort you home?" he asked.

Madie hesitated, then said, "No thanks."

He gave a casual shrug of his wide shoulders. "I don't mind. I'm going that way anyhow."

Madie's brow furrowed. "How do you know where I live?" She didn't bother to hide the sudden wariness that had crept into her voice. Safety and security had been drilled into her at a very early age. It wasn't something you just forgot because of a handsome face.

"I don't." Damon ran his fingers through his hair, then shoved his hand back into his pocket. "I assumed because you're a student, you live in or near student housing by the older part of town."

"Good guess," Madie said, but suspicion lingered in her mind.

"He's just being nice," Sarah said. "Lighten up, Madie."

Damon's eyes sparked. "Forgive my impertinence, but it's not safe for two beautiful women to wander the streets at night. You never know what is lurking in the shadows."

Madie shuddered as she replayed her ghostly encounter from the previous night.

Damon's expression turned serious. "I should walk you both home."

Sarah jumped up, purse in hand. "Great."

Damon acknowledged Sarah with a quick nod and swept his hand out for them to precede him. They left the pub and headed down the street. Sarah happily gave Damon her address when he asked, the longing in her eyes sending out an unmistakable invitation. He politely deflected it with a quick smile, then asked Madie where she lived.

The relief Madie felt that Sarah and Damon wouldn't be hooking up tonight was undeniable, but she was still reluctant to hand over such personal information. "It's really not necessary. I walk these streets alone all the time."

"Humor me. I'd feel better if I escorted *you*." Damon's voice dropped, his persuasive tone left no room for argument.

"Honestly, I'll be fine," she countered. Madie watched his expression subtly change to annoyance. She was giving him the perfect opportunity. He should be happy that she was stepping aside.

"I really must insist," Damon said in a clipped tone that said he was anything but happy.

His smoldering eyes seemed to reach through the darkness and pierce Madie's soul. She felt strangely compelled to accept his offer. A minute later, she surrendered her address. Why had she done that? There'd been no thought, no reasoning, like a moron she's simply complied.

More like caved, her mind taunted.

It had nothing to do with the fact that she *wanted* Damon to walk her home. She was doing this for Sarah.

Yeah, right. Even Madie didn't buy that one.

Her muddied thoughts cleared the second he looked away. Later, she'd wonder again why she'd ever said yes.

8

They ambled down the desolate streets, their footsteps echoing off the cobblestones. The brightly lit stores had closed hours ago, leaving nothing but darkened brick buildings in their stead. The night was crisp, despite the promise of spring. The inescapable odor of ocean and fish permeated the area.

Sarah managed to hook her arm around Damon's while they strolled. Madie tried to ignore the stab of discomfort she felt from the not so innocent action. She should be happy her friend was taking him off her hands. Not that she had him on her hands, but still...

Madie made sure she stayed a few steps behind. She already felt like a third wheel. She sighed. Maybe once she made it through graduation and her initiation, she'd be able to find someone who could overlook her family's past long enough to fall in love with her.

Get out of the pity pool, before you start to prune.

The temperature had dropped significantly since sunset and fog rolled in from off the coast. Madie brushed her arms to alleviate the chill. They rounded the final corner that led to Sarah's house. They had a few more businesses to pass before they reached the residential area. Madie could see Sarah's porch-light glowing on the next block.

As they moved between the dress shop and the corner market, a rumble emanated from the alleyway.

Hair prickled at Madie's nape as she relived the fear from last night's mysterious encounter. Startled, the group halted and turned toward the noise. Sarah's grip tightened on Damon's arm. His muscles tensed beneath his leather jacket.

Madie stepped back, her eyes trying to discern animate from inanimate objects in the shadows. The memory of the piercing howl from the night before seared her mind.

It's back, she thought, as blood crystallized in her veins.

Before they had a chance to think or react, a white blur lunged from the darkness. Sarah screamed. Her eyes rolled back in her head and she dropped with a thud onto the sidewalk.

A cry seized in Madie's throat. It couldn't be. She stared at the large pale white wolf. Her mind worked to make sense of what her eyes were telling her. The wolf took a step sideways.

It's real. *They're real.* Madie's heart slammed into her ribs, taking the breath from her lungs.

A musky animal odor surrounded her as the wind shifted. Unable to move, Madie stared in horror as the wolf crept forward, gray eyes glowing and fangs bared. Bits of saliva dripped from its mouth, pooling on the dull cobblestones before freezing. The creature sniffed the air, then dropped its head dangerously close to Sarah's face.

Madie's terror grew. The crazed beast was going to kill her best friend and there wasn't a thing she could do about it. Her mind scrambled to find Damon. He'd been standing next to Sarah when the commotion began. Where was he now? Had he gone for help, leaving them to fend for themselves? Or had the wolf frightened him away?

She longed to look over her shoulder to see if he was there, but dared not take her eyes from the beast. The wolf sniffed Sarah twice, before giving her cheek an unexpected lick.

"Get away from her," Madie croaked, finally finding her voice.

The wolf's head shot up and its eyes flashed.

Madie watched the wolf stalk toward her with its tail up. It had lowered its head and the hair on its neck stood on end. Its deadly claws clacked on the cobblestones each step bringing her closer to death. A low growl emanated from deep inside its throat as the pale menace hunched to leap.

Her heart lodged in her throat, choking her. Madie's pitiful life played before her eyes. She'd done so little and now she'd never get the chance to do anything else. The wolf lunged. In slow motion, she watched it hurdle through the air toward her. Closer…closer…closer. This was it.

The moment before contact, Damon yanked her out of the way. She stumbled, twisting in his grasp. He clutched her sweater in his fist. His eyes glowed amber. Madie screamed and struggled to get away.

In a blink, the gold was gone and the hazel had returned. Damon glared at her. "Get behind me," he growled, then slowly released her.

Madie took a step back. The wolf circled them and lunged again. She ducked. The wolf missed her, but hit Damon, knocking him to the ground. Its teeth snapped viciously, latching onto his jacket. The material ripped like tissue paper.

Strong white teeth sank into Damon's flesh. Madie shrieked as blood spurted out of his chest like a fountain, steaming upward in the cold night air.

The wolf was going to kill him if she didn't do something fast. Scrambling her feet, Madie looked for anything that could be used as a weapon.

There was nothing.

She clenched her fists and felt the leather of her purse strap biting into her palm.

Fury the likes of which she'd never experienced surged through her body, propelling her toward the melee. Madie swung the purse a couple of times around her head to build momentum. On the third swing, she brought the purse down.

The heavy section that held her wallet and water bottle smacked the wolf in the middle of its back, drawing the beast's attention away from Damon. She swung her purse again, hitting him in the muzzle and clipping his nose. He yelped.

If Madie didn't know any better, she'd swear a look of surprise crossed the wolf's features.

Madie swung the handbag once more and lost her footing on the frost-covered road. She fell hard, slamming her head onto the cobblestones. Blinding pain shot through her. Her vision faded in and out, then comforting blackness enveloped her.

Fear squeezed his chest as Damon watched Madie fall. He wanted to rush to her side, but he couldn't. Luc, his Beta tried to rush her, but Damon latched onto his leg. His flesh burned from the wounds the wolf inflicted, but he didn't cry out.

Luc had no right to interfere. As Beta, he had not only overstepped the boundaries set by the pack—he'd demolished them. The attack was a direct challenge to his position as Alpha and Damon wasn't about to let it slide.

Damon growled menacingly at the youth, as his teeth and fingernails began to grow. The beast within struggled to break its leash. Pain ripped through him and his clothing fell away as he willed his body to make the change.

Between the injury and the lack of full moon, shifting was difficult.

The pale wolf sensed the danger and jumped away from him, lowering his eyes from Damon's gaze. Too late for that. Damon lunged, his jaws clamping down on Luc's neck. He shook him, tearing bits of flesh. Blood covered his white fur. Luc whimpered, but did not fight back.

Damon continued to squeeze until Luc's air was cut off. His Beta dropped to the ground and rolled over, baring his belly and throat to Damon's sharp teeth. He held Luc for another minute, then slowly released him. Damon wanted him to know that the only reason he lived was because he'd allowed it.

Luc stayed down. He didn't try to challenge him again. Why would he give up so easily? Understanding flashed in Damon's mind. The Beta came for Madie tonight, not to try to take over the pack.

Leave now, Luc, while you still can, Damon barked out the mental command. *We'll settle this later*. He fought for some semblance of control as he slowly shifted back. His mind switched violently between wolf and man, as Damon struggled to his feet, then quickly dressed.

Luc tucked his tail between his long legs, then limped off. He faded into the darkness, rumbling under his breath—a cowardly action, considering his hasty retreat. Damon watched until he knew he was gone, then held his leather coat out in front of him.

Damn, this was his favorite jacket. Puncture marks dotted the leather. Thank goodness, the coat took the brunt of the attack. The pup owed him a new one.

Damon glanced up and down the street to see if any cars approached. The last thing he needed was to have to explain to a bystander what had just occurred. He heard a moan and hurried toward the women. It was stupid of Luc to jeopardize the pack this way. Unnecessary exposure was not tolerated.

The biggest surprise had been the care Luc displayed for Sarah. Tenderness in the face of viciousness was not the norm. Damon planned to have a serious talk with his Beta about his brash actions. Later. When he didn't feel like ripping Luc's throat out.

Damon looked down at his torn T-shirt. Blood seeped through in a steady stream. He inhaled. The coppery odor seemed at odds with the fresh sea air. His elongated canine teeth began to recede, along with his claws.

He squatted next to Madie. Her face was pale set against the mossy cobblestones. She'd fought Luc like a true she-wolf defending her mate. Her actions surprised him, though he knew that they shouldn't. Something in the vicinity of Damon's heart softened.

Her breathing was regular and even, but he could smell her blood as it mingled with her flowery perfume.

Damon brushed a wisp of blonde hair from her brow, the texture soft as silk against the thick pads of his fingertips. With the back of his hand, he gently skimmed her cheek. She was warm and supple.

Heat spread to his groin and he groaned. Despite the gravity of the situation or perhaps because of it, his need returned with a vengeance.

Damon's fingers fisted in her hair.

A trickle of blood rolled down Madie's forehead. Her eyes were still closed. Damon waited to make sure that she wasn't going to open her eyes, then he leaned forward and lapped at the wound with light strokes of his tongue. Spice mixed with sugary fire hit him like a rocket, exploding across his senses. He sucked in a startled breath.

His question from last night had been answered. Madie did taste as sweet as she smelled.

A soft moan to his right brought his attention back to the situation at hand. Damon released Madie's hair and turned to help Sarah.

Sarah stumbled to her feet and glanced around. Her wary gaze darted to Madie's still form. "What happened? Is Madie all right?"

"She'll be fine. She wasn't out long," Damon said. "She slipped on the frost and hit her head. She's coming around now."

"Is the monster gone?" Sarah asked.

Anger filled him. His jaw tightened as Damon fought his knee-jerk response. It was typical of humans to call anything they didn't understand a monster. He nodded curtly. Sarah looked back at Madie and her returning color started to drain. She swayed.

Her fingers shook as she pointed to her friend. "She's not moving. Are you sure she's still alive?"

Damon's gut clenched at the thought. He didn't think to stop and ask himself why it should unsettle him so. "She's strong." He forced Sarah to sit down on the edge of the curb and put her head between her boney knees. "Take deep breaths," he demanded, before tending to Madie.

Tenderly, he felt around Madie's head. Her lashes fluttered. There didn't appear to be any fractures, but she'd probably have one whopper of a headache.

He patted her hand. The fleshy skin heated under his touch. Her eyes slowly opened. She looked at him, her gaze unfocused for a full thirty seconds, before sucking in a violent breath. Madie bolted upright in a panic. She swayed and her hand flew to her head.

"You're okay," he reassured.

Madie gasped. "The wolf. Where's the white wolf?"

"It wasn't a wolf, it was a wild dog," he said matter-of-factly.

A look of confusion crossed her face. "That was no dog. I saw it attack you. It was a wolf. I'm sure of it. Are you all right?" she fired out in rapid succession.

"I'm fine." He released a heavy breath. "I got an up close and personal look at the animal." Damon pulled out his T-shirt for emphasis. "I think you should take my word for it, when I say it was a dog."

"I saw it, too." Sarah raised her head.

"I hit it on the snout," Madie insisted.

Yes, you did. Damon caught himself before he smiled. He made sure his expression was stern when he spoke. "You and Sarah saw it for a split second, before she fainted and you fell."

Heat rushed to Madie's face. She'd never passed out before in her life. Now at the first sign of danger, she'd rushed in without thinking and ended up knocked out cold. The fall could have killed her, if the wolf didn't.

Gaston would be so proud.

She shook her head, pain splintering her thoughts. She strained to recall the few seconds before the attack and subsequent fall. "I suppose the animal *could* have been a dog," she conceded.

"Of course it was," Sarah, concurred. "No way would a wolf come this far into town. It would have to be rabid."

"Exactly," Damon seconded. "Everyone knows wild wolves are extinct to the area. It was probably someone's malamute or more likely a hybrid. People are breeding wolf hybrids for pets these days."

"It was white and it did have a lot of fur." But Madie didn't believe her own words. She knew what she'd seen, and it wasn't a dog. Dogs rarely behaved like that, did they?

Her eyes were drawn to the burgundy slashes and puncture wounds across Damon's shirt. Her stomach lurched. He saved her life. Whatever attacked was intent on killing her.

Madie rubbed her throbbing temples, trying to clear the fuzziness. She looked around at her surroundings as if she'd never seen them before.

Damon his hand held out. Madie let him help her up. She wobbled and he caught her before she could fall. He brushed her hands and face using a gentle touch, then picked debris from her hair.

After tonight, she owed Damon Laroche. Big time.

That single thought caused her whole body to shudder. She shook her head in silent denial. The pain rushed back. Her heart pounded as a second rush of adrenaline pulsed through her.

"Are you okay?" he asked. "I didn't feel any fractures, but you should go to the hospital to get checked out. Both of you should."

"I'm fine. Luckily, I have a pretty hard head." Madie winced. "I'll make sure I get checked out by the student health clinic in the morning before class. For now, I just need to go home." Unable to stop herself, Madie reached out and touched his chest. She traced the slash marks with her fingertips. He was warm, despite the temperature.

She felt wetness and looked down to see blood glistening on her skin. She attempted to pull away, but Damon captured her hand before she could do so, holding it flat against his chest for a few seconds. His eyes locked on her face, his heartbeat steady and strong.

Madie once again felt like she was falling, only this time it was into his heated gaze. She pulled her hand away slowly, reluctant to break contact. She swiped her palms along her clothes, wiping away the blood and the warmth of his body. "Y-You need to see a doctor. That wol-dog could have rabies."

"He doesn't." Damon ran his hand over his arm. "I mean I'm sure there haven't been reports of rabies in the area. I'll see to it in the morning. Are you sure you are okay? You don't feel sleepy, do you?"

"No. If I thought I had a concussion, I'd go to the emergency room immediately. I think I'm more stunned than anything."

Damon and Madie walked Sarah home. After the fright, Sarah wasn't as eager to have him come in. He bent from the waist and brought her fingertips to his lips. He pressed a chaste kiss to her knuckles and then released her.

"Sleep well," he said.

Sarah blushed bright enough to be seen under the porch light. She scurried up the steps and into her building, holding her hand all the way.

Damon shifted and his gaze flicked to Madie. "I assure you that you are perfectly safe with me—tonight."

Madie shivered. "After what just happened, you'll forgive me if I don't take your word for it."

Despite his reassurances, she didn't feel safe. Madie wasn't sure if she'd ever feel safe again. They walked in silence and reached her door without further incident. She turned to Damon before entering her apartment.

Her eyes were drawn again to the slash marks across his T-shirt. She could see the ripple of muscles next to the wounds, but the bleeding appeared to have stopped. Her gaze followed the spattering of hair that led down into the waistband of his pants. She swallowed hard as she pictured his naked body once more.

Damon cleared his throat.

Madie jumped, embarrassed by her inappropriate thoughts. "That looks like a pretty nasty gash." *The man was attacked. What do you expect?*

"It's fine." Damon knew exactly what she'd been thinking. Her changing scent left no doubt. He grappled with his need to dominate, to take what she so willingly, albeit innocently, offered.

Damon forced his mind to focus on her words. Madie's scent changed again. He was surprised to find the longing replaced with genuine concern. The realization that she cared was…*disturbing*. She was even more dangerous than he'd first suspected.

"It doesn't hurt anymore," he added coolly, speaking the truth. The wounds were almost healed, thanks to the wolf blood in his veins.

Her gaze darted everywhere but his face. "Thank you for saving my life. I-I guess I owe you one."

Damon reached out and gently grasped Madie's hands. Their gazes locked. He massaged her delicate knuckles with his callused thumbs. The lazy circles made her heartbeat skitter beneath his touch. Color dotted her milky cheeks and her teeth worried her lower lip.

"You blush a lot, you know that?"

She nodded. "It runs in my family. You should've seen my mom. She walked around the majority of her life the color of a fire hydrant."

Damon chuckled, then took a long breath. He was finding it difficult to tear his eyes from her full mouth. The predator inside threatened to rear its ugly head again, to take, to possess. He released her hands and cleared his dry throat.

"I know of a way that you can pay me back," he whispered.

Madie glanced at him, her suspicion clear. Her voice sounded tight, when she asked, "How?"

Damon grinned. *Definitely an Alpha female.*

For a second he allowed the beast to flash, answering her fire with his own. Madie took a step back, her eyes widening, before dropping her gaze. Her instinctive response satisfied him, until she looked up again.

A spark of challenge lit her cobalt eyes. He stared at her unblinking. Not trusting what his senses were telling him, Damon breathed in her scent.

Her lust struck him like a bolt from the sky, electrifying his senses, flowing through him down to his toes and back to his groin. His cock hardened painfully and Damon shuddered, tasting her unspoken need on the air.

He yanked his jacket closed to keep her from touching him again. Her scent was driving him crazy. Damon couldn't imagine what it would be like when she was in heat. Already, he longed to rub against her, lap up her innocence and drink from her very essence.

Alarmed by his thoughts, Damon took a desperate step back. He needed to get away, to put some distance between them, while he still grasped a straw of restraint. If not, he'd do something they'd both regret.

He gruffly cleared his throat. "If you'd do me the honor of letting me escort you to dinner tomorrow night, we'll call it even," he said, sure she'd be unable to resist the temptation. If not, he'd guilt her into saying yes.

Madie hesitated, clearly surprised by the invitation, then her chin firmed. "Sorry, but I have to work at the diner."

"I can pick you up after you get off," he said. "Berta's right?"

"Yes, how did you know?" she asked.

"It's the only one around here," he said.

"I don't think us going out would be a good idea," she said.

"So you keep saying. I just don't understand why," he said. "Are you involved with someone?"

Madie shook her head. "No." Not unless Gaston had his way.

"Then come out with me. It's just dinner," Damon said, looking like temptation incarnate.

Madie had waited years to meet someone that was truly interested in her as a person, not as a freak. Someone who saw past the frumpy clothes, who had a passion for art, who couldn't be bought by her father. Someone who could make her heart flutter with just a look—the kind of look Damon was giving her right now.

Madie stared into his haunting eyes. Hadn't they been a different color earlier? A trick of light perhaps? Without thinking, she took a step forward, longing to bask in their ethereal glow.

Damon's pupils dilated.

Awareness prickled her skin. Her long stagnant body came to life in an instant. The throbbing in her head ceased, quickly replaced by a raging fire within.

He bent down until their lips were but a whisper apart. The warmth from his labored breath fanned out across her face, soothing, beckoning. He smelled of spice, blood, and red wine. Madie took in the curve of his sensual mouth. He wet his lips with the tip of his tongue. And all she could think about was what it would be like to taste him.

She took another exaggerated breath, and her sweater rasped across her tender breasts.

Damon's gaze held her, all but daring her to act. Madie tried to smooth her cardigan by tugging at the ends. He stilled her hands.

"Go out with me," he murmured, so close she could feel the heat radiating from his body.

Breathless, Madie waited.

Please let him kiss me, the only mantra going through her head.

"Say yes."

Madie was ready to agree to anything, as long as he kissed her. "Okay." She closed her eyes, but the embrace never came.

"I'll see you at closing," he said.

She looked at him.

Damon had the courtesy not to gloat.

9

Madie locked all three deadbolts, before peeking out the peephole. Damon stood outside her door, staring directly at her, his gaze unwavering. She drew back in surprise, then peeked out once more. Damon flashed a devilish smile and winked at her, then strode away into the darkness, down the deserted street.

It wasn't possible. There is no way he'd seen her through the peephole. Yet, he'd known she was there. The heat of lust faded, as she replayed the events of the evening.

Madie turned away from the peephole, leaning her back against door for support. She refused to let her imagination ruin an otherwise perfect moment. She closed her eyes and pictured Damon's face. How close he stood, and how bad she'd wanted him to kiss her.

A howl shattered the night.

Madie's eyes flew open and her heart lodged in her throat. She jumped away from the door and bolted up the stairs to the security of her bedroom. Madie shut the door and locked it, then pressed her body against the wood.

The cry came again. This time closer.

Her legs shook as she forced herself to walk to the window. Madie frantically searched the darkness for the source of that eerie howl. At the same time, she prayed she wouldn't find it. Shadows faded in and out as clouds crossed over the half moon. Something flickered. The slight movement caught her attention. It happened again.

There.

Lurking in the darkness.

Watching.

Waiting.

Madie's heart tripped as the shadows shifted and began to take form.

"No." She closed her eyes and opened them again. "It's just a bad dream. Wake up."

Madie froze like a deer in a hunter's sight as glowing red eyes stared at her from behind Johnson's Bookstore up the street.

The creature took a step forward, stopping under a pool of pale yellow light. The white wolf sat down under the streetlamp, its gaze focused on her window—on her. An unnatural intelligence glowed in its eyes as it studied her as closely as she studied it.

Madie stood at the window, an abnormal stillness taking over her body. The massive animal growled and then threw its head back, releasing another blood-curdling cry. Her heart dropped to her knees.

Turning away from the chilling sight, Madie numbly reached behind her for the plastic handle on her blinds and slapped them shut. Her legs buckled and she slid down the wall, hugging her knees to her chest.

That thing was stalking her. She knew it with all certainty. But why?

Gaston's booming voice echoed in her head, *"Girl, werewolves exist, as sure as I'm standing here."*

There had to be a logical explanation.

A sardonic laugh escaped her. She was beginning to buy into her father's hysteria.

She couldn't allow that to happen. Not when she was so close to obtaining her dream. Covering her face with her hands, Madie succumbed to tears.

Damon saw Madie turn away from the window a second before the blinds closed, terror clearly etched on her face. His incisors lengthened as anger tore through him. He slipped behind his SUV and quickly undressed.

Claws replaced fingernails as sable fur covered every inch of his skin. Damon crept behind the pale menace, who lingered beneath Madie's window like a harbinger of death. How dare Luc interfere again! He'd obviously not learned his lesson.

When he was in range, Damon's muscles bunched and he leapt, blindsiding his Beta. Snarling, he rolled Luc beneath his massive paws. It took all Damon's control not to rip Luc's throat out with his razor sharp teeth.

He clamped his jaws onto Luc's soft belly and drew blood. Luc snarled. Damon released his abdomen and lunged for his throat. He squeezed, his teeth ripping the tender flesh.

Luc gurgled, then whimpered.

The sound of distress drew Damon out of his killing frenzy long enough to release the youth.

I warned you to stay away. You disobeyed a direct order.

Their eyes met and held.

This is your final warning, Luc. Damon slammed the words into his Beta's head. *Next time you won't live to walk away.*

Luc glared at Damon. *I am here to protect the pack.*

That's no excuse for defying your Alpha. Damon growled.

Luc lowered his eyes, then raised his head to expose more of his throat and belly.

Satisfied by his submission, Damon stepped back, allowing Luc to rise. Blood covered the pup everywhere, but his tail, turning his pale blond fur to black.

I won't let you destroy the pack, Luc said.

Trust me, I have not forgotten my orders. Damon coughed violently, dispelling bits of Luc's flesh and fur from his mouth. He had a feeling this wouldn't be the last time they butted heads over this woman.

Still in his wolf form, Damon returned to Madie's building. He could still smell her intoxicating scent permeating the area. Even in his Other form, he wanted her. Driven by instinct, he lifted his leg and relieved himself on the side of the brick wall that faced the alley.

No one could touch her now, except him.

His territory marked, Damon bounded into the darkness, his paws falling silent on the cobblestones. He would worry about the repercussions of what he'd just done later.

Damon arrived home within the hour. He'd spent the time in his wolf's form racing through the woods, leaping over downed trees and chasing night creatures. He felt carefree, almost child-like as a wolf. No worries, no troubles, only the world in shades of gray.

He entered the house through the back door, as naked as the day he was born, and headed to the living room. He'd return tomorrow morning for his SUV and clothes. They'd be safe for the night. If an emergency came up, he could always take his sedan.

His fingers itched to phone Madie, but he couldn't, since he hadn't actually *asked* for her number. As skittish as she was, she'd cancel on him tomorrow night if she grew anymore suspicious. Despite Luc's interference, Damon was pleased with how the evening went.

He walked to the crystal decanter on the end table and poured himself a glass of Scotch, enjoying the darkness surrounding him. Damon retrieved the file on Madie from his dining room table. He'd only skimmed it the first time. Now he wanted to read it again. Since he'd spoken to her, Damon was more convinced than ever that he'd missed something vital.

He sat down on the arm of the couch and thumbed through the file, stopping when he reached the section on Hunter history. It was thin. Much thinner than it should be after all these years. Damon read it anyhow.

Nothing stood out.

He was about to throw the folder onto the coffee table, when a handwritten note scribbled in the margins caught his eye. The writing was so tiny that he had to flip on the lights to read it. *Valois family members only become the Hunter after an initiation.* The exact details remained sketchy, having been well guarded throughout the centuries. Had Madie been initiated? If not, when did this initiation take place?

Damon read the page again. If an initiation was required, maybe there was a way to stop it without having to kill anyone other than the person who'd killed his brother, Jacque. He flipped the page over and continued to read.

The word 'purity' leapt out. Did that mean what he thought it meant? Damon's mind reeled. No way *that* had anything to do with it. But Damon couldn't let the tantalizing thought go.

If one's becoming the Hunter was contingent to one's purity during the initiation then...that certainly explained a lot about Madie's awkwardness.

Damon's heart bounced against his ribs. He had sensed that first night that she was untouched, untainted, but he'd assumed he'd been mistaken. Now that he'd met her in person, there was no doubt in his mind that Madie was innocent. But was she truly a *virgin*?

In this day and age, it was highly unlikely. Especially given her age... *but what if she was?*

His lips canted as Damon sipped his Scotch, letting the fiery liquid burn down his throat. He could *definitely* do something about that. For the good of the pack of course. The smile spread across his face.

Would fucking her actually break the cycle?

He swirled the Scotch around the glass, his mind racing with possibilities. It was certainly worth a try—or two. After all, he'd already decided that he'd take her, long before he'd come across this latest information.

Damon laughed. The sound lifted a weight from his shoulders that he hadn't known he'd carried. He had never liked the idea of killing a woman. It didn't sit well with him. If there was a pleasurable way to work around it, then he'd most definitely give it a try.

"Soon, *mon chéri*..." he whispered.

10

Madie's head still throbbed. The doctor had examined her and sent her for x-rays, then given her the all clear. She returned to her apartment with a bottle of aspirin shortly thereafter. The pain wasn't going to keep her from going on her date tonight. Wild horses—or even wolves—couldn't keep her away. The sun shining bright outside lifted her spirits out of the glums.

She glanced in the mirror. The circles under eyes from crying last night made her look like a raccoon with water retention problems. Madie did her best to cover them with makeup, then dressed quickly, grabbed her sketchpad, then headed out the door to get some drawing in before work.

Madie practically floated into the classroom. The students' voices were at a dull roar, since only ten people had bothered to come in on a Sunday. A quick scan of the room told her that Sarah wasn't there. Was she just running late or had something else kept her from class?

Hopefully she'd recovered from last night's scare as quickly as Madie had. *Scare?* The little voice in her head snorted. *You were almost killed by a wolf.* She wanted to deny it, but it *had* been a wolf, no matter what Damon said to convince them otherwise. Maybe he'd been trying to convince himself, too.

She shivered at the thought, then walked across the room and put her backpack on the stool next to hers to save Sarah a seat in case she arrived.

Madie took out her pencils and placed them in front of her pad—at least she'd managed to remember them this time. She flipped the cover of her sketchpad over and her breath caught. The chatter in the classroom faded away.

Damon's face stared back at her, haunting in its masculine beauty. She wasn't sure until that moment if she'd captured his eyes, but she had. They practically glowed on the page, even though the image wasn't in color.

Breathe, Madie, breathe.

Madie was so wrapped up in drooling over Damon's likeness that she didn't hear Sarah's approach.

"Can you believe last night?" Sarah's voice burst with excitement.

Madie glanced at her and smiled. "It was something all right."

"What do you mean *something*?" Sarah frowned. "We were almost killed. I came this close to death." She held her thumb and finger an inch apart.

Not unless dying involved being licked to death. Did wolves even do that type of stuff? Not in any documentary she'd ever seen.

"Now who's being the drama queen?" Madie glanced at the other students and tried to downplay Sarah's declaration. Their conversation was drawing unwanted attention.

"I think Damon likes me. What do you think?" Sarah moved Madie's backpack and slid onto her stool. A dreamy expression flitted over her face as she glanced at Madie's drawing. "You've captured him perfectly. The muscle definition in his arms, chest, even his—" Her eyebrows shot to her hairline. "You have an amazing attention to detail. Are you sure you're a virgin?"

Several students snickered.

"Sarah Ann!" Madie squeaked. "Keep your voice down."

Her friend's unfocused gaze returned to her. "It was just a question."

Madie stared at the torn carpet at her feet. In her mind, she'd gone over every square inch of Damon at least a million times. His sheer physical perfection had caught her artist eye, but it was the man who fascinated her.

She toed the small hole with her clunky black shoe. "Let's talk about something else."

Sarah rolled her eyes. "Madie, don't be such a buzzkill."

"I'm not a buzzkill," she said.

"Then why don't you want to talk about Damon?" This time when Sarah looked at her there was speculation in her eyes.

"No reason." Madie took in an uneasy breath. She didn't think Sarah would freak when she found out about their date, but it wasn't something she felt comfortable discussing.

"I think I'm going to ask Damon out." Sarah tapped the side of her chin with a dainty finger as if in contemplation. "Tonight."

Madie's gaze snapped to Sarah's face. "Tonight! Why tonight? Couldn't you give it a day or two?" Panic rose inside of her. She was going to have to say something before Sarah went any further.

"I'm sure the professor has his number." Sarah smirked as she tossed a glance toward the woman in question. "She practically threw herself at him."

He's mine, the little voice in Madie's head screamed out like a petulant child who'd been asked to share her favorite toy.

But it was more than that. Madie felt an uncontrollable attraction to Damon. She didn't just want the man. She *needed* him.

Gaston's outrageous warning rang in her head. "*When you encounter a werewolf, you'll be inexplicably drawn to it. This is a warning sign, the Hunter's only defense.*"

Except, Damon wasn't a werewolf.

He was attacked by one.

There are no such things as werewolves. Do not allow Gaston to poison your mind. Madie concentrated on her drawing.

An image of the pale wolf flashed before her eyes. Madie ignored it, focusing on Damon's perfect form instead.

The dark lines on the paper brought out the rough planes of his face. Disheveled sable-colored hair now looked black from the charcoal pencils. His washboard stomach rippled with minute detail, realistic enough to look as if she could reach out and touch the hardened muscles, run the pads of her fingers in the indents.

Madie stopped before she actually followed through with the action. She rubbed her fingers along her skirt, fighting the overwhelming urge to lean forward and sniff the sketch to see if she could detect his delicious scent.

Sarah poked her in the arm. "Earth to Madie?"

Madie jumped. "I'm sorry, what did you say?"

"I asked what you were thinking," she said. "Though it's fairly obvious." Sarah glanced at the drawing.

Madie blinked, clearing her mind of the erotic thoughts. The classroom felt absurdly warm. "I was just studying the drawing."

Sarah scrutinized her for several seconds. "You have that look on your face again."

"What look would that be?" Madie prayed her face didn't actually show what she'd been thinking about. That would be beyond embarrassing.

"The look that the proverbial cat gets before it swallows a fat rat."

Madie fidgeted.

"What gives?" Sarah pushed.

"Nothing."

"Fine, don't tell me," she said. "Be right back."

"Where are you going?" Madie reached out to stop her, but her friend was too fast.

Sarah marched up to their instructor and pulled her aside. Madie heard whispers, and then saw Sarah write something down. She returned triumphant, waving the scrawled number like a victory flag.

"I've got it." Sarah chirped.

"Good for you." Madie felt anything but happy for her friend.

"Do you want to grab a coffee tonight before I call him?"

Madie avoided Sarah's eyes. "No, I have to work."

"What about afterwards?" Sarah asked.

"Sorry, but I have plans." Madie avoided her gaze.

"Plans? What kind of plans?" Hurt tightened her voice, making it rise a register.

"I-I have to sketch out my thesis after I get off work." She glanced at Sarah.

"Your thesis?" The hurt was quickly replaced with incredulity. "You finished your thesis last month. I helped you research it, remember?" Sarah's eyes narrowed until only a thin slice of jade showed beneath her lashes. "What's really going on?"

"The truth is," Madie paused and took a calming breath, "Damon asked me out to dinner tonight. It's not really a date, it's just dinner. I didn't want you to be upset." She expelled the air in a rush.

Madie had never been good at lying to anyone, especially her best friend. Who was she kidding? Her only friend. She didn't want to lose Sarah over a man. And she wouldn't. Madie would phone Damon right this minute, if it meant keeping her friendship intact.

Sarah stared at her for what seemed like an eternity, her mouth agape. Her expression changed as a kaleidoscope of emotions swirled over her face, running the gamut from shock to genuine excitement. "Oh, Madie," she squealed. "I am so happy for you." Sarah jumped up and down clapping her hands together in glee.

"What? Why?"

"Because I knew you really liked him. I've just been waiting for you to admit it. Why do you think I flirted so hard and threw myself at him last night?"

"I thought it was because you wanted him," Madie said.

"Oh sure, I wanted him. You'd have to be dead not to. But that's not why I did it," Sarah said.

"Then why?"

"I was trying to provoke you into acting on your attraction. For as long as I've known you, Madie, you've never been attracted to anyone. At least not like this," Sarah said. "I didn't want you to miss out on something special just because you're scared."

"I'm not scared," Madie said, but they both knew it was a lie.

"It's okay to be scared. Everyone is at one time or another," Sarah said.

"You're not," she said.

Sarah laughed. "Well I'm different. I've always been fearless."

"It's just dinner," Madie said, overwhelmed by Sarah's admission.

Sarah grinned. "It's a start."

Madie glanced around at her peers, who were doing a poor job of pretending not to listen to their conversation. She clenched her drawing pencil and heard a slight crack. Madie put the pencil down before she snapped another one in two.

"Do you think he'll be 'the one'?" Sarah lowered her voice and looked at her meaningfully.

"To early to tell, but I doubt it. When you don't know how to drive, the last thing you want to do is jump behind the wheel of a Ferrari." But Sarah's question had already planted a bug in Madie's ear. She could almost hear it buzzing as the idea took flight.

The class volume dropped. "I've seen the way he looks at you, when he knows that you're not looking," Sarah said. "It's seriously intense. There's more than lust happening. Let me tell you."

"Really? He said that he didn't notice me in class," Madie asked.

"I know what he said, but it was a lie. He probably didn't want to come off as eager in case you blew him off. As if you're that stupid." Sarah bent her head to Madie's ear. "It's hard for me to admit it since it hurts a girl's ego, but last night at the pub Damon couldn't take his eyes off you."

"But—" Madie's confusion was growing in leaps and bounds.

"Trust me, I know men." Sarah gave her a knowing smile. "I've never seen a guy work so hard to show disinterest. I bet he had eye strain this morning from fighting to keep from looking at you." She squeezed Madie's hand. "I just want you to be happy."

"I know but—"

"But nothing. You deserve to be happy, Madie. You can't do that if you're constantly trying to please everyone but yourself." Sarah leaned in closer. "Besides, did you see the way that blond guy in the bar last night was looking at me?"

"Yes." Madie grinned. "It was impossible to miss."

"If you tell anyone I said this, I'll kill you." Sarah's face was fierce. She looked to her right and then to her left before turning back to Madie. "He made my panties wet."

Madie laughed. She couldn't help it. That was the last thing she'd expected Sarah to say. As secrets went, it wasn't a surprise, but it certainly lightened the mood.

"I'll have Mr. Tall, Blond and Sexy eating out of my hand in no time." Sarah sat back on the stool and crossed her arms over her chest. "So, I don't want to hear any more protests from you. Go out with Damon. Have a good time. Don't do anything I wouldn't do." She waggled her eyebrows.

Madie wasn't so sure Mr. Tall, Blond and Sexy could be so easily manipulated. There was something different about him that she couldn't quite put her finger on. Well if anyone could tame the savage beast, Sarah could. Of course she had to find him first.

Since that was the only time they'd ever seen him that could be a problem. Madie decided to keep that thought to herself. A little challenge in her life might do Sarah some good.

"Don't get any crazy ideas," Madie said. "It's just dinner."

"Yeah, keep telling yourself that." Sarah gave Madie's hand a knowing pat. "I better get the lowdown Monday morning. No censoring allowed."

"What are you going to do tonight?" Madie asked.

"Be vewy, vewy quiet," Sarah said doing her best Elmer Fudd impression. "I'm hunting bwondes."

Madie laughed. "Be careful. He looks like he bites."

"Only if I'm very lucky." Sarah grinned.

11

Damon's day was a total wash. He hadn't been able to concentrate on work and lost a chance to buy a valuable Renoir sketch because of it. Luc had disappeared, or was avoiding him. If he were smart it was the latter.

He knew the pup was young and impetuous. Hell, Damon had been the same way at that age. Luc was only looking out for the pack, unlike his Alpha, who was finding it harder and harder to distinguish between loyalty lines. Once he had calmed down, Damon realized he'd overreacted.

Luc was his friend, his Beta. He trusted him with his life.

Yet, it was Madie who'd haunted him all day. Visions of her lush body danced before his eyes. Her skin soft and pliant, her mouth inviting. His palms itched at the thought of touching her. Damon imagined her in so many phases of undress that his shaft became engorged and he needed to stand.

Damn her. He was the one who was supposed to be doing the seducing.

Her sinfully full lips taunted him. She'd welcome his need there, too. He'd envisioned her snowy hair, so much like silk, splayed across his down pillows. Silk on silk. Body on body. Wolf on prey.

In his mind, he'd removed her clothing repeatedly, sometimes ripping the cloth from her, at other times peeling the fabric away in layers, excruciatingly slow. His fingers trembled at the thought and his cock jerked.

Damon shook his head and gripped the edge of his maple desk, trying to clear the unwelcome fantasies. He heard something snap and looked down to find that he was holding part of his desk.

Crap! Now he'd have to replace the desk. Damon dropped the wood and examined his palm. Instead of seeing a wound, Madie's face flashed before him again, taunting. This was not good. He needed to take things slow. If she truly was a virgin, he couldn't pounce on her and rut like a beast or he'd scare her away.

Damon glanced at the clock and cursed. He'd have to make it a quick shower, if he was going to catch Madie before she got off work at Berta's Diner. It was time he made her *suffer* like he was.

The bell on the door clanged against the glass. Madie shook her head. Only Sarah managed to make that sort of a ruckus. She turned to playfully chastise her friend. Instead of Sarah, Damon stood in the doorway a sexy grin on his lips.

He wore snug fitting blue jeans that lovingly cupped his sex and a black long sleeved shirt that could easily be mistaken for a second skin. The matte fabric clung to his chest like a barnacle, outlining his wide shoulders and every ripple of his washboard abdomen.

Madie sucked in a surprised breath and glanced at the clock on the wall. "W-what are you doing here so early?"

"I wanted a cup of coffee." He smiled disarmingly. "Is that all right?"

"No. I mean sure." She stammered. "Sit down. I'll get you one."

Damon glided the rest of the way into the little shop and sat on a bar stool at the counter. She could feel heat radiating from his body like a furnace or maybe it was just her nerves. Madie scooted around the counter with a pot of coffee in her hand and refilled the cups of the few people seated at the tables.

She couldn't even focus on their faces with him so near. Her fingers trembled until she had to use both hands to steady the pot.

What had really brought Damon here? It couldn't be the coffee. It wasn't that good.

Madie walked back behind the counter and put the coffee pot on the warmer. Picking up her pad, she strolled over to Damon. "What can I get you?"

His eyes raked her from head to toe, then he said, "I'm in the mood for something sweet." A wicked grin slashed across his handsome face. "Since I can't have what I want, I'll start with coffee and a slice of pie."

"You're going to ruin your appetite," she said without thought.

His smile widened. "Don't worry, I'm always hungry."

Madie swallowed hard. She wasn't about to touch that one. She pointed to a chalkboard behind her, which listed today's specials, along with the diner's selection of fresh baked pies. "What kind of pie?"

"For some reason, cherry comes to mind."

The line was corny, but effective. Her heart gave a hard jolt.

He licked his lower lip.

Her gaze subconsciously followed his tongue's movement. The look in his eyes should be illegal, but she was glad that it wasn't. Madie's dormant body responded in an instant, leaving her breathless.

Out of self-preservation, she retreated to fetch the pie. Her mind searched frantically for something to talk about, since she'd never had anyone flirt this hard with her.

Get a grip, Madie. The man just ordered pie, for goodness sake.

She sliced him a large piece and put it on a plate. Madie's hand trembled as she reached for the whip cream can. She shook it hard and aimed the nozzle at the pie. White foam shot out of the can, covering the pie and the wall behind it.

This wasn't happening.

Madie closed her eyes and counted to five, before cracking one eyelid open. Whipped cream oozed down the wall in white fluffy clumps. *Please don't let him have noticed.*

She glanced over her shoulder, praying for a miracle. No such luck. Damon's eyes sparkled and his whole body shook as he tried his best not to laugh.

Madie walked over to where he sat and dropped the plate on the counter in front of him. "Here's your pie."

Damon laughed even harder.

It wasn't that funny. "Coffee?" Madie asked through gritted teeth.

"Please." He gave her an innocent grin that on anyone else might have been convincing.

She grabbed a clean cup, filled it to the brim, and handed it to him. "Would you like cream with your coffee?"

He snorted. "Why not?"

Madie glared, then reached for the cream. Damon stopped her. He lifted her captured hand to his lips and proceeded to lick off a spot of whip cream that she hadn't noticed dangling from her fingers.

Madie's breathing stuttered and her senses locked onto the velvety rough texture of his tongue. Moisture fled from her mouth and headed south between her thighs. If he could do that just by licking her hand, what he could to the rest of her?

She bit back a groan and closed her eyes as her thoughts shifted to where else he could use that tongue.

Damon released her fingers and Madie's eyes flew open in time to see him wink.

"Tease," she muttered under her breath.

He laughed again. "Never."

Damon finished his pie and paid Madie, leaving her a generous tip. He walked toward the door, stopping short before opening it. He looked over his shoulder at her, holding her gaze for what felt like hours, but was only a few seconds.

The world seemed to stop.

Damon smiled. "See you later," he said, then glided out the door.

12

Madie walked around for the next few hours in a haze. Berta greeted her with a smile, when she came in. The grin slipped off the woman's face the second she got a good look at Madie.

"Only one thing puts that kind of expression on a woman's face, and that's a man. Come over here, honey, and tell Berta all about it." The woman took Madie under the arm and led her to a booth in the back. "Charles," she shouted to her husband, "you take care of the customers for a few minutes. I've got a crisis to solve."

Madie let Berta seat her. Berta then wobbled over to the counter and picked up two cups. She filled them with coffee and ambled back. She placed one in front of Madie and the other across the table. She returned to the counter for a couple of forks, and then swiped the chocolate cake from the mini-fridge. She placed the confection between them and sat down.

"I've got a feeling this talk is going to need chocolate." She nodded her head knowingly and shoved a fork into the side of the cake, producing what passed for a bite in Berta's book. "You know Berta don't work well, when she's hungry."

Madie laughed despite herself. She picked up her fork and dug into the chocolate cake. It was moist, sweet and decadent. Just what the doctor ordered. She took a sip of coffee, and then looked into Berta's big brown eyes.

"Tell all, child, I'm dying of curiosity. Who is this man that's got your panties so wound up?"

Madie sighed. "You don't know him."

Berta brow furrowed. "I know everybody. Now spill."

"His name is Damon Laroche."

Berta whistled between the gap in her teeth. "Mmm-mmm, he's a fine looking man. Could put the giddy-up in any girl's drawers." She giggled and took another bite of cake.

Madie played with the crumbs on the table.

"You'll feel better once you get it all out." Berta took another bite. "Lordy, that's good."

"I really like him, but I'm worried he's way out of my league," Madie said. "He's really *worldly*."

"Girl, whatchu mean by worldly? Is he foreign or something?" Berta asked.

Madie shook her head and heat flooded her face.

Berta stared at her as she licked the frosting off her fork. "Now I understand." Her brown eyes softened and she lowered her voice. "I don't think you have anything to worry about. If Damon is as worldly as you say, he's going to know patience. He'll be understanding when it comes to…you know what. Just don't let him rush you, if you're not ready."

"You probably think a twenty-four year old is stupid for worrying about something like this," Madie said.

Berta jabbed her fork into the cake and shoveled out another hunk. "Nothing stupid about it. Sometimes I wish I would've waited for 'the one', but I am not a patient woman." She chuckled, causing the extra layer of love around her stomach to jiggle.

Madie felt better after talking to Berta. If nothing else, it helped calm her nerves.

The woman smiled and patted Madie's hand. "You think about what I've said, child. I have to get Charles out of here and to bed. All this talk of sexy men has got me itchin', if you know what I mean?"

Berta rose from the table. "You still okay with closing by yourself?"

"Sure." Madie nodded. "It'll give my mind something else to think about."

"Don't think too hard. Men like Damon Laroche don't come around often." Berta laughed, and then hollered for Charles.

Madie watched the older couple exit the diner hand in hand. She picked up the cake, took it to the back, and placed it in the refrigerator. The last of the customers wandered out five minutes before closing. Madie wiped down the stove area and workspace. She dropped the used rags into the laundry bag and brushed her hands on her apron.

She was about to leave the kitchen when she heard the bell clang on the door. Madie looked at her watch. It was eight-thirty, well past closing. She'd already turned off the 'open' sign and was pretty sure she'd locked the door. Maybe it was Damon. She'd hoped to have a few minutes to get ready before he arrived, but didn't mind that he was early.

"Hey," Madie yelled out.

No answer came.

It was probably just Sarah messing with her again. Madie walked through the kitchen. She was headed toward the counter, when the lights went out. She stopped in her tracks

"Sarah?" she called out tentatively. "This is so not funny. Now turn the lights back on."

Nothing.

Something wasn't right. Madie crouched down on her knees and crawled forward until she could peek out from behind the counter. In the doorway stood a man. From the streetlight, she could see that he wore a mask.

Blood roared in her ears. She could taste her own fear as bile rose in her throat. She ducked back behind the counter and searched for another way out.

The man took a step forward. His boots scraped over the tile floor like there was a pebble caught in the tread. He walked past the cash register, not even breaking stride. If he was there to rob the place, why didn't he stop to check it?

Madie couldn't seem to slow her breathing. She looked around the counter again. The man now stood ten feet away from where she was hiding. Up close he was big—really big.

Where was Damon? He should've been here by now.

Madie crawled back into the kitchen as silently as possible. Her ears strained to hear telltale footsteps that would let her know that the man had followed. She made it across the kitchen floor to the back storage area, which had an outer door that was used for delivering fresh produce.

The outer door stuck and had always been hard to open. It also screeched loud enough to wake the dead. Berta had planned on replacing it eventually, but she hadn't gotten around to it yet. The second Madie went for the door the man would hear her. She had to slow him down somehow.

Madie turned the knob and slipped inside the storage room as quietly as she could. It was impossible to see in the darkness. By feel, she went around the room, searching for anything that could be propped against the door. She needed something to buy her a few precious minutes, while she pried open the other door. She found a couple of crates full of what felt like cabbages off to the side. It wasn't much, but it would have to do.

Pots and pans hit the floor.

She used the clatter to cover the sound of her dragging the crates across the floor. Madie stacked them against the door as quietly as she could, then made her way to the back entrance. The alley lay on the other side. Madie's fingers trembled as she tried to open the door. As per usual, it wouldn't budge.

She heard the doorknob to the kitchen rattle.

Madie yanked hard, putting all her weight behind it.

The door leading into the kitchen clicked, then hit the crates with a bang.

Madie started screaming and banging on the outer door, trying to get out. The crates she'd placed as an obstacle fell over and were quickly pushed aside. Madie wheeled around and hit the light switch. She scanned the room for a weapon. Any kind of weapon. There was nothing, only produce. "What do you want?"

The masked man stepped through the door, holding one of Berta's kitchen knives.

Madie let out another bloodcurdling scream and wrenched the door with all her strength. The door came off its hinges.

She dashed through the opening, still clutching the door knob. She looked back over her shoulder as she ran down the alley to the side street. The man shoved the door out of the way and loped behind her, as if he were enjoying the chase.

She hung a quick right and headed for the main road. She turned a corner and ran face first into Damon Laroche.

Madie screamed and started to struggle.

"Madie, it's me," Damon said. "What's wrong?"

She gulped in a ragged breath, then blurted, "Someone broke into Berta's and tried to attack me. We have to call the police."

Damon's eyes shimmered until they looked molten gold in the low light. "Wait here. I'll be right back."

He started to walk away, but Madie grabbed him. "No, Damon. He's huge and he has a knife."

Damon inhaled. "Where was he?"

"In the alley. He chased me around the building," she said as panic gave way to nausea.

"Let me at least make sure that he's gone," he said.

She clung to him. "Please, don't leave me." Madie knew she was begging, but she couldn't help it. She was scared out of her mind and she didn't want Damon to get hurt.

He hugged her close. "It's okay. Everything will be okay."

Damon stared into the darkness. He needed to get into the alley before the scent faded. From here, he couldn't detect much beyond the garbage and odors of fried food. Madie's fingers fisted his jacket. Her whole body trembled with fear and residual adrenaline.

He reached into his pocket for his cell and hit a button to summon the police. "Help is on the way," he said, even though help was standing right in front of her. "Did you get a good look at him?"

Madie shook her head. "He wore a mask."

"You said he had a knife?" Damon asked.

"He grabbed it from the kitchen," she said. "I recognized it as one of Berta's."

"That's a weapon of opportunity. Are you sure you didn't disturb a robbery?" He hoped that was the case.

"Positive." She sniffled.

Damon pulled her back until he could look at her face. "Why do you say that?"

Madie scrubbed at her watery eyes. "Because he didn't even touch the cash register. He walked right by it."

"Maybe he didn't see it," Damon said.

"I suppose it's possible, but then why did he shut off the lights, when I called out to see who it was?"

Damon stiffened. If what Madie said was true, then the person who'd come here tonight had planned to kill her. Luc's face flashed in his mind. Would his Beta be so stupid as to try again so soon after he'd failed? It was possible. Luc was determined to protect the pack at all costs. Why would he bother with a knife? His claws were built in weapons and far sharper than any steel blade. Was he trying to cover his tracks? Too many things didn't make sense, but Damon couldn't rule it out.

The police arrived within minutes. They took Madie's and Damon's statements, though he had little to contribute. Berta and Charles were contacted to go over inventory. Other than the knife, nothing appeared to be missing.

"Can I take her home?" Damon asked. "She's pretty shaken up."

The officer nodded. "I know how to get in touch if we need anything else."

"Let's get you out of here." Damon led Madie to his car and opened the door for her. She slipped inside, but couldn't buckle the seatbelt because her hands were trembling too bad. "I'll get it." He clicked the buckle into the slot and loosened the strap.

"Sorry I ruined our dinner plans." She hugged herself.

Damon climbed into the driver's seat. "You didn't ruin anything. We'll go out tomorrow, if you're feeling up to it."

"I'd like that," she said, then stared out the window in silence.

Damon dropped her off, but not before checking her house from top to bottom. It was all for show. He already knew they were alone. He would've smelled any intruder the second they stepped over the threshold. But seeing him look, put Madie at ease.

"I'll see you tomorrow," he said, once he got her settled on the couch. "Lock the door behind me and don't open it to any strangers."

Madie laughed. "Does that include you?"

Damon grinned. "We aren't strangers anymore. Not after tonight." He stepped out onto her porch. "Try to get some sleep."

"I will, but I'm not making any promises," she said.

"Understandable." He grasped her hand and kissed her palm, lingering over the fleshy part. His tongue darted out just long enough to taste her skin, then he pulled back. "Maybe that will give you something pleasant to dream about."

Madie stared at her hand for a moment, then looked at him. "Thank you," she said sincerely. "For everything."

"See you tomorrow," he said.

She nodded and shut the door.

Damon waited outside the door, listening for the locks to fall. "Madie, stop playing around."

He heard a soft giggle, then the snick of locks falling into place. Good girl. As he stepped off her porch, Damon's smile faded. Time to find Luc.

* * *

It took several hours, but Damon finally found his Beta sniffing around Sarah's house. He didn't know why he was surprised, given the young pup's reaction to the dark-haired beauty last night. But that wasn't why he was here.

Damon needed to know what had happened tonight. He wouldn't let Luc go until he found out the truth.

"I tried to call you earlier," Damon said, his voice calmer than he'd expected it to be.

Luc glanced at him. "I've been busy."

"I can see that. How long have you been here?" Damon asked.

"Why do you ask?"

Damon's jaw tensed. "Just answer the question."

Luc turned from the spot he'd been occupying in the shadows. "I've been here a few hours. You want to tell me what's going on?"

Damon inhaled, allowing his wolf senses to tell him what his human senses might miss. "You're not lying."

"I know," Luc said. "Now what are you doing here?"

Damon arched a brow. "I could ask you the same thing. You nearly scared that girl out of her mind last night."

Luc's cheeks flushed. "That wasn't my intention."

"Regardless, it was the outcome," Damon said.

"Why are you here, Alpha? If it's to bust my chops, consider them busted." Luc held his head high and stared at Damon's chin, a sure sign that despite their earlier disagreements that he still respected Damon's position in the pack.

"Someone broke into Berta's Diner tonight and tried to attack Madie with a knife." Damon watched Luc's reaction closely.

"What? When?" Luc asked.

"An hour and a half ago," he said.

"Who was it?" Luc stepped closer to Damon. It was a natural reaction when a wolf was concerned about their safety.

Damon shook his head. "I don't know. She was so shaken up that I didn't get a chance to sniff the alley."

Luc's expression sobered. "I didn't do it."

Damon looked at him. "I know you didn't, but I had to be sure."

"What if I had?" Luc whispered. "What would you have done?"

Claws sprang from Damon's fingertips. "Fortunately, those are questions I'll never have to answer. Now get out of here before Sarah sees you."

Luc grinned, his gray eyes shimmering in the darkness. "She won't know I'm here unless I want her to."

"Take some advice, my friend."

"What's that?" Luc asked.

"Hunt other prey. This one will be more trouble than she is worth," Damon said.

Luc laughed. "You know me. I never could follow good advice."

13

Butterflies invaded Madie's belly as she searched for something to wear. The sun was sinking low in the sky, giving her about an hour and a half before Damon arrived. Despite her reservations about this evening, she decided to enjoy herself and try to look extra special. No hiding under baggy clothes tonight.

She bathed, luxuriating in her tub. Warm water caressed every pore, washing over her sensitized skin. Madie closed her eyes and allowed herself to relax. She should wear something practical, something she'd be comfortable in. Her mind flashed to the black lace lingerie she'd purchased months ago, but never wore. Definitely not practical, but perfect for tonight. She grinned.

Madie grabbed a nearby towel and got out of the tub. She dried herself, puckering her nipples in the process. Her near-death experience last night had made the world brighter and her senses somehow sharper. Madie paused as she moved the towel lower to the damp curls at the apex of her thighs. Her flesh throbbed for an instant as she brushed over her sensitive nub.

For a moment, Madie closed her eyes and imagined Damon touching her there. She trembled, her body electrified by the thought.

Madie expelled a ragged breath and dropped the towel, then walking into her bedroom. She gazed into the full-length mirror on the back of her closet door and bit her lip.

For years, she'd tried to hide her full figure. No amount of dieting would produce the skinny look so popular with glamour magazines. She dreamed of the day that the hourglass came back into fashion.

"A man should like you for who you are," she told her reflection. No other option was acceptable.

Would tonight be *the* night? Not likely. She cursed Sarah for planting the thought in her mind. Or maybe they were *her* thoughts, which meant her friend was finally rubbing off on her.

Madie threw on the lingerie and dressed quickly, giving herself no time to chicken out.

The black outfit she chose was businesslike, but also sexy. It struck just enough of a balance to make her feel secure, confident. The skirt hugged her curves, showing them to her best advantage. She added a tight black V-neck sweater that displayed her generous cleavage. A quick dab of perfume behind her ears and she was ready.

For the life of her, Madie didn't know why she was worried. This was just dinner.

Her mind flashed to his naked form.

Who was she trying to fool? Madie knew she was hoping for far more than food…eventually.

The bell buzzed at seven-thirty on the dot. Madie peeked out the peephole. Damon stood outside her door dressed in a deep brown suit. In his hand was a bouquet of blood red roses.

Madie took a deep breath, pasted a smile on her face, and opened the door. The intoxicating floral scent engulfed her as she stared at Damon.

His face had been freshly shaven, accentuating his chiseled jawline. The ends of his whiskey-colored hair were damp, curling enticingly over his collar. The expensive suit made his shoulders look impossibly wide, and those hazel eyes...

He was a walking, talking Molotov cocktail of sexuality. A truly lethal combination destined to make her heart explode and her underwear melt away.

Damon smiled and handed over the blooms.

"Thank you." Madie grasped the roses tight, holding them to her chest.

Desire flared in Damon's eyes as his gaze traveled over her body, carefully taking in all the curves. After his leisurely perusal, he shifted his attention back to her face, lingering on her mouth. The air heated around them, making her painfully aware that they were alone.

"You look utterly delectable." Damon smiled, his appreciation genuine.

Madie blushed, but remembered to invited him in.

She smoothed her hand down her outfit, over her not too subtle curves. The lace on her thong tickled across her belly and backside. Madie desperately needed to pull the creeping material out, but that wouldn't be very sexy.

"Please, take a seat." She managed, hoping her nervousness wasn't as obvious as it seemed. "Would you like something to drink?"

"What do you have?" Damon sat on the couch.

"Not much. Just tea, OJ, and water. I don't really have people over," she admitted.

He looked around, since in his rush to eliminate the threat last night he hadn't gotten the chance. "OJ would be great."

Damon knew that she didn't have people over. He'd already scented her place. For some reason, it made him unduly pleased that Madie didn't have men around.

Not that he cared one way or the other. It was just nice not to have any interruptions.

As Madie disappeared into the kitchen, his eyes followed her swaying bottom until she was out of sight. He glanced around the small living room. It had few homey touches, mainly art pieces from her classes.

A number of photos sat on a curio shelf. Damon walked over and picked up a photo, lightly caressing the frame with his fingertips. It showed Madie's smiling face, when she was a child. She was seated next to a blonde-haired woman with similar features, obviously her mother, the resemblance astonishing.

Beauty ran in the family.

In the other photo, her smile had been replaced with a frown. She looked tiny and overwhelmed, surrounded by men with bright red hair and grim expressions.

Damon bristled.

He knew those men by reputation, without knowing their names. The oldest man's eyes were cold, almost dead. He looked as if his soul had long since departed his body, leaving behind an iron-hard shell of a man.

Gaston…

Madie returned, teetering in her high-heeled boots, carrying two glasses of OJ. Her smile radiated from within and Damon found himself responding despite his resolve to keep a part of himself distant.

"Thank you." He took a glass from her unsteady hand. "How did you sleep?"

She smiled. "Not bad all things considering."

"Have you heard anymore from the police?"

Her smile dropped. "Yes, they phoned this morning. They didn't go into any details, but they did mention that there have been several robberies in the area. I think they think last night was a robbery gone bad."

"What do you think?" Damon asked. "Now that you've had some time to sleep on it."

"Honestly, I don't know what to think." She glanced at the picture in his hand. "That's my father's side of the family. I look like a cotton ball in that picture."

"You definitely stand out," he said.

"I don't look like I belong to any of them, except Mom." Madie pointed to the picture next to it. "They're a grim bunch when they are around, but I suppose since they're family that you've got to love them." She laughed.

Damon flinched. "They're not around anymore?"

"No, that was our last family reunion. It's probably been fifteen years ago. Some have passed on, since that photo was taken. My other uncles and cousins live all over the planet. It's hard to keep up with them," she said.

He doubted she'd love them so much, if she knew what they did for a living. Perhaps she already knew. Madie gazed at the photos lovingly. Damon tensed. He didn't want to hear about her emotions. His were already interfering with the task at hand. He didn't need to know anymore personal things about her, unless they helped him with his goal, which was to bury himself between her thighs and retrieve the Book of Lycan. The sex would get her out of his system once and for all and hopefully break the Hunter line of succession in the process. It had to work.

For his sake—and hers.

"Your family wouldn't happen to be related to the Valoises from France?" he found himself asking despite his resolve.

Madie hesitated. Fear shadowed her eyes. "Why do you ask?"

"I've heard that the family has an antique collection of first edition books. As an art collector, I'm interested in a lot of different mediums."

Madie exhaled and the tension in her shoulders relaxed.

"I'm sorry, did I say something wrong?" Damon hoped he hadn't played his hand too soon.

She shook her head. "No, not at all. I just thought you might have been referring to something else. It's not important."

Damon changed the subject. "It's a shame you don't live around more of your family." He indicated to the picture.

"It's probably a good thing." Madie laughed.

"Why would you say that?" he asked.

"My uncles had some kind of falling out with my father. They're no longer speaking." She shrugged like it was no big deal, but sadness crept in her voice.

"I'm sorry." *What was he saying? It was better for all Moonlight Kin, if the family rift continued.*

"Don't be. It's been a while and it really doesn't hurt near as much as it did in the beginning. To be honest, we don't have a lot in common."

Damon studied her. Today she smelled like apple blossoms in the spring, succulent and tempting. Too tempting. He sniffed again trying to pick up her natural scent.

Her hormones shifted. In another day or so, Madie would be in heat. *Luperca* help him, when that happened. He already found her hard to resist.

Damon's cock hardened as his body digested the news. His mouth started to water. He tried to concentrate on drinking the orange juice, but it was no use. He took a couple of sips and dropped the glass on the end table, spilling some in the process.

"I'm sorry." He ran a trembling hand through his hair. "We better go. Our reservation is for eight-thirty." His voice came out in a low rasp.

Madie grabbed a towel from the kitchen and bent over to mop up the juice. Her bottom tilted up another inch as she reached across the table. With every swirl of the rag, her hips jerked.

Damon rubbed his itchy palms along his pants. He had to get her out of her apartment or he'd end up taking her right here and now.

14

Madie's heart raced as they pulled up to the restaurant in Damon's Jaguar. After parking, he escorted her inside, resting his hand at the small of her back. The heat from his palm burned right through her sweater, making her skin tight.

Neptune's flashed in blue neon at the entrance. It wasn't much to look at from the outside, just your standard eastern seaboard whitewashed brick, but inside it was warm and cozy. A crackling fire blazed in an over-sized hearth of worn stone on one wall. The rest of the rectangular room was bracketed by floor to ceiling windows.

White linen tables were spread about the space, along with a smattering of booths. The candlelight from each table flickered enticingly like jewels upon a foamy sea. The flames danced as the bustling staff stirred the air. There appeared to be a good view from every seat.

They checked their coats at the door. The hostess, a plump woman in her late forties, gave Damon a secretive smile, but he didn't seem to notice. The woman led them toward a table next to a window.

When they reached their table, Damon's eyes locked on Madie's face. He gave her a slow, sensual smile. Her breath caught as he moved behind her. His fingers casually brushed her arm, as Damon pulled her chair out and waited for her to take a seat.

The heat from his touch practically burned a hole through her sleeve. Madie sat down. She'd been on so few dates in her life and none had come close to giving her this kind of treatment. Almost all the men that she'd encountered had arrived on her doorstep via her father's matchmaking.

They didn't care about her, only her inheritance. Damon treated her like a lady, like she was more than just an obligation. He didn't know Gaston and he didn't need her money. It was refreshing.

Madie smiled and decided to enjoy herself. What she did or did not do with Damon Laroche was her choice, and her choice only.

Damon took his seat. A waitress arrived with menus and a wine list.

"Would you like a glass of wine?" he asked, scanning the vintages.

"Red, I think." She pondered for a second before deciding what to order for dinner. "Definitely, red."

Damon arranged for a bottle of Cabernet Sauvignon to be brought to the table, along with a crab appetizer. They placed their orders for the main course, then the waitress scurried off.

He turned to Madie. "Trust me, you'll love this."

The wine was dropped off discreetly. Damon swirled the wine in his glass, then held it up to the flame of the candle to examine the color. "Looks good." He inhaled, then took a sip. "Tastes even better, though I think it may need to breathe some more."

Madie followed his lead, so that it appeared that she knew what she was doing. The ruby colored liquid slipped over her tongue and down her throat, leaving the taste of currants and a trail of wonderful warmth behind.

The appetizer arrived as they finished their first glass of wine. Damon selected a crab-filled pastry square and held it up to Madie's mouth.

She looked around the restaurant. Couples dotted the corners, laughing and chatting over their candlelit dinners. No one looked in their direction. Flushed from the wine and being too close to Damon, Madie nervously shifted in her seat.

"It's just the two of us. Nobody is watching." His eyes dared her to accept his offering.

Madie opened her mouth and the buttery delight slid inside, melting on contact. Crab juice squirted out the center as she bit down. She closed her eyes for a moment and savored the succulent morsel. "That is delicious."

"Told you." Damon brushed a bit of crumb and butter from the side of her mouth with a slow swipe of his finger. His hazel eyes ignited against the candlelight as he raised that same finger to his mouth and sucked it, his tongue lapping the remnants of butter.

Madie imagined that sinful mouth closing over her sensitive nipples. Despite the wine, her throat went dry. With trembling fingers, she lifted a pastry off the plate and held it to his lips.

Damon grabbed her hand, holding it steady as he devoured the pastry. Before Madie could pull away, he sucked one of her fingers into his mouth, swirling his tongue around and around, until the butter had been removed.

The ache that started between Madie's thighs turned into a steady throb. No amount of crossing and uncrossing her legs could diminish it. He was making her feel things that she'd never felt before and he hadn't even kissed her yet.

Madie was so engrossed in her fantasy that she didn't hear the waitress approach. She jumped when her steak was placed in front of her. After the waitress left, Madie forced herself to focus on her plate. She cut into the medium rare meat grateful that her hands had something to do. Blood dripped from her fork as she raised a slice to her mouth and took a bite.

Heaven.

Damon's eyes held undisguised appreciation. "You prefer your steak rare."

"You sound surprised."

"I am. Most women don't eat their meat that way," he said.

She laughed. "I like my steak practically mooing. I'm a serious carnivore." She looked at her plate. "I hope it doesn't offend you or gross you out." Her smile faded. What if Damon was a vegetarian? She glanced down at the bloody steak on her plate and suddenly it didn't look nearly as appealing as it had a moment ago.

"Not at all," he said. "Most people order fish when they come here."

The waitress returned with Damon's order. It was a steak, too.

He sliced into a corner and held it up for Madie's inspection. It looked as if it hadn't been cooked at all. "It appears we have similar *appetites*."

"If you love a woman with an appetite, then you're sure to love me. I eat like a horse." Madie realized how bad that sounded as the last word left her mouth.

Damon stared at her, but said nothing. A myriad of emotions passed across his handsome face.

Heat rushed to her cheeks. She'd embarrassed herself again. She knew dinner was a bad idea. "I didn't mean anything by that. I wasn't trying to imply… I have a bad habit of speaking before I think." She covered her face with her napkin.

"Don't worry about it." His lips quirked in a half smile.

They ate companionably. Madie found herself telling Damon things she shared with few people. She told him about her mother fighting for her to go to school and how afterwards she'd worked her way through college at the coffee shop.

"So it's true about the…books?" Damon asked.

"For a second there, I thought you were going to ask me about my family's odd reputation."

Damon looked at her, his gaze intense. "I find gossip tedious and rarely truthful. Don't you?"

"Yes, I do." Madie swallowed the last drops from her third glass of wine. She was feeling so good, better than good, and Damon's response made her feel even better. "It's true that my father has a large collection of musty old books."

Damon sat up straighter in his seat. "I'd love to see them some day. I admit I'm a bit of an antiquarian," he said. "It's just a hobby, but goes nicely with my other interests."

Madie hesitated.

"We could swap," he said, before she could reply. "I'll show you my collection and you can show me yours."

As ideas went, Madie thought she got the better end of the deal. "Okay, but given the size of my father's collection, you may want to narrow it down a bit. I can't bring you the whole library."

Damon took a sip of wine. "Fair enough." He tilted his head in thought. "How about you bring me the three oldest titles?"

Madie frowned. "You don't care who the authors are or the subject matter?"

"Not in the least." He shook his head. "I'm more interested in the book's age and its bindings."

"It's a deal." She held out her hand to shake his. He took her hand gently and brought it to his lips, then placed a kiss upon her knuckles.

Damon released her and picked up his wine glass. "Here's to our mutually satisfying agreement. May we both find what we're looking for." He clinked her glass and downed the last of his wine.

15

Damon wined and dined Madie over the next few days. Each night he dropped her off at her house, but never tried to kiss her. He was a perfect gentleman. Beyond a perfect gentleman. And it was driving Madie absolutely insane.

At first she'd been grateful that Damon had taken things so slow, but her gratitude had quickly morphed into frustration. Every casual touch, every heated glance only ratcheted up her need.

If he didn't do something soon, she was going to. Madie had read enough books and watched enough videos to know what to do—at least in theory. She figured once she got things started Damon would take over.

It was a good plan, but success rested solely upon his cooperation.

What if he didn't respond? What if he wasn't interested in her that way? The thought dampened some of her enthusiasm. It didn't help that Sarah asked her every day if they'd "done it" yet. It was Friday. Graduation was tomorrow. If something didn't give soon, Madie was going to scream.

Damon picked her up for dinner at eight. They drove through New Salford. Instead of making a left toward the restaurant, he made a right.

"Where are we going?" she asked.

He glanced at her. "To my house. I want to show you my collection."

"Oh, good. I've been looking forward to seeing it." Nerves coiled in

Madie's stomach. This was it. This was the chance she'd been waiting for.

They drove in silence to the section of town that would be considered exclusive, if it weren't for the fact that the entire town was only a few miles wide.

Damon's home overlooked the wild Atlantic. It had a marker outside the door that listed it as a historical site like every other building in New Salford.

The two-story stone brick house had been painstakingly restored, making its colonial heritage obvious. A garage had been built nearby. Vines grew wild across the side of the house, giving the structure and its surroundings an untamed feel. Every nerve ending in her body prickled.

She waited in the Jaguar until Damon walked to her side of the car and opened the door. Madie hesitated. She wasn't sure if she could go through with this. She'd waited a long time, saving herself for someone special.

Damon more than qualified on that front, but did he feel the same way about her? It was a schoolgirl question, but the woman in her needed to know. He held out his hand to help her out of the car. The second he clasped her fingers a jolt of awareness shot through her.

The electricity sparking between them continued as they headed to his front door. Damon held her hand, positioning himself so that his wide shoulders blocked the harsh Atlantic wind.

His front door had a Celtic design woven into the thick wood. Madie found herself tracing it with her eyes, its pattern strangely soothing. She followed the design up to the top of the frame. The carved face of a snarling dog greeted her. The teeth and snout were elongated, its fierceness frozen forever in the chunk of wood.

A shiver raced down Madie's spine.

"Are you cold?" Damon circled her, mingling his scent with her own until a single scent remained.

"No," she said, which was the truth. "Just a little freaked out by the dog."

He glanced up. "He's meant as a warning."

"For what?" Madie asked.

"Trespassers." Damon grinned and opened the door, then put his hand on the small of her back to guide her inside. He pulled her coat off her shoulders and hung it in the cloak closet next to his own.

Madie rubbed her arms.

"Wait here." He walked into the darkness and flicked on a light switch.

Bright light bathed the room. Damon dimmed the lighting until it was a seductive glow.

So maybe he was tired of waiting, too, Madie thought.

He walked to the massive gray marble fireplace that took up much of one wall. Taking a match from the mantel, he lit the kindling until it caught onto the larger logs. A warm blaze rose from the stone hearth.

Madie walked a couple of steps in and studied the room. The floors were made of stone, unusual flooring for the area, but a nice compliment to the home. A large animal skin of some kind lay in front of the fire and beneath the chocolate colored over-stuffed sofas. White spiral candles sprung up from the top of a wrought iron coffee table.

A golden tapestry hung on the far wall depicting some kind of hunt. As she studied the fabric her gut clenched and her palms began to sweat. It depicted a large animal surrounded by the band of hunters. From the looks of it, the creature was about to be slaughtered. Madie looked away. The scene reminded her too much of reality.

Her whole life she'd despised hunting, since it was always done for sport, not for food. To her family, hunting was a form of recreation, even though Gaston often referred to it as a *calling*.

The *call* must have skipped a generation, since Madie certainly didn't hear it. Her lack of bloodlust was just one of the many reasons she didn't fit in at home, since her mother passed.

Damon cleared his throat to get her attention. Madie turned. He held two crystal goblets of wine. Despite his jeans and sweater, he looked otherworldly like he could have easily existed in another time, another place. She could almost see him wearing a formal jacket and ruffled shirt. His wild hair tamed only by being pulled back in a tight queue.

"What?" Damon asked, as he handed her a glass.

"Sometimes you just seem so different…so old world. You know what I mean?"

Damon stilled. "Yes, I do. Sometimes I feel quite out of place in this world." He walked over to the fire.

"Me, too," Madie admitted. "I've always felt a little odd. Never quite fit anywhere, especially with my family."

"You do seem different," he added absently, "at least from what you've told me."

"You've never mentioned anything about your family." Madie rolled the glass between her palms. "Do they live nearby?"

Damon poked the fire a couple of times, sending embers flying through the air. "Some."

Madie walked over to the mantel and picked up the photo perched there. "Is this your brother?"

He took the picture from her and put it back where it was. "Yes, it was."

"Was?"

"He's dead." Damon stared at the photo.

"Sorry." Madie gave him some space. Her gaze returned to the tapestry.

"It's called 'The Hunt'," he said, coming up beside her. Coldness seeped into his voice as he spoke.

Madie scrunched her nose in disgust. "It looks more like a slaughter to me."

"Really?" One eyebrow rose.

"Have you taken a good look at it? It's horrible. That poor animal doesn't stand a chance. They have bows, spears, and knives. There's nothing sporting about having an animal surrounded."

"No there isn't," Damon answered, truly surprised by her reaction.

This doesn't make sense. How could she be against hunting? She's supposed to be the Hunter, yet she allows her emotions to get in the way.

The initiation Damon had read about came to mind. Something about the ceremony must change the person. But he had a hard time imagining Madie becoming a cold-blooded killer.

"Haven't you ever been hunting?" Every muscle tightened, waiting for her response.

Madie's face dropped. The reaction was as good as an admission.

"So you have killed—" His stomach churned as she confirmed his worst fears.

"No!" Her eyes burned with anger.

Damon kept his gaze locked on her. He wanted more than anything for it to be a lie. He was looking for any excuse to keep his distance.

She's telling the truth.

"You let the animals get away?"

Madie smiled. "I covered their paw prints when my father wasn't looking."

Damon laughed as he pictured Madie as a child crunching her way through the woods. He wondered if she would be as uncensored when she had him between her lush thighs. The thought brought an uncomfortable tightness to his groin.

She was so unguarded…*so innocent.*

There was that word again. Her fate had already been determined by the Elders. It wasn't his decision to make.

Still, if he could break the initiation, then the Elders would possibly reverse their ruling.

He watched her take a sip of the wine. Stray drops lingered on her full bottom lip. Damon had the overwhelming urge to lick them off. He'd purposely avoided kissing her. He wanted to build the tension between them.

In that, Damon knew he'd done a bang-up job because he was wound so tight he was near bursting. He had to fight the desire to act for now, but before the night was through—he would taste all of her.

"Would you like to sit down?" He curbed the urge to direct her to a seat. "Or would you rather see the collection first?"

"I can wait." Madie eyed the sofa and the chair, then glanced at the fire.

Damon waited to see which one she would choose. If she picked the chair, he'd have to take things even slower, but if she chose the couch…

He smiled when she sat down on the large leather sofa. Damon settled in beside her. "Are you enjoying the wine?" He hated small talk, but this time it was necessary.

"Yes, it's delicious." She glanced back at the flames, her nervousness obvious.

The blaze grew high now that the wood had caught on, warming the main room nicely. Madie's blue eyes mirrored the flames. He took the wine glass from her hand and set it down on the end table beside his.

Damon reached for her hand and brought it to his mouth. Pausing, he waited to see if she'd pull away. Madie didn't. He smiled and began placing tiny kisses on each knuckle, savoring the taste of her delicate skin.

He would take great pleasure in discovering the intricacies of Madie's body, savoring her like a fine wine. He'd allow her spicy sweet bouquet to breathe and blossom under his masterful touch, before he consumed it, consumed her.

Damon's firm lips feathered kisses across her hand. Madie's nerves jumped beneath her skin, leaving gooseflesh in their wake. Each caress, each touch drove her nearer to madness. Maybe he was doing it on purpose? She didn't know. Didn't care. As long as he didn't stop.

This isn't a romance novel, girl.

It may not be a book, but it sure felt like one. Damon slid his mouth down each finger, paying special attention to the fleshy web in between. Madie's eyes closed as the sensual assault continued.

His tongue slid between her fingers and flicked up. Madie's eyes flew open as an answering pulse started in her clit. Her breathing hitched as he flipped her hand over and nipped at the tender skin on her palm.

"Damon, please," she muttered.

Her nipples beaded against the lacy cups of her bra. Heat rushed through her and her whole body began to tingle. Her eyes grew heavy as she watched him slowly seduce her.

Damon stared boldly at her, his gold-flecked eyes giving off an unholy glow. A low rumbling growl rose from deep within him. She lowered her lids for a second before returning to his heated gaze. He blinked and then lifted his chin to smile at her. She wasn't quite sure why he looked so pleased, but she liked it. She loved his smile.

In fact, she loved a lot of things about Damon. He made her feel special—unique. He could have any woman, yet he chose to be with her. Madie smiled back, letting him know without words that it was okay to continue.

Damon released her hand and moved in for a kiss, capturing her mouth completely. Madie sighed. Finally.

His lips were firm, yet pliant upon hers. The kiss seared her to her toes. Madie had waited so long to feel him, to taste him. The wait had been worth it. He had been worth the wait.

She found herself drawn deeper into the embrace. His tongue traced the seam of her mouth. Madie opened for him. Damon dove inside, exploring every inch of her mouth, teasing, taunting, devouring.

Madie's head spun, but she'd never been happier. She longed to wrap herself in the safety of his strong arms and never leave.

Where had that thought come from?

She should be worried, but the longer his magical lips kissed hers, the harder it was to concentrate on anything but the awakening of her body.

Damon angled his head to deepen the kiss. He couldn't seem to get close enough to Madie. Without breaking the embrace, he pulled her onto his lap. The soft cushion of her breasts deflated against his hard chest. A groan escaped him when she melted further, settling her bottom against his straining erection.

Suddenly too many clothes separated them. His resistance reached the breaking point. Damon pulled back from the kiss. Staring into her passion filled blue eyes, he willed his body to wait, even though he longed to feel her petal soft skin stretched beneath him.

"Slow down. We have all night," he said, though the comment was aimed at himself. He attempted to catch his breath.

Madie sucked his lower lip into her mouth and worried it with her blunt teeth. The blood in Damon's ears roared, deafening him. He tried in vain to reorient himself, but the fog remained. He was too far gone. He had to have her now, but he wasn't about to take her on the sofa. Not for her first time.

He stood up, lifting her into his arms.

Madie gasped.

"We need to go somewhere more comfortable," his voice rasped. "If that's okay with you."

They stared in each other eyes for a few seconds, then Madie nodded.

Damon carried her through the house and up the staircase. They walked down the narrow rose-colored hall to a set of double oak doors at the end. Gaslight sconces lit their way.

He threw the doors open and stepped inside. The room was dark. Damon set Madie down. "Don't move."

She took a tentative step forward, then stopped.

The flame of a candle burst forth, casting the room in shadows. Other than a large sleigh bed and a single nightstand, very little furniture filled his room. Damon liked it that way. Thick navy drapes hung from rings on the ceiling, giving the bed a medieval vibe. It also ensured privacy when the pack stopped by.

"That's some bed," she said. "Did you get it at a castle yard sale?"

"No." He laughed. "I got it in Paris. Don't you like it?"

"It's lovely. Opulent," she said. "Just not what I expected to find in a colonial home." Madie glanced around the room. "But the simplicity is nice."

He smiled and continued to light the candles in the wrought iron candelabra. "I want everything to be perfect."

"It already is," she said coyly.

Damon studied her for a few seconds. She looked lost and little scared, but she was also turned on. He could tell by her delicious aroma.

Damon called on the wolf's power as he concentrated on the double doors behind her. They slowly closed. Madie swung around at the sound of the click.

"Are we alone in the house?" Fear crept into her voice.

"Yes, I would've told you otherwise. The doors close automatically." They didn't, but she did not need to know that right now. Damon set the burned match next to the candle and slowly approached her. "A safety precaution, nothing more."

"Damon, I need to tell you something before this goes any further," she stammered.

Damon watched her expressions change, blowing across her face like the seasons. In her eyes, he saw hope, fear, and excitement. The wide blue liquid pools gave away her every emotion. Any man would be happy to bask in the cool depths, given half the chance.

"I've never done this before." Madie motioned to the room, while her gaze darted to the bed.

Although he'd been aware of her innocence, her admission fueled the fire within him. Damon curled his fingers to keep from grabbing her.

She was his—only his. No one else would ever touch her.

"I suspected as much," he said.

She looked startled. "You did?"

Damon smiled. "Don't worry, we'll take it slow." He held his hand out. Madie had to come to him willingly. "If you don't want to do something, just tell me to stop. Hell, if you want me to take you home right now, I will."

What was he saying?

He had no intention of taking Madie anywhere, but his bed. Damon held his breath, waiting for her answer.

"I don't want to go home." Madie grasped his hand.

Her aroma changed as she stepped forward into his arms. Damon couldn't wait to see what she would be like once he got her clothes off. He scented the air. *Heat* filled his lungs. Her hormones cried out for his body. She was ready, even if she didn't realize it yet.

Damon held her for a few seconds, giving her time to get used to his body once more. He didn't want to frighten Madie. As much as she presented a brave face, he knew that she was scared.

Hell, he was nervous.

He felt like a young pup the first time a werewoman put her sex in his face. He'd been so overwhelmed by the delicious scent that he couldn't remember what he was supposed to do. Thankfully, nothing happened that time.

Had Damon acted on his instincts then, the Alpha would have challenged him. Choosing to leave the pack for a while, he'd existed as a loner until his father requested his return.

Damon was as shocked as anyone, when he was named the Alpha's successor over his brother Jacque. He'd been Alpha for over fifty years now and that wouldn't change unless he named a successor of his own or produced young.

Candlelight bathed Madie in its soft glow, her skin the color of fine cream, her full mouth still swollen from his kiss. She was so young and innocent. Totally unaware of the world in which she was about to be plunged into.

Yet, he had to have her.

For a second Damon wished he could tell her the truth, but that wasn't an option.

He kissed her, ravishing her mouth with a hunger he'd never experienced before.

There was no escape for her now—or ever.

Damon stalked her like a predator. Madie felt like the proverbial rabbit being chased by the fox. His tempered stride did nothing to ease her growing nervousness. She was no match for this man. He was sex incarnate.

She stood frozen in place. Her frenzied heart hammered out an unsteady beat against her chest. She didn't blink. She didn't move. Deep down Madie didn't want to. He held her in his arms, then he kissed her like she'd never been kissed before.

This man was going to make love to her.

This is just sex, girl, don't ever forget it, the voice in her head admonished.

Madie ignored her good sense. Tonight she wanted the fairytale. She wanted Damon. She needed his warmth. His attention. His love, even if it was only in her mind. She had to believe that some part of this man cared for her or she wouldn't be able to go through with this. The moment meant too much to her.

His mouth was firm as he deepened the embrace. He devoured her, leaving her breathless. The candlelight threw shadows across his handsome face. An untamed wildness lit his eyes.

She looked up into his smoldering eyes and for an instant saw something melt. Her heart rejoiced. Damon reached out and clasped her hand, the gentleness disarming as he led her toward the bed.

When they reached the mattress, he kissed her again, tenderly this time. With trembling fingers, he reached down to the hem of her black sweater and eased it up over her head.

Madie made no move to stop him. He tossed her shirt aside, then sucked in a ragged breath, drinking in the sight of her. Her bra plumped her breasts up impossibly high. The rose of her nipples peeked out over the lacey cups, drawing his rapt attention.

"You are perfect," he said.

Madie shook her head in denial. "My thighs are too big. My shoulders are too narrow. And my butt deserves its own zip code."

Damon pressed his finger to her lips. "Shh…you're perfect. Trust me, I know."

He slid his callused hands over her shoulders, taking the straps of the bra with him in one smooth motion. His eyes raked over her bare skin. Madie's breathing deepened, sending the rosy peeks tumbling out of the lace.

Damon stared transfixed by her nipples. He reached around her back and unclasped her bra, and she trembled as his fingers brushed her heated skin. The lacy material floated to the floor. Madie had never been more turned on in her life.

Those milky mounds could easily feed his offspring.

Damon quickly dismissed the dangerous thought and nipped Madie's earlobe. He worried the flesh a moment before nibbling his way down the column of her throat. His hands massaged her back in slow sensual circles, kneading her tension away. Her frantic pulse beat beneath his lips.

"Relax," he murmured, giving her neck another lick.

Inch by inch he lowered his head, biting and licking every inch of her bare skin. Just above her nipple, Damon stopped to look up. He'd gladly drown in the desire he saw burning in her eyes. Madie's lids lowered.

He couldn't wait a minute longer. Damon captured her nipple and began to suck. The first taste nearly brought tears to his eyes as the turgid flesh kernelled in his mouth. He heard Madie gasp a second before she grasped his head with both hands and drove her fingers into his hair.

He found her other nipple and pinched it between his thumb and finger, then began to pull and tease, while his mouth worshipped her. He rolled the tight nub, until Madie moaned.

Damon released her and raised his head. He waited until he'd trapped her gaze, then said, "Do you have any idea how much I want you?"

Madie shook her head.

"You are my fantasy come to life." He brushed his knuckles against her cheek. "Your skin is like the finest silk, soft and smooth."

She pressed her face against his hand. "You're driving me mad."

"I haven't even started yet." To prove his point, Damon lowered his head and suckled her until her knees gave out.

16

Damon swept her up in his arms effortlessly before she could hit the floor and laid her on the bed. He continued to feast upon her generous breasts, turning her nipples a bright rose. The sweet aroma of Madie's arousal was driving him insane.

He leashed his desires and reluctantly pulled his mouth away long enough to remove her boots and skirt. Damon dropped them over the side of the bed. Now only her black lace panties remained.

"Aren't you going to get undress?" She reached for the sheet to cover herself.

"Don't!" The request came out more like a command, but Damon couldn't help it. He wanted to look his fill. Remember this moment. Soon he would learn every nook and cranny of her body. He'd know every valley, every secret patch so well that he'd be able to identify her by touch.

He removed his sweater and flicked open the button on his jeans.

Madie seemed transfixed by his hands. She watched him undo another button, then reached out to stop him. "Please let me."

Damon moved his hands away.

Madie placed her fingertips on the front of his pants. His arousal jutted out under the denim material. He was painfully hard and more than ready. She ran her palms along his length. He felt his shaft thicken with each stroke.

She fumbled with the button clasp, but eventually got his jeans open. Damon's cock sprang out from the tight confines. Madie licked her lips as she openly gazed at him. Gone was the virginal hesitance. Damon waited to see what she'd do next.

"You're so…big," she gasped. "I mean I knew you were large in the art class, but now, you're…intimidating."

Damon read her mind easily. "Don't worry, it'll fit."

Madie wrapped her hands around his girth. He pulsed beneath her fingers. She looked up, her eyes wide with wonder and blatant sensuality. Damon's jaw clenched. There was a reason he stayed away from virgins.

She squeezed him and he gasped. Madie snatched her hand away. "I'm hurting you."

Damon barked out a strangled laugh. "No, you're killing me."

"What?"

"Just…touch me," he murmured and nearly exploded when she did.

Madie focused her attention back on the fascinating flesh before her. She stroked up and down, watching it grow before her eyes. Damon emitted a low moan, when she picked up her speed.

If he likes this, I wonder if he'd enjoy…

She leaned forward and placed tiny kisses around the head of his cock. It jumped beneath her lips. Tentatively, she stuck out her tongue and gave it a quick lick.

Damon expelled a long, strangled breath.

Feeling empowered, Madie took the head of his cock into her mouth and began to suck like the books said to do.

His whole body trembled.

Madie licked and sucked him, swirling her tongue around the thick head, then traced a vein down to the base of his shaft before giving his sac a quick swipe of her tongue.

Damon sank his hands into her hair. "Enough!"

He pulled her up until she was kneeling on the bed.

"Did I do something wrong?" Madie whispered, afraid that she'd somehow ruined the moment. Her head dropped.

"Hardly." Damon tilted her chin until she was looking at him. His rough thumb lightly stroked the side of her face. "I want to be inside of you." His eyes pleaded, the haze morphing to molten gold. "Now."

Madie sat down on her knees. "I've brought—"

"Shh—don't worry. I have everything we need in the nightstand."

Madie tried to shimmy her panties off, but stopped when Damon's hands closed over hers.

"Not yet," he said. "I want to be the one to remove them." His voice was hoarse, yet coaxing. "With my teeth," he added, flashing a wolfish grin.

Madie's heart skittered.

"Lay back and let me look at you." He rummaged through the nightstand.

The sheets cooled her heated skin as she reclined against the pillows. Every nerve-ending hummed with excitement. Madie squirmed, trying to get comfortable, but it was impossible. She was far too nervous.

Heat flooded her as she pictured Damon removing her underwear with his teeth. He set a couple of foil wrappers on top the nightstand, then dropped to his knees beside the bed. He looked hungry, starving in fact. And there was no doubt that she was on the menu.

Damon leaned over and captured her nipple between his teeth, then swirled his tongue around the tip. Madie's back arched and groaned as fire shot through her. He nibbled a while, then opened his mouth wide to take in the top half of her breast. Damon sucked hard. Each pull of his mouth drove her higher, made her body a little tighter, until Madie thought she'd explode.

Tension built in her abdomen, then spread. She writhed beneath him as he released one nipple only to take in the other. Madie's hips bucked of their own volition.

God, make him stop the ache. It's driving me crazy.

"Not yet." Damon answered, as if she'd spoken aloud. He reached between her thighs and stroked her until her body felt like it would snap in two. When he pulled his hand away, Madie whimpered in frustration.

"Please, don't stop." She barely recognized her own voice.

Damon looked down at Madie. Her eyes were glazed with passion. He trailed kisses down her stomach, teasing her tense muscles. He stopped just above the black lace covering her mound. Damon closed his eyes and inhaled. Her arousal washed over him, racing through his canine senses.

He nipped at the band playfully, causing her to raise her hips, then he grabbed the edge of the material with his teeth and tugged. He could've easily snapped the lace in two with his sharp teeth, but what was the fun in that? Madie lifted her bottom. Damon tossed her underwear over his shoulder, then let his eyes devour what he'd uncovered.

He stared at her naked form, drinking in its beauty, its *purity* and began to drool. Damon couldn't help it. The canine in him sensed that she was in heat. A guttural sound escaped his throat. "You are truly beautiful, never doubt that. I want you like I've never wanted anyone else." It was the truth, though he hated to admit it.

Madie blushed. "You're probably only saying that to be nice, but don't stop. I love hearing it."

"You are a gift that only I've been allowed to unwrap, and for that, I thank you." His senses went into overload as he lowered his head to the pale triangle of hair between her thighs and took in her rich womanly aroma.

Damon closed his eyes and dipped his tongue between her nether lips. Her juices flowed over his tongue. She was sheer ambrosia. A strangled cry broke from her throat as he continued to explore. Carefully he separated her delicate petals to expose the succulent bud beneath. Hunger struck with such ferociousness that Damon struggled to breathe.

He lowered his face and began to suckle the sensitive flesh. Madie's body flooded with moisture. Her velvety entrance called out to him, but Damon knew she wasn't ready yet. He needed to prepare her, stretch her, if he hoped to ease some of the pain that came with deflowering her. Damon slowly worked one finger inside her, curling it up until he reached the knot of internal nerves guaranteed to drive her insane.

Madie shimmied and rolled her hips.

Damon was determined to ensure that her first and only time would be forever imprinted on her mind and body. He refused to look too closely at why it was so important to him that she find pleasure in his arms.

He swirled his finger around until Madie liquefied. She was so hot. So naturally sensual. Untapped in her sexuality, yet primal in her needs—the perfect Alpha female. Damon imagined her as a she-wolf. Her fur, white as a cloud, her eyes blue as the sky. She'd welcome him in that form, too.

Damon needed to rut inside her. Feel her tight body glove his cock until he didn't know where he left off and she began. The urge to plant his seed was strong and it scared the hell out of him. Where were these thoughts coming from? This was sex. That's all he wanted from her—at least until she gave him the Book of Lycan.

Madie dug her fingers into his hair, shoving his face into her sex.

"Mine." Damon growled low against her wetness, before swirling his tongue her clit. He plunged a second finger inside of her and began to work them in and out. She was tight. So deliciously tight and she was all his.

Madie was on fire. Never in her life could she have imagined the sensations shooting through her body right now. Damon's tongue swirled around her until she couldn't breathe, couldn't think. Her back arched, bringing her off the bed. Stars burst behind her eyelids and her whole body shuddered in delight.

His strong hand splayed across her stomach, holding her in place, while his mouth and fingers continued to work their magic. Moisture flooded her until she grew even slicker with need.

Madie wanted to scream. And if he kept doing what he was doing, she would.

He was driving her insane. Her skin heated, over-sensitized by his blatantly sexual massage. Tension reached the breaking point, the pain-pleasure so great that she couldn't stand it.

"Please stop! I can't…it's too much," she cried out.

"Trust me." Damon intensified his movements. His long fingers picked up the pace inside of her, while his mouth explored every inch of her nether regions.

Madie's head thrashed against the pillows. She was coming unglued. Damon added a third finger, before withdrawing them all. Her body cried out for their return.

"No!" she screamed.

"Tell me what you want, Madie." His voice was strong and confident—determined.

Why was he torturing her? He'd been so nice before.

"What do you want?" he repeated. "You need to tell me or I will get dressed and leave this room."

"You," she whimpered. "I want you."

"Where do you want me?" he asked, his voice strangled.

"Here." She pointed between her legs.

Damon's fingers returned in a flash, slipping even deeper inside her. Madie's sex clenched around them, but it didn't impede his movements. Damon flowed in and out of her with ease, her moisture drowning his fingers. Madie's hips picked up the rhythm he set.

She felt Damon shift a little higher. His breathing deepened, sawing in and out of his lungs. His mouth came down on her once again. He sucked her clit between his teeth and bit down. Hard

A buzzing noise started in Madie's ears. She cried out as her whole body shook, then exploded in a million pieces. The orgasm ripped through her, scattering her thoughts, lifting her to a level of bliss she never knew existed.

Damon continued to lick her, while making happy gurgling sounds in the back of his throat. When the shudders lessened, he rose up and gave her a blistering kiss. Madie tasted her own essence, as his lips lingered over hers.

She dug her fingers into his hair, luxuriating in the feel of it. His erection stood proud against her soft skin. Madie's eyes fluttered shut for a moment, relishing every sensation. She was shocked when her own arousal flickered to life once more.

"I had no idea." Madie released him and ran her hands over her naked body, truly feeling it for the first time. "This was incredible. You are incredible."

Damon cracked up, his laughter shaking his flat belly. "I do aim to please."

He reached down and stroked her again.

"Damon, I'm not sure I can do it again—oh, that feels good."

He smiled. "Just wait."

Madie's eyes closed as she relished his gentle ministrations. His fingers were tender, yet insistent. Demanding that she respond, and she did.

Tingles danced up her spine as she felt the pressure building anew. *The romance novels got it right.*

Damon climbed onto the bed beside her. A second later, his hard body blanketed hers. The weight was odd, but strangely comfortable. Madie felt his massive erection brush against her stomach. Damon reached over to the bedside table and picked up the foil wrapper. He tore it with his teeth and quickly sheathed himself.

Madie felt the color drain from her face as her nerves returned. "I guess this is it."

Damon's face blanked. "Say the word and we'll stop."

She shifted uneasily beneath him, shoring up her courage. "I-I don't want to stop."

"Last chance." He stoked the head of his cock against her entrance, teasing her flesh.

"I want you. All of you." Her body flooded with moisture and her hips undulated.

Damon stopped her movements. "Don't do that or this isn't going to last very long," he gritted out.

Madie lowered her lashes and concentrated on the various sensations. She noted the scrape of his chest hair over her breasts, his hard muscles tensing above her, the soft steel of his shaft stretching her opening.

"Look at me, Madie," Damon demanded.

Her eyes flew open to meet his gaze.

"I want you to know who you belong to tonight." With that, Damon plunged inside of her, tearing through her hymen.

Pain shot through Madie, causing her to gulp in air. The discomfort lasted but a minute, as her body tried to rapidly adjust to his brutal thickness.

"Relax. Breathe." His voice sounded garbled as his whole body tensed.

"Does it hurt you, too?" she asked.

He swallowed hard. "Not in the same way." Damon brushed the hair away from her face. "Are you all right?" He hadn't moved a muscle since he entered her.

"Yes, I think so," she said. "It feels…different. Like my body is stuffed."

"It will feel a lot better in a minute. You just need time to adjust." The strain in his voice was evident. "The first time always hurts, but not for long. It should be easing up now."

Madie squirmed. Her body needed to move. "Damon?"

Without a word, he began to slowly thrust, the torture exquisite. Madie felt the thick glide as her body worked to accommodate him. He was right. The pain was fading quickly, becoming a distant memory thanks to the pleasure building inside her.

Her body was made for this man. The thought shocked her, but she was honest enough not to deny it.

Damon trembled and his eyes darkened to deep amber. Sweat dampened his brow. He slid his hands under her bottom and lifted her hips, allowing his long shaft to embed even deeper. Madie let out a soft moan as desire snatched her up and carried her back toward the abyss.

If she died right now, she'd die a happy woman.

He continued his hard and steady assault on her senses. Madie clung to him as their bodies came together only to part the next second. She raked her nails down Damon's back and nipped at his shoulder, eliciting a pleasurable growl from him. His hips bucked, then moved faster as he lost some of his steadfast control.

Damon felt impossibly long and thick inside of her. Bigger than he'd been at the start. Madie could feel him swell within her. He continued to grow until the fit became uncomfortable.

She'd never done this before, but something about the situation didn't seem right. Madie had read about sex in several books, but none of them mentioned anything like this.

As the pressure increased, so did the internal stimulation. Her orgasm struck out of the blue and with such intensity that Madie nearly blacked out from the pleasure of it. When her breathing calmed and she'd floated back to Earth, she realized Damon was still inside her, as hard and hot as ever.

Stretched to the limits, Madie couldn't take much more. "Damon, is this normal?"

The look of horror on his face told her that it wasn't.

Madie stilled beneath him. "What's happening? What's wrong?" She had no idea what to do or how to help.

"Don't move." Damon's mind screamed in agony and utter disbelief. The only time a werewolf experienced the melding was when he encountered his bondmate.

This couldn't be happening—she was the enemy. She was human.

Werewolves didn't bond with humans, but his body didn't seem to care. He tried to pull out, but couldn't. His cock felt like it was going to explode as it continued to grow.

Damon had heard tales of mating with ones bondmate, but he hadn't believed the stories because they'd seemed like old wives' tales concocted to scare the newly bonded. There was only one reason for a werewolf's cock to swell—to guarantee the continuation of the species.

"Shit!" Damon's world crashed around him. He tried to pull out again, but his shaft didn't move. Panic hit as he realized he was locked inside Madie and would remain that way until the wolf decided it'd had enough. Damon thrust forward, hoping to ease some of the tension, but it had the opposite effect.

Damon groaned aloud as the intensity of the pleasure became nearly too much to bear.

He looked down into Madie's face. She'd gone pale. He could smell the fear wafting from her pores. "Everything's all right." His voice took on as much of a comforting tone as he could manage under the circumstances. He had to admit that it wasn't much.

Madie gasped. "It hurts."

Damon stroked her hair. "I know and I'm sorry. It should stop hurting soon." He prayed that was true.

She stared at him with eyes so trusting that something inside of him shattered. "I need you to move," she said.

"Okay, but let me know if it hurts." Damon made a short teasing stab forward and his cock pulsed. He moaned.

Madie's sighed against his cheek. "Do that again."

"Are you sure?" He wasn't sure how much more he could take.

She nodded.

He did. It was her turn to moan.

"Harder this time," Madie said.

Damon drove into her once more. His cock slid forward…right through the end of the condom. The sensation of skin on skin scalded him and was nearly his undoing. She felt amazing. So hot. So tight. So perfect. Damon cursed long and fluently inside his head. This could not be happening. But he knew that it was. The wolf would not be denied.

"Are you on any birth control?" he asked, already sure of the answer.

"No." Her eyes widened. "Is everything okay?"

"It's fine," he said, but it wasn't.

Unless he could figure out a way to pull out of her without injuring them both, Damon knew that there was a very good chance he'd impregnate Madie. It shouldn't be possible since she was a human, but the bonding changed everything.

"Let me know if this hurts." He slowly pulled his hips back. Pain shot through him. It felt like his dick was coming off.

Madie yelped.

He immediately pushed back in until he nudged her womb. "Better?"

She nodded.

He wasn't going anywhere, anytime soon. Damon closed his eyes and waited for the revulsion to hit. It never came. Instead, a surge of unexpected happiness coursed through him. He reached between their bodies and stroked her clit.

Madie wiggled and her channel moistened even more. When the first flutters of her orgasm hit, Damon felt them all the way to his core. The powerful contractions took him over the edge with her. His body shuddered as he exploded inside her.

Damon moved as much as he could, as more and more of his essence filled her. Forty-five minutes later, his cock began to shrink back to normal size.

He took a long look at Madie's dreamy expression and his heart began to pound as the ramifications of this moment registered once more. She was the Hunter. She would also always be from this day forward…

His bondmate.

He mentally berated himself. If he hadn't been so bent on revenge, this would never have happened. He also would've never found his mate. The truth humbled Damon. There was no way he'd be able to kill her now, even if he couldn't stop the initiation.

He'd sooner take his own life than destroy hers.

Madie snuggled closer, then smiled at him. "That was amazing."

Damon kissed her hard, his mouth foraging for the sweetness hidden there. The urge to dominate was strong. "Let's try it this way." He withdrew from Madie and carefully flipped her over onto her stomach. Damon ripped away the shattered condom and tossed it onto the bedside table. It was useless now.

He pulled Madie to her hands and knees, then grasped her hips. Instinct took over, Damon positioned his shaft at her dripping entrance, then thrust as he bit down on the side of her neck just enough to draw blood. Her hands curled into the pillows and she cried out, but didn't try to pull away.

Madie's molten channel gripped him tight as he lapped at her neck, tasting her delicious blood. His hunger for her grew to ravenous as he took her in true Moonlight Kin fashion.

Damon's hips pistoned in and out of her willing body with blinding speed. He felt tension rising inside Madie, as her inner muscles clenched around him and her knees quivered.

Suddenly, his wolf surfaced and Damon went wild. His hips slammed into Madie's lush bottom, as he speared her deep, hard, and fast. She screamed out his name as her arms collapsed beneath her.

Damon held her hips, keeping her lower half in place as her channel milked his shaft. Pleasure exploded behind his eyelids at the delicious friction. He wasn't going to last much longer. His sac drew up as he thrust forward and he felt his body tense.

With a loud bellow, Damon came hard, exploding inside of her. His shaft pulsed as he pumped his rich seed deep into her channel, sealing their fates once and for all.

17

Madie lay stretched across the bed. Damon's warmth seeped into her, capturing her heart, imprisoning it, even though she'd been determined to keep it safe. His even breaths tickled her ear, brushing her hair away from her face with their gentle cadence. She was boneless.

At least that's what if felt like, since her body refused to move. She twisted her head until she could see more of Damon's handsome face. As she stared, she relived every moment of their love-making. At times, the intensity of it had frightened her. The pain and pleasure had blurred into an endless spiral of release.

In all her years of reading about sex and imagining it, nothing had prepared her for the real thing. She'd entered his bed as a scared girl and came out a woman.

She continued to stare at Damon. Sweat still dampened his forehead and neck, making his hair curl up at the ends. He smelled of musk and man, a heady combination that nearly took her breath away.

Sleep brought out his true beauty, making him look younger, almost innocent—though Madie knew after last night he was anything but. His soft snores lent credence to his level of satisfaction.

It made Madie's heart flip to know that she was the reason for his peaceful slumber. Whether she'd planned to be or not, she felt connected to Damon and knew she would always be joined to him in some fashion, even if they parted ways.

Though she didn't care to think about them no longer being together, Madie had no regrets. How could she regret the best night of her life?

She rose from the bed and tiptoed to the bathroom. Madie closed the door and looked in the mirror. Her hair was a mass of blonde tangles and her body felt tender to the touch, especially the massive hickey on her neck.

Damon had been so carried away by their love-making that he'd actually bit her. It had been shocking at the time, but the stinging pain had faded so quickly that she hadn't given it another thought until now.

It looked like she was going to have to wear a turtleneck today at graduation.

Madie turned on the tap and splashed cold water on her face. The chill brought with it a fresh pink glow. She could still smell Damon's lingering scent on her skin and wasn't in a hurry to wash it off.

She used the facilities, then crept back into the bedroom. The sheets were in disarray and Damon was nowhere to be found. Madie walked around the bed and picked up her scattered clothing. Damon's shirt lay on the floor next to her lace panties, but his pants were gone.

Madie lifted his shirt to her face and inhaled. Her eyes closed as she took his distinctive scent into her lungs. The door banged opened, startling her. Madie dropped his shirt and clutched her clothing to her chest to cover her nakedness. The bright morning light illuminated Damon's grim face.

Dread squeezed her stomach. "What's wrong?"

His solemn gaze slowly faded as he took in her exposed skin. Hunger leapt into the gold flecks, lightening them with desire. Madie's breathing hitched, then accelerated. The muscles in his bare chest bunched and flexed as if he fought the urge to move.

All it took was one look from Damon, and Madie was ready to throw herself back on the bed. She'd gone from virgin to nymph overnight.

When he finally spoke, the deep timber of his voice sent delicious shivers through her. "Something's come up," he said. "I have leave town for a while."

"I thought maybe you'd come to graduation." Madie could feel him pulling away and there was nothing she could do about it.

"No, I'll be leaving shortly after you do," he said.

The statement smacked her back into reality. This wasn't a romance novel or a fairytale. This was real life. There would be no happy ending. Last night might have been perfect for her—okay, was perfect to her, but in the harsh morning glare it was plain to see that Damon viewed it as a one-night-stand. Madie felt heat rise in her cheeks. She'd been so stupid.

Madie's chin lifted and she threw back her shoulders. She might've been naïve about their future, but she still had no regrets. She wasn't going to give Damon the satisfaction of knowing that he'd hurt her. "Just let me get dressed and I'll get out of here." *Out of your life.* "I don't want to keep you." Her words dripped with sarcasm.

"You don't have to hurry." Damon ran his hand through his hair, sending it spiking in all directions.

Madie snorted. "I wouldn't dream of delaying your trip." She clutched her clothing and walked into the bathroom. She'd just started to dress, when the bathroom door flew open.

Damon crossed the room in two long strides. His hands clasped her arms, halting her movements. She looked down at his hands, and then up into his face. His eyes were practically glowing.

"You don't understand," he said, his voice low and guttural as if he were in pain.

"Actually, I understand perfectly." She shrugged out of his hold. "Last night was fun. I had a blast. Maybe we can do it again sometime…once you get back in town."

"Madie?"

She tossed her clothes onto the counter by the sink. "What do you want me to say, Damon?"

He took a step back and ran a hand over his shadowed jaw.

"Do you want me to beg you not to go? If so, I'm afraid you've got the wrong girl." She pulled on her sweater. "I may have been a naïve virgin last night, but I'm not stupid. I can take a hint. Now if you don't mind,

I'd like a bit of privacy while I finish getting dressed."

He opened his mouth to speak, but stopped short. Instead, Damon shook his head and left the room.

Madie fought back tears. It was just sex. She knew that going in, but sometime during the night something had changed—at least for her. She swiped her hand across her eyes, wiping away any telltale moisture. She finished dressing, then took a deep breath and exited the bathroom.

She found Damon downstairs in the living room perched on the edge of the couch, his arms crossed over his chest. He stared at two cups of steaming coffee that had been placed on the end table.

"You never saw my collection," he said softly. "I have it in a fireproof vault."

"Maybe some other time." Madie had been so caught up last night that she'd forgotten all about the real reason she'd come over in the first place.

"Do you at least have time for a cup of coffee?" His brow furrowed and his lips firmed into a straight line.

Why did he want her to stay now? He'd all but asked her to leave only moments ago. "I didn't think you had time. You said you needed to leave after I did, *right*?" Madie hadn't called him a liar directly, but she'd certainly implied as much.

Damon didn't dispute her nor did he answer. Instead, he picked up the coffee mug and silently held it out in front of him.

Madie sighed. "Fine." She lifted the mug from his hands. Damon's fingertips brushed hers before releasing the cup, sending a jolt of electricity through her. She fumbled with the cup and almost dropped the coffee onto the floor.

Damon watched her, his gaze unreadable.

Madie brought the steaming mug to her lips and blew on the pungent liquid. She took a tentative sip. The bitter coffee held a hint of vanilla. Before she could ask for cream, Damon produced a small pitcher.

"Thanks." She took it from him and added some to her cup. "I don't suppose you have sugar hiding somewhere?"

He pushed off the couch and walked into the kitchen to retrieve the sugar.

Damon picked up the sugar bowl and strode back into the living room. Madie was hurt. He could see it in the tension around her mouth and smell it on her skin. And it was all because he couldn't keep it in his pants. He'd messed up big time and there were no easy fixes.

To make matters worse, he'd handled this morning all wrong. He should have prepared breakfast for Madie and brought it to her in bed. Instead, he'd freaked out and burst through the door to tell her that he was leaving town.

It sounded like a lame excuse to his ears, even though it was the truth.

He had to speak with the Lycanian Elders. They needed to know these latest developments, before he explained a word to Madie. Given her background, Damon knew there was no way she'd believe him.

Hell, he wouldn't believe him, if he were on the receiving end. The whole thing might be funny, if it was happening to someone else, but it wasn't.

Damon handed her the sugar. She placed two cubes in her cup and took another drink. Who would have thought that an encounter with the Hunter would lead to the discovery of his bondmate? Certainly not him. Damon shook his head at the irony. Of all the women on this planet, why did it have to be her?

Just one of many things that he needed to discuss with the Elders.

He picked up his cup and stared at Madie over the rim. She was beautiful, even with anger and hurt coloring her soft cheeks. Her full lips were still swollen from his kisses. Damon had no doubt other places were, too.

When he'd walked in on her holding his shirt to her face, his heart had skipped a beat and something inside of him had shattered. The burgeoning tenderness had scared him. He'd had no choice, but to mask it with anger.

The lush skin he'd explored at length last night was now hidden beneath her sweater and long skirt. Damon longed to touch her again.

Taste her wetness. Bury himself so deep inside her that she'd feel his shaft nudging her heart.

Damon's cock hardened at the thought of Madie's wet sheath closing around him. He cleared his throat and shifted casually to ease the tension in his jeans. He had to tamp down the need for her, at least until he could get things cleared up with the Elders.

Of course none of that would matter, if Madie stopped speaking to him. He had to smooth her hurt feelings. So Damon said the first thing that came to mind, "I'd like to see you, when I get back in town."

Her surprise showed for a second, but a cynical expression quickly masked it. "Sure, I'll wait for your call." Madie tipped her cup back and finished her coffee. "I'd appreciate it, if you'd call me a taxi."

Damon frowned. "I can take you home."

"No, I wouldn't want to be a bother. Besides, I've delayed you long enough."

Damon's voice came out on a growl. "I'll get the car." He bounded up the stairs to retrieve a clean shirt and get his keys. When he strode back into the living room, Madie was gone.

Every instinct told him to go after her, but Damon couldn't. Not now. She would be fine until he got back. She'd have to be.

Too much was riding on his meeting with the Lycanian Elders. Their decision could mean the difference between life and death.

18

Madie phoned Sarah the second she got home. Her best friend hadn't been able to come over, but she had commiserated with her and cursed Damon sideways for being such a fool.

Sarah had told her the only way to get over the pain was to get right back in there and go out with someone else. She'd said sleeping with a new man would wipe Damon's memory from her mind.

Madie had her doubts. She didn't think anything would take away the memory of making love to Damon, but she promised to give it some thought.

Commencement turned out to be a mixture of joy and sadness. Graduation meant saying goodbye to long time friends and moving out of the area. Sarah and Madie sat a row apart, their faces glum.

Madie looked over her shoulder into the crowd, but there was no sign of Damon. She knew he wasn't going to be there, but part of her had hoped that he'd show. She refused to admit it aloud, but she was disappointed with the way things had ended. After all the wining and dining, she thought he was different.

The truth hurt.

Sarah's name was called and she rose to receive her diploma. Her parents rushed forward to take a few pictures, then she returned to her seat. The next few names were a blur to Madie.

She sat there thinking about what was going to happen with her life now. She hadn't seen her father, but that didn't mean Gaston wasn't here, lurking somewhere in the back of the crowd.

One thing she had decided after last night was to keep her apartment. Madie knew her father wasn't going to be happy about it, but she needed a place of her own, a place she could escape to if things at home went south like she expected.

The announcer eventually called out Madie's name. She walked to the front of the crowd and looked out across the sea of faces. With the exception of Sarah and her family, none were familiar.

Madie's fingers trembled as she accepted the scrap of paper that was the culmination of all her years of college. Teary-eyed she looked at her graduating class, and then at the bleachers beyond. She could almost imagine her mom sitting in the crowd cheering her on.

This is for you, Mama.

Madie waved her diploma in the air and caught sight of *Damon* in the crowd. A thrill shot through her until she looked again, then her stomach sank. It wasn't him. She could see that now. Though the man did look a lot like him.

He had the same sable-colored hair and classically handsome face. His upper body was corded with muscle just like Damon's, but he had broader shoulders and a thicker frame. From a distance, the resemblance was uncanny.

He stared at her as she walked back to her seat and sat down. The ceremony droned on, until the students squirmed.

Finally, the words they'd all been waiting to hear were announced, "Ladies and gentlemen, I'd like to introduce you to the latest New Salford Art Institute graduating class."

The crowd went wild. On cue, the class tossed their caps into the air and it was done.

Sarah raced to Madie's side and embraced her. "We made it. Can you believe it?"

"No, I think I'm still in shock," she said.

"I know. Me, too." Sarah removed her graduation gown. "My parents are planning to take me out to dinner, want to come?"

"I'd love to, but—"

"She already has plans," a male voice said.

Sarah's eyes widened and she grinned at Madie. "Lucky girl," she said, squeezing her hand. "Glad you decided to take my advice."

Madie turned to find a stranger behind her. It was the same man that she'd seen in the crowd earlier, who'd looked so much like Damon from a distance. "I'm sorry, do I know you?"

"I haven't had the pleasure to meet you until now," he said.

Sarah's parents called her name.

"You kids have fun getting to know each other," Sarah said with a wink. "Don't do anything I wouldn't do."

Madie snorted. "I'm not about to take that advice again."

"I'll call you later," Sarah tossed back as she walked away.

Madie watched Sarah leave, then turned back to the stranger. "Now that my friend is gone, do you want to tell me who you are and why you interrupted my plans?"

The man hesitated, then stepped forward. "My name is Jack Hanson." He shook her hand. "I'm a friend of your father, Gaston."

"My father doesn't have any friends." Madie kept her gaze trained on the crowd. "Is Gaston here?"

Jack shook his head. "No, he couldn't make it."

"Couldn't make it or didn't want to come?" Madie asked, meeting his level gaze. Her diploma meant nothing to Gaston and never would. He'd already decided what she needed to do with her life and he'd do everything in his power to see that she followed his wishes.

Jack laughed. "He's your father, what do you think?"

Her brow furrowed. "I think you're one of Gaston's hunting buddies. And that you're here because he's trying to set us up."

"Don't hold that against me." Jack grinned. "At least not until you get to know me."

Madie smiled. She couldn't help it. She may not be interested, but the man was charming. "Fair enough."

Jack's smile widened. "If you wouldn't mind, I'd like to take you to dinner."

She opened her mouth to protest, but he stopped her before she could.

"For no other reason than to celebrate your graduation," he said. "I wasn't exactly thrilled by the idea of springing this blind date on you."

Until now, was left unsaid.

Madie weighed her options. She could try to find Sarah, go home and dig into a gallon of ice cream to drown her sorrows, or she could accept Jack's offer and go have a nice dinner.

Damon hasn't called and probably won't. You don't owe him anything. It was just a fling. Her heart sank at the thought. *You have a handsome, charming man in front of you, who is going out of his way to make you feel comfortable. Don't be an idiot. Why pine over a man, who's obviously not into you?*

"Sure," she found herself saying. "That would be nice." As a bonus, it might get her father off her back for a while.

They walked toward the parking lot where Jack had left his truck.

"I thought we'd go to that fabulous fish place up the coast," he suggested.

Madie's stomach clenched. "Are you talking about Neptune's?" That was where she and Damon had had their first date. She didn't want to go there, it would only make her more miserable.

"Yes, that's the place." He unlocked the truck and walked to the driver's side.

Madie opened her door and climbed inside. "Do you mind if we go to Bob's steakhouse instead? I'm not in the mood for fish." Nor did she think she'd ever be again.

Jack grinned. "Sure, no problem."

His mannerisms were so much like Damon's that Madie found herself nearly calling him the wrong name on several occasions. She didn't think Jack would appreciate that much. And she wouldn't blame him.

Throughout dinner, Jack remained charming, but aloof. He asked her questions about what she'd studied, what she liked, didn't like, and what her future plans were. When Madie inquired about his past, Jack's demeanor changed and he became evasive.

Madie chalked it up to being around Gaston too long. He had that effect on people, her included. It wasn't like she was looking for a relationship with the man, so it really didn't matter what he chose to confide.

After dinner, they drove back to Madie's apartment. The food had been delicious and she was still stuffed. She'd been ravenous all day, but considering how she'd spent last night that was hardly a surprise.

Jack's cologne mingled in the air between them as they strolled down the sidewalk toward her apartment. He smelled woodsy and fresh with a hint of citrus. Madie sniffed again, not citrus, orange. It was a nice combination and suited him from what she could tell.

When they reached the front door, Madie turned to face Jack, resting her back against the wooden frame. "I had a lovely time tonight. Thank you for taking me to dinner."

"You only graduate once," he said. "I'm glad I got to share this night with you."

She smiled. "Me, too."

Jack leaned closer. He was taller than Damon by an inch or two and he looked as if he out weighed him by at least twenty pounds. She wouldn't want to meet him in a dark alley.

Madie paused, surprised by her wayward thought. Jack had been nothing but a gentleman all evening. He deserved her respect.

"I'd better get inside." She gripped the doorknob behind her back. "I'm sure Gaston will be here first thing in the morning."

Jack shook his head. "No, you have a slight reprieve. He plans to come next weekend. He's been experiencing problems on the estate."

Madie straightened. "Is everything all right?"

"Yeah, just business stuff." He crowded her with his large body, then paused as if gauging her reaction. "I was hoping that maybe you'd invite me in for coffee, before the long drive back."

Madie hesitated, then said, "Sure." It wasn't like he was going to do anything with the threat of Gaston hanging over his head. She unlocked the door and stepped inside.

Jack followed her and shut the door behind him. He slipped off his coat and dropped it beside him as he sat on the couch. Madie walked into the kitchen to get some instant coffee.

When she returned to the living room with the two steaming cups, she found Jack rubbing his hands all over her worn throw. His eyes were closed and his head was thrown back as if he were in ecstasy. Madie almost laughed. He reminded her of a cat lounging in a pile of catnip.

She cleared her throat and asked, "What are you doing?"

Jack's eyes flew open and he stilled. "Your apartment is nice. Did you decorate it yourself?"

Madie rolled her eyes as she handed him a cup. "What do you think?" She laughed as she slid into her overstuffed chair. "I call this collection early college student cheap."

As if he couldn't help himself, Jack clenched the throw again, squeezing it through his fists.

"Seriously, what's up with the couch?" she asked.

"Sorry, it just smells so good." His eyes nearly rolled back in his head.

Madie sniffed, then wrinkled her nose. She couldn't smell anything. "Really?"

His eyes fluttered open. "Yes, I can't get enough of it. What do you use on it?"

She hadn't used anything, but she had spent a good amount of hours napping on it. "It's *Eau de Madeleine*, I guess." She giggled.

Jack's expression went from lazy to intense. "You should bottle it."

Madie flushed and glanced down at her cup. "You said you had a long drive. Where do you live?" She'd been wondering all night how Jack and her father had met. Personality wise, they didn't seem anything alike. Maybe they lived in the same area.

Jack sipped his coffee. "I've been staying with Gaston for the past couple of months."

"Months?" He'd been living with her father and she hadn't even known about it. What else had been going on that she didn't know about? Before Madie could ask, Jack's cellphone rang.

"Excuse me," he said, then answered. "Gaston, what's happened?"

Madie's heart raced. What was wrong?

"I see," Jack said, his expression grim. "I'll be there as soon as I can." He hung up.

"What is it?" Madie asked. "Is Gaston alright?"

"He's fine," Jack said. "Someone or something's been setting off his traps. I have to go." He stood and slipped his jacket on.

Cold enveloped her. For a few hours, she'd managed to forget that Jack was her father's hunting buddy. The call brought everything into perspective. Madie walked him to the door.

The playfulness had left his eyes, replaced by a hard unforgiving mask. The coldness that she saw there frightened Madie. "Thank you for the coffee," he said.

She nodded and started to shut the door. Jack's hand sprang out and gripped the frame. "I'd like to see you again."

"I-I don't know, Jack." Despite the wonderful evening and her best friend's advice, Madie wasn't ready to jump back into dating.

His gaze locked onto hers. Before she realized what he was about to do, Jack leaned in and tried to kiss her. Madie turned her head at the last second and his lips brushed her cheek. It was an awkward moment for them both.

Jack let go of the door and pulled out a card from his wallet. He handed it to her, pressing it into Madie's palm. His hand lingered over her fingertips. She tried to pull away, but he wouldn't allow it.

"At least think about it." He released her hand. "I had a good time tonight and I know you did, too. Give me another chance." With that, he left.

Madie shut the door and looked down at the card. It was a simple white design with embossed gold lettering. The only thing written on it was a phone number. It struck her as odd, since most people have their name engraved on business cards, but she shrugged it off as she placed it by the phone.

If Jack had been living with Gaston for months, then it had to have affected his behavior somehow. Gaston soiled everything he touched and that was never a good thing.

19

Jack smelled Damon Laroche all over Madie. It had been excruciating to sit through dinner with his stench so thick in the air. Even the smell of the food hadn't helped. And it had only gotten worse, when they reached her apartment.

Damon was all over it and so was her heat. The second he'd sat down on her couch it had hit him like a sledgehammer to the gut. No wonder the wolf had rutted inside her. He'd barely been able to keep his hands to himself. Had Gaston not phoned when he did, Jack was pretty sure he would've acted on his instincts.

Of course, he would've had to bathe her first to get Damon's scent off. The Alpha had marked her well. Jack doubted there was an inch of Madie's skin that hadn't been covered in Damon's pheromones. What Jack didn't understand was why?

Sure, Madie smelled delicious, but so did all women when they were in heat.

The Moonlight Kin and the Valoises were enemies. That had not changed nor would it ever, if he had anything to say about it. Had the Alpha fucked her to somehow get back at her family? That made the most sense given their long convoluted history.

Jack thought about Madie. Gaston was under the impression that she was innocent. Pure. The old man would pop a blood vessel if he knew the truth. He laughed at the picture that leapt to mind. His daughter was anything but innocent, if she'd spread her legs for Laroche.

He wondered if Madie knew the truth about her lover.

Jack thought about telling her just to wipe that smug look off her face. She'd rejected him, when he'd tried to kiss her. How dare she reject him! He wasn't the one betraying his family. He'd been betrayed. Jack knew how it felt, which was why he only looked out for himself.

He jumped into the truck and put it into gear. Madie would come around once she realized that she'd been used. He wouldn't have to tell her. Damon would, since werewolves never mated with humans. Madie was an easy fuck, another weapon to be used on Gaston. Nothing more. Eventually, she'd figure out the true score and give him a call. Jack was sure of it. No one resisted his charm for long.

When she did, he'd follow Laroche's example and fuck her into submission.

Jack found Gaston deep in the woods. He'd gathered up all his destroyed traps into a pile, so they could examine them. His face was flushed from exertion and whiskey. His fetid breath nearly knocked him over when he spoke.

"How did it go?" Gaston asked. "Did you manage to sleep with her?"

Jack's jaw clenched and he purposely focused on the traps, so Gaston couldn't read his expression. "No, but we did have a nice dinner after her graduation."

"Graduation?"

"Yeah, that's what you bowed out of today," Jack said, but there was no censure in his voice.

Gaston tossed another trap onto the pile. "Good to know that I didn't miss anything important."

"Madie was upset," Jack said, just to see the old man's reaction.

"She's too much like her mother for her own good." Gaston indicated to the traps. "What do you think?"

Jack examined them closely. Someone had taken a blowtorch to them. "It's sabotage like you thought. These have been burned until they fell apart."

"Damn it! It'll take at least two weeks to replace all of these." He scrubbed a hand through his red hair. "The full moon is in seven days."

Jack glanced at him. "What would you like me to do?"

"Put them in your truck," Gaston said.

"We could set up a blind in the trees. Pick them off as they make their way through the woods," Jack suggested.

"They'll smell us a mile away, even if we slather ourselves with bait goo."

Jack nodded. "True. We're not dealing with regular wolves." An idea started to form in his mind. It might be just crazy enough to work. Jack loaded the traps into his truck and waited for Gaston to climb inside the cab. The old man was sweating and grunted like he'd run a marathon.

"What are you looking at?" Gaston's eyes narrowed.

"I have an insane idea of how we can catch the wolves, but I'm not sure you're going to like it," Jack said.

"Try me," Gaston replied.

"It involves using your daughter," he said.

Gaston's eyes narrowed even more. "Using her how?"

"I saw the Alpha wolf sniffing around her, when she was at work."

Gaston stiffened. "Why didn't you kill him?"

"Didn't get the chance," Jack said. "Anyway, I'm thinking that maybe we can use her as bait to lure him into an ambush. We kill the Alpha and the pack will be in disarray. What do you think?"

Gaston sat back and eyed him for what felt like an eternity. "You sure it was him?"

Jack nodded. "No doubt in my mind."

"Do you think he likes her enough for the plan to work?" Gaston asked.

"Pretty sure." *If his stench was anything to go by.* Jack kept his expression neutral. Gaston would grow suspicious if he appeared too excited. "If nothing else, we could have it as our backup plan."

Gaston grinned. "Now you're thinking like a Hunter."

20

Damon stood in front of the Lycanian Elders. His head pounded and his throat was raw from pleading his case for two days. He'd missed Madie's graduation, something he was sure she'd find unforgivable.

He still couldn't believe his bondmate had turned out to be a human and not just any human, but the Hunter herself. Her face swam before his eyes, a vision of loveliness upon the ocean of uncertainty stretching before him.

Aidan Fortier stared down at him with a fierceness that reflected the intensity of his emotions. Damon's first cousin had been the most vocal when Damon had announced that Madeleine Lucine Valois was his bondmate. And he wasn't finished reading the riot act to Damon yet.

"It would be an abomination for you to take this woman as a mate," Aidan thundered, his eyes sparking with renewed fury. "Our species does not bond with humans."

"Cousin—" Damon stared at Aidan, trying once again to reason with him.

"You will address the Lycanian Elders formally or you will be sanctioned. Do you understand?" Aidan snapped.

Damon nodded. "I apologize to the Elders." He lowered his head as a sign of respect. "If I can have but a moment to give you my side of the story, I'm sure you will see that I have grounds to support my plea."

"Proceed," the Elders chimed in unison. Aidan glowered.

"Thank you." Damon looked up, but did not make eye contact with any of the Elders. "As you know, I was tasked with assassinating the Hunter. I staked out Madeleine and realized that she had no werewolf blood on her hands. I thought this discovery warranted further investigation. In order to do that, I had to gain access to her inner circle."

Aidan growled. "I don't see why that was necessary."

"I'm getting to that." Damon made eye contact with Aidan just long enough to let his cousin know that he wasn't going to be pushed around for much longer. "As I was saying, I needed to get closer, so I concocted an excuse for us to meet. We talked. I asked her out to dinner. It didn't take long to realize that she wasn't a willing participant in the initiation ceremony. In fact, she hates hunting."

"That's all fine and well, but why did you feel the need to plant your seed in this woman?" Aidan bellowed. "Of all the females that you could've chosen, you picked the Hunter." His face turned bright red and his sharp gaze bore into Damon.

Why had he done it? He couldn't exactly tell the Elders that it had been lust at first sight. Damon faltered for a second, then stood at attention. "I did it to stop the initiation. If any of you had bothered to read the Hunter files that you sent me, you would have noticed the paragraph discussing the future Hunter's purity status." He took a heaving breath, trying to rein in his temper. "It states that a Hunter must be pure at the time of the ceremony for the initiation to take."

A collective gasp was heard throughout the room.

"I wasn't positive it was referring to her virginity, but it seemed like a safe bet at the time," Damon said. "I did what needed to be done in order to stop the cycle—to end the Valois reign of terror."

He didn't bother to mention the fact that he'd planned to bed Madie with or without that tidbit of information. Or that she'd smelled so fresh and welcoming when he drove her to dinner that he had no choice but to seduce her.

Damon closed his eyes. He could almost hear Madie's soft moans of pleasure ringing in his ears as she came during sex for the first time.

He'd been her first and he'd be her only. No man was going to take his bondmate away from him, and that included her father.

"What about the murders?" Aidan asked. "Have you forgotten about your brother? Are you sure she is not responsible?"

Damon swallowed hard and his jaw clenched. "I'm sure Madie is innocent. As for my brother, I have forgotten nothing." The tone of his voice left no doubt that he spoke the truth.

Aidan's expression darkened. "If she isn't behind the killings, then who is murdering our people?"

This time Damon met his gaze squarely and answered truthfully, "I don't know. I think there may be a new player in town."

"Working alone?" Aidan asked. "Gaston would never allow that."

"That remains to be seen," Damon said.

"How will we find out if that's the case?" Aidan asked.

"I plan to investigate upon my return to New Salford."

The Elders spoke amongst themselves, using a private communication path. There were a lot of red faces and unhappy glances sent in his direction. Damon's heart pounded in his chest as he waited for their judgment. Finally, Aidan spoke for the group.

"You have until the moon. If we do not receive definitive proof by then of another Hunter, the pack will be ordered to carry out Lycan law."

"She's my bondmate," Damon said.

Aidan looked at him. "Then I suggest that you do not fail."

Damon bowed at the waist, even though all he wanted to do was punch his cousin in his smug face. Aidan didn't understand. Didn't want to understand. Hopefully someday that would change. He had little time to find who was killing members of the pack, but for Madie's sake, he had to try. He turned to leave the room.

"Damon?" Aidan called out, stopping him in his tracks. "When the time comes, do not stand in our way. We will not tolerate one of our own siding against us. If you choose to stand with your bondmate, then be prepared to die with her."

"I was prepared for that the second the wolf chose her as my bondmate." Damon saw the shock on Aidan's face as he spoke. Now maybe his cousin would understand. Damon nodded to the Elders, then left their chamber.

* * *

Monday morning was bright and sunny when Madie opened the door. Damon stood in the frame grinning. Her heart fluttered.

"Good morning." He leaned in to kiss her, but she backed away.

"What are you doing here, Damon?"

His brow furrowed, but his smile stayed firmly in place. "I came to see you. I wanted to take you to breakfast."

"I've already eaten."

He shrugged. "Well then, why don't I take you to get a cup of coffee?"

She shook her head. "I don't think so." It hurt Madie to say those words, but she had to stay strong. He'd treated her badly. She wasn't about to let him off without receiving a heartfelt apology and a lengthy explanation.

"Aren't you going to at least invite me in?" he asked.

She felt herself crumble. She called herself seven kinds of stupid, but Madie still stepped aside. She told herself that asking him in was only inviting trouble, but her heart didn't care. She was glad to see him. Her body came alive just looking at him. She didn't know how Damon had gotten under her skin so quickly, but she couldn't deny the fact that he had.

Damon walked into Madie's living room. She was barefooted and freshly showered, dressed in a loose pair of jeans and a red T-shirt. She didn't have any floral perfume on, but her natural scent was intoxicating and driving him to distraction. He wanted to drag her onto the floor and bury himself deep inside her until the world slipped away.

He took a seat on the couch, while she walked into the kitchen to get some water. Damon watched her bend forward to turn on the tap. Her jeans tightened over her rounded ass and need hit him. In that instant, he wanted her just as clearly and sharply as he had the first night he'd taken her.

She was his bondmate.

Damon's head dropped back onto the couch and he closed his eyes, trying to will his hard-on away. He took a deep breath and the unmistakable scent of wolf smacked him in the face. His head shot up and his body tensed. Damon's senses went on full alert.

He leapt up off the couch as if it had burned him, then turned to examine it closer. The scent was familiar, but he couldn't place it as he mentally ran through the remaining members of his pack.

Madie returned with two glasses of water. "What are you doing?" she asked. Her face scrunched in confusion.

Damon turned, his eyes narrowing to dangerous slits. "Are you sleeping with someone else?"

Madie put the water glasses down on the coffee table with a loud *thunk*. "What?"

"I asked if you were fucking another guy." Pain welled up inside him with such intensity that Damon thought he'd die. He'd just spent two days fighting with the Lycanian Elders to spare her life and now she did this to him. She was *his,* his bondmate. Didn't she understand that?

Something inside him shattered and cold enveloped his limbs. His whole body went numb. He'd kill the wolf that touched her with his bare hands when he found him. "What is his name?" he ground out between clenched teeth.

"I don't know what you're talking about." Madie planted her hands on her hips. "But you need to leave. Right now!"

Damon approached her, his fists clenched at his sides. "I asked you a question." He sniffed Madie, circling her a couple times as he did so.

"What is the matter with you?" She jerked back. "Have you lost your mind?"

He shot her a sharp glance, but said nothing. Damon couldn't detect another's scent on her skin, other than his own. His rage eased a fraction.

Madie's body trembled with anger and awareness. Damon's

overreaction should have scared her, but instead she felt elated. If he was angry, that meant he was jealous. And he could only be jealous, if he cared. Her heart swelled in her chest.

"Are you going to tell me who you've been seeing?" His voice had softened a bit, but still had bite.

"No!" She shook her head defiantly. "I don't have to answer you because it's none of your business."

Damon was on her before she even saw him move. He pinned her against the wall, his big body crowding hers. "Whether you realize it or not, you are my business."

His lips came down on hers with a hunger she didn't think existed within him. He savagely ravished her mouth, seeking entrance with his skilled tongue, while his hard body demanded her surrender.

She should have resisted, but Madie didn't. It felt too good to be in his arms again. Warmth filled her body, flooding her, swamping her with emotion. She clutched his broad shoulders. The pressure of the kiss intensified, until Madie felt like she was falling.

Today, Damon tasted like peppermint, sharp and sweet with a touch of heat as his tongue sparred with hers. Madie couldn't seem to get close enough to him. She pulled at his jacket until it fell to the floor. The white T-shirt he wore was taut across his muscled chest. Her nipples tightened as she brushed against him.

Damon moaned into her mouth and reached for the front of her shirt. He pulled back, his breathing ragged and his eyes glazed. "Is this one of your favorites?" He looked down at the material filling his hands.

"No," she whispered against his lips.

"Good," he muttered and recaptured her mouth.

Madie heard material rip, then cool air caressed her skin. The now useless garment slid off her shoulders and onto the floor, joining Damon's jacket.

"I'm sorry, but I can't wait. I have to have you now." He panted. "Your scent is driving me wild."

Damon's heated words caused her channel to flood. She wanted him.

Right here. Right now. Nothing else matter.

He removed her jeans and panties, then hiked her up higher until she straddled his waist. Damon braced her back against the wall. He held her with one arm as he fumbled with his pants.

Madie heard the glide of a zipper a second before he spread her thighs wide. Damon positioned himself at her entrance, then thrust hard, filling her completely. Madie wrapped her legs around his hips as he pulled out.

Damon groaned and drove into her again.

His rhythm gained momentum, and pretty soon he was pounding into her, claiming her body, while branding her soul. Madie's hips moved of their own accord, matching Damon's frantic pace.

He shifted her even higher until he was hitting her sensitive nub with each stroke. She threw her head back and moaned at the overwhelming pleasure coursing through her.

Madie felt the pressure building inside. Each glide of his thick shaft brought her nearer to blissful release. He was everything she'd remembered and more. And she couldn't get enough. Higher and higher she climbed, until Madie teetered on a precipice.

He drove deep and rotated his hips.

Madie cried out as her orgasm slammed into her, driving her over the edge.

Sweat dripped down the side of Damon's face. His hands tightened on her thighs and he rocked his hips, driving even deeper inside of her to draw out her release. Madie's sheath clamped down on his shaft.

Damon groaned and closed his eyes.

A second later, she felt his cock pulse and warmth explode inside her. The sensation triggered another orgasm, which left her limp.

Musk from their lovemaking filled the air. Damon's chest brushed Madie's sensitive nipples with every breath he took. She decided she could stay like this forever in the arms of the man that she loved. Madie tensed as the thought slipped into her mind.

"Let me down," she said, trying to prevent full-blown panic.

He slowly complied.

Once he did, she pushed Damon away.

Oh god, she loved the man. When had that happened?

Damon pulled his pants up and fastened them. "Are you going to tell me who you've been seeing now?" He picked up his jacket.

"Really? That's the first thing that comes to mind after what just happened?" Madie asked. She was too shaken by her sudden revelation to discuss something so inanely stupid with him. Why couldn't he just let it go?

Damon's nostrils flared. "Fine! If you change your mind, you know where to find me."

"And you know where I'll be." At least for a few more days.

He stormed out of her house, slamming the door behind him.

Madie released the breath she'd been holding. She knew that she could have salvaged an otherwise perfect moment by answering his stupid question, but she'd been miserable since she left his house.

He hadn't called or texted while he'd been gone. He'd let her think that he didn't want anything to do with her. It was about time Damon felt some of her pain. She wasn't about to call him. He could just sit and stew for a while.

<h1 style="text-align:center">21</h1>

For better or worse, Madie's period had always been like clockwork. She was now officially two days late. *There's no reason to be concerned yet*, she told herself, but that didn't stop Madie from phoning her ob-gyn and begging for an appointment.

The doctor slipped her in at noon and immediately drew her blood. Madie read every magazine in the office and chewed off all her fingernails, while she waited. An hour later, her doctor walked into the room with a smile plastered on her face.

"Congratulations, you're going to have a baby," she said.

And just like that, Madie's whole world changed.

Madie drove back home in a daze, the doctor's words ringing in her ears. One part of her was scared out of her mind. The other part was thrilled. She just wasn't sure which part would prevail in the end.

She hadn't spoken to Damon since their fight. She'd felt off the past couple of days, but had chalked it up to the excitement of graduation and the fact that she'd been eating more than normal.

Madie laughed. That should have been her first clue.

Who in the world has sex for the first time and ends up pregnant a few days later? Madie shook her head in dismay. She was going to have a baby. This was serious. There was no time to cling to her foolish pride.

Whether she was ready or not, she had to let the father know. Madie had no idea how Damon would take the news. She prayed he'd be happy, but they hadn't known each other long enough for her to be sure.

Known each other long? She cackled again, sounding insane.

Before she could chicken out, Madie turned the car toward the nice part of town and drove to Damon's house. She parked the car and sat in it for a few minutes, staring at his front door. Her hands were shaking, when she finally opened the car door and stepped outside. Her head came up as she smelled smoke. That's when Madie noticed the flames.

"Oh, my god, the house is on fire." She screamed and raced to the front door. Madie pounded on it, but Damon didn't answer.

The thought of losing him terrified her. Madie dug into her purse and grabbed her phone. She called 911, then ran around the house to the back door. If Damon was home, then he was in danger and needed her help. Madie banged on the back door and threw her shoulder against it. The door didn't budge.

Flames shot out of the roof, licking at the old timber with glee. Madie ran back around the house. She spotted Damon's car in the garage as the sound of sirens reached her ears. She pounded on the front door again and listened for footsteps.

None came.

Damon choked. The flames were preceded by a thick cloud of noxious gases. His senses were so overloaded, he couldn't find the front door. His eyes watered, blurring any chance of seeing, and his lungs burned as he fought for each breath.

The sealed vault would protect his priceless collection, but did little to help him. The room swirled before his eyes. Damon knew if he didn't get out soon, there would be no escape.

In the distance, he heard sirens. Or was his mind playing tricks on him? A twisted wishful thinking in his last moments of life. Thoughts of Madie swamped him. He'd failed her. He'd failed the Elders. He'd failed his pack. Perhaps it would be better if the flames took him.

Even as the distressing thought crossed his mind, the wolf's instinct to survive was too strong to allow it. His hands hit glass and Damon realized he was at the window. He took a step back and shifted to his other form, then threw himself through the pane of thick glass, shattering it into a million tiny pieces.

Pain ripped through his body as the glass worked its way through his fur to the tender skin below. Bleeding, he staggered to his feet and forced himself to move. The sirens grew louder. Their haunting wails signaling that help had arrived.

Damon limped to the edge of the woods and waited for his eyes to stop burning. The house was engulfed in flames. The fire splintered and attacked from every angle, hungrily eating every beam before devouring the interior walls.

The emergency crews arrived and rushed forward hoses in hand. Water spewed out, attempting to thwart the blaze, but it was too late. The house was a total loss. Damon heard a scream and saw five firefighters attempting to hold back Madie. She fought like a banshee, throwing one of the men to the ground. She screamed out his name as she was lifted off her feet.

The cry was primal, tortured like a creature that has lost its mate. Damon stood on shaky legs. Hearing her cries of pain renewed his strength and he stumbled to the edge of the tree-line.

Madie kicked the fireman holding her. "Let me go, damn it. I've got to get inside." She struggled, wrenching one man's hand from her wrist. "You don't understand, the father of my child is in there."

The firemen turned weary eyes toward the blaze. When they looked back at her, their faces reflected their sadness. "If he's still in the house, then I'm afraid we've lost him."

Tears welled up in Madie's eyes. Damon couldn't die. Not now. Pain ripped through her body, so strong it felt as if it would tear her in half. Her hands automatically dropped to her abdomen to protect it as grief enveloped her.

The fireman moved her back away from the house. She was lying on the grass, when Madie caught a flash of movement in the trees. Standing on the edge of the woods was a magnificent sable wolf. His gold eyes were eerily intelligent in their perusal of her.

She stared at the animal, transfixed. He took a step back, and then another. Logic told Madie to run, but she didn't—couldn't. She found herself drawn to the creature. Before she realized what she was doing, Madie had crossed the lawn and stopped at the edge of the woods. The wolf was farther in, but had somehow waited for her. Instinct told her that the wolf wouldn't hurt her. Logic called her every kind of crazy.

How could Gaston kill so many of these beautiful creatures? You'll think differently if that wolf eats you. The little voice in her head retorted.

The wolf continued to stare at her, then stepped even deeper into the woods. Madie followed him, fascinated by the creature's bizarre behavior. When she'd lost sight of the yard, the wolf stopped.

Suddenly the sable fur started to glow. It grew brighter and brighter, until Madie had to shield her eyes.

When the light finally faded, Damon stood in front of her completely naked. Madie couldn't seem to remember how to breathe. The earth tilted on its axis and the ground beneath her feet fell away. Emotions flowed through her. She went from relieved that he was alive to angry, confused, and scared.

Damon took a step toward her.

"Don't move." She held up a shaky hand to ward him off. Her other hand subconsciously moved to her abdomen to protect her child.

"Now you know what I am." He paused mid-step.

The trees started to spin and Madie stumbled back. "No, I don't."

He stood solemnly, soot covering half of his handsome face. Damon coughed, then his lip curled in a sneer. "I'm your bogeyman." His voice held bitterness and resignation.

"You're a monster, an abomination." Tears filled her eyes.

He laughed, then coughed again. "It's funny, that's what the Lycanian Elders said about you." Damon took another step closer.

"Stay away," Madie screamed. "I mean it." She choked on the words. Her heart hurt worse than if someone had taken a knife to her chest and cut it out.

"We have to talk."

"There's nothing left to say," she said. "You're a liar. You've lied to me from the beginning." Madie gulped in air, trying to steady herself. She couldn't afford to pass out. "This explains everything." She indicated toward him. "Why you rushed me out the morning after we had sex, the attack in the alley, all of it."

Damon's eyes narrowed. "You know I made love to you that night."

"Do I?" Her mouth twisted painfully. "How would I know? It was my first time."

"Madie…" He sighed. "I had nothing to do with that attack in the alley."

She held up her hands. "Stop lying. I'm so sick of people lying to me." She swallowed the bile that threatened to rise. "Tell me, did you do all this to hurt my father?"

He didn't answer fast enough.

Her hand covered her mouth. "No, it's not him you're after. You want the book."

Damon's face hardened and his honey-colored eyes lost some of their brilliance. "I did what I had to do to protect my people," he bit out. "If I made any mistake at all, it was falling for the next Hunter."

"Well I'll remedy that mistake right now. As soon as I get my inheritance, I'll leave town and you'll never have to see me again." She turned to leave.

"Madie, don't!" Damon reached out to touch her, but she wretched her arm away. "I won't beg. Not even when the baby comes." The determination on his chiseled face held little doubt about the sincerity of his words.

Madie was stunned. He knew about the baby.

Of course he knew about the baby, she'd told the firemen. *Oh my god, the baby.*

She wasn't carrying a baby she was carrying a monster. Visions of *Rosemary's Baby* and the *Alien* movies went through Madie's mind in quick succession. What was she going to do?

"I don't want to ever see you again," she said, but couldn't meet

Damon's eyes for fear she'd glimpse the hurt lingering in his amber depths.

Madie stumbled through the woods and ran when she reached the yard. Her body quaked as she ripped the door of her car open and crawled inside. Her fingers shook as she pressed the lock button and started the engine. The flames were gone, but the firemen continued to douse the house.

She drove away in tears, refusing to look in the review mirror for fear of what she'd find. Madie glanced down at her stomach, cupping it tenderly. "It's just you and me now, squirt."

Tears made it difficult to see the road. The lines blurred as she drove aimless around New Salford. She was crazy, plain and simple. Losing her mind could be the only explanation for what she'd just witnessed. Werewolves did not exist. They couldn't exist. Because if they did, then everything her father had told her had been true. She couldn't accept that. Wouldn't accept that.

Madie had always thought it was only a matter of time before she and Gaston suffered from the same delusions.

Today, her nightmare had come true.

Damon knew he shouldn't have transformed in front of Madie, but she'd seemed so distraught over his presumed death that he couldn't help himself. What had he been thinking? She was human and frightened out of her mind.

What had she called him after he'd transformed? *An abomination.*

He winced as he recalled her exact words. His people had spent centuries trying to outrun that ugly word and now after all these years it was back again.

The pain that he felt was palpable. Madie would never accept him now. She'd never accept their child. Fear gripped Damon. She thought she had a monster growing inside of her.

Would she take the obvious way out and get rid of their baby?

It was her choice, but still…

Damon dropped to his knees. The thought of losing his bondmate and his child clawed at him, leaving deep welts on his soul. He reached out, hoping to connect with Madie's mind, but found only darkness.

The howl that escaped his throat was one of pain and for the first time in his life—*fear*. He'd never cared about his own safety. He'd recklessly rushed into danger over the years with complete abandon. But that all changed with the bond. Now that he had a wife in the eyes of the pack and a child on the way. Loss took on a whole new meaning.

22

adie locked herself inside her apartment and spent the next forty-eight hours trying to process everything that had happened. She'd picked up the phone a dozen times to call Sarah, only to remember at the last minute that her friend was on a cruise with her family in the Bahamas. She wasn't going to ruin it just because she was going insane.

Damon hadn't phoned. Not that she'd expected him to after their last conversation, but the loss still hurt. She had no idea what she was going to do. Gaston would freak, if he found out about the pregnancy. It didn't matter that she was almost twenty-five. His views of the world hadn't changed since the fifties.

The phone rang. Madie stared at it, debating whether to answer. She decided to let it go to voicemail. The phone stopped ringing for a minute, then started up again. What if it was her father calling to tell her that he'd be over tomorrow to pack up her things? Madie sighed and picked up the receiver.

"Hello," she said tentatively.

"Hi," Jack said. "What are you doing for lunch?"

Madie tried to hide the disappointment in her voice, but wasn't successful. She knew she couldn't stay in her apartment forever, eventually she'd have to come out. She cleared her throat. "I have no plans."

"Great, now you do," he said. "I'll pick you up in an hour."

"See you then."

Lunch was great, just like dinner had been the night of her graduation. The problem wasn't with Jack, it was with her. No matter how awful the circumstances were, she couldn't shake thoughts of Damon. It was almost as if she could feel his pain and confusion, though Madie knew it was all in her imagination.

She dreamt about him at night and obsessed over him in the harsh light of day. In her dreams, Damon seemed utterly alone. It was difficult to resist the urge to go to him—comfort him, even though she knew it would be a mistake.

Jack tapped her hand and smiled.

He was such a nice man. One thing she couldn't do any longer was lead him on. Jack deserved a woman who cared about him, and him only.

Madie had decided to let Jack know that she couldn't see him anymore by the time they returned to her apartment. She unlocked the door and stepped inside, then turned to face him. "Thank you again for lunch. It was really kind of you, but—"

"May I come in?" he asked.

"Umm, uh, sure." Madie stepped aside.

Jack came in and shut the door behind him. "How come I get the feeling I'm not going to like what you're about to say next?"

Madie looked down at her hands. She'd never had to do this sort of thing and for that she was grateful because it sucked.

Jack nudged her. "Cut to the chase. Tell me what it is that you wanted to say."

Madie took a deep breath. "Jack, I think you're a really great guy. You're nothing like I expected."

He gave her a tense smile. "You make it sound like that's a bad thing."

"No." Madie shook her head. "It's not, but I have a lot going on right now and I don't think we should see each other anymore. Not even casually."

"You just said that you thought I was nice," he said. "I thought we were getting along well."

"We were, I mean are, but the truth is I've been seeing another man. I met him before I met you. And things between us are complicated right now," Madie said. "I don't want to make it more so, if I can avoid it." She didn't mention that the man she'd been seeing was a werewolf because she was conscious of who she was talking to. As angry as she was at Damon, she did not want him harmed or hunted.

Jack leaned against the doorframe. "What's his name?"

Madie's brow furrowed. "It's not important."

"Then why don't you tell me?" Jack asked.

Madie sighed. "Damon."

Jack's eyes flashed with fury and his whole body tensed. The surprising emotion disappeared as quickly as it had arrived. Did he know? Fear beat at her as she fought to keep her placid expression. Before Madie could probe to find out what had caused the sudden change, Jack smiled.

Would he react that way if he knew Damon's secret? She didn't know. Madie had never understood the mind of a Hunter.

"I understand," he said. "When things don't work out with this guy, you know where to find me."

Madie blanched. That hadn't been the response she'd been expecting, but she was grateful that Jack was taking the news so well. "Thanks for understanding," she said.

"No problem. Well, I'd better scoot," he said.

Madie walked over to shut the door behind him. At the last second, Jack turned and pulled her into his arms. Stunned by the sudden move, she froze. His lips came down upon hers, firm and unforgiving. Jack's tongue pushed its way into her mouth, attempting to coax a response from her.

When none came, he released her.

Madie gasped, trying to slow her racing heart. "Why did you do that?"

"I've wanted to do that since I first saw you at graduation," Jack said. "And," he smiled, "I thought you'd like to see what you'll be missing."

Madie tried to laugh, but the sound came out strained and patently fake. "Goodbye, Jack."

"See you soon," he said, then strolled off down the sidewalk.

Jack's smile slipped the second he turned away from Madie. How dare the bitch dump him for a mongrel! He'd planned on seducing her after lunch, but Madie had kept him at arm's length the whole time. At first, he'd thought she was playing coy.

It wasn't until they'd reached her apartment that he'd smelled the changes in her body. Fury had engulfed him as the truth hit his nose and was later confirmed by her damning admission.

Madeleine Lucine Valois was pregnant. And Damon Laroche was the father.

Paternity was never in doubt, since Damon's stench coated her skin. It shouldn't have been possible given that she was human, but there was no denying her rise in hormones. It was one thing to sleep with the wolf, it was quite another to get knocked up by him.

The stupid bitch had screwed up everything.

Jack pulled out his phone and stared at Gaston's number. His finger hovered over the talk button. No telling how the old man would react to the news of his only daughter, only heir being impregnated by the Alpha of the Moonlight Kin pack.

Gaston might do something insane like shoot her on sight and ruin all their well-laid plans. Jack couldn't take that chance, not when he was so close to achieving his goals. He shoved the phone back into his pocket. There was only one way to fix this mess.

He had to get rid of Madie. If that didn't work, there was always the backup plan.

23

It had taken Madie an hour to get to her family home and an hour to get back. Somehow she'd managed to sneak into the house and retrieve the Book of Lycan without being caught. She only hoped that Gaston wouldn't notice the book was missing before she could return it. Madie had shoved the old tome onto a shelf in her kitchen, then left for work.

Her mind was so distracted by what she had done that Madie didn't see the black Mercedes coming down the street as she crossed the road by Johnson's Bookstore.

Mr. Johnson's bellow interrupted her thoughts.

Madie glanced up in time to see the car coming straight for her. The windows had been blacked out, making it impossible to see inside. The engine roared as the driver gunned the vehicle.

For a split second, Madie didn't move. She was too surprised. Then her thoughts leapt to her unborn child and she dove for the sidewalk.

The Mercedes clipped her ankle, sending shards of pain streaming through her leg. Madie turned expecting to see brake lights. Instead, the driver punched the gas and sped away. Mr. Johnson came running across the road with his phone in his hand.

"Did you catch the license plate number?" he asked.

"It didn't have one." Madie bent to examine her leg.

Mr. Johnson helped her up. "Are you alright? That was a close one."

Madie could stand, but her ankle was already turning blue.

"I think you should have that looked at," he said. "Come into the store and I'll call an ambulance." Mr. Johnson put one arm around Madie's waist, supporting her weight while she limped back across the street to the bookstore. He plopped her into a seat and moved a stack of books aside so she could put her leg up.

Madie winced as she lowered her leg onto the small table. "Did you see the driver?"

"No, but I have no doubt it's one of those crazy drivers from the city." He sniffed and his moustache twitched from side to side. "They don't pay a mind to the speed limit and they always drive like they're in a hurry. Wish the mayor could fine them for coming into town."

Madie feigned a yawn to hide her smile behind her hands. Mr. Johnson believed all of New Salford's woes were caused by the city drivers that regularly came to their little town to get away from the crowds. He blamed everything from the price of milk to the cost of printing on out-of-towners, so it was no surprise that he thought the Mercedes was an evil city-dweller, too.

The ambulance arrived and took Madie to the hospital. While she waited, she phoned Berta to let her know that she wouldn't be in. After Madie was treated with the world's most expensive gauze wrap, she called a taxi to come pick her up and take her home.

Madie stumbled in the door and landed on the couch. She decided to sleep there for the night, instead of wrestling with the stairs. In the morning, she'd call her father to come pick her up. She could've dismissed the break-in at the diner as a random act, if it had been the only thing that had happened to her. But when she coupled it with nearly being rundown in the street, then the random act suddenly looked *intentional*.

Someone was trying to hurt her, though she didn't understand why. She'd never consciously hurt anyone in her life. Her mind leapt to Damon. Had he been behind the hit and run? It wasn't the model of car that he drove, but given his level of deception, Madie knew he was more than capable. Yet somehow she couldn't bring herself to believe it.

Now you're just being stupid and naïve, the little voice in her head said. This time Madie didn't argue with it because she knew it was right.

Damon flooded her mind as soon as her head hit the decorative pillow. He smiled. His face radiated glowing warmth that felt so real in the darkness that her skin tingled. Just as the dream was getting good, the doorbell rang. Figures.

Madie grabbed her crutch and struggled off the couch to peek through peephole. Damon stood on the other side of the door, looking none too happy.

"Open the door, Madie. I know you're in there," he grumbled impatiently.

Madie closed her eyes and counted to five, then unlocked the door. "What are you doing here, Damon?"

"I'm here to make sure that you're alright. That our baby is alright," he said in strained voice. "Can I please come in?"

She stepped aside. "How'd you hear about the accident?"

"I didn't." His gaze darted over her, looking for any sign of injury. He locked onto the scratches on her hands, then traveled to the bandage on her ankle. "I just knew."

Her suspicions rose again. Had he been the one behind the wheel? The thought sent ice through her veins. Before she dared voice the question, Damon lifted her hands to his mouth and kissed every scrape, every bruise. His tongue darted out over the deeper wounds.

When his eyes met hers again, they were filled with unshed tears. "I'm sorry I wasn't there to protect you and our child from danger."

A lump formed in her throat and the muscles in her chest tightened, threatening to cut off her air. "That's alright." Madie carefully pulled her hands away. She could think with him touching her. His tenderness was hurting her heart.

She couldn't allow that to happen again. She couldn't survive any more pain. Madie had to stay strong for herself and her child. The only way to do that was to keep Damon away.

His mere presence brought danger to her, to her way of life, to her sanity. They came from two different worlds. Heck, they were two different species. They had no chance at a future.

"What happened?" His face was pale and drawn with worry.

"I almost got run down. Guess the driver didn't see me, because he kept going afterwards."

"You don't really believe that, do you?" he asked.

"I don't know what to believe," she said truthfully. "I'm tired. I am confused. And I really need to be left alone."

"Are you sure you're all right?" he asked.

"I'll be fine." Madie wobbled, not used to the foreign feel of a crutch under her arm. "The doctor said I was lucky, no broken bones, just lots of bruising. I'll have to keep it wrapped for a couple of days and put lots of ice on it." Madie's foot was almost black, but she could put weight on her ankle.

Damon stared at her bandaged foot.

If he continued to look at her like that, she was going to cave. She could feel the walls inside her already beginning to crumble. She had to get him out of her house, out of her life before that happened.

"You need to go." Madie ignored the pain welling inside.

Damon flinched, but didn't say a word. His eyes sought hers, their amber depths fathomless.

"Before you leave, I have something for you." Madie limped into the kitchen to retrieve what he'd wanted all along. When she returned, she dropped the battered tome onto the coffee table. "Here, this is what you really came for. Isn't it?"

"Madie." Damon reached for her.

"Don't!" She jerked back. "Take it! Take it and leave. It's what you wanted. What you've always wanted." Madie laughed bitterly. "You never wanted me."

She'd been such a fool to believe that a *man* like Damon Laroche would want a sheltered, naïve woman like her. Gaston's overprotective nature had done her no favors. Madie was far from worldly. She might as well have "stupid" tattooed on her forehead.

"That's not true," Damon said.

"All these years I thought Gaston was wrong," she said. "But he was right about you."

Damon stiffened and red bloomed in his cheeks.

"A werewolf really can rip your heart out before you realize what has happened. I'm living proof."

He flinched and pain flashed across his face. "Don't go," he murmured.

It hurt to look at him, but Madie forced herself to meet Damon's eyes. "There's no reason for me to stay. Now if you'll excuse me, I have an initiation to get ready for."

Damon walked to the door, then stopped short, gripping the frame until his fingers turned white. Through gritted teeth he said, "If you need me, just call and I'll come for you." With that, he pushed forward and strode into the darkness.

Madie watched him until he disappeared from sight. With each step he took, her heart sank a little further in her chest.

It was for the best, she told herself again. They couldn't possibly remain together. Could they? *Definitely not.* Their whole relationship had been based on lies.

She'd given Damon exactly what he wanted, what he'd really come for. Madie had made the right decision, she was sure of it.

Then how come it feels like my heart is breaking?

Anger boiled through Damon. He knew Madie wanted him—wanted their child, but she insisted on pushing him away. Her birthday was tomorrow, which meant the ceremony was upon them and he was no closer to solving the murders. To make matters worse, the killer was now after Madie.

Why would he target Madie?

It made no sense. She's human, not wolf.

Damon stopped. Madie may not be wolf, but she was carrying one. He could smell the babe on her skin. Taste it in her blood, when he'd cleaned her wounds. She may be human, but what was growing inside her wasn't. Did the killer know that?

Was it possible Madie was being hunted by another Hunter?

Damon couldn't dismiss the thought outright. Anything was possible. He was pretty sure that Gaston would not hunt his own, even though the Hunter's behavior was getting more and more erratic. The risks he took grew bolder and bolder, as if he were no longer worried about being caught or violating the treaty. There was no telling what he'd do next.

Had he hired an outsider to kill Madie, so that her blood wouldn't be on his hands?

In the end, it didn't matter. Damon had to stop whoever was doing this or die along with his bondmate and heir.

Damon returned to the home that he'd rented, while his other house was being rebuilt. Thoughts of Madie flooded his mind. He was missing something, but what? He pulled out the folders the Lycanian Elders had given him about the pack members that had died. There had to be a common denominator. He just hadn't noticed it yet.

He scanned the papers until his eyes burned. All the members that had died had been from the Fortier line, except Jacque.

Why had the killer picked Jacque? He wasn't part of the pattern. Was it because he was heir apparent? Damon didn't think so.

His hands shook as he picked up the Book of Lycan. The leather was soft and pliant beneath his fingertips. Damon had spent years trying to get his hands on the records written on these pages. In this book, he'd finally discover the truth about what had happened to his brother and the others.

And the information had only cost him his bondmate and unborn child.

24

Madie phoned Gaston the morning of her twenty-fifth birthday. She thought he'd be happy to hear from her, but his gruff tone told her otherwise.

"I'm ready to go through with the initiation, but I'm keeping my apartment. I want a place in town, so I can be near my gallery," she said, sounding braver than she actually felt.

"We'll discuss it when I arrive," he said. "I'll be there in late afternoon." Gaston hung up before she could respond.

So much for wishing her a happy birthday.

Jack and her father arrived, when Gaston said they would. Madie had dressed in slacks and flat shoes because she wasn't sure what she'd have to do once the initiation started. To be honest, she didn't care as long as the whole thing went by quickly.

They piled into the front seat of her father's pickup truck and drove to her family home. Jack sat on one side of her and Gaston on the other. Madie felt like the filling in a rancid sandwich. Broad shoulders brushed hers, squeezing off any chance of movement. She reached for the radio in hopes of relieving the tension in the cab, but Gaston stopped her. Instead, they drove in silence.

The sun slowly faded on the horizon, its waning rays winked over the treetops before saying goodbye. Madie felt the chill to her bones and snuggled deeper into her sweater.

After a quick fuel stop, they finally reached the long familiar driveway that led to her childhood home. Gaston didn't put on his blinker nor did he slow down as they approached.

"Gaston, you're going to miss the driveway." Madie watched as they drove right past it. "We have to turn around."

Gaston glanced at her. "We aren't going to the house, girl."

She frowned and looked back as the drive faded into the distance. "But I thought…what about the ceremony?"

"Isn't held at the house," he said, finishing her thought.

Jack kept a watchful eye on the woods. His sharp gaze scanning the tree line for any sign of movement.

"Anything yet?" Gaston asked, without taking his eyes off the road.

Jack shook his head. "Not yet."

Suspicion rose inside her. "What are you looking for?"

"Company." Jack's eyes fastened on her abdomen and his expression slowly twisted into hatred, before carefully resuming its stony façade.

Madie crossed her arms defensively and looked straight ahead.

Gaston pulled onto an unpaved road that was full of ruts. The truck bounced its way to the woods, then stopped. "We're here." He shut the engine off.

They all climbed out.

Madie was stiff from the long ride. She stretched her arms above her head, then touched her toes.

"Stop fooling around!" Gaston said. "We still have a ways to go." He led them down a trail, deeper and deeper into the forest.

Fear and her crutch slowed her footsteps. "Where are we going?" Madie asked.

"You'll see." He dismissed her question.

Jack nudged her forward, but continued to watch their surroundings.

"Father?"

"Don't ever call me that!" he bellowed.

Madie flinched as his words struck her. Something was wrong, very wrong. "I want to go back to the house."

Jack reached out and grasped Madie's arm, his grip tightening to the point of pain. "You aren't going anywhere."

She tried to pull away, but he only increased the pressure. "Let go! You're hurting me."

"I'll do more than that, if you don't come along." Jack leaned in close to her ear, so that only she could hear what he was saying. "I can smell him on you," he growled. "You carry his heir in your womb."

He knew about Damon and the baby. But how?

Madie struggled to break Jack's punishing grasp. "Gaston, what is going on?"

Gaston's lip curled. "You always were weak." He shook his head in disgust. "I should have rid myself of your existence when I found out your mother had that affair in Boston. She said you were mine, but the Valoises breed true, and they always breed male."

The shock of the admission numbed Madie to the core. Tears flowed freely down her cheeks. All the years of trying to get Gaston to love her. All the years of thinking that she wasn't good enough in his eyes, finally made sense. So much wasted time. Well no more.

She stared at Jack and Gaston. The two men looked as if they were possessed. Their pale faces were sunken, their eyes reduced to slits, and their mouths were no more than twisted lines of determination. They upped the pace and Madie found herself having to hobble quickly to keep up, which sent pain spiking through her ankle.

They reached a clearing in the center of the woods. Someone had gathered stones and laid out in a circle. Four torches were perched around the crude structure. Jack released Madie long enough to go light them.

She looked around.

The center of the stone circle held four stakes with leather tethers attached to each one. She didn't like the looks of this at all. Madie gauged the distance back to the truck, but knew with her bum ankle that she'd never be able to outrun Jack.

"What are you planning?" she asked.

Before Gaston could answer, Jack lifted her off the ground and carried her into the circle. He held her down, while the man she'd thought was her father tied her arms and legs to the stakes.

"He'll come for her," Jack said. "He has no choice. She carries his spawn."

Gaston gasped in horror. "She's been tainted?"

Jack nodded.

"How do you know?" Gaston's gaze examined Madie closely.

"Isn't it obvious?" Jack asked. "She doesn't cringe from my touch. She's used to male hands being upon her body. If she were pure, that wouldn't be the case."

Gaston's face flushed. "But you said there was a babe, perhaps you're wrong?"

Jack shook his head. "No, I followed her to the Alpha's house. I heard her tell him that she was carrying his heir."

Gaston's eyes burned with hatred. "You whore!" He spat. "If you weren't my sole heir, I'd shoot you this instant." He slipped the safety off on his gun.

Madie's heart slammed into her ribs. "I can explain." She pulled against the restraints, but it only made them tighter.

"Don't say another word. I raised you as my own and you've dishonored me. You've dishonored this family," Gaston said. "Jack, get the head strap. We'll have to pry her jaw open to get her to drink the potion."

In that moment, Madie knew they were insane. She had to get away from them or she and her unborn child were going to die.

Jack hesitated. "Will it kill the child?" he asked, but there was no concern in his voice, no feeling whatsoever. The utter disregard for her safety chilled her.

"What does it matter?" Gaston countered. "She's already ruined everything."

Unholy light filled Jack's eyes. "Perhaps not," he said. "I've been giving her pregnancy some thought. We might be able to use it to our advantage."

Gaston turned to him. "How so?"

"She's carrying what will in all likelihood be the future Alpha of the Moonlight Kin pack," Jack said.

"So?" Gaston glowered.

"So, if I was to, say, marry Madie, and she had the baby, then we'd eventually have total control over the pack," he said. "They wouldn't be able to deny their Alpha once the child got a little older."

Jack's reasoning, though sound, terrified Madie. No way would she agree to any of this. She'd die before she'd allow her child to be used in this fashion.

"If the abomination lives," Gaston said with a disgusted snort. "You can do whatever you want with it. It's not like it's human."

Jack retrieved the potion and handed it to Gaston, who stirred the paste until it thinned into a semi-liquid state.

Madie pulled on the tether as Jack strapped her head in. The restraints locked her forehead in place and yanked at her jaw down until her mouth hung open. "Don't do this!" she pleaded.

Jack leaned in close. "This is the only chance you and your baby have of making it out of here alive. I suggest that you shut up and take it, before I remove the offer from the table and move on to our backup plan. It's not like I'm happy to be getting Damon's sloppy seconds."

Gaston approached. There was no love in his eyes as he poured the potion down her throat. Madie tried to spit it out, but the tether prevented it. She held it in her mouth for as long as she could, but with Jack massaging her throat, she eventually had to swallow.

The bitter taste made her gag, but the potion stayed down.

"Now we wait," Gaston said. "It shouldn't take long for it to take effect. When it does, she'll do whatever we want."

25

Damon had spent the night and all morning reading the Book of Lycan. He was still in shock over what he'd discovered. The pain that followed was nearly unbearable. He had to contact the Elders, then he'd go find Madie. If what he'd read was true, then she was in serious danger.

It was early evening by the time Damon reached Madie's home. He pounded on the door, but there was no answer. She was gone. Had been gone for a while, if her fading scent was any indication.

He recognized Gaston's stink and the same elusive werewolf scent that he'd caught earlier. This time it was fresh. His blood went cold. Fear gripped his heart like icy tentacles.

"Why?" he asked, but the empty house held no answers.

There was only one place that Madie could be—at her family's estate. He had to reach her. Save her. It wasn't until that moment that Damon realized how much he loved her.

He raced away from the house, his heart beating a mile a minute. Damon turned a corner and slammed into a wall or at least that's what he thought. When he looked up, he was face to face with Luc.

Damon stumbled back, ready to fight his Beta if need be. "What are you doing here?" he asked, a growl forming in his throat.

"I've come to warn you that the pack is after your mate." Luc grumbled. "But I can see I'm too late."

Damon smiled at the sour expression on Luc's face. "I should have known I could count on you, my friend." Then the words Luc spoke finally sank in. Damon's face drained of blood. "How long have they been on the hunt?"

Luc glanced at his watch. "At least an hour or two. They were headed out to the Hunter's estate."

"Then we must hurry. My mate and child are in even greater danger than I realized."

Luc grabbed Damon by the shoulder and guided him to his waiting vehicle. "I'll drive. You talk," he said.

Damon explained that Gaston had Madie.

Luc's eyes narrowed. "But Gaston is her father. Surely no harm will come to her."

"There is another." Damon raked a hand through his hair. "I thought it was you. The scent was familiar. I didn't know the truth until last night. I still can't believe it."

"Werewolf? Are you saying the Hunter is working *with* a wolf?" Luc's shocked expression was mirrored by Damon's.

Damon nodded, then leaned forward to grip the dashboard. His claws sprang out of his fingertips, digging into the leather as if that would somehow make the car go faster.

Luc punched the accelerator.

"If the wolf doesn't get her, then the pack will." Damon spoke the words they were both thinking.

"We'll make it." Luc's voice was soft and menacing.

"For all our sakes, I hope you're right."

They reached Gaston Valois's home in record time. Damon jumped out of the vehicle before it had even stopped. His nose was in the air, sifting through the clues that had been left.

"They're not here." He dropped to his knees. He couldn't lose her. Not now.

Luc raced into the woods. Five minutes later, he returned. "They've headed this way." He pointed back in the direction he'd just come from.

"I can smell the pack."

The two men sprinted through the woods until they came upon a trail. Their senses alert to an ambush. Damon heard voices grumbling in the distance. He stuck a hand out to halt their silent pursuit.

"What should we do?" Gaston asked. "He should have been here by now."

"Be patient, Gaston. He'll arrive soon," Jack said.

"You said that before."

"And I'll say it again. Be patient." The quiet threat behind the innocent words went unnoticed by Gaston. "Check to make sure that she's ready."

Madie felt strange, really strange. The concoction she'd drank left her sluggish. She looked around at the shifting shadows. What were they doing in the woods?

"Look at me," Gaston said.

She did as he asked. She could do no other.

"You will do everything that I tell you to do," he said. "You shall have no fear, no hesitation."

"No fear. No hesitation," she murmured.

"When Damon Laroche arrives, you will kill him," Gaston said.

Madie hesitated.

"What did I tell you?" he snapped.

"I will do everything you tell me to do," Madie parroted.

He stepped closer. "What did I tell you to do?"

"Kill Damon Laroche," she said. His orders surrounded her, filling her brain until nothing else remained.

Gaston slipped one of the rifles off his shoulder and handed it to her. "Good! Now take this."

Madie held the weapon. She knew how to use it. He'd taught her how from a young age.

"Remember to aim for the heart," Gaston said.

"Aim for the heart." Madie couldn't feel her limbs. Nothing in her body seemed to be working except for her brain. And it didn't feel like her own. She needed to kill Damon Laroche. She just couldn't remember why.

Growls emanated from the woods.

"They're here," Jack said. He and Gaston drew in closer to be ready for the impending attack.

Several sets of red eyes glowed in the darkness. Excited cries broke from the wolves' throats. Gaston and Jack stood back to back. Damon broke from the trees.

"Kill him!" Gaston shouted.

Madie raised her rifle and aimed.

Damon slowed his approach. "Madie, it's me."

"I must kill Damon Laroche," she said in a voice that sounded nothing like her own.

"Madie, honey. Put down the gun. You're in danger," he said.

"Must kill Damon Laroche," she repeated as she stared straight through him.

"What have you done to her?" he bellowed.

Jack looked at him. "We didn't do anything to my future wife."

Damon reeled back in shock. "Wife?"

Gaston barked with laughter. "Tell him how you plan to marry Jack."

"Marry Jack," she said.

"Like hell you will." Damon rushed forward.

The rifle in Madie's hand rose with blinding speed, her finger resting on the trigger. He ran straight into the barrel.

"Go ahead," Damon said. "My heart is yours to do with as you please. I can't live without you. Without either of you." He reached out and gently touched her abdomen.

Madie's hands trembled and tears filled her eyes. "Must kill Damon Laroche."

"Do it now!" Gaston shouted as the pack came out of the woods.

Pain blossomed in Damon's side as the bullet ripped through his flesh. Blood spread across his T-shirt. He looked down in disbelief. She'd shot him. Madie had shot him. He glanced at where the barrel of her gun now rested. Only moments ago, it had been over his heart, but not now. She'd moved the rifle at the last second, sparing his life.

"Madie?"

She stared at the blood, transfixed, unseeing, then took a deep breath and let out a scream so loud, so mournful that it could've curdled blood. Madie dropped the gun, her hands shaking. She blinked as if to clear her head and looked around in confusion. "Damon? What are you doing here?"

"Oh Madie, I thought I'd lost you." He pulled her into his arms and hugged her.

She pulled back and looked at her hand, which was now covered in blood. Madie glanced at his shirt. "You're bleeding. Why are you bleeding?"

"It was an accident," he said. "I'll explain later. Luc?"

Luc stepped out of the woods.

Madie glanced over Damon's shoulder. "You're the man from the pub." Her brows furrowed in confusion. "I don't understand what is happening."

"You've been drugged," Damon said. "Luc, I'm trusting you to keep my bondmate safe."

Luc nodded solemnly, then gently pulled Madie out of Damon's arms and shoved her behind him.

Gaston pulled a gun from behind his back and pointed it in Damon's direction.

"He's mine," Jack said. "Keep us covered. Shoot any of the pack that gets too close."

Gaston's eyes widened as he tried to cover everywhere at once, but it was impossible with the wolves circling around them.

Jack started clapping as he approached Damon. "Well done, brother. You've managed to break the drug induced spell that Valois put on your mate," he said the last word with so much venom that it actually burned the air between them.

Damon watched Jacque's head drop into attack position. He could feel the pull of the moon in his bones, but it hadn't risen yet. When it did, there would be no holding the wolf at bay.

"You have no idea how it sickened me to smell you on her body, every time I was around her," Jack sneered. "The stench just would not go away."

Damon smiled, baring his teeth.

"I tried to get her to take me in your stead, but she'd already been brainwashed." He shrugged as if it were no big deal.

Damon kept his eyes on his brother and on Gaston, who was looking more and more desperate as the pack moved in for the kill. "Why, Jacque?"

His jaw tightened. "It should have been mine," he growled.

He looked at his brother and pain filled him. They'd grown up together. Shared everything. What could he possibly want that would make him betray his pack, his family? "What should've?" Damon asked.

"The pack, the leadership." Jacque ran a hand through his hair, which was getting shaggier by the seconds, thanks to the moon. "Even the bitch." He shot a glance in Madie's direction. "She should be carrying my heir. Not yours. I am the true Alpha of the Moonlight Kin pack."

Damon sighed. "You know I never wanted the responsibility."

Jacque laughed. "Yeah, well you didn't exactly turn it down when it was offered."

"I couldn't. Father wouldn't let me," he said. "You're going to have to face the Elders for what you've done." Damon knew he was sentencing his brother to death, but there was nothing he could do about it.

Jacque looked at him and snorted. "You know I can't do that, brother dear. They'll kill me and I'm not ready to die."

Damon had so many questions. Needed so many answers. "Why kill the pack?"

Jacque growled and snapped, trying to shake off the moon's pull. "Those bastards voted against me. If it wasn't for those members, I'd be pack leader."

Damon shook his head. Numb from the shock that his brother was alive. He'd hoped that the Book of Lycan had been wrong. "Father decided who'd lead, not Daniel, Rachel, and the others."

"Don't stick up for them," he growled. "I know they sided with our sire."

"That is our way, Jacque," Damon said. "We all know the rules. They're drilled into us at birth."

"That may be your way, but it's not mine, brother." Jack stepped within striking range. "I tire of talking. It's time for me to finish what your mate could not."

Damon and Jacque circled each other. He was woozy from blood loss, but that wouldn't stop him from fighting to the death.

Jacque leapt into the air.

The full force of his body came down on Damon's chest. Damon went down with a thud and wheezed when he tried to take a breath.

"Let me go!" Madie tried to break loose, but Luc held her steady. "He's going to kill Damon," she cried.

Luc glanced at her, but went back to staring at the fight. "Our way will settle things. Have faith in your mate. There is a reason that he's Alpha."

The pack stayed close to the tree line. All eyes were upon the two fighting in the center of the ring. Damon's fist made contact with Jacque's jaw. Blood spattered as Jacque's lip split. Damon managed to get his knee up and pushed his brother away.

He rolled to his feet, attempting to regain the breath he'd lost. He heard the crack and watched Jacque transform. The black wolf bounded across the hard ground and jumped, sinking his teeth into Damon's shoulder.

Damon cried out as his muscles were ripped away from the bone. Jacque's jaws snapped again, coming dangerously close to Damon's exposed throat. Spittle clung to Jacque's teeth. Madness possessed his eyes.

Damon's muscles strained as the change took him. His powerful jaws latched onto his brother's neck and he shook him with all his strength. Jacque struggled to break free, but Damon's hold was too tight.

Blood sprayed across Damon's face in a shower of red as his sharp teeth punctured an artery. He knew the blow was fatal. They both knew it was. It was over. Damon released Jacque and slowly walked away, transforming as he did so.

"No! This was not how it was supposed to be," Gaston raged. "He can't be one of them." He pointed to Jacque's body.

"Father." Madie rushed forward, but Damon caught her.

Gaston raised his gun and pointed it at them. "I will see you in the grave before I let you soil this family!"

Damon shoved Madie behind him.

Luc came out of nowhere and slammed into his body. His powerful jaws latched onto Gaston's arm and ripped it out of its socket. The pack closed in for the kill.

Madie turned away. She couldn't watch. She tried to drown out Gaston's cries, but it was impossible. The wolves began to howl and slowly circle them.

"What's happening?" Madie asked.

"The Lycanian Elders ordered our deaths," Damon said.

Madie frowned. "Our deaths? Why?"

"They believe you're behind the deaths of the pack members," Damon held her close. "I will do my best to protect you."

"I'm done hiding," Madie said.

The pack drew in, each one daring the other to get closer. Madie turned in time to see Damon transform again. His teeth were bared and the hair on his sable back was standing on end. His head was lowered, ready for attack. He snapped his jaws viciously, daring them to approach.

Madie put her hand on his head, her fingers sinking into his soft pelt. "This is my fight," she said. "I cannot allow you to die because of me." She took a step, placing herself between Damon and the pack.

Damon nudged her away, but Madie resisted. She shook her head no and took another step forward, until she was within five feet of the nearest pack members.

They growled and circled her like sharks sensing blood in the water.

"I didn't kill them," she said. "I didn't even know you guys really existed until a few days ago."

The clouds parted, revealing the full moon.

Madie felt pain rip through her body. Her legs buckled. "What's happening?" she cried, as another debilitating stab brought her to her hands and knees.

The pack stepped back. The earlier yipes of attack changed to barks of excitement. Madie couldn't breath and she couldn't move. Every muscle in her body felt as if it was stiffening and contorting at the same time.

She looked at her hands. A thin layer of white hair appeared, then thickened before her eyes. She sought Damon. "Help me."

He licked her face, laying his heavy bulk against her side. What felt like hours, only took minutes.

When Madie finally stood, she felt different…but somehow the same. The wolves continued to bark. The sound loud to her sensitive ears.

She took a step and stumbled, glancing down at the thick paws that had replaced her hands and feet. Pale hair now covered her entire body. Strength coursed through her, along with a confidence she'd never experienced before. For the first time in her life, she felt comfortable in her skin.

Damon hadn't moved. His presence lending her love and support.

Madie, can you hear me?

She heard Damon's voice whisper in her mind.

Madie turned until she met his amber eyes. He licked her face and snout, then nudged her with his head. There were shouts of glee from the pack members as one by one they approached her, each lowering its head in deference to her new position.

Why aren't they killing us? she asked Damon, hoping he understood.

Because I told them not to. A giant black wolf stepped out of the woods.

Damon jumped up and ran over to him. *Cousin, I knew I could count on you.*

I am not here as your cousin. I am here on Elder orders, he said.

Damon looked at him, his long tongue bobbing out of his mouth. *Whatever you say, Aidan.*

But how? Madie asked. *I'm not wolf.*

Are you sure? Luc asked.

Pretty positive, since I've never changed into one until now.

It's our child, Damon said. *Though I wouldn't rule out having some wolf blood in your family tree.*

Aidan approached. *Welcome to the Moonlight Kin pack.*

Thank you, she said.

Damon nipped at Aidan's tale.

Do that again and you'll be sorry, Aidan said.

It's hard to look noble when you're getting bit in the butt, Damon said and took off as Aidan turned to chase him.

Madie watched the exchange. Somehow, she'd lost one family, only to gain another. In her wolf form, she could feel her baby growing inside her. It's tiny heartbeat echoing in her head. Was that why she was able to transform? Or had Gaston been right about her mother's affair all along?

Damon returned to her side out a breath and laughing. Madie gave him a quick lick that had been meant as a thank you, but threatened to turn into something altogether different if the look in his eyes was any indication. Damon had saved her life and she'd saved his. They were equals, partners—bondmates.

EPILOGUE

Madie Laroche glanced out the kitchen window. The house smelled of fresh baked bread and roast beef. Her stomach growled at the thought of eating. She couldn't seem to get enough food these days.

Instead of rebuilding his house, she and Damon had moved to her family's estate, giving the wolves a ton of acres to roam on without having to worry about being hunted.

She glanced down. Flowers grew in the garden below, their multicolored blooms giving off a cacophony of scents.

In the grass, Damon lay with his eyes closed, a drooling baby boy sprawled across his wide chest. They awoke at the same time, as if they sensed her watching them.

Madie smiled and waved. Damon returned her smile, then picked up their son and rolled to his feet. He held the baby above him, not seeming to mind the drool running down his arm as the baby smiled and gurgled at him.

Gurgles turned to giggles, as Damon made silly faces at his son. Madie shook her head and sent Damon a vivid picture of just how sexy she thought he was at that moment. Damon's attention shifted from the baby to her, a promise clearly written in those amber eyes.

Madie's body responded instantly just like it had the first time she'd laid eyes on him in art class. She didn't think she'd ever tire of looking at the man. Other than having a family, life had pretty much returned to normal.

If being surrounded by a pack of werewolves could ever be called normal.

She'd opened her art gallery in New Salford and had employed Sarah as manager. Damon's Beta, Luc had left the pack, but hadn't gone far. He'd told Damon it was time that he made his own way in the world.

Damon had just snickered and told him that he wanted an invitation to the wedding. Luc's face had blanked, but they'd parted as friends. Madie had seen him more than once around the gallery, but she hadn't said anything to Damon.

For the first time in her life, her best friend was playing hard to get. Madie wondered how long Sarah would be able to hold out with Luc hot on her tail.

They had buried Gaston in the clearing where he'd fallen. There hadn't been much left of him after the wolves finished their feast. Some days it still made her sad that her father hadn't been able to see past his prejudices, but Madie rarely dwelled on the past.

With Damon's help, she'd found out that her inheritance was never in Gaston's hands. He'd squirreling her money away, hiding it, so she wouldn't find out and take it from him. It had been another brutal blow, another lie, but like everything else, she'd gotten over it.

Over him…

She glanced down at the ruby and diamond ring on her swollen finger, watching it catch fire in the dazzling sunlight.

Madie had a new life, a new baby, and a wonderful husband who loved her dearly. She couldn't ask for anything more. Madie glanced down at her swelling belly. Except for maybe a little girl.

# # #

Moonlight Kin 2: Aidan's Mate

DEDICATION

Dedicated to Bernard Lee DeLeo and Sasha White. Bernard, thank you for sharing your automotive expertise and lending me your eagle eyes. Anything I got wrong is entirely my fault. Sasha, thank you for not being afraid to tell me when something was wrong with the story. Your honesty is greatly appreciated and desperately needed in the world.

1

The wolves stood in the clearing, their bodies quivering with a mixture of tension and excitement. The cool summer breeze wafted through the branches of the thick copse of trees, rustling the leaves.

Aidan Fortier stepped away from the group toward the center of the grass-covered clearing, his dark head held high. His gaze drifted over the assembled members of the pack. *His pack.* The wolves showed the proper respect by lowering their heads and dropping their gazes.

All but one.

René Dubois lost his wolf form and rose to his feet. Naked, he walked into the clearing until he stood a few yards from Aidan.

A big man and powerful wolf, René had more brawn than sense, which would be proven for the last time tonight. He'd openly disagreed with Aidan's decision to back his cousin, Damon's choice for a mate. René had considered the endorsement a betrayal of sorts, a sign that perhaps Aidan wasn't up to the task of running the pack.

René wasn't the only wolf who'd taken Aidan's decision as a sign of weakness. There'd been others who had voiced concerns, as was their right, but René was the only wolf that had come forward to present Aidan with a formal challenge for his position.

The brawny wolf wanted to be Alpha. Convinced his size would get him the coveted position. Tonight would determine who would rule the west coast Moonlight Kin pack.

Aidan had no intention of losing his Alpha position. He'd fought hard to get it and planned to keep it. The last few months aside, Aidan had done a good job of running the pack, both financially and politically.

But tonight wasn't about his money acumen or his diplomatic abilities. It wasn't even about the pack being in a better position now than they'd ever been. Tonight was about proving who was the strongest, fiercest, and most brutal male standing in this clearing. And the only way to do that was to fight to the death.

Aidan didn't relish the idea of killing René. He was a good man, a good wolf, and a productive pack member, but he'd never been the brightest bulb.

René was easily led, easily persuaded. Initially, Aidan wondered if that was why René had challenged him in the first place. Had he been goaded to act?

His gaze strayed to Robert LaBeouf. Aidan had absolutely no proof, other than a gut feeling, that his personal assistant was involved. Unfortunately, he couldn't present 'feelings' to the Lycanian Elders. They wanted evidence, especially when a charge carried a death sentence. Until Aidan found proof, he'd keep LaBeouf close.

Ultimately, the machinations behind the challenge didn't matter. Whatever or whoever was behind René stepping forward would mean nothing in the end. The challenge was issued and accepted. It could not be halted now.

Perhaps it was good that René had challenged him. The pack needed a reminder that despite his controversial decisions, he was still their leader and the most powerful wolf in the territory.

"A challenge for the position of Alpha has been issued by René Dubois and accepted by me," Aidan said. "As with all Alpha challenges, it will be a fight to the death. Does anyone have anything to add? To contest?"

Murmurs swept through the pack, but no one stepped forward.

"Very well then. Let's get this over with." Aidan shucked his clothes, dropping them carelessly onto the ground. Once he was naked, he turned to face René.

René slammed his meaty fists against his bare chest, then threw his head back and howled. Several of the wolves joined in until a chorus rang out.

Aidan waited, feeling no need to participate, since it was all for show. His wolf rose to the surface. Claws sprouted from his fingertips, replacing his blunted nails. Dull human teeth quickly became sharp incisors. His jaw stretched and grew until he sported a snout. It wasn't a complete change. That would come later once first blood was drawn.

René stopped howling and looked at him, his green eyes glowing in the darkness. Aidan nodded, then took a step back, so the big man could prepare for battle. René's body went through a partial shift, then he circled Aidan.

Aidan's claws clacked together in anticipation of René's attack. Despite being Alpha, it wasn't his place to strike first during a formal challenge. Had René chosen to go the informal route, then all bets would've been off.

The burly Were snorted as he stepped left, then right. At nearly six foot four, Aidan wasn't as big as René, but he made up for the difference with his speed and cunning. René growled and lunged at Aidan, his claws spread wide for the strike.

Aidan dodged and quickly whipped around to rake René's back. The Were hissed and jerked to the side, before Aidan could take off another strip from his hide. With first blood drawn, they both shifted the rest of the way.

René's body was still reshaping when Aidan launched himself onto the Were's back. He dug his claws into René's side and sank his teeth into his shoulder.

The Were twisted, getting a claw into Aidan's flank. He jerked his powerful arm and sent the Alpha flying through the air. Aidan crashed into the trunk of a tree, then quickly scrambled to his feet. René was strong. Incredibly strong. He shook his head to clear it and warily watched the Were, attempting to gauge his next move.

René quickly finished shifting, then charged him. Three hundred and some odd pounds of werewolf steamed toward Aidan.

He jumped to the side, but wasn't quick enough. René caught his shoulder and sent him sailing through low hanging branches. This time when Aidan looked up, there were two Renés standing in the clearing.

He blinked several times. The images wavered, then morphed into one. Aidan couldn't take another hit like that. The fur on his neck rose and he bared his teeth.

Aidan sat back on his haunches and launched himself at René. His claws caught the Were in the neck, taking them both down to the ground.

They rolled, snarling and growling, each trying to get the upper hand. Jaws snapped, as they tore out chunks of flesh. Aidan raked René with his claws, shredding fur and strips of skin.

Blood filled Aidan's mouth, fueling his instinct to go in for the kill. He ignored the pain searing his side, where René latched onto him. It was a desperate move, an attempt to get him to loosen his hold. Aidan refused to release him and bit down even harder.

René's gasps turned to strangled gurgles, as Aidan's jaws closed around his throat. The claws digging into Aidan's sides lost some of their intensity. Aidan shook his head and heard a distinctive *snap*. The Were's heavy mass slumped over him.

Aidan growled some more, then struggled to push René off him. The Were's lifeless body fell to the side. Sweat and blood covered Aidan from head to toe. As he rose, his body shifted into human form. He swayed, but somehow kept his feet beneath him.

"It is done," he gasped, his lungs bellowing. He glanced down at René. "If anyone else thinks that they can run the pack better than me, then say so now. Let it be known that I welcome all challenges, all discourse, but will not tolerate disloyalty."

Aidan walked over to where he'd left his clothes and dressed quickly. His head throbbed and the trees swayed before his eyes, but anyone looking at him would think that he was fine.

He made his way back to the house, wanting nothing more than to take a hot shower and crawl into bed. Aidan could still taste René's blood on his lips and feel it matting his hair.

What a waste.

The others would burn the Were's body and dispose of all his belongings. Tomorrow, he and the rest of the Moonlight Kin pack would celebrate René's life and mourn his death in the traditional Lycan way. The day after that, preparations would begin for the upcoming moon run.

2

Two Days Later…

The bed creaked as Aidan turned to nuzzle the plump breast beside his face. He inhaled deeply, taking in the deliciously ripe aroma of feminine heat.

Aidan's canines grew as he sucked the rosy nipple into his mouth and nipped at the sensitive nerve-endings, his tongue soothing the sting.

The dusky tip beaded eagerly in response, stabbing the roof of his mouth. A sensual moan came from the female beside him.

His ears perked. Aidan loved that sound. To him there was no greater sound on the planet, except perhaps a woman's cry of release, when he took her over the edge.

He swirled his tongue around her again, then leaned back to view his handiwork. The woman undulated, revealing more of her nakedness.

Beautiful, as only a female werewolf could be, she ran her sharp claws over her taught abdomen, then licked her lips and smiled.

Aidan grinned back, then threaded his hands into her long, red hair, successfully tangling his fingers. He used the silky strands to pull her closer, then captured her mouth in a blistering kiss. Their tongues tangled as they fed each other's passions.

Her ample body flooded in preparation for their joining. The woman's grip tightened around his neck. She moaned and her back bowed, crushing her breasts into his chest. Aidan's body tensed as his shaft hardened.

Was this it? Was she the one? He waited a beat, but felt *nothing...* beyond the usual physical pleasure.

Disappointed, he slowly released her lips.

Face flushed and panting for air, it took the woman a moment to recover her composure. She nudged his shoulder with her head, encouraging him to return. Her yellow-green eyes searched his longingly, even as her brow furrowed.

Aidan knew what she wanted. It was the same thing *all* the single females of the Moonlight Kin pack wanted when they came to his bed, but he couldn't force himself to take a bondmate. No amount of lust or sexual gymnastics would make it happen. Werewolf nature didn't work that way; though there were times he'd like it to be otherwise.

He stared at the gorgeous Were, her eyes still clouded with desire. Aidan couldn't deny the attraction sparking between them, but there'd be no love lost when they parted ways.

Her beauty and attentiveness didn't change the fact that this was nothing more than a chance at the lottery to her, a way to better her position in the pack. When she left his bed, there were fifteen others—literally—waiting to take her place.

Each more determined than the last to try her luck at becoming Alpha female of the west coast pack before the end of the moon run.

Unfortunately for this woman, sex held little interest to him now that his wolf had determined that she wasn't a match. His withdrawal made that obvious, but that wouldn't stop her from trying to *forge* a bond. They all tried.

Send her away, his wolf snarled.

The next female Were on the list currently waited down the hall in a small parlor for her chance to 'test' the Alpha. Aidan opened his mouth to tell this woman to leave, but stopped short when he spotted the determination in her lovely eyes.

"You are not my bondmate." The fact left no room for

misunderstandings.

"I know," she said.

"If we do this, it means nothing." *Take the opportunity to back out gracefully.*

She shrugged. "I understand. I'd still like to…"

Did she understand?

Really?

Or was she simply hoping he was mistaken? As if such a thing were possible.

Aidan scrubbed a hand over his face. "As you wish." He'd fuck her like he did all the others, then send her back to the east wing, where she'd stay until the moon run next weekend.

Before he had a chance to act, the female Were hooked her foot around his leg to drag him closer.

Aidan growled, holding the urge to rut in check in order to remind her who was Alpha.

The woman immediately lowered her gaze and moved a small distance away. He would not allow any Werewoman to make demands upon him, especially one who wasn't his mate. It could lead to misunderstandings within the pack and unnecessary power struggles.

Aidan didn't play favorites. His wolves knew it, but that never stopped them from trying to change his mind.

To prove his point, Aidan rose out of the bed, leaving the woman tangled in the sheets. Naked, he strode across the room toward the French doors that led out to his balcony.

Not even a willing female in heat could hold his wolf's interest for long, once she'd been ruled out as a mate.

Aidan was beginning to believe nothing but his bondmate would satisfy his growing appetite and ease his restlessness. Years of searching and countless bedmates only added to his discontent.

Sex shouldn't be one long fucking audition, he thought.

A flash of gold caught his eye, stalling his hand on the door latch. His gaze wandered unerringly to the framed photo of the dark-haired child seated on his father's lap.

Two sets of amber eyes stared back at him, confirming that the wolf had bred true. Aidan's fingers hovered over the shiny frame. He drew his hand back, as if it had been singed.

Damon looked so damn happy holding his son. The toothy grin aimed at the camera would shame a Labrador.

Stupid pup, Aidan thought, then shook his head.

If he hadn't gone to the east coast to save his cousin's ass, Aidan was convinced that he wouldn't be suffering from this incessant longing for a mate now.

He'd succeeded in saving his cousin's life, but the act came at a steep cost. Damon had ended up bondmated to a female Hunter—a very *human* Hunter.

A fate worse than death in Aidan's mind. It was one thing to fuck one or accidentally eat one, but you didn't *bond* with humans and you certainly didn't convert them.

Technically, there were no Lycan laws against mating with a human, though Aidan had searched high and low to find one, convinced they should exist.

The best he and the other Lycanian Elders had come up with was an obscure reference in an ancient text that mentioned two instances of wolves successfully bonding with humans. Two, out of the thousands of years of Lycan history. Even Vegas wouldn't take those odds.

Aidan glanced at the woman in his bed, taking care to conceal his ambivalence. He'd spend a few useless hours with a Werewoman any day, if it meant avoiding Damon's fate.

Saddled to a human. He bristled. Never!

Damon's recklessness coupled with the added pressure from his fellow Elders cemented Aidan's resolve to remain true to the pack, true to his bloodline. Someone had to now that Damon had failed.

His gaze settled on the photograph once more. *Why did he have to look so damn happy?*

Something twinged inside of Aidan. Something he refused to

acknowledge or name. Until he found his bondmate, there would be no smiling heirs for him.

Aidan growled and shoved the French doors open. They banged against the outside wall of the house, the glass panes rattling, as he stepped out onto the balcony, allowing the darkness to embrace him.

He inhaled to calm his racing heartbeat. The scent of pine trees surrounded him, their needles rustling in the mild summer breeze. The sharp tang mingled with the delicate aroma of the roses growing in his garden.

In the distance, he scented deer as they made their way through the woods, their silent hooves falling on the soft blanket of ferns below the green canopy.

Their careful efforts weren't enough to slip past the predator in him. Nothing came onto his property without him knowing about it, especially not prey.

Insects buzzed and frogs croaked in chorus, creating a symphony of night sounds. Their steady hum a soothing balm to his werewolf soul.

Aidan tilted his head toward the night sky and his blood pulsed, pulling him forward. The moon's gentle tug would turn into a riptide strong enough to yank his feet out from under him by the end of the week.

He closed his eyes and took a deep breath, his body shuddering with the urge to shift. Aidan threw his head back and let out a mournful howl, strangely diminished by his human form. Creatures scurried. Aidan's eyes opened and he scanned the tree-line. Instincts demanding that he give chase.

He turned away from the lure of the night and returned to the warmth of his bed. No sense putting things off any longer, when there were others waiting.

"Last chance," he said. *Please go.*

"I want to stay." Her thick lashes concealed her emotions, but not the strength of her voice.

Aidan nodded. Without preamble, he dipped his fingers between her lush thighs, seeking her core. He stoked her, fueling her desire as he gathered the moisture needed to mount her. As soon as he had enough, Aidan climbed between her legs and thrust hard, entering her with one stroke.

He rode her relentlessly until she came, leaving her gasping and shuddering beneath him, then pulled out spilling his seed onto the sheets. Aidan rolled onto his side, his chest heaving.

"I'm sorry," he said.

"So am I." She rose quickly and pulled on her robe, then opened the door to leave.

Aidan's voice stopped her. "Send in the next woman."

Her mouth tightened and her shoulders tensed, but she managed to give him a clipped nod.

Tonight, like every night, he would sleep alone. That would remain the case until he located his bondmate or another Alpha managed to oust him from his position. Since the latter wasn't likely to happen anytime soon—thanks to René's recent challenge—Aidan would have to continue his search.

He closed his eyes and tried to imagine what it would be like, what she would be like. A soft knock on his bedroom door interrupted his thoughts.

"Enter," he said, reminding himself once again that this was his duty.

3

Aidan held the phone to his ear, listening to the other Lycanian Elders. They'd been droning on about his duties to his pack for an hour with no sign of the conference call coming to an end.

He lifted his cup of coffee and took a sip. Aidan grimaced. Cold. It had been hot, when his personal assistant brought it to him first thing this morning. Aidan put the cup back on his desk.

Robert LaBeouf knocked once and entered the library, which doubled as Aidan's office. His P.A.'s normally stony face sported a light blush and he wore a queer expression. Aidan held up one finger.

Robert nodded and kept his position by the door.

"I am well aware of my duties as Alpha," Aidan spoke into the receiver. "I do not need to be reminded again and again and again." He pinched the bridge of his nose to stave off a headache. "Yes, the women are here." Aidan took a deep breath to calm his temper. "No, I do not want to discuss my progress. If anything of import occurs, you all will be the first to know. Now I have to go." He disconnected the call before they could respond.

Robert stepped deeper into the room.

"What is it?" Aidan asked, grateful for any excuse to get off the phone.

"Sorry to bother you, Alpha," he said. "But we have a bit of a situation at the front gate."

Aidan tensed. "What kind of situation?" And why hadn't his wolves handled it already?

"We have a visitor." His normally monotone voice rose, belying his true emotions.

They never had visitors, unless the Lycanian Elders called a meeting or there was a moon run. Since he'd just got off the phone with the Elders and most of his pack was already here for the run, then that meant the visitor was a stranger.

"Hunter?" he asked.

His personal assistant shook his head. "Don't think so."

"Send them away." Aidan didn't have time to entertain any more guests. His house was already overflowing.

Robert's gaze darted back to the door. "I tried, Alpha, but she sat down in front of the gate and has refused to leave."

Aidan blinked in surprise. "She?" A sliver of premonition coursed through his veins, as he leaned against the edge of his desk. Aidan was careful not to disturb the neatly stacked papers he'd intended to read this morning, before the Lycanian Elders phoned and interrupted him.

"Yes, a human female, Sir." Robert nodded.

Human? Disappointment welled in Aidan's chest, though he didn't know why. It wasn't like he needed another female in his life right now. He gone through three Weres last night and still had thirteen to get through. "Send one of the wolves out," he said. "That should change her mind."

The crimson color in Robert's cheeks reached cartoonish levels. It took two tries for him to clear his throat. "That didn't work either," he said. "Byron came running back to the house with his tail tucked between his legs. He said that when the gate opened, he growled at her and she growled right back."

Aidan's brows rose. Either the woman was really brave, really stupid, or she was... "Are you sure that she's human?"

His assistant's gaze met his for a moment, then skittered away. "Once Byron came back, I went out to see for myself. There's no mistaking that *odor.*"

Robert's disgust for humans was well known within the pack. He never bothered to hide his feelings about them, griping to anyone who'd listen. He thought they were all vermin that needed to be exterminated. Fortunately for humans, most *Weres* weren't so intolerant.

Aidan scratched his chin. "Did she say what she wanted?"

"She mentioned that her car broke down and that she needs to use a phone, but who doesn't have a cell phone these days?"

"Not many people," Aidan said. "It's possible that she has one, but it isn't charged."

"I suppose so. She certainly looks like someone who's been walking awhile. She's sweaty, but she doesn't smell right." Robert's nose wrinkled.

Aidan leaned forward. "What do you mean?"

"My senses tell me that there's more to her than meets the eye. I can't explain it, but I'm not convinced that her story isn't an elaborate trick to gain entrance to the residence. Humans can be so deceptive."

So could wolves, Aidan thought, eyeing the man.

The woman's arrival could be a ruse. It wasn't out of the realms of possibility. His success in business dealings had garnered an unusual amount of attention—unwanted attention, considering the secrets Aidan kept. Reporters phoned constantly. Everyone wanted an exclusive from the famous software *recluse*.

If the woman was a reporter, she'd regret this bold move. No one came to his house uninvited. By the time Aidan finished with her, she'd be so frightened that she'd leave the area.

Of course, if she were as she said—a stranded motorist, he couldn't exactly leave her out there to wander around unsupervised. Aidan could not afford for her, or anyone else, to be traipsing around the estate this close to the full moon.

"Show her in." Aidan already regretted his decision, but at least he'd know if she were lying.

Robert's gaze shot to his face and his eyes widened. "Alpha?"

"You heard me."

"But she seems dangerous," Robert said.

Aidan pressed his lips together to keep from laughing. "I'm sure that a pack of werewolves can handle one human female. Don't you?"

"Yes, sir. Of course, but it can't hurt to keep an eye on her." Robert left, pulling the door closed behind him.

Aidan shook his head. He had no doubt Robert would keep watch, waiting for the unsuspecting human to cross the line, so he could invoke Lycan law.

Robert would use any excuse to kill one of them. Luckily, he needed permission to do so and Aidan wasn't likely to grant it.

He glanced at the phone on his desk. He should've called the authorities to have the woman removed for trespassing. That was the prudent thing to do, but Aidan couldn't shake his curiosity.

What type of woman growled at a wolf?

The same type who was foolish enough to come here on their own.

Aidan stepped in front of the antique mirror on the wall to inspect his appearance. His unfashionably long black hair fell past his shoulders in desperate need of a cut. He checked his teeth to make sure there wasn't raw meat stuck in them.

The move stretched and twisted the jagged white scar that ran across his chin, cutting into his otherwise polished appearance. He ran his finger over the thin line, admiring the memento he'd gotten the night he became Alpha.

Sharp amber eyes stared back from the mirror. In a few more days, they'd begin to glow and the façade he presented to the human world would disappear. His beast would rise and Aidan would be more instinct than man.

He smiled in anticipation of the full moon and the freedom it brought him. A knock sounded on the door as he turned away from the mirror. "Enter."

Robert poked his head in. "I've put her in the parlor."

Aidan gave him a curt nod, then walked out of the library across the marbled entry hall to the closed door on the opposite side. Aidan raised his hand to knock, stopping short in surprise, unsure why he found the need to do so in his own home.

He frowned and turned the knob. This was his house. He damn well didn't need to announce himself. Aidan entered the parlor, his footsteps silent on the hardwood floor.

The woman's back was to him, her slender frame partially obscured by the cascade of strawberry blond ringlets flowing over her narrow shoulders and down her back. A worn camouflage bag lay at her feet.

Aidan's gaze locked onto her heart-shaped bottom as it swayed to some internal beat. Her long legs were bare where her brown walking shorts left off. Strong thighs, made for grasping a man's waist, flexed with each side-to-side motion.

A wisp of bare abdomen peeked out beneath a short white cotton shirt. Aidan couldn't see her breasts or her face, but it didn't matter. She already had his undivided attention.

He inhaled to get a read on her before she had a chance to open her mouth and lie. The scent of lilacs in the spring slammed into him.

Aidan scanned the parlor to ensure that Robert hadn't placed a bouquet in the room. He hadn't. *She* was the source of the delicious aroma.

She bent over to get a better look at the photos in the curio cabinet. The move caused the material of her shorts to pull tight and cup her bottom. Aidan's mouth watered and a rumble came from his chest.

The woman gasped and spun around, knocking the lamp off the end table in the process. She fumbled to catch the base, but missed.

Aidan rushed forward, using his preternatural speed, and caught the lamp before it shattered on the ground. When he looked up, their eyes met and the breath froze in his lungs.

The woman had the face of a road-weary angel, who'd taken flight one too many times. Wide ice-green eyes, the color of pale peridot, watched him in shocked silence. A strong chin supported full lips that dipped and swelled, all but begging to be kissed.

Those same luscious lips parted, breaking into a lopsided grin. That silly smile drew attention to the freckles dotting her high cheekbones and pert little nose. That same nose crinkled, as he continued his undisguised perusal.

"I'm Jenna." She scrubbed her hand on the side of her shorts, then held it out for him to shake.

"Aidan." For a second or two, he simply stared at her, unable to move, then ever so gently he clasped his big hand around her smaller one.

The jolt hit like a shock from a wet plug.

Aidan's jaw clenched, as part of his body inconveniently stirred to life. He forced himself to release her, then pulled his shirt down to hide his perplexing condition. Aidan opened and closed his hand to dispel the remaining tingles.

A single curl dropped onto her forehead. Jenna tucked the stray behind her ear, exposing an angry purple slash that bisected part of her eyebrow. Although he could see no blood, the wound smelled fresh.

"Did you have an accident?" he asked. "My assistant was under the impression that your car broke down."

"It did," she said. *Truth. Lie.* No wonder his wolves were having such a difficult time reading her.

"The wound on your eyebrow says differently." His voice chilled the air around them.

Jenna's hand flew up to cover the area. Her smile faded. Her clear bright eyes dimmed, overshadowed by wariness.

Aidan sniffed, scenting her again.

Underneath the sweet aroma of lilacs a faint odor of a man's cheap cologne lingered on her clothes. His thoughts took a dark turn. Was he the one who'd struck her?

A growl came from his throat. Aidan coughed twice to cover up the unbidden noise. The urge to shake her until she told him everything about this man besieged him. He clenched his fists at his sides to keep from acting on the impulse.

She's human. A stranger. And most definitely not his responsibility.

Aidan fought to regain control of his turbulent emotions. His mind flashed to the hearing he'd attended on Damon's behalf. His cousin had professed his love for the human woman, his bondmate. He'd said there was no denying the wolf once it made up its mind.

A buzzing noise sounded in Aidan's head, before being drowned out by his own heart beat thundering in his chest.

Well it wasn't going to happen to him, damn it. He was a Lycanian Elder. He had responsibilities. He didn't think with his dick.

Aidan ignored the strange feelings of possession that had momentarily overwhelmed him. It was just the pull of the full moon and his instinctual need to protect everything in his territory. It had to be.

The fact the woman was human was coincidental.

Jenna had sensed his presence a moment before he'd cleared his throat. She'd turned too quickly and lost her balance, knocking an expensive looking lamp off the end table.

He'd moved with incredible speed, catching the fixture before it hit the floor.

When Jenna had looked up, an unusual pair of amber eyes had immediately captured her. The warm honey hue had heated and cooled as the man assessed her. His eye color was made all the more striking due to the contrast to his ebony hair. Jenna normally didn't like guys with long hair, but for some reason the style suited him.

She'd actually felt her heart skip a beat. Jenna thought that kind of thing only happened in fiction, not real life. Of course, men that looked like him didn't exist in real life either. Yet here he was, standing in front of her.

Never in all her years had she ever seen a man so devastatingly handsome. Nothing, not even the scar on his chin, could detract from his perfectly chiseled features. It was the one blemish that stood between him and the definition of pretty.

Her heart tripped again. Once could be dismissed as coincidence, but twice pointed to attraction.

Jenna had given up on being attracted to any man after her ex-boyfriend, Ethan Manning's betrayal three months ago, so to find herself drawn to this man, this stranger was disconcerting.

Muscles rippled beneath his form-fitting shirt, as he lifted the lamp and gently set it back onto the table. Power oozed from his pores. Not the kind of power that Ethan flaunted, but a more subtle strength that he wielded like it was his birthright. At no point did he look away.

The room shrank around them, cocooning them in a fragile bubble that one wrong word would pop.

As he straightened to his full height, Jenna had to crane her neck to maintain eye contact. She'd murmured her name or at least she hoped that she had. He'd responded in kind.

Aidan…

It was the kind of name that swirled on your tongue and bore repeating. She swayed toward him, sucked in by the odd gravitational pull happening between them. The second Jenna noticed that she'd moved closer, her face flamed and she stepped back.

What was wrong with her? Had she learned nothing in the last few months?

Jenna swallowed hard. "Sorry about the lamp."

He remained silent.

She fidgeted. "Thank you for letting me in to use your phone."

Amusement lit his amber eyes. "You didn't give me much choice." He watched her closely.

Oops! She hadn't, had she?

Jenna had already apologized. What else was there to say or do? "Sooner I use your phone, the sooner I'll be out of your hair."

Aidan pointed to the phone on the desk. "What about your car?" he asked.

Jenna tensed. No way could she afford a tow truck. It would cost a fortune to get the Bug to Breakbend. If she had her garage handy, this wouldn't be a problem. But thanks to her conniving ex, she didn't.

Ethan had taken the only thing of value she'd ever owned, the only place she'd ever called home, and the only family she'd ever known. And for what? So he could build a stupid luxury condominium complex? Like the world needed another one of those.

Jenna gritted her teeth. "I'll get the car when I can."

Her scent soured at the mention of her vehicle. Aidan watched her dig into her pocket and pull out a crumpled piece of paper with a number scribbled on it. Jenna picked up the phone and punched in the number. She tapped her fingers against the desk as she waited for someone to answer.

He heard a woman come on the line.

"May I please speak with Paul Welling?" Jenna asked.

Sirens went off in his head. Aidan instantly recognized the name of the Gazette editor. Had Robert been right about her all along?

"Hi, Mr. Welling. It's Jenna Dane."

"Jenna, where have you been?" he asked. "I expected you here hours ago."

"I ran into car trouble."

"Where are you?" he sounded dubious.

"I'm not sure." Jenna looked at Aidan and mouthed '*Where am I*'?

Aidan blinked. She didn't know? How could she not know? "The Fortier estate," he said casually, waiting for some sign of recognition to cross her face. None came. Jenna stared blankly at him. She had no idea who he was. Aidan's tension eased a notch.

"I'm outside of town," she said.

"If you're not here in the next two hours, don't bother coming," Paul said.

Jenna turned her back to Aidan and whispered into the phone, though she needn't have bothered. Aidan had been listening to both sides of the conversation and didn't feel an ounce of guilt about eavesdropping.

"Please, Mr. Welling. I need this job." Her desperation was palpable.

For some reason, Aidan found himself responding to it, to her.

He slipped out of the room and summoned Robert. "Take Nic and go find her car."

"What do you want us to do with it once we find it?" he asked.

"Bring it to me. Something is off about her and I want to know what it is. In the meantime, have the Range Rover brought around to the front of the house. She needs transportation."

Robert gaped. "You're going to give the Rover to a human?"

His hackles rose. "Yes, do you have a problem with that?"

Robert's gaze dropped. "No, sir."

"Good." Aidan strolled back into the room in time to see Jenna wipe moisture from her face. The tears clinging to her eyelashes were the only evidence that remained to prove she'd been crying.

She gave him a strained smile. "Thanks for the use of the phone."

"Anytime," Aidan heard himself say.

Jenna hoisted her bag onto her shoulder and walked to the door. Her hand hesitated on the knob. "I know it's rude of me to ask, but you wouldn't happen to have any tools I can borrow, would you?"

"Tools?" What in the world did she need with tools?

"Yeah, socket wrenches, pliers, things like that? I'll give them back. I promise."

Intrigued by the request, Aidan asked, "What do you need them for?"

"I thought maybe I could fix Stan," she said.

"Stan?" *Who was Stan? And why was he just hearing about him?* Unexpected anger flared inside of Aidan.

Jenna laughed, oblivious to his mood change. "Stan is my car."

Aidan's brow quirked. "You have a name for your car?"

She shrugged. "Don't you? I thought all guys did."

His eyes scrolled over the front of her T-shirt, taking in the soft slope of her full breasts. Aidan watched her nipples harden and tore his gaze away. "You are most definitely not a man," he said in a garbled voice.

Jenna crossed her arms over her chest. "I know, but it doesn't stop me from naming cars—or fixing them."

"You're a mechanic?" He'd assumed she was a reporter.

"I used to be." She bit her lip and looked away.

His gaze was drawn to her mouth like a lodestone. Oh, the things he could do with those lips. The part of his body he refused to acknowledge, twitched behind his zipper.

Aidan shook his head to clear it. What was wrong with him? He shouldn't be thinking about her mouth or how her body responded to him. She was human. He shouldn't be thinking about her at all.

Jenna stared at him. "Do you have the tools or not?"

Robert knocked on the door and stepped into the room. He scowled at Jenna, then handed the keys to Aidan and left.

"You only have two hours to reach town. There's no time to fix your vehicle."

"How did you know about—?"

"Take these." He handed her the keys to the Range Rover, effectively cutting off a question he could not answer. "My *men* will retrieve your car."

Jenna reached for the keys automatically. "You don't have to do that."

"I insist." Aidan dropped them into her hand. "I'll have your car repaired."

"No!" she snapped. "I mean it's not necessary. You've done too much already. I can fix it myself."

Was she in trouble or was she worried about getting caught in a lie?

Aidan opened his mouth to tell her that he'd do as he damn well pleased, but stopped when he glimpsed the panic in her eyes. "There's a garage on the estate. I'm sure you'll find everything you need there," he said instead.

"But…"

He held up his hand. "No arguments. Your car will be there tomorrow." What was he doing? Aidan had obviously lost his mind. Her and her stupid lilac scent was making him crazy. "I'll show you to the front door.

Aidan practically shoved her out of the room and down the hall. He needed to get Jenna away from his home and out of his head.

Jenna trotted to keep up, but said nothing more. She climbed into the Rover, then turned to thank him again.

Aidan didn't give her the chance. He spun on his heel, and like prey evading a predator, bolted for the front door.

4

The drive to Breakbend took longer than Jenna thought. She'd overestimated the distance she'd driven and would never have made it to her new job by the end of the day had she continued walking.

Jenna kept watch in the rearview mirror for any sign of Carl Rich. She might've changed vehicles, but she couldn't afford to underestimate the private investigator her swindling ex had hired to find her. The man was doggedly persistent.

Of course with millions riding upon obtaining her signature, Jenna wasn't surprised. That kind of money would motivate anyone.

Her fingers brushed the healing gash over her eyebrow and she winced. The wound reminded her just how close Carl had come to capturing her a week ago. She'd barely escaped his grasp. Jenna didn't think she'd be as lucky next time.

Carl had learned the hard way that she wasn't a victim. She got some satisfaction from knowing that her swift kick had landed squarely in Carl's crotch. If there was any justice in the world, his balls still ached.

Breakbend trickled into view. Trees slowly gave way to frontier storefronts and trendy coffee shops. Some of the buildings looked original, but most were manufactured to appear 'old'.

A few high-end restaurants stood out amongst the mom and pop establishments, along with the usual array of fast food chains that invaded every town.

Two billboards advertised a nearby lake that touted great fishing. The lake appeared to be Breakbend's only claim to fame.

The Breakbend Gazette had pride of place on the main drag, between a diner and a jewelry shop. She spotted a car pulling out of a space in front of the paper and quickly slid the Rover into the vacated spot.

Jenna checked her appearance in the rearview mirror. If she'd been going for the deranged lion with mascara issues look, she'd be set. Unfortunately, she'd been going for 'urban professional', which wasn't going to happen today. On the bright side, at least she'd stopped sweating.

She fixed her face the best she could and rearranged her hair to hide the cut above her eyebrow, then killed the engine. Jenna took a deep breath, then climbed out of the SUV. A bell clanged as she pushed the door open to the Breakbend Gazette.

A receptionist sat near the entrance, filing her nails. Her orange floral print dress accentuated her wide hips and generous belly, while leaching color from her peachy complexion. A brown bob haircut stopped at her jawline, exposing her double chins.

Her strategic position guarded the spattering of worn desks beyond. Most were empty, but a few still held what Jenna assumed were reporters. They varied in age from pimple-faced to geriatric.

Jenna approached her desk.

The receptionist wrinkled her nose. "Can I help you?"

Jenna straightened the front of her sweat-stained shirt and brushed a stray curl behind her ear. The woman's gaze shot to the bruised cut by her eyebrow.

"I had an accident," Jenna said.

The woman's gaze softened. "I understand."

No, she didn't. No one could comprehend the hell Jenna had gone through these past three months.

"Mr. Welling is expecting me."

"Name?" she asked.

"Jenna Dane."

The receptionist's eyes widened and her face transformed once more.

"I'm Molly. Molly Jones." She held out her hand. "Nice to meet you. Welcome to the Breakbend Gazette," she said, then swiveled her chair around and shouted toward a closed office door at the back of the small space. "Paul! Jenna's here."

The door flew open, hitting the wall with a loud bang. "Molly, how many times have I told you not to shout for me? It's unprofessional. Why do you think I installed that fancy phone system?" The closer Paul Welling got, the more rumpled he appeared. His suit had been new…in the seventies, along with his haircut.

Jenna stepped forward to introduce herself.

"It's about time you got here." He ignored her outstretched hand.

"Sorry." Jenna dropped her arm. "I had car trouble."

"Nice car." Molly stared at the Range Rover, a devilish gleam in her eye. "Wish I had that kind of trouble."

So it was going to be like that, Jenna thought. Her lips thinned, but she didn't say anything to Molly. She couldn't afford to lose this job.

Reporting for the Gazette was her big chance—her last chance to earn enough money to hire an attorney to fight Ethan.

"It's not mine," Jenna said.

"Whose is it?" Paul's brown eyes narrowed. "I was under the impression that you were new to the area. If I find out that you're lying to me, then you're fired."

"I'm not. I've never been to Breakbend." She'd never even heard of the town before answering the ad. "I broke down near the Fortier estate. A man named Aidan loaned me the SUV, until I can get my car repaired."

Molly gasped. Everyone in the room stopped what they were doing and stared at Jenna.

She flustered. "What?"

"Aidan Fortier?" Molly asked.

"I don't know," Jenna said. "I didn't catch his last name."

"Who else could it be?" Molly asked Paul.

"There's only one Aidan in the area," he said.

Molly shook her head. "I can't believe he let you inside the estate."

Jenna was confused. "Why wouldn't he?"

Molly glared at her. "He never lets anyone in, aside from his employees. He's very secretive."

Maybe no one had tried sitting in front of his gate and refusing to move. Jenna almost smiled as she recalled the look on everyone's face, when she'd done so. Aidan hadn't exactly rolled out the welcome mat, but he had helped her. In Jenna's book, that counted for a lot.

"Is it true that he has wolf packs running around his property?" Molly asked.

Jenna had seen one wolf, but not a pack. She decided to keep that information to herself. "Is he part of some kind of weird cult?"

Molly waved her question aside. "No, nothing like that. He's just peculiar."

One of the male reporters came over to where they stood. "I heard he was horribly disfigured and that's why he's rarely seen in public."

Jenna frowned. "Are we still talking about Aidan?" They couldn't be referring to the gorgeous man she'd met.

"Duh." Molly rolled her eyes, as if she were dense. "Is it true he runs around in robes and has a harem?"

Jenna snorted. "Where are you guys getting your information from?" Aidan had gone from eccentric wolf whisperer to a sheik in seconds.

"Don't laugh." Molly grabbed her arm. "There are tons of rumors surrounding Aidan Fortier. Some people in these parts don't think he's human. They say he howls at the moon with his wolves."

The male reporter nodded in agreement. Paul Welling watched Jenna. She assumed he did so to see how she'd react.

"You're kidding, right?"

"It's no joke," the male reporter said.

Coming to Breakbend was obviously a mistake. These people were crazy. "You honestly believe Aidan's a werewolf?"

"Don't be ridiculous," Molly said earnestly. "He's probably a vampire. These parts attract creatures of the night."

Jenna waited for her to laugh.

Molly didn't.

She looked at all the somber faces in the room. This had to be a prank. Why weren't they laughing? They couldn't all be delusional. Could they?

Fear prickled the skin at the base of her neck. Jenna needed to defuse this situation before it got worse. If they honestly believed Aidan was some kind of monster, how long would it be before they convinced themselves that he should be hunted down and destroyed?

"I assure you, Aidan's as human as you or I." Jenna extracted her arm from Molly's grasp. She hoped whatever had made them crazy wasn't catching.

"Come into my office," Paul said. "I'll get you your paperwork and explain everything."

Jenna followed Paul Welling to the back of the small space. If anything, his office was even more dingy than the outer area.

A scratched wooden desk sat in the center of the room. Piles of papers and a laptop covered much of the surface. An old office chair missing half of its padding rested behind the desk, while two folding chairs faced the front of it.

"Take a seat." Paul pointed to one of the folding chairs.

Jenna perched on the edge of one, but didn't settle in. She was afraid to after everything they'd said to her. How could these people believe all the crazy stories circulating about Aidan? Weren't newspapers supposed to deal in facts?

Paul typed a few keys on his laptop, then turned the screen toward her. "See this?"

Jenna frowned. "What am I looking at?"

"That's all the information the world has on Aidan Fortier," he said. "Pretty interesting given he's a multi-millionaire, isn't it?"

"Not really. It's common for wealthy people to keep a low profile for security reasons." It was obvious Aidan had money. People didn't get to live on a fortified estate without it. "Have you ever thought that maybe he likes his privacy? I know it's a rarity in this world, but it does still occur on occasion."

"Oh, I'm sure he does." Paul made it sound as if Aidan's wishes were of no consequence. "The question is why?"

"I'm sure there are a multitude of reasons," she said.

"Do you have any idea what an exclusive interview with the famous software developing recluse would fetch? A lot!" he said, before she could answer. "If we can't get an interview, I'd settle for something scandalous like a photo of him howling at the moon."

Oh, is that all?

She inched forward. "Do you really believe he's a werewolf?"

"Recluse, eccentric, werewolf, vampire, I don't care what he is, as long as it helps me sell papers."

Okey, dokey. Jenna's lips thinned. She didn't like the direction this conversation was taking.

"One page on Aidan Fortier would get us both out of this town and into the journalistic big leagues," he said.

Jenna didn't care about the 'big leagues'. All she wanted was to earn enough money to give Ethan a good legal fight.

"I didn't come here to write gossip pieces or fiction. Had I known that you'd have me looking for Bigfoot on my first day, I wouldn't have bothered to apply for the job."

"Aidan Fortier isn't Bigfoot," Paul said.

"Well he sure as heck isn't a werewolf!" Jenna snapped. "What someone does with their spare time is none of our business, as long as they aren't harming anyone."

She had experienced firsthand what lies and sensationalism could do to someone's reputation. That had been the first blow Ethan Manning had struck after cheating her out of her garage.

Instead of a David meets Goliath story, the press had sided with her ex and made her out to be a lying, thieving, gold-digger. Customers stopped bringing their cars in for repair long before Ethan put locks and chains on the doors.

Jenna had managed to hang onto the land the garage had been built on, but if she didn't get legal help soon, she'd lose it, too.

"How dedicated are you to this job?" Paul asked.

"What do you mean?" Jenna didn't have enough cash to leave town.

"I hired you, even though technically you didn't have enough experience."

"Thank you again for giving me a chance." It pained her to say those words.

Paul sneered. "I don't want your thanks. I want you to get an interview with Aidan Fortier or some information about his private life. If you do that, it would go a long way toward proving to me that you are committed. That you deserve this job," he said. "I'd hate to think that I'd made a mistake by giving you the position."

"You haven't."

"Then prove it!" He bellowed. "Reporting isn't about being nice. It's about uncovering the truth."

Jenna's eyes narrowed. "You're not talking about the truth. You're talking about sensationalism and possible libel."

Paul leaned forward. "The truth comes in many forms. Some just pay better than others."

Jenna's stomach knotted. Manipulating the facts to accommodate an agenda wasn't her idea of journalism. And ultimately that's what Paul was asking her to do.

Any other time, she'd tell him to stick this job up his butt, but Jenna was down to her last fifty and pride wouldn't buy food or gas. Still, she didn't like the idea of taking advantage of someone who'd shown her kindness.

"I'll give it some thought." She choked on the words as they lodged in her throat.

"You do that." Paul gave her a knowing glance. "I expect you to report back to me in the morning with your answer."

Jenna left his office, nausea replacing her earlier hunger. Molly stood nearby, casually flicking through back issues of the Gazette. The second Jenna appeared she pounced.

"So what's he like?" Molly asked.

"Paul?"

Molly frowned. "No, Aidan," she said. "Everyone knows that Paul is an asshole."

"I heard that, Molly," he said.

"Knew you would," she said.

Jenna sighed. At least that was one thing they could agree upon. "Aidan seemed like any other mega successful business man. Slightly aloof. Cultured. Intense." And way too sexy for his own good.

There it was again. That unbidden attraction that cropped up every time she thought about the man.

"What does he look like?" Molly asked.

Jenna shrugged. "Dark hair. Longish. Tall."

"You're going to have to do better than that, if you're going to work for my parents' paper. People like description," she said.

Well that explained why Molly could do or say whatever she wanted. If her folks owned the paper, she had no fear of getting fired.

Molly clasped her hands against her chest. "What's his body like? Is he fit? Fat? Thin? Somewhere in between?"

Jenna pictured Aidan's wide shoulders and flat stomach. Fit didn't begin to describe his banging body. Something inside her fluttered. Something she promptly squashed before it could take form.

"Don't keep me in suspense," Molly whined.

Jenna cleared her suddenly dry throat. "Yeah, he's in good shape."

"I knew it!" She grinned. "He sounds dreamy."

"I hadn't noticed," Jenna lied. For some reason, it bothered her that Molly was so interested in Aidan. It shouldn't matter. It wasn't like she and Aidan had any connection beyond his vehicle. "I'll see you tomorrow." Jenna rushed to the door, hoping she didn't follow.

"Where are you going?" Molly asked.

"To my motel. I'm beat." The lie slipped easily from Jenna's lips. She couldn't exactly say that she planned to sleep in the SUV. Businesses rarely employed homeless people.

She left quickly before Molly could ask any more questions. The little bell chimed loudly behind her as she stepped onto the sidewalk. Jenna sucked in the fresh air to clean the mental filth Paul had left in her mind.

She walked, needing to get away.

Maybe you had to be scheming or insane to do the job. If that were the case, Jenna wouldn't last long.

She found a fast food restaurant to dine in and used their bathroom to get cleaned up. Jenna got a few strange looks when she came out of the restroom with a wet head, but no one said anything.

She waited until the Gazette closed, then walked back to the Rover. Jenna studied the navigation system to see what was around.

A campground located five miles down the road looked like her best bet. They tended to be cheap and rarely asked questions.

Jenna drove in silence, her body and mind weary from the day's events. She put aside Molly's ridiculous ideas and thought about everything Paul Welling had told her.

Was it true that an interview with Aidan could fetch big money? Could she afford to pass up the opportunity, if there was even a remote chance that was the case?

The truth was no, she could not. Paul might be willing to settle for something scandalous about Aidan, but Jenna wouldn't. She couldn't. And she prayed that her desperation never reached that point.

Jenna pulled into the campground and found an out-of-the-way spot to park and settle in for the night. She grabbed a jacket from her tote, then climbed into the backseat.

With a click of a button, Jenna locked the doors, then tried to get comfortable. The Rover had a lot more space in the backseat than the Bug, which was probably why she found it so difficult.

She was used to being cramped. The tight fit made her feel protected, even though it was an illusion. Jenna plucked a shirt out of her bag and rolled it up, creating a makeshift pillow.

Thanks to Molly's ravings and Paul's veiled threats, sleep didn't come easily.

* * *

Aidan couldn't get Jenna out of his mind. Her lilac scent lingered in the parlor and clung to his skin. He shook his head and snorted, but it did little to alleviate the aroma.

He walked into Robert's office. "I'm going to my room to grab a shower. Send up the next Were on the list," he said, more gruffly than he'd intended.

Robert nodded. "Right away."

Hair still damp, Aidan stood on his balcony inhaling the night, while he waited for the woman to arrive.

There was a soft knock at the door.

"Come in," he said without turning around. He heard the woman enter the room.

"Alpha, you called for me." Her sultry voice whispered over his skin.

Aidan tore his gaze away from the view of the backyard. Golden hair framed a narrow face, making her skin glow. A blue silk robe did little to conceal her lush curves. Aidan held out his hand.

"Come here, Sydney," he said.

She strolled across the room, her hips swaying teasingly with each step. When she was within arm's length, she reached out and placed her fingers into his hand, allowing him to pull her into his arms.

Soft breasts met his hard chest and Aidan inhaled. Sydney's warm scent tickled his nose. She smelled buttery like fresh baked bread—and all wrong. Aidan inhaled her delicious scent again. This time he sneezed, wrinkling his nose.

"Bless you," Sydney said in surprise.

"Thank you."

She rubbed her hand over his chest, trailing her fingers down until she found his soft shaft. Sydney stroked him, then waited for a response. There was none. She ran her palm over his length again and squeezed.

Aidan's cock twitched, but remained flaccid. Fear crept from his gut to his head, leaving tension in its wake. He took an awkward step back. This had *never* happened before.

He'd been with three women yesterday and hadn't experienced any problems. Maybe that was it. Maybe he'd overdone it yesterday. Or maybe he was ill. But even as the thought whispered through his head, Aidan knew that wasn't the case.

Werewolves didn't get sick and they certainly didn't have performance issues. Their hormones ran hot year around.

Aidan cursed under his breath and glanced down at his limp dick. *What the hell is the matter with you?*

Sydney took a step back. "Alpha?"

"I've changed my mind," he said. "I want you to leave. Now!"

Her face reddened. "I understand."

Aidan gritted his teeth. "You understand nothing." How could she, when he didn't understand what was happening? "Go!"

Sydney rushed to the door and slipped out of the room, before he could say another word. No doubt she'd report his 'condition' to the others.

Aidan swore again. This was the last thing he needed. *First his cousin, then the challenge, now this.* Aidan's chest squeezed. He needed to get outside. He couldn't breathe.

He shed his clothes and leapt off his balcony, transforming into a massive black wolf in mid-air. With silent paws, Aidan landed on the grass and took off running for the trees.

He ran hard, until exhaustion took him.

No longer on estate property, Aidan loped through the woods, searching for a place to bed down for the night. He couldn't bear to return to his room. He wasn't ready to face the shame or the failure.

He settled on a spot in the park under a canopy of trees, not far from a campground. Aidan scented the area for danger one final time, then dropped down onto the soft ferns. For a moment, he thought he smelled lilacs. First his body, now his nose was betraying him. He shook his head in disgust, then rested his muzzle upon his paws.

Aidan slept fitfully, dreams of curly, strawberry blond hair and the smell of fresh lilacs, haunting him until dawn.

Through the thick trees, in a secluded campsite nearby, Jenna tossed and turned in the backseat of the Range Rover. For the first time in three months, Ethan Manning wasn't taking center stage in her dreams. He'd been replaced by a dark-haired demon with amber eyes, whose smile could quite literally melt the clothes off any woman.

5

Ethan Manning nodded patiently at the bloated banker sitting across from him. On the outside Ethan appeared calm, but inside, his anger roiled, churning with the need to smash something.

"You have until Monday," the banker said. "After that, we'll have no choice, but to remove our offer."

"I need more time," Ethan smiled through clenched teeth. Only a fool would mistake it for a friendly grin. How much cash had his family stored within those re-enforced walls? How many investments had they made?

Too many to count. Certainly enough to afford him some leeway and keep the banker in thousand dollar suits for the rest of his life.

The pompous ass straightened his food-stained tie and squinted against the setting sun. "We've already extended the deadline twice in deference to your family, but we cannot extend it again. We have a board of trustees to answer to and other investments to consider. You understand."

Ethan understood all right. If he didn't get his hands on Jenna Dane soon, he'd lose more than his initial investment. He'd leveraged over half of his inheritance on this land deal. He wouldn't be *poor* by most people's standards, but by Manning family standards he might as well be destitute.

This was the type of business blunder that tarnished family names.

Something his father and mother would not tolerate—not even from their son.

It was a good thing the private detective he'd hired had found Jenna Dane. Ethan didn't want to think about if he hadn't.

The banker rose and extended his hand. Ethan glared at it until the man slowly brought it back to his side. He grabbed the glasses perched on his nose and carefully wiped them with a handkerchief. "I'll expect to hear from you before the deadline." He placed his glasses back on and walked to the door.

Ethan watched him leave, then picked up the crystal candy dish on his desk and hurled it toward the wall. The dish exploded on impact, raining multi-colored mints and shiny glass shards onto the Persian rug. No one was going to fuck up this deal for him, especially not a low-class, second-rate mechanic.

He needed to find out exactly where they were. Carl and Jenna should've arrived in town by now. Ethan glanced at his calendar. Had it been a week since they last spoke?

That couldn't be right.

It didn't take a week to drive back to Vancouver. He waited to get his temper in check, then buzzed his executive assistant. "Cynthia, get me Carl Rich on the phone."

"Right away, Mr. Manning."

A moment later the phone rang. Ethan picked it up and without preliminaries said, "Where is she?"

There was a pause, then Carl's gruff voice said, "I lost her, but I have a couple of leads to follow up on."

"What do you mean you lost her? The last time we spoke you'd found her and had Jenna in your custody. You told me that you were on your way." Ethan clutched the receiver, his knuckles white. "What the hell happened? I expected you to be here by now." Something akin to panic clawed at his chest until he could barely breathe.

"She's pretty resourceful when she needs to be. She gave me the slip at a gas station, when I stopped to fill up," he said. "Hitchhiked back to her car and disappeared."

Fury over the man's incompetence made his shake. "How did a woman give you the slip? I thought you were a professional."

"She's tougher than she looks and obviously very persuasive when she needs to be," Carl ground out.

Ethan was beginning to understand that about Jenna. Somehow she'd eluded them for three months, but her admirable survival skills didn't change his objective. He'd paid a lot of money and expected results.

"I don't pay you for excuses," Ethan said. "Find her now or you won't see another dime. And just so we're clear, if you fail me again, I'll have your license yanked. You won't be able to get a job parking cars in this town. Got it?"

"Understood." The word was ripped from his throat. "Trust me, sir. She will not get away again," he said with menacing promise.

"Call me the second you spot her. I want to be there to make sure there are no more screw-ups. You have until Saturday." Ethan hung up before Carl could respond.

He was so tired of dealing with inept people. He should've gone after Jenna himself or at the very least gotten her to sign over the deed to the land before she ran. The garage that sat on the property was useless without it.

Stupid bitch!

She should know better than to try to strong arm him. He'd just have to consult his attorney to see if there were any charges he could level against Jenna for hindering the business transaction.

Every day she was out there running around the countryside cost Ethan thousands of dollars. Thanks to her, he was hemorrhaging money.

He should've known that someone with Jenna's spotty background would only cause him trouble. Ethan hoped his family never found out that he'd slept with the whore.

* * *

Jenna's first day on the job at the Gazette had been frankly boring compared to the unconventional introduction she'd received yesterday.

Paul had spent the morning badgering her about the interview with Aidan. He'd only stopped once she'd agreed to try her best, but Jenna had made it clear that her acceptance wasn't a promise of success.

Half the time the phone stopped ringing before Molly answered it. For a receptionist, she didn't seem overly concerned about the missed phone calls.

Instead, Molly continued her barrage of questions about Aidan. By noon, she had finally stopped calling him a vampire—thanks in large part to Jenna's assurance that she'd seen him in sunlight.

After being worn down all morning, Jenna had agreed to go to lunch with her.

Molly turned out to be a font of information. Jenna now knew that Ted was dating Alex. Though she hadn't met either one yet. And that Carol had finally 'come out' to her family, which as it turns out wasn't a surprise to anyone.

Thanks to the little gossip, Jenna also found out a lot about Paul Welling. According to Molly, he used to be a big city reporter. He'd fallen on hard times once it was discovered that he'd fabricated a couple of major stories. His previous employer had been sued and Paul had been let go. He'd been trying to carve his way back ever since.

That didn't bode well for Aidan. Paul's shady past coupled with his need to regain his reputation could lead him to do just about anything, print anything.

Five o'clock arrived after what felt like an eternity. Jenna rolled her neck to ease the stiffness and scanned the road behind her. Nothing. Forty-five minutes later, she spotted the entrance to the driveway and made a right.

The estate gate opened the second she buzzed to announce that she'd returned. Thanks to her co-workers fanciful stories, Jenna found herself scanning the woods for wolves. She'd seen one yesterday, but one hardly accounted for the rumors.

A couple of times Jenna thought she caught a flash of movement amongst the trees, but whatever it was disappeared too quickly to be positively identified.

The trees parted and the estate appeared. A mix of old world charm and modern architecture, the design fit its owner. Her heart raced as she scanned the yard. Was she really hoping to catch another glimpse of Aidan Fortier?

If Jenna were being honest with herself, then the answer would be yes. There was something about him that drew her to him. Sure, he was gorgeous and rolling in money, but that wasn't what fascinated her. Aidan was a puzzle.

Jenna had never been able to resist puzzles. She loved twisting the pieces to see how they fit together. It was one of the reasons she'd become a mechanic. Engines were like giant landscape jigsaws. They only worked when they were assembled in the right order.

Aidan had only presented her with a few pieces. Not nearly enough to form a clear picture of him. The stories she'd heard at the paper only added to his mystique and made her itch to know more.

"Like you need that kind of trouble," she muttered to herself.

Paul's thinly veiled warning rang in her ears. *Get the job done or get out.*

What choice did she have?

The driveway forked near the house. Jenna veered left and continued on another hundred yards. She pulled up in front of what she hoped was the garage. Several vehicles were parked haphazardly in the gravel lot.

Jenna tucked the Rover into a space and cut the engine. She jumped out, not bothering to lock it. Pebbles crunched under her feet as she walked to the door on the side of the building.

She heard men laughing inside and the sound of tools hitting metal. The combo drowned out the soft music playing in the background. Jenna poked her head inside. Her presence killed the conversation.

"Who are you?" one of the men asked, stepping away from a Lincoln MKX. "And what are you doing here unescorted?"

Unescorted? What did he mean by that? "I'm Jenna." She gestured to the Bug. "I just wanted to make sure my car made it here." She loved her car and was determined to get it running again. "Aidan said it would be okay to work on it."

The man glanced at her car and scratched his head. "Not sure when we're going to have time to get to it. We have our hands full right now." He jerked his chin toward to the Lincoln and the truck on racks beside it.

Jenna bit back a smile. He wasn't the first man to assume that she needed help. He wouldn't be the last. "That's all right. I think I can handle it on my own."

The man's gaze turned more assessing.

"Don't worry, I won't get in the way." The smell of grease and sweat greeted Jenna as she entered the garage, reminding her of home.

The large space had several bays, but only three were used for repair. The rest held luxury sedans and sports cars. Each work bay came equipped with hydraulic lifts and enough diagnostic equipment to open a shop.

Various sized tires were stacked against the right wall. Shelving units containing standard parts lined the back. To the left of the tires, a row of tools hung above a long workbench, organized from small to large and by type.

The man who'd questioned her stepped forward and gave her a sheepish grin, which was at odds with his hulking size. "I'm Nic. That's Bernie." He hiked his thumb over his shoulder to point to the man under the hood of the Lincoln. "And that's Josh." The latter stood near the rear of the car and didn't look old enough to drive. He smiled and waved as their eyes met.

"Nice to meet you," Jenna said. "I'll let you get back to it."

Nic continued to stare at her.

"I'll call you, if I need you," she said.

"Sure." Nic hesitated, then backed into a tray of tools. The tray crashed onto the ground, sending socket wrenches and screwdrivers skittering across the concrete floor.

"Might help if you look where you're going," Bernie said.

Jenna watched crimson creep into Nic's cheeks.

He spun around, took one step, and tripped over a crowbar. Nic grunted and somehow kept his feet under him. That didn't stop Bernie and Josh from busting a gut though.

"Something got you distracted, Nic?" Josh howled with laughter.

"Keep it up, pup," Nic muttered.

Jenna poked her head under the Bug's bonnet, so Nic wouldn't see her laughing, but she couldn't stop her shoulders from shaking.

The laughter gradually faded and the men went back to work.

Jenna grabbed a nearby light and clipped it to the metal frame, then slowly examined the engine. While she did, she couldn't help but overhear the conversation taking place beside her.

"I changed out the right rear hub bearing assembly," Nic said. "That got rid of the noise, but caused a glitch in the ABS braking system. Now I have speed sensor code being set during the test drive."

In her peripheral, she saw Josh glance her way, then quickly turn his attention back to the job. "I can't figure out why you're getting an ABS light and no speed signal from the wheel with the new hub bearing assembly in place."

They bantered various theories and suggestions back and forth, but no one was coming up with a solution. Jenna stopped what she was doing. "It's none of my business," she said, "but did you happen to use an aftermarket assembly?"

Three sets of eyes locked onto her. Nic hitched his hip against the side of the car. "Let's say that I did."

"Then that's your problem," Jenna said. "You need to use the Ford OEM assembly. The aftermarket assembly's toner ring doesn't play nice with the Ford sensor."

"How many days have you been working on the problem, Nic?" Bernie asked. "Three? Four?" He laughed. "Jenna here just fixed it in five minutes."

Nic flushed.

"Don't bust his chops too bad," Jenna said. "The only reason I knew what the problem was, is because I went through the same issue at my... at the," she corrected, "garage I worked at a few months back. Course it only took me two days to figure it out." She winked at Bernie.

The men roared with laughter. Jenna joined in, feeling relaxed and at home for the first time in months. She missed this kind of camaraderie. It seemed like a lifetime ago that she'd stepped foot inside a garage.

Until now, she hadn't dared. It would've been the first place Ethan and Carl Rich would've looked for her, the first place they would've checked.

"See, that proves you're a better mechanic than old Nic here." Josh playfully dug his elbow into Nic's ribs.

"He would've figured it out eventually...once he stopped staring at my butt," she said.

"Busted!" Josh shouted.

Jenna grinned at him, then went back to work on her car.

6

Aidan tried to keep his distance, but he couldn't ignore Jenna's sweet scent floating on the breeze. The alluring aroma wrapped around his senses, leaving him dizzy.

He'd intended to work, instead he found himself following his nose all the way to the garage. As he passed the Rover, he spotted Jenna's bag in the back.

Why hadn't she dropped it off at her motel last night? He shrugged it off and continued to the door.

Aidan stepped inside. A wrench hit the concrete with a loud clang. All three men slipped out from beneath the hood of the car to face him. Jenna didn't notice that he was there, until Nic muted the music.

She popped her head up. "Hey, that was my favorite song."

Aidan moved into her personal space and cleared his throat. Jenna spun around, pressing a hand to her chest. Her eyes widened, when she saw him. Was it his imagination or had her pupils dilated?

"Aidan," she croaked. "What are you doing here?"

He did his best to ignore the men's gaping mouths. "I thought I'd check to see that you had everything that you need."

"Uh. That's kind of you. Thanks!" Jenna took a step back and focused on her car.

She probably thought he wouldn't see her blush.

"I believe I have everything I need," she said.

"Good. How is the Rover working out?" Aidan rolled his shoulders. He didn't like having an audience, especially when the conversation was so awkward. He'd never had trouble speaking to women, not even when he was a pup. Being tongue-tied was a new experience for him. One Aidan didn't like one bit.

Jenna rubbed her face, smearing grease across her cheek. "It's great. Thanks again for letting me use the space."

"Sir," Nic interrupted. "Did you need something?"

Aidan's attention remained on Jenna. He didn't bother to glance at Nic. "No."

"It's just that you never come down here," Nic said.

Aidan's wolf brushed his skin as he slowly turned to face his mechanic. "Then it's high time that I did."

Nic's blue eyes glowed.

Aidan bristled.

Nic's gaze immediately dropped to the floor. "Of course. Let us know if you want to see anything in particular." He glanced at Jenna, which only made Aidan's hackles rise even more. The tension in the space increased.

"I will." He showed more teeth than was necessary. Aidan didn't like the wolf's interest in Jenna, but he let it go...for now.

It shouldn't matter to him if Nic and Jenna went out. If anything, he should try to encourage the relationship. It would take her off his hands and hopefully get her out of his thoughts.

His wolf snarled in protest.

Before Aidan could examine his wolf's odd response, Robert LaBeouf popped his head into the garage.

"Sir, you have a phone call," he said.

Aidan sighed. The work of an Alpha never ended. He rubbed the back of his neck. Aidan wasn't ready to leave yet. He hadn't gotten his fill of Jenna's lilac scent.

"I'll be there in a moment," he said.

Robert hesitated like he was about to say more, but caught Aidan's censorious glare. "I'll let them know."

"You do that."

"Your garage is incredible." Jenna's comment drew his mind away from the unwanted distractions. "Better than…" She stopped short. "I should get back to work. It was nice seeing you again."

Aidan nodded, feeling oddly disappointed as he left the garage. She'd dismissed him. Dismissed him like he was some kind of annoying pup, nipping at her heels. Aidan had never been dismissed before. Not by a woman. He had no experience with this type of rejection and wasn't altogether certain how he should act.

Bernie followed him out. "Alpha, can I have a word?"

"Can it wait?" Aidan needed to get away from the garage. Away from *her.*

Bernie glanced toward the open door, then lowered his voice. "No, it's about Jenna."

Aidan halted immediately. "What about her?"

Bernie's nervous gaze darted to the garage once more.

"She's human," Aidan said. "She's not going to be able to hear us."

His shoulders slumped in relief. "I think she's been living in her car," Bernie said.

Shocked by the statement, Aidan moved them away from the entrance. "Why would you think that?" His chest clenched at the thought of Jenna being in such a vulnerable position.

"I don't have proof," Bernie said. "But her scent is unusually strong in the Bug's backseat. And I found a tremendous amount of food packaging material scattered throughout the car."

"Are you sure she's not a slob?" Aidan asked. It wasn't unusual for humans to use their cars for trash heaps.

Bernie shook his head. "Don't think so. I also found a blanket rolled up and tucked into a side panel. Taken individually, I wouldn't think much of it, but when you add in her scent…" Bernie tapped his nose. "I just thought you should know."

Aidan nodded his thanks, then walked over to the Rover and opened the back door. He leaned in and inhaled deeply.

Jenna's scent filled his lungs. Aidan breathed in again and frowned. "You're right. Her scent is all over the backseat. There's only one reason for that. She must've slept in here last night. But why?"

Bernie shrugged. "The stuff I found in the Bug was old—at least a couple of weeks. I wouldn't be surprised if some of it is even older."

Had she been living in her car for months?

Aidan stared at the backseat. It didn't make sense. Why was Jenna living out of her car? She obviously had skills. Without them, she wouldn't have a job at the paper or be able to repair her car.

Bernie stepped toward the garage and stopped. He glanced back. "I've got an extra room in town—"

"No!" The vehemence in Aidan's response shocked them both. "I mean that's not necessary."

"She can't stay in the SUV," he said.

"She won't be," Aidan said.

Bernie's brow furrowed. "I've only known her for a couple of hours, but I can tell you right now that the girl is proud. No way is she going to let us help her, if she thinks we're trying to give her a handout."

"Leave it to me." Aidan's mind raced, but kept coming back to only one option. It was sheer insanity on his part, but what choice did he have? He couldn't let Jenna sleep in the vehicle. It wasn't safe. For some reason Aidan *needed* her to be safe.

He glanced at the sky. The moon peeked out from behind the tops of the trees. Not quite full yet, but it would be soon. When that happened, the estate would transform. He would transform.

It will only be for a couple of days. She'll be gone long before the moon run, he told himself.

Aidan stared at her bag in the back of the Rover. What kind of Alpha would he be, if he let her leave without at least trying to convince her to stay?

The phone call could wait. If it were important, they'd call back. Aidan shut the Rover's door and walked back into the garage. Jenna was once again under the hood of her car. "I was thinking," he said.

She gasped. Her head shot up and hit the hood. "Ouch! Stop sneaking up on me."

"Sorry." Aidan fought the urge to walk over and examine her. Touching her was a bad idea, especially when he needed to convince her to stay. "You okay?"

Jenna rubbed her head. "I'll be fine. What were you saying?"

"I was thinking about the repairs you need to do on your car," he said, not entirely sure where he was going with this idea.

She paled. "What about them?"

"It's ridiculous that you aren't able to work on the vehicle anytime you like," he said.

Confusion marred her face. "I can't. I have a job."

"I know." His nose wrinkled in disgust. "That's not what I meant. I thought it might be easier for you, if you stayed here at the estate—at least while you're working on the car. That way you could do the repairs anytime you felt like it. You wouldn't have to worry about driving back to your motel every night."

The last of the blood in her face drained away and her scent soured. It was as Bernie suspected.

Aidan pretended not to notice her reaction. What if she turned down his offer? What would he do then? He couldn't order her to stay. Jenna wasn't part of his pack. He couldn't hold her against her will. Though that thought held some appeal.

His wolf perked up. *Forget about it. Not going to happen.* Aidan's heart pounded. The need to protect thrummed in his head, as he waited for her answer.

Everything inside of Jenna screamed for her to say no, but Aidan was right. If she were here, she could spend every moment of extra time that she had working on her car. It would be a relief to not worry about driving back to the campground every night.

Staying on the estate would also give her the opportunity to interview Aidan. Jenna liked the idea of getting to know the real man behind the success, solving the puzzle that was Aidan Fortier.

Jenna bit her lip. "I don't want to put you out." Pride reared its ugly head.

"You won't," Aidan said. "As you've seen, the house is quite large. There's plenty of room for one more."

"If you're sure?" Say yes! Her brain screamed. She'd never get a better chance than this.

"I am." Aidan cleared his throat. "Now if you'll excuse me. I've kept whoever is on the phone waiting long enough."

"They've probably already hung up," she said.

Aidan smiled. "That's highly unlikely. When you're finished here, find Robert. He'll have a room waiting."

"Thank you," Jenna said.

Their eyes met fleetingly, long enough for Jenna to see the heat burning behind Aidan's amber gaze. In a blink it was gone, but there was no doubt in her mind that it had been there. Most shocking of all was her reaction to it. To him.

With one look, Aidan made her want. Made her ache. Her body had been dormant for three months. Now suddenly it was awake, aware of what it had been missing. And Jenna wasn't sure how to handle that.

When in doubt—run!

Jenna opened her mouth to tell Aidan that she'd changed her mind.

"Please excuse me, I really must go," he interjected, before she got the chance.

She glanced over her shoulder. All three mechanics busied themselves, pretending that they hadn't been listening to every word.

Bernie looked at her.

"What?" she asked.

"Nothing." He grinned, then grabbed the remote from Nic and turned up the music.

Aidan spent twenty tedious minutes on the phone, listening to all the areas that the southern Moonlight Kin pack Alpha would like to see reformed.

Some of his ideas were genuinely innovative, while others simply rehashed old notions and outdated concepts. Aidan tried to concentrate on what Pierre was saying, but his thoughts refused to leave Jenna.

He didn't like the idea of her out there in the garage surrounded by his wolves. She was perfectly safe, but Nic had shown far too much interest in her for his peace of mind.

Now that she was under his roof, Aidan felt responsible for her. It was his duty to protect her, especially from his wolves.

Pierre said something else that Aidan missed. This was ridiculous. They were going to have to have this whole conversation over again, but not tonight.

"Rest assured that I will bring up your suggestions at the next Lycanian Elder meeting." He gave the southern Alpha his standard political reply and excused himself.

The second he hung up, Aidan pressed a buzzer to summon Robert into his office. His assistant entered, his face drawn in concern.

"Sir, I noticed that Ms. Dane is still here," he said. "Should I tell her that it's time to head back to town? I can't help but think she's taking advantage of your hospitality."

No one took advantage of him. Aidan wouldn't allow it. "Jenna will be staying with us for a few days," he said. "I'd intended to let you know before I answered the phone, but I'd kept Pierre waiting long enough."

"Jenna?" Robert startled. "But Alpha, the wolves were planning to run tonight."

Aidan played with the miniature Zen garden on his desk, but the repetitive sand raking did little to bring him inner peace. "Make sure that they shift in the woods and tell them to keep away from the house."

"But Alpha, we risk exposure with her here," he said.

Aidan set the tiny rake down. He was well aware of the risks. He didn't need reminding. Perhaps he should be more concerned about Jenna given the phase of the moon, but she'd already faced down one wolf without batting an eyelash. He didn't think she'd wilt, if she accidentally caught sight of a few more.

"My orders are clear," he said. "Prepare a room for her in the west wing."

Robert shifted in place. "Wouldn't she be more comfortable in the east wing?"

"With the pack?" Aidan arched a brow. "Do you think that would be wise?"

Robert shook his head. "I was merely concerned for your safety. Humans are untrustworthy vermin. If it were up to me, I'd send her away or have her exterminated, before she has a chance to 'infect' the pack."

Aidan rose from behind his desk. "Of that I have no doubt, but since you are not in a position to give orders..."

It was rare that he had to remind any of his people of their position in the pack, but today Aidan found himself doing so twice.

It was his fault. He'd given Robert far too much leeway, too much responsibility in hopes that he'd slip up and reveal where his true loyalties lie. He hadn't yet. But the small shift in power had gone to his head and made Robert forget his place.

Robert paled. "If that is all, I'll notify the maids to prepare her room."

Aidan nodded. "You do that."

He stopped at the door, pausing with his hand on the knob. Color had returned to his face, but Robert couldn't meet Aidan's gaze. "Do you still want me to send another female to your room tonight? Or would you rather *rest*?"

Aidan ground his teeth. The gossip from his encounter with Sydney had obviously reached his assistant's attentive ears. Robert's gleeful expression only made matters worse.

Last night was an anomaly. Tonight he'd prove it. "I have no need to rest, when duty calls."

Robert coughed. "Nine o'clock okay?"

"That would be perfect." His wolf grumbled. Aidan ignored it. Just because Jenna Dane was staying at the estate didn't mean that anything in his life had to change.

Jenna settled into the bedroom that Aidan had selected for her. Soft cream colors and earth-tone browns served to decorate the cozy room. A small dresser sat against one wall, while a queen-sized bed smothered in pillows graced another, leaving Jenna spoiled for choice.

How long had it been since she'd slept in this kind of bed? Three months? Longer? She'd certainly never owned anything this nice. Jenna had poured every penny she earned back into her business.

The bedroom had an ensuite bath attached that came fully stocked with shampoo, soap, and several fluffy towels. She stared at the bathtub longingly. Jenna couldn't wait to take a long soak.

She leaned down to turn on the water, but was interrupted by a knock at the door. Jenna gave the tub a longing glance, then crossed the room to open the door.

Robert LaBeouf stood in the hall with a tray of food in his hands. He didn't wait for her to invite him inside. He simply stepped by her and placed the tray on a small table situated by the sliding glass doors.

"I wasn't sure what people like you normally eat, so I had the chef put a little bit of everything on the tray. It should keep you until morning. There should be no need to leave the room."

His tone was perfectly polite, but his words and demeanor gave Jenna pause. Robert made it sound like she was a prisoner, not a guest. Was Molly wrong about this being a cult?

Aidan didn't strike her as the type to pass around the Kool-Aid, but he was certainly charismatic enough to garner a lot of followers. She made a mental note to check the door to make sure it couldn't be locked from the outside.

Jenna didn't know why Robert didn't like her, since they'd had very little interaction. Maybe protecting his boss was part of his job description?

Made sense. Aidan's wealth automatically made him a target.

Or maybe Robert had a distrustful nature? Of course, there was always a possibility that he was just a dick. For some people that state of being came naturally.

Aidan didn't strike her as the type of man who needed defending, but Jenna couldn't say for sure, since she really didn't know him.

"Please tell Aidan thank you again for the use of the room." She hoped her gratitude would smooth Robert's ruffled feathers. If anything, it made matters worse.

Robert stiffened at the familiar use of Aidan's name. "*Mr. Fortier* is *occupied* this evening." He paused, letting the words and their meaning sink in. "I'll be sure to tell him in the *morning* that you find the room adequate."

Jenna waited for Aidan's stuffy assistant to leave, then checked the door. To her relief, the only lock was on the inside.

Once she was convinced that Robert couldn't trap her, she sat down to eat. The food should've been delicious, but instead, it dropped like boulders into her stomach.

Who cares what—or *who* Aidan was doing tonight? Certainly not her. Their relationship was purely professional. And it needed to stay that way so she could remain impartial during the interview.

Jenna snorted. Fat chance of that after everything he'd done for her.

Besides, Aidan hadn't agreed to an interview yet. If his history was anything to go by, he would likely decline her offer.

Jenna put her fork down and pushed the tray aside. She needed air, but didn't feel like facing Robert's misplaced scorn. Her gaze strayed to the sliding glass doors. Jenna pulled the curtains aside and glanced out. The stone patio appeared to be vacant.

Perfect.

The lock opened with a soft click and she stepped out into the temperate air. Jenna wrapped her arms around herself and took a deep breath, feeling some of the tension leave her body. The aroma of freshly mowed lawn greeted her, but it was the movement in the woods that surrounded the yard that captured her attention.

Red eyes glowed in the darkness like demonic fireflies amongst the trees. Jenna caught a glimpse of fur and saw a bushy tail swish.

Wolves!

And not just one from the looks of it. A whole pack.

The stories from town came rushing back. "Every story holds an element of truth," she murmured.

Just because the man had wolves on his property didn't mean he was a werewolf or a vampire.

The wolves nudged each other with their massive heads, yipping playfully as they darted amongst the tree trunks. If they noticed her, they didn't care. They were obviously used to seeing humans.

Jenna's dour mood lifted as she watched them scamper about. What would it be like to belong to such a tightknit family?

She couldn't even imagine. She'd spent her life moving trash bags full of clothes from one foster house to the next, doing her best to avoid getting too attached, while dodging the occasional molester. That had been her life, her only world, until she'd aged out of the system.

The process had taught Jenna that she couldn't count on anyone but herself. There was no such thing as the perfect family. It was an illusion, a fairytale, a dream she'd stopped believing in a long time ago.

Better to live vicariously through animals than to delude herself. At least their instincts were honest.

Jenna watched the wolves interact, marveling at their closeness. If only people could learn to work together for the good of the 'pack', the world would be a much better place.

7

Tonight was the night. Aidan stood in his room, wearing nothing but a pair of low-slung black jeans. His feet were bare as he paced across the carpet, nerves on edge.

Even though Jenna's room was on the floor beneath his, Aidan kept thinking that he could *hear* her. It was his imagination. The walls and floors in his home had been soundproofed for Were privacy. What he hadn't imagined was the sweet aroma of lilacs wafting on the air. The scent followed him wherever he went.

He heard shuffling in the hall outside his door. What if Jenna was lost and needed his help? Without thought, Aidan crossed the room and opened the door before anyone could knock.

Lisa's arm hovered in the air. Her gray eyes widened in surprise. She lowered her hand and took a step back.

"You called for me, Alpha?"

"Yes, come in." Aidan concealed his disappointment, ignoring the *wrongness* in his gut.

The sooner they got this over with, the sooner he could prove to himself and the pack that everything was normal. *He was normal.* The presence of one human female wasn't going to stop him from performing his duties.

"It's been a long day, so if you don't mind I'd like to get started." Aidan wanted to find his bondmate and put an end to the tryouts.

Lisa flushed, but stepped inside the room and shut the door behind her. "As you wish, Alpha." She quickly stripped off her clothes, revealing her womanly body. "Where do you want me?" There was huskiness to her voice that hadn't been there before.

Aidan pointed to the bed, then his hand moved to the buttons on his jeans. He shucked his clothes quickly.

Lisa licked her lips as her gaze traveled down the length of his naked body.

Aidan had never seen the need for modesty. Like all wolves, running through the woods kept him in shape. He was proud of his form, happy that it pleased both Were and human females, though he'd never acted upon any attraction with a human.

The memory of Jenna's dilated pupils popped into his mind. He hadn't imagined the heat simmering between them. Her scent had warmed, grown richer, deeper, when she'd looked at him.

What would it be like to hold her in his arms? Sink into her body? Have her writhing beneath him? His shaft hardened at the thought.

"Alpha?"

Aidan blinked and the room came back into focus. Instead of Jenna, Lisa lay on his bed, her firm thighs slightly parted, giving him a tantalizing glimpse of the moisture gathering in her soft folds.

The sight should've enhanced his erection, instead his shaft wilted like an over-watered plant.

She pursed her lips. "I want to touch you."

Touching was good. Touching would help bring his mind and body back into alignment. Aidan mentally smacked his wolf upside the head to get its attention.

Once he had it, Aidan nodded to Lisa to proceed. He could do this. Last night was a fluke. His hands clenched at his sides as he kneeled on the foot of the bed to give her better access.

"Wait," he said, before Lisa could grasp him. Aidan leaned over and dug his nose into the soft curls between her legs.

She mewed and her eyes drifted shut. "Yes!" she hissed.

Her deliciously musky scent filled his lungs. He could do this. It was just like riding a bike.

Aidan's wolf snorted.

"Touch me," he said, ignoring it. He was in control, not his beast.

Lisa grasped his shaft and stroked him, trying to bring it back to life. The normally dependable part of his anatomy once again refused to rise.

His inner wolf snickered. It had won this battle, but the war for control of his body wasn't over.

Aidan pulled away and slid off the bed, hoping Lisa hadn't noticed. He scrubbed his hands over his face and through his hair. "I'm sorry, but you are not the one," he said.

Lisa's lower lip poked out. "But we haven't tried yet." Panic seeped into her voice.

"I don't need to. I can tell by your scent that you're not my bondmate," Aidan said.

Her brow furrowed. "I thought you needed to be inside me to be sure."

He did and he didn't. Aidan shook his head. In this instance, he just knew.

Lisa spread her legs wider. "Maybe you didn't get a good whiff. Why don't you try one more time?"

"I beg your pardon?" Aidan's brow shot to his hairline. How could she question his scenting abilities? "My nose is *not* broken."

She glanced at his flaccid shaft and mirrored his expression. The implication clear.

Heat infused his face. Aidan snatched his denims off the floor and jerked them on without looking at her. "Leave!"

Her scent sharpened as anger replaced need. Lisa threw on her clothes and stomped to the door. "Sydney was right about your impotence," she muttered under her breath, just loud enough for him to hear.

"Get out!" Aidan bellowed.

Lisa slammed the door behind her.

Aidan rolled his shoulders, but it did little to alleviate the tension and fear building inside of him. He wasn't impotent. How could he be? He was a werewolf. His hand trembled as he scrubbed it over his chest.

Lisa's sour scent lingered in the air, choking him. Aidan couldn't breathe. He needed to get out of his bedroom, out of this house before the walls closed in and crushed him. He walked over to his French doors and threw them open.

The evening air smacked his face, clearing his lungs of the female Were's scent. Aidan walked to the balcony wall and leaned over it, hanging his head between his arms. He took several deep breaths.

What was he going to do? He couldn't go on like this? It had only been two days, but soon news of his 'affliction' would reach the ears of the Lycanian Elders, then there would be questions. Questions he couldn't—wouldn't answer. If this continued, he'd have no choice but to step down as Alpha. The pack needed a mated leader.

He inhaled once again, filling his lungs. This time he caught Jenna's floral aroma. He heard the tread of a shoe scraping against stone. Aidan's ears perked. He leaned over the balcony, balancing on his stomach, and spotted Jenna standing on the patio below.

She didn't notice him, didn't hear him. Her gaze remained trained on the trees. Aidan followed her line of sight and saw his wolves moving beneath the branches.

He cursed under his breath and strode back into his bedroom. Three minutes later, Aidan found himself dressed and standing at the foot of the stairs that led to the lower patio.

Aidan watched Jenna from the shadows, unable to look away. Her hair glowed like fairy-fire in the burgeoning moonlight, giving her an ethereal appearance.

She'd make a beautiful wolf. The thought came unbidden into his mind, leaving him shaken. As tempting as it was, biting her would be sheer madness.

He might be temporarily 'afflicted', but Aidan wasn't insane enough to act upon the impulse. His gaze drifted over her.

Jenna wore a pair of black leggings that clung to her like a thin layer of paint, cupping her lush bottom. An over-sized sweater and T-shirt concealed her firm high breasts, but Aidan knew they were there.

She leaned over the wall, her head dropping down to look at something on the ground. The move lifted her ass, making her appear submissive.

Aidan's wolf shoved him aside to get a better look. When he tried to push the beast back down, it snapped and growled at him. Aidan couldn't tear his gaze away from her. He wanted. He needed. His mouth watered as blood from his brain rushed south.

It wasn't until the buttons on his denims bit into his shaft that Aidan noticed how hard he'd become. He glanced down in disbelief at the bulge filling the front of his denims.

You picked a fine time to start working again. He stared at his erection in bewilderment.

His wolf barked inside his head to get his attention, then urged him to act.

Not going to happen, Aidan spoke directly to his beast. *You're only interested in her because she's human. That makes her unique to you. To us. That's the only reason you want her. It's also the reason you can't have her.*

The wolves in the woods sensed his presence and howled. Jenna didn't even flinch at the sound. Instead, she leaned even further over the short wall. She was killing him. Aidan closed his eyes and prayed for strength.

"I wouldn't do that if I were you." He adjusted himself, then stepped out of the darkness.

Jenna nearly toppled before catching herself. "You really have to stop sneaking up on me."

"I wasn't sneaking. You were too preoccupied with the wolves to hear me."

She glanced back at the trees and scowled. "I think you scared them away."

Doubtful, Aidan thought.

"Aren't you afraid?" he asked.

She edged away from him as he drew nearer. "Of what?"

Of me? Of the beast you sense lurking inside of me?

"The savage beasts in the woods." He motioned to where the wolves had been milling only moments ago.

Jenna stopped her retreat and her green eyes narrowed.

Aidan's lips canted at her sudden mood change. She had a lot of courage for a human. He'd give her that.

"They're not beasts." She chided. "Not in the sense that you mean. And they're certainly not savage, unless they're starving. As someone who keeps wolves on his property, I would think you'd know the difference."

Jenna was scolding him, actually scolding him. No one scolded him. So why did that make him so damned pleased?

"I didn't mean to offend you." Aidan planted his hip against the wall. "It's just that a lot of people don't see wolves that way. They look at them as pests, nuisances in need of extermination. Instead of an apex species that keeps the animal population healthy and in balance."

She looked at him. "If humans had half the sense of family that wolves do, then there wouldn't be so many abused and neglected kids in the world."

"Are you speaking from experience?" The idea enraged him, but there was no denying the shadow of pain in her eyes.

Aidan tried to imagine what it would be like to have had his family reject him. He couldn't fathom it, the concept far too alien in the Lycan world.

"People take family for granted." Jenna's voice cracked as she dodged his question. "I don't."

What had happened to her? Was that why she was living in her car? She was too old to have runaway from foster care, but that didn't mean she hadn't grown up in the system. He clamped down on his anger. If he didn't, Aidan would end up shifting in front of her.

"What are you doing up?" He moved the conversation to a less volatile topic.

"Couldn't sleep. Thought maybe some fresh air would help, then I noticed the wolves and I guess I lost track of time. I didn't disturb your evening, did I?"

He shook his head. "No." At least not directly.

"Are you sure?" she asked.

Aidan crossed his arms over his chest and narrowed his eyes. "Why do you ask?"

Jenna's fingers curled around the top of the stone wall. "Your P.A. implied that you'd be occupied for the rest of the night and you were not to be disturbed."

What in Freki's teats had Robert told her?

"My plans changed," Aidan said.

Her gaze flicked to his, then skittered away. "Sorry." Her words didn't match the pleasing scent emanating from her skin. Was he the cause of it? For some reason, Aidan wanted to know.

"Don't be." He moved closer.

Her floral scent changed, became richer, muskier. With infinite care, he pushed a stray curl away from her face. Jenna's heart pounded so hard that he could hear it. His gaze flicked to the pulse jumping in her neck.

"So soft," he said.

"Thanks." She brushed a hand through her hair and cleared her throat. "Is this some kind of animal sanctuary?"

The question brought him up short. Aidan had never thought about his estate in those exact terms, but the idea was close enough. "Something like that."

Jenna tilted her head. "You know people in town talk about your wolves."

His heart slammed against his ribs, but Aidan managed to maintain his calm exterior. "What exactly do they say?" He touched her hair again, the silky strands slipping through his fingers.

Jenna gave him an odd look, but she didn't pull away. "Honestly, I don't know where to start. They are a crazy bunch." She shook her head. "And when I say crazy, I mean *crazy*. They think you howl at the moon with your wolves like some kind of werewolf." She giggled, missing Aidan's startled expression.

"That's quite a theory," he said softly. "Wonder how they came by it?"

"You haven't heard the best one yet," she said.

"Can hardly wait," he deadpanned.

Her grin widened. "One person in town is convinced that you're a vampire." Jenna roared with laughter. "A vampire! Can you believe it?"

Aidan snorted. "As if I'd ever stoop to *that* level."

He was quiet for quite some time, then asked, "What do you think?"

Her gaze drifted to his sensual mouth. No fangs there. Were his lips as soft as they appeared to be? The urge to close the distance between them and find out nearly overwhelmed her.

Jenna shoved her hands in her pockets and tore her gaze away from his mouth. "It's true that you allow wolves to run loose on your property, but I haven't seen you howling at the moon." She winked.

She was actually flirting with him. Jenna hadn't flirted with anyone in months. It felt good. Felt right. Even if it was a little awkward.

"It's not full yet," Aidan said dryly.

She laughed. "Right. I forgot." Jenna glanced at the moon, basking in its soft glow. Her smile faded. "I think people start rumors to make themselves feel better, feel superior to others. They don't know you, which makes them even more jealous of your success." Her gaze strayed to the house.

Aidan sighed. "Material things do not define who I am. You should know that by now."

His words shamed her. Aidan had gone above and beyond to help a total stranger. But Jenna had allowed a handsome face to sway her before. The consequence of which had destroyed everything she'd worked for.

It pained her to admit, but other than striking good looks, Aidan didn't have much in common with Ethan. It wasn't fair of her to compare them.

Jenna had been comparing people to her ex for three months and all it had done was make her bitter. She was tired of being bitter. She was tired of the distrust. Jenna was tired period.

She needed that chapter of her life to be over, so that she could be open to new things. Perhaps the things right in front of her.

Aidan's sharp amber eyes glowed the longer he stared at her. A trick of the light no doubt. The intensity of his gaze made it hard to breathe. Hard to think.

She casually moved to the side to give herself some space. If Aidan noticed, he didn't say anything. He turned his attention toward the trees.

"Why are you really here?" he asked.

Ice encased Jenna, leaving her shivering inside. "What do you mean?"

"Why Breakbend? Of all the places to settle, why did you come here?" he asked.

Some of the tension left her body. "Like a lot of people, I needed the work."

Aidan glanced at her. "That doesn't explain why you're on the run."

She flinched. "Who said anything about...I don't know where you got that idea from, but you're mistaken."

"Am I?"

Jenna nodded, but couldn't meet his gaze.

"Do you know why I'm so successful in business?" he asked, throwing her off balance.

She shrugged stiffly. "Because you've developed innovative software?"

Aidan shook his head, sending his black hair into his face. "No, it's because I have an uncanny ability to read people. My competitors, my business associates, my enemies, and my friends. I know without fail, when someone is lying to me." He reached out and clasped her hand.

Fire shot up Jenna's arm, melting the ice as it spread throughout her body. She couldn't catch her breath.

Pull away, her mind screamed, but her hand refused to cooperate.

"You're not a liar," Aidan said, "but you're definitely hiding something."

Her stomach ricocheted off her knees, then bounced into her throat. "I'm tired," she said abruptly. "I think I'm going to head to bed. Thanks again for the room. I'll do my best to get the car fixed tomorrow, and then I will be on my way." She took a step toward her room, forgetting that he still held her hand.

The warmth of his fingers scalded her. Their gazes met and lingered.

Aidan stepped closer and leaned in next to her ear. His warm breath brushed her skin, making her nipples harden.

"You're safe here, Jenna," he murmured. "I'm a good friend to have." *And a worse enemy*, was left unspoken. "I offer you my protection freely. No strings attached." His lips brushed her jawbone.

Jenna closed her eyes and shuddered. Her resolve wavered. The urge to come clean burned her esophagus as the words tangled in her throat.

She wanted to trust him. Wanted to believe what he was saying was true, but she didn't know Aidan Fortier. And he certainly didn't know her.

Still, it was a tempting offer, but he didn't realize the trouble she was hauling in her wake. Aidan might genuinely mean what he'd said, but Jenna had been wrong before.

Jenna couldn't risk it—not even for him. She wouldn't survive another betrayal.

"Goodnight, Aidan." This time when Jenna stepped back, he released her.

His jaw tightened, but he didn't say another word. Aidan simply nodded, then turned back to face the woods.

Whatever she was running from had Jenna spooked. You didn't have to be a werewolf to see that. He'd only known her for two days, but Aidan needed her to trust him. He refused to look at why it was so important. Her scent faded, replaced by the thick green growth of the woods.

Something moved to his right. Aidan's hackles rose. He swiftly inhaled, scenting the night air. He caught a wisp of sweetness and expected to see a female Were.

Robert stepped from the shadows.

How long had he been standing there watching and listening? The fact that Aidan hadn't noticed him until now was testament to how much Jenna distracted him.

Aidan checked to make sure that Jenna's sliding door was closed. "You were supposed to order the wolves to stay in the woods." Without another word, he moved them to the far end of the porch.

"I relayed your message," Robert said. "But I cannot make them follow orders. Only the Alpha has that power."

Aidan bristled. "The Alpha is who gave them the order to stay away."

Robert looked down at the stone floor. "Did they scare the human?" He sounded hopeful.

Aidan watched him closely. "Their appearance intrigued her. She wanted to get closer, to know more. Maybe even become part of the pack." The idea wasn't as appalling as it should be, but he'd said it to see how Robert reacted.

"We can't let in strays! She wasn't born Lycan. She's not one of us." Robert's eyes glowed with barely contained fury. "What did you tell her?"

Interesting...

"I didn't tell her anything," Aidan said. "She came up with her own conclusions."

Robert searched his face. "And what conclusions would those be?" he asked.

"She believes the estate is a wildlife refuge." Aidan kept his expression bland and crossed his arms over his chest. "I saw no need to correct her assumption."

Robert sighed and deflated under scrutiny. "I suppose there are worse things for her to believe," he said. "It isn't safe for her to be here. For her or for the pack."

Aidan strode down the stairs into the backyard, leaving Robert scrambling to catch up. "I will handle Jenna Dane. There's no need for concern."

"I'm only looking out for the pack, Alpha."

"As am I!" He growled low in his throat. "The only reason I allow you to question my judgment is because of your loyalty to the pack. Do not make me regret my decision."

Aidan was under no illusion, when it came to Robert's loyalty to him. Because of his lack of strength, Robert would suck up to any Alpha—or potential Alpha in order to maintain his current position. Without his job, Robert would drop to the bottom of the pack.

"Yes, Alpha." Robert's gaze burned holes in the grass, but he never looked up.

Aidan stripped his clothes off. "I'm going to go for a run." He walked to the edge of the woods and glanced at Jenna's darkened room. Aidan saw the curtains part, then he felt her heated gaze upon his bare skin.

She might not trust him, but she did *want* him. That was a start.

Aidan stood in plain view for longer than he normally would have. He wanted Jenna to see him. Wanted her to want him as much as his wolf wanted her.

It shouldn't want her at all, something inside him snapped.

Aidan waited a few seconds more, then stepped behind a tree. Black fur rippled over his skin and claws sprang from his fingertips as he shifted, freeing his Other form. Aidan threw his head back and howled, then took off in search of the rest of the pack.

Jenna was convinced that she'd swallowed her tongue. That was the only reason for the strangled gasp that had come from her throat, when she watched Aidan strip off his clothes and walk toward the woods.

She couldn't hear what he was saying. There'd been no reason that she could see for him to stop walking, but he had. And for that, Jenna would be eternally grateful.

Never in all her years of existence had she ever seen anything more shocking or more spectacular. The man was gorgeous from his head to his...oh my.

Her body clenched.

That particular part of his anatomy had to be a trick of the light. Jenna gulped and tried not to drool.

Too bad he was crazy as a loon. Because only a crazy person would walk into woods, teaming with wild wolves. Naked as the day he was born.

Jenna watched until he'd disappeared, then slipped into bed. She closed her eyes, doing her very best to erase Aidan's naked body from her mind. But no matter how long she laid there, Jenna couldn't forget.

The more she thought about him, the more she ached. She turned over and punched the pillow.

His perfect male form haunted her, turning her thoughts carnal, before she drifted to sleep.

8

Long, strawberry blond curls brushed Aidan's abdomen, causing gooseflesh to rise over his skin. His stomach muscles contracted as moist lips brushed an open-mouthed kiss over his navel.

"Jenna," he hissed, sinking his fingers into her hair.

Her green eyes sparkled mischievously, as she moved his hands away and placed them on the bed beside him. She grinned and went right back to raining kisses over his chest.

Aidan fisted the sheets to keep from reaching for her again. His swollen shaft ached as her lips skirted around it, teasing him, tormenting him. She was trying to destroy him.

Her curls caressed his thighs and Aidan trembled. Jenna's blunt nails dug into his legs as she pushed them apart and positioned her body between them. She looked at him once more from beneath her long lashes. Their gazes locked and embers burst into flames.

Jenna lowered her head. Her lips drew closer and closer to the place he needed them most. Aidan's shaft bounced against his belly. He stared, transfixed by the sight of her and held his breath. Jenna's lips parted and she...*chirped*.

Aidan was too far gone to care. "Please don't stop," he begged, his desperation dire.

Chirp! Chirp! Chirp!

Aidan frowned. What the hell? Why was she making that sound?

Strike that—how was she making that sound?

Her breath brushed over him and he shuddered. Forget about the noise. Aidan wasn't going to let anything interrupt this moment. He was too close.

Chirp!

The sound was louder now. More insistent. Aidan squeezed his eyes closed, willing it to go away. When he opened them again, Jenna was gone.

"No!" He shot straight up in bed.

Sunlight poured into the room, temporarily blinding him. *Chirp! Chirp!* His gaze strayed to the alarm on the table.

Aidan closed his eyes and groaned. He hit the snooze button and fell back onto the bed, his body hot, hard, and trembling with need.

A dream.

It had all been a dream.

Disappointment hollowed his chest, leaving behind a soul-deep yearning he could no longer ignore.

* * *

Jenna didn't have to be into work until the afternoon, which was a good thing considering how fitfully she'd slept. Every time she'd tried to close her eyes, she'd seen Aidan's naked body. The image had been burned into her retinas.

In the moments she'd managed to catch some sleep, the dreams had taken over. Vivid, active, and so intense that they'd felt real. *He'd felt real.* She and Aidan had devoured each other, their bodies twining like boa constrictors in the middle of a mating frenzy.

Jenna threw back the covers and climbed out of bed. She might as well get some work done on the car, since there was no way she was going back to sleep. At this point, she didn't dare close her eyes.

She showered quickly, making good use of the adjustable massage head, then went to the garage. Her body still ached, despite the orgasm, but at least she'd taken some of the edge off. Jenna had had to do something, before she faced Aidan again.

The garage was empty when she arrived. It didn't take long to realize that her beloved Bug needed several new parts in order to run properly. Parts that weren't available in the garage. Parts that cost money. Money she didn't have. Wouldn't have, unless she could get an interview with Aidan.

She was still under the bonnet, where she'd been for an hour, when Nic and Bernie arrived. "Morning, guys." She peered beyond them. "Where's Josh?"

"He drove into the city last night to pick up more parts. Should be back later this afternoon," Bernie said.

Nic stared at her face and frowned. No doubt noticing the circles under her eyes. "You're up early," he said.

"Couldn't sleep. The wolves kept me up," she lied.

It hadn't been the wolves occupying her thoughts, but she wasn't about to tell them that she'd dreamt about their boss.

Both men froze and exchanged an odd glance. Bernie recovered first. "You should stay away from the monsters in the woods. They're dangerous. Every child familiar with Little Red Riding Hood knows that."

Was he kidding? Jenna couldn't tell, but something in his cautious expression told her that her response mattered. "The only monsters I've ever encountered are the two-legged variety." Without conscious thought, her hand moved to the healing wound above her eye.

The men exchanged another telling look.

"What?" Jenna asked.

Bernie once again broke the silence. "You're not like most people that I've met."

Jenna laughed. "I'll take that as a compliment."

He picked up a wrench and polished it. "You should."

"Now that we've bonded, you're not going to ask me to join your commune, are you?"

"Commune?" he asked, his confusion evident.

"Just checking," Jenna said, only half kidding.

"Oh, I get it." Bernie shook his head and chuckled. "This isn't the type of club that you can just join." He winked. "You don't have worry about anyone trying to *convert* you."

Jenna snorted. "Good to know." But she did wonder what type of club Bernie was referring to. All the clubs she knew about had special jackets, funny handshakes, or silly hats. She hadn't seen any of those things on the estate. Maybe they only trotted them out for special occasions? Or maybe they only wore them when outsiders weren't around?

Nic walked over to a coffee maker tucked between the shelves and poured himself a cup. "Thanks for making a fresh pot," he said, then added, "Want one?"

"Sure." Jenna smiled. "As long as you promise not to trip over anything while you're bringing it to me."

Nic smirked. "I'll do my best."

Jenna had forgotten all about making the coffee once she'd popped her head under the hood of the Bug and calculated the cost of repairs.

He poured her a cup and brought it over. "Figure out what's wrong with it yet?"

"Thanks." Jenna took the coffee from him. "Still working on it."

Nic brought the cup to his lips. "Need help?"

Jenna shook her head. "Nah, but thanks for the offer. I've worked on her so many times that I know this car inside and out. She doesn't keep her secrets for long."

She wasn't keeping secrets at all. The Bug had pretty much shouted that she was badly broken.

"If you have time later, I'd like to get your opinion on some diagnostics I ran on the truck," Bernie said.

"Yeah, I'd love to help," Jenna said. "Just let me finish up here." It felt good to be included, to once again be part of a team.

Nic walked over to the Lincoln and set his coffee cup down. He didn't go back to work. Instead, he glanced at Jenna. His mouth opened and closed a couple of times, then his hand moved to the back of his neck. Nic rubbed the tendons absently.

The whole thing was odd and slightly unnerving. "What's up?" she asked.

"I was wondering." He bit his lip. "Do you have any plans tonight? If you do that's fine," Nic said in a rush. "But if you don't, I thought maybe we could...I mean if you're not busy."

Jenna blinked in surprise. *Was he asking her out?* She thought they'd just been teasing each other and hadn't taken the bantering seriously. Her gaze sharpened.

Nic was an attractive man with his sandy brown hair and dark blue eyes. He had the kind of disarming smile that drew people in and made them want to smile back. Any woman would be flattered to catch his attention—even Jenna, if only she hadn't...

Hadn't what? Met Aidan? Seen him naked? Been on the run? The truth sucked.

Jenna didn't want to hurt Nic's feelings. He'd been nothing but nice to her. At the same time, she couldn't in good conscience lead him on.

She was about to let him down easy, when a clack, clack, clack of claws scraped the concrete behind her. Jenna swiveled in time to see a huge black wolf come strolling into the garage.

It was so large that the top of its massive head reached her chest. Its ears were up. Alert. While its amber eyes watched her every move. It took another step, then hesitated.

A jolt of fear struck. Jenna's first instinct was to run from the pony-sized beast. The urge was followed by an equally strong impulse to stay put.

Bernie and Nic didn't say a word, but their shocked expressions spoke volumes.

So this wasn't something that happened every day.

"Is the wolf tame?" she asked softly. After all, it had walked into the garage filled with humans. Not typical behavior for a wild animal.

"Hardly!" Nic replied.

Jenna reached for a wrench, then visually examined the animal's mouth. She detected no foam or any other sign that would indicate that the wolf was rabid. She dropped the wrench back onto the tray of tools.

"Slowly come toward my voice." Nic cupped his hand, beckoning her to move away.

The hair on the wolf's back rose and he growled.

Jenna's legs locked. "Easy." Her hand trembled as she held it out and cooed quietly to calm the animal.

The wolf sniffed the air, then glanced at the men and slowly approached. Jenna continued speaking to it, her cadence low and soothing.

When her fingers were within an inch of the creature's massive muzzle, its tongue darted out and licked her hand.

She gasped in surprise. "Did you see that?"

"We saw it." There was an odd tone to Bernie's voice. One Jenna didn't recognize.

Encouraged by the wolf's response, Jenna inched closer, until she could touch the wolf's head. The creature flinched, but didn't shy away. Jenna took that as encouragement and petted the animal. She watched in amazement as his amber eyes closed.

"Oh my gosh! I can't believe this. Have you guys ever seen anything like this?" she whispered.

"No," they said in unison. "Never."

"This is amazing. I never thought in a million years I'd ever get the chance to do anything like this. I wish I could get a picture. He's beautiful. Truly magnificent."

Bernie and Nic didn't respond.

"Are you sure he's not tame?" she asked, unable to tear her gaze away. He sure seemed tame enough to Jenna.

"Positive," Nic said. There was tightness to his voice that hadn't been there before.

"Do you guys feed the wolves?" she asked.

"No, they hunt," Nic said. "If you don't stop petting him, he might just follow you home."

That would be a trick, since she didn't have a home. Still, Jenna couldn't hide her delight. "You know that only makes me want to pet him more, right?"

Nic took a step toward her. The wolf lowered its head, this time baring its teeth. Nic paled and stopped.

"I don't think he likes you," Jenna said.

Nic's color drained completely. His gaze dropped to the floor and he slowly backed away.

"I was only kidding," she said.

Without another word, Nic went back to work.

The wolf allowed Jenna to pet him one more time, then he left the garage, trotting off toward the woods.

"Pinch me. Seriously. I cannot believe that just happened," she said. "I'm pretty sure that's the coolest thing that has ever happened to me." She squealed like a little girl. "I've got to tell Aidan. He's never going to believe it."

Bernie shook his head, then went back to work.

"Come on, you guys. A wild wolf walks into the garage and you have nothing to say. Really?" She threw her arms up in exasperation. "I can't believe you are so nonchalant about what just happened. You act like this kind of thing happens all the time."

"It's not as unusual as you might think," Nic muttered.

"Whatever." Jenna walked to the door of the garage and paused. "Nic, about tonight..." Her voice trailed off.

He turned away from the engine, but didn't meet her gaze. Instead, he focused on the wrench in his hand. "You know what, I completely forgot that I had a meeting tonight. Can I take a rain check?"

That was odd, but Jenna was grateful for the excuse he gave her. "Sure." She nodded, then bolted out the door in search of Aidan. No doubt he would appreciate her wolf story.

Robert LaBeouf cut her off in the driveway before she reached the house. "Shouldn't you be at work?"

Jenna slowed, not wanting to get caught up in a conversation right now. "Not until this afternoon." She tried to move past him, but he stepped into her path. Clearly there was more on his mind than simple chitchat.

Robert straightened the sleeves on his impeccable suit and picked at invisible lint. "Any luck with the car?"

Jenna sighed and did her best to hide her impatience. "It's coming along." It would be a lot faster if she had the parts.

"So you'll be out of here soon?" he asked. "Before the weekend, perhaps?"

Why was he in such a hurry to get rid of her? "Should be," she said noncommittally. "Do you happen to know where Aidan is?"

Robert's jaw clenched. "Mr. Fortier is a busy man," he said. "He doesn't have time for you..." Robert sniffed. "Can I be frank?"

Like there was any way she could stop him. "By all means." Jenna grinned to hide her clenched teeth. Anything to speed up this unpleasant conversation.

"You're not his type," he said.

She stumbled back. Jenna struggled to come up with an appropriate response, but failed miserably, so she blurted the first thing that came to mind. "What makes you say that?"

He stared pointedly at the back patio. Several women milled around. A moment later Aidan strolled up the stairs. The women turned as one to greet him, bright smiles on their beautiful faces.

One woman stepped away from the others to approach Aidan. When she reached his side, she ran her hand down his back. It was an intimate gesture that indicated she had more than a passing familiarity with his body.

Aidan grinned at the woman and lovingly brushed a kiss across her cheek.

Jenna swallowed the lump that formed in her throat. How could she possibly compete with women like that? She glanced down at her grease-stained jeans and dirty hands. She couldn't.

Aidan's smile faded, when he caught sight of her in the driveway.

Pain raked her, but Jenna made sure not to show it. She wouldn't give either man the satisfaction of knowing that they'd hurt her. She stared at Aidan.

Was this the same man, who'd offered her assistance last night? The same one who'd stripped naked and stood beneath the moonlight in full view of everyone? The one who'd nearly kissed her? Last night, she'd convinced herself that he'd done all that for her benefit.

I'm such an idiot, she thought.

"As you can see, he's busy." Robert gestured to the women. "What did you want to tell him? I can relay a message if you like."

"That's okay," Jenna said, voice tight. "It's not important. I better go in and get ready for work."

Robert's dark eyes glimmered, then he glanced at his watch. "I thought you said you didn't have to work until this afternoon?" A shadow of a pleased smile crossed his lips, before his stern expression returned.

"I forgot that I had errands to run. If you'll excuse me." Jenna rushed off, before he could reply.

Robert watched her go. He needed to get rid of the human. She was distracting the Alpha from his duties to the pack. It proved once again that Aidan's blood was weak like his cousin's.

His lip curled in disgust.

How could anyone be attracted to vermin?

If René had won the Alpha challenge, he wouldn't have had to worry about the pack's future. René was easy to control, to lead. Robert thought for sure that the dumb wolf's size would give him an advantage in the fight. And it had, but not for long.

He'd underestimated Aidan.

Robert wouldn't make that mistake again.

He watched Jenna walk stiffly to the house, and couldn't help but smile.

If Aidan wouldn't run her off, then he would.

Jenna didn't understand the pain that she was experiencing. There was no logical reason for it. None whatsoever.

There was nothing going on between her and Aidan. *Nothing at all.* Better to know that now, than after it was too late.

She rubbed her chest to ease the ache and hurried toward the house. Jenna paused at the threshold and glanced back.

Robert LaBeouf still stood in the driveway. This time he was smiling at her. He'd dropped all pretenses.

She clenched her fists. Jenna had the sudden urge to stomp over there and punch him in the face. Maybe then, he'd lose that smug expression. But she wouldn't, because he wasn't worth it. None of them were.

With one last smirk, Robert strolled off toward the garage.

Something wet hit her cheek. Jenna violently scrubbed it away. "Knock it off," she muttered. "You've only known him for a few days."

She ran to her bedroom and shut the door, resting her back against the wood. Laughter filtered in from the outside. The joyful sound slicing her deep.

How had she convinced herself that Aidan wasn't like her ex? Through the curtain sheers, her gaze swept the patio. The women were all flawless like they were auditioning for a photo shoot.

Aidan's dark head stood out above the crowd of females, a king holding court, a sheik surrounded by his harem. So there had been an element of truth to that story, too.

Jenna marched across the bedroom and snapped the thick drapes closed, plunging the room into darkness. It didn't entirely shut out the sound of the party, but at least she wouldn't have to watch Aidan take his pick of the women.

How could she have been so wrong about him?

She was determined now more than ever to get her interview. The wolf encounter would add a nice spin to the piece. Soon, she'd earn enough money to leave Breakbend. The thought should've filled her with excitement, but it didn't.

Aidan's not going to miss you. Given the bevy of beauties on the patio, he probably won't notice that you're gone.

Jenna wished that she could forget him as easily.

9

Aidan had *felt* Jenna's gaze on him. Even surrounded by all the female Weres, he could distinguish her from the others. When he'd glanced toward the driveway, he'd seen Robert and Jenna locked in a serious conversation.

A conversation only interrupted by Robert pointing to him. Jenna's body had tensed and her lush mouth had thinned. Their eyes met briefly. Long enough for him to see the pain, then it vanished. The connection he'd felt in the garage disappeared with it.

Jenna had been happy when he'd left her a few minutes ago. Ecstatic even. Aidan had taken a huge risk showing her his Other form.

He'd expected her to run away, but had hoped that she wouldn't. He should've known that Jenna would be brave given the courage she'd shown last night.

Aidan had sensed her fear, but her trepidation hadn't latest long. Jenna's curiosity was far stronger. When her fingers had sank into his fur, Aidan had nearly whimpered from the overwhelming wave of pleasure that came from her touch.

Even now, he could feel her stroking him, hear her cooing softly in his ears. It took every fiber of his being not to rush to her side and confess that he and the wolf were one and the same.

A suicidal act if there ever was one.

Jenna had secrets. Secrets that were potentially dangerous to him and the pack. As Alpha, he couldn't overlook that. Of course, his secrets were even greater. Of that Aidan had no doubt. There was a reason why the Moonlight Kin and humans rarely mixed.

Of course, none of that explained what Robert was up to. Aidan made a mental note to find out, once his assistant returned from his visit into town.

Still angry with herself for getting emotionally attached so quickly, Jenna drove to town. The patio was clear by the time she left. No sign of Aidan or any of the model wannabes.

Unfortunately, that only made her mood worse. Jealousy scalded her insides, burning like acid. Where was he? Who was he with? What were they doing? And why weren't they still on the patio?

Carnal images flooded her mind. Tears threatened to return. "You're being ridiculous!"

Jenna pressed a button to roll down the window. Air rushed in, blowing the moisture away.

You're not his type. Robert's seething statement rang in her ears.

Judging by the appearance of those women, he'd been telling the truth. Jenna glanced in the rearview mirror. Other than the healing cut, she didn't look too bad.

A little underweight maybe, but that's what happened when you couldn't afford to eat everyday.

She examined her features carefully. Her green eyes were okay. Better with a little makeup. Her mouth was too wide, her lips a little too full. Nothing could be done about her crooked grin or strong jawline.

Face it, without plastic surgery you're never going to be model pretty.

Her gaze strayed to the road behind her. It was empty.

She felt the same way inside. Like part of her chest had been carved out and she'd been haphazardly sewn back together.

It dawned on Jenna that this was the first time she'd checked to see if someone was following her. She'd gone a whole day without looking. That had never happened before she'd met Aidan.

There was something about the man that made her feel safe and protected.

Jenna snorted in derision. "Don't get used to it." Today proved that wouldn't be smart.

Robert had made it clear that he expected her to be gone by the weekend. That didn't give her much time. Since he was Aidan's personal assistant, he could very well be speaking for his boss. What if that were the case? What if Aidan really didn't want her around? Pain returned, shoving the unreasonable jealousy aside.

Jenna pulled into Breakbend. This time she wasn't lucky enough to score a parking space in front of the paper. She found a spot in a lot a couple of blocks away. Jenna gathered her purse, then locked the Rover.

Busy shoppers had Main Street humming with energy. Several men wearing lure-covered fishing hats strolled down the sidewalks.

Must be some kind of tournament going on, she thought. Either that or the worst fashion show ever!

Jenna got her first inkling that something wasn't right, when she passed the coffee shop on the corner. It started with an itch between her shoulder blades. The itch became a crawl that crept down her spine. Carl's dogged pursuit had taught her never to ignore her instincts.

He was here.

It was only a matter of time before he caught up with her.

Jenna kept her pace even, taking care not to break stride or look around. Her gaze strayed to the windows that lined the storefronts. She searched the reflections for sudden movements, anything out of place.

It had to be Carl.

Who else could it be?

Once Carl caught her, he wouldn't go easy on her, especially after their last encounter. No doubt he didn't appreciate having his balls shoved into his intestines.

Somehow Jenna had to evade him for another day or two, until she could secure her interview and get her car repaired. Would be easy enough if she were in a city, but how could she hide in a town this small?

The paper came into view. Jenna passed the entrance. She saw Molly wave, then frown as she kept walking. She waited for the crowd of people to thicken, then she ducked down and darted into a side street.

The narrow lane gave her access to Puck Street, which ran parallel to Main, and went by the back of the Gazette building. When she came around the corner, Paul Welling was leaning against the back door, enjoying a long drag on a cigarette.

"What are you doing? Why didn't you use the front entrance?" He dropped the butt onto the ground and stubbed it out with his heel.

"Got turned around in the crowd. Missed the door. Lucky I found you," she said.

"Turned around in this town?" Paul scoffed, then his brown eyes narrowed. "How's the interview coming along?"

"Good." Her gaze strayed to the street. She didn't see Carl, but that didn't mean he wasn't there. "I should have it finished by tonight. In the meantime, is there any chance of getting an advance on my first paycheck?" She needed money to run.

Paul laughed. "After less than a week on the job?"

Jenna wasn't surprised by his answer, but it didn't hurt to ask. She was out of time. It was either get the interview tonight—or never.

"Let's go inside." Before Carl found out where she worked. He wouldn't hesitate to cause a scene. He'd made that clear, when he'd tried to abduct her. Jenna's hand touched the cut on her forehead. Never again.

10

Jenna's heart was in her throat. She'd stayed at work until five, long enough to make sure that Carl wouldn't wander in looking for her, then she'd snuck out the back door and made her way down side streets and alleys until she'd spotted the Rover.

She didn't immediately climb into the vehicle. Instead, Jenna watched the car and the streets for ten minutes before deciding it was clear enough to make a run for it. She jumped inside and sped off.

Her gaze flicked repeatedly to the rearview mirror, as she drove toward Aidan's estate. Twice she'd thought someone was following her, only to have them turn off on one of the streets leading out of town. Somewhere in Breakbend, Carl was searching for her.

I thought I'd have more time. Damn it, Ethan!

Jenna's sweaty palms slid across the steering wheel. It wasn't until she caught sight of the massive gates blocking the entrance to the estate that some of the tension eased in her shoulders.

She pressed a button and those imposing gates opened. Jenna glanced one last time at the barren road, then hit the gas, sending gravel spraying behind her as she barreled down the driveway. Shadows filled the woods as the sun sank below the horizon. Jenna kept seeing movement where there was none.

"Keep it together," she muttered, glancing once more in her rearview, even though she was safely behind the tall walls.

A black mass darted in front of her. Jenna screamed and jerked the wheel to the left to avoid hitting it. Something large thumped the bumper and sent her skidding out of control. The Rover fishtailed toward the trees.

Brush scraped the paint as she wrestled with the wheel. The front tires dipped, throwing Jenna sideways. Her head hit the driver's side window, stunning her. The seatbelt tightened, yanking her back against the seat.

She hit the breaks, but it was too late. The front of the SUV collided with the trunk of a pine tree. Glass shattered. Metal crunched. Then the airbag exploded in her face.

Dazed, Jenna glanced in the rearview mirror. A naked man lay on the other side of the driveway. That couldn't be right. She shook her head and squinted. His dark hair and muscular body came into focus and looked...*familiar*.

For a second, Jenna couldn't breathe, couldn't move, then adrenaline hit. "Aidan!" she cried.

Jenna struggled out of her seatbelt. What if he was hurt? What if he was... She couldn't even bring herself to think it. He had to be okay.

"Hang on, Aidan. I'm coming." Jenna threw the door open in a panic and fell onto the ground, her legs trembling too bad to support her. She pulled herself up, using the Rover for leverage. She had to get to Aidan.

Jenna scrambled up the short embankment and out of the woods. From here she should be able to see if he was breathing. She glanced across the road.

Aidan's body was gone.

It wasn't possible. She'd seen him. Did that mean he wasn't hurt? Jenna glanced down the driveway, hoping to see him walking toward the house. There was no sign of Aidan.

Where did he go? Had he wandered into the woods?

Blood roared in her ears. Fear enveloped her. If Aidan had stumbled into the woods, then he was definitely hurt. She had to find him before the wolves did.

Jenna crossed the road, her gaze scanning the ground, searching for clues that might indicate which way he'd went.

"Aidan, where are you?" She turned in a circle, the trees blurring before her eyes. "Aidan!" Jenna couldn't lose him. Not like this. Not yet.

The shadows hid him at first. His black fur blended so well that she'd nearly stumbled over him. Her *wolf.* Lying next to the trees not far from where Aidan had been.

Or had he?

Had she really seen him?

Jenna wasn't sure.

Just how hard had she hit her head? She thought she'd only been momentarily stunned. Jenna felt the wound on her forehead, but other than being a little sore from the airbag, it didn't feel too bad.

Had she imagined the whole thing? Aidan had looked so real in the rearview mirror. She glanced across the driveway at the tilted SUV. The angle out the back wasn't perfect. It wouldn't give her the clearest view.

Jenna shook her head and looked down at the ground. Maybe she'd just wanted to see Aidan again. So much so that her brain had conjured him up for her. She didn't want to examine why too closely.

It dawned on her that he hadn't been wearing any clothes. Jenna groaned.

Terrific! Even during an accident, she couldn't escape thoughts of his naked body.

Jenna stared at the black wolf. The wolf stared back. She had hit something. Of that there was no doubt. Since Aidan wasn't here, it stood to reason that she'd struck her wolf.

She needed to make sure he was okay. If he wasn't, then somehow she'd coax him into a vehicle and get him to a vet. Jenna tried to imagine lifting over two hundred pounds of wolf into her car. No way could she do that without hurting him worse. He had to be okay.

"Easy, fella." Jenna held her hands out and kept her voice soothing. "How's my pretty boy?"

His ears perked up as he watched her approach. There didn't appear to be any visible injuries, but she wouldn't know for sure until she could examine him. Jenna kneeled as she neared the animal.

"Come here. I need to make sure that you're okay." She reached out and slowly felt his legs before making her way over his body, checking for tenderness.

There was no blood that she could see or feel. And nothing seemed to be swollen. Did that mean he was okay? Maybe she'd simply stunned him, too.

Please let him just be stunned.

"That's a good boy." Jenna carefully examined him again, making sure she hadn't missed anything. The wolf didn't whimper or flinch.

Relieved that he was unharmed and that it hadn't been Aidan that she'd hit, Jenna's composure shattered. She threw her arms around the wolf's neck and buried her face in his fur. The tears she'd held back released in a flood. All the pain and frustration she'd suppressed came bubbling out.

"I'm so sorry." Her shoulders shook as she cried. "I never wanted any of this to happen. I thought I'd have more time. But he's here," she said between hiccups. "I don't want to betray his trust...But I can't fight him without money." She sobbed. "He'll just keep coming...Won't ever stop... Maybe someday Aidan will forgive me."

The wolf licked the tears off her cheek, then swept his tongue over the wound on her forehead. Jenna could feel his muscles quiver beneath her hands, but he didn't try to pull away or try to bite her. She rubbed his head and ran her hand over his muzzle. "I'm glad you're okay."

He licked her hand.

She sniffed loudly and wiped her face with her sleeve. He couldn't understand a word she was saying, but that was okay. She'd just needed someone to listen.

"Thank you for letting me hold you. I'm glad you're all right." Jenna stroked the wolf's sides one last time, then slowly rose to her feet.

The wolf waited a moment, as if to make sure she was all right, then bounded into the woods.

Jenna watched him go, paying special attention to his strong legs. No limps. No favoring of sides. No whimpers of pain. She sighed. Thank goodness.

She walked back to the Rover and climbed behind the wheel. Jenna had no idea how she'd pay for the SUV's repairs, when she couldn't even cover the Bug's, but she'd get the money together somehow.

"Please start," she whispered.

The engine sputtered, then turned over. Jenna slipped the Rover into reverse. Twigs snapped and limbs creaked as she backed out of the woods and did a three point turn to get the SUV headed in the right direction. Jenna drove sedately down the rest of the way the driveway.

Aidan rushed outside when she reached the house.

Despite her encounter with the wolf, Jenna's gaze roamed over him, examining every inch. She needed to see for herself that he was unharmed. Her relief was palpable.

So much for keeping her emotions in check.

Aidan opened the driver's side door and pulled her into his arms.

Jenna allowed herself to sink into his warmth, feeling his strength beneath her fingertips. His chest rose and fell against her cheek. She could hear his powerful heartbeat, its steady cadence reassurance that he was in fact all right.

"Are you all right?" He brushed her hair away from her face, his gaze carefully examining her.

People from the household gathered outside to see what the commotion was. They watched her and Aidan's exchange closely, their expressions registering various levels of surprise.

Uncomfortable with the growing audience, Jenna stiffened. "How did you—"

"Security cameras," Aidan answered before she could finish her question. "They saw everything. We were just about to come out and get you, when someone spotted the headlights. Are you sure that you're alright?" He moved her inside without waiting for an answer.

Robert stood in the doorway, his wiry frame ramrod straight. He took one look at the Rover and scowled at her. His frown deepened, when he noticed how tightly Aidan held her.

Jenna slipped out of Aidan's embrace. She felt guilty enough over having to betray him. She didn't need or want him to take care of her. His concern for her well-being only added to the heaping pile of self-loathing, growing inside of her.

Aidan didn't acknowledge the move. Instead, he countered it by wrapping his arm over her shoulder and maneuvering her up the stairs.

"Where are we going?" she asked.

"My room. I've called for our staff physician to meet us there."

His room. Warning bells went off in her head. Jenna didn't think going to Aidan's room was a good idea, stunned or not, but there was no deterring him. She had a feeling if she dug in her heels and refused, he'd pick her up and carry her.

Aidan threw open the double doors to what could only be described as a decadent master suite. Jenna took in the room in a glance.

It was no surprise that Aidan's bed garnered center stage in the space. The massive sleigh frame carved from cherry wood appeared to be custom made. Jenna's suspicions were confirmed when she caught sight of the extra large mattresses.

Soft cream sheets met a mountain of pillows. Two matching side tables flanked the bed. There were books stacked on top of both.

Aidan was a reader.

Jenna wasn't sure why that surprised her or why it pleased her so much. She scanned the titles quickly, recognizing a few familiar names before her gaze was drawn to a set of dual French doors. The doors led out to what looked like a large balcony.

The perfect spot for the king to survey his kingdom, she thought. A soft knock interrupted her musings.

"Come in, Gabe." Aidan didn't look to see who was at the door.

A man with sandy blond hair and gold-rimmed glasses entered the room, carrying a brown leather bag. Jenna had never seen him before, but he seemed familiar with the space. He walked past them straight into Aidan's bathroom and set the bag on the counter. "Bring her in here."

Aidan guided Jenna into the bathroom.

"I can walk by myself you know?" she said.

Aidan's amber gaze assessed her. "You've no doubt bumped your head and had an airbag explode in your face. I want to make sure you're okay."

Several painful finger probes and a barrage of pointless questions later, Dr. Gabe declared that she didn't have a concussion. Jenna could've told him that.

The doctor gave her a couple of aspirin.

Jenna dry swallowed them.

He removed his latex gloves and tossed them into the trash, then closed his bag. His gaze returned to the healing wound on her forehead. "You should've had someone take a look at this right after it happened. It might've prevented scarring."

Scarring had been the least of her concerns. Jenna hadn't had the money to see a doctor. Nor had there been time when she was running away from Carl. She didn't have the money now either.

"I don't have health insurance," she said. Not an oddity in this day and time.

Dr. Gabe turned to Aidan. "She'll be fine. It's just a knock. Let me know if she gets sleepy or her speech slurs."

Jenna glared at him. "*She* can hear you. She's standing right here."

Gabe didn't spare her a glance as he waited for Aidan's response. "Stay close." He glanced at Jenna. "Never know when trouble might arrive."

11

Aidan's heart continued to race in his chest. When he'd seen Jenna skid off the road into the woods, something inside him had shattered.

The bone deep sense of loss had struck him to the core and he could no longer ignore the growing connection between them or the need to find out where it would lead.

Terror was not a feeling Aidan was used to experiencing or one he cared to repeat. It didn't sit well with his wolf.

Thank goodness she'd been driving the Rover and not her vehicle or the accident could've been a lot worse.

She'd been crying so uncontrollably. Each tear had battered his Lycan soul. In his wolf form, Aidan had had difficulty following her conversation. Though he doubted that it would've made sense in his human form either, since she'd had her face buried in his side.

He'd caught enough to know that Jenna intended to betray him, but he still didn't understand why. The odd part was it didn't make him angry.

By rights, he should be furious with her. Instead, all he could think about was who had arrived in town?

Just the thought of Jenna around another male brought out some very uncomfortable feelings. On a normal day, it was hard to fight his nature. This close to the full moon made it damn near impossible.

Jenna was in danger. Of that there was no doubt. Aidan had suspected as much, but her disjointed, tear-soaked confession proved it.

Someone was after her. Someone she feared. That same fear drove her now to do things she wouldn't normally do. His Alpha instincts quickly rose to the surface. The urge to protect what was his burned through his body. Aidan wanted to sink his claws into the threat and eviscerate it.

But he needed more information. He had to be able to identify the threat. Once he did that, Jenna wouldn't have to worry anymore. Now the question was, how would he ferret out the truth?

Demanding that she tell him everything would only drive Jenna away. She was stubborn to a fault. There was only one way forward. Aidan had to let her go through with her 'plan'. Whatever it may be. Convince her that he was falling for her ruse, then like any good wolf, he would pounce.

Aidan felt her gaze scroll over him. She'd been doing that ever since she had entered the house. He would've been flattered, if he didn't think there was more behind the look than plain lust.

"What are you looking for?" he asked.

She jumped and her voice squeaked. "What?"

Aidan tilted his head. "You keep looking at me with a funny expression on your face. What is it you're searching for?"

Jenna hesitated. "It's ridiculous."

He brushed a strand of hair away from her face. "Tell me anyway."

She bit her lip, drawing his gaze to her mouth. "It's going to sound crazy."

Aidan smiled. "Promise I won't laugh."

She took a deep breath. "For a moment back in the woods, I thought I'd hit *you*."

Aidan didn't blink, didn't show any emotion at all. "Why would you think that?"

Jenna shook her head. "When I looked in the rearview mirror after the accident, I could've sworn I saw you lying by the side of the road. Obviously, I didn't. You're here. Unhurt. The accident scrambled my mind and somehow I incorporated all those wild stories I heard in town."

His brows rose.

She rubbed her arms, quelling the gooseflesh. "Told you it was crazy."

Aidan closed the distance between them. "There are a lot of things that cannot be easily explained away by logic. If you say that you saw me in the woods," he shrugged, "then maybe you did."

Jenna's lips flattened. "Don't patronize me. I know you weren't in the woods. I hit a wolf."

"Was he okay?" he asked.

She nodded. "I checked."

He waggled his eyebrows. "So you're saying that I look like a wolf?"

Jenna grinned. "When you look at me like that." She pointed at his face. "Yeah, you could do a passing impression."

"I'm flattered." Aidan held out his hand. Jenna hesitated, then slowly took it. Her fingers were so fragile beneath his. One squeeze would crush every bone in her hand to dust. Aidan closed his fingers around hers and led her out of the room.

"Sorry about the Rover," she whispered. "I'll pay for the repairs. In fact, I'll do the work myself to make sure it's done right."

"It's not important. The vehicle is insured." Aidan led her down the stairs.

She pulled back. "Please stop being so nice."

Aidan snorted. "No one has ever accused me of that."

She rolled her eyes. "Then they don't know you very well."

Aidan's chest filled with warmth. He liked that she thought he was nice. Liked doing nice things for her, if it got him a smile.

"I'm hungry." And he was, just not for food. The taste of her sweet skin still lingered on Aidan's tongue, burning its way through his body in a rush. He desperately wanted another taste, a far more intimate taste.

His wolf surfaced. Aidan felt his shaft stir behind his zipper. He waited, but it didn't go down. If anything, he grew even harder.

Fine! Aidan growled at his wolf. *You'll get your way this one time, and one time only.* He was desperate enough to make a deal with the devil, if it meant the end of his 'affliction'. *Tonight I'll have sex with her and prove to you once and for all that she's not the one.*

His wolf yipped with excitement.

After we've had her, you'll change your mind. You will see that there's nothing remarkable about humans, then we can get back to the business of sorting through the Werewomen. Do we have a deal?

In his head, Aidan heard his wolf howl.

He escorted Jenna to her room. "Take a quick shower and we'll head into town."

"Town?" Jenna's eyes widened and she pulled her hand away. "Why would you want to go there?"

"To get something to eat," he said slowly.

Her scent turned bitter. "Why not eat here?" Panic squeezed her voice, making the pitch higher.

"I eat here most nights. I'm in the mood for something different." That was the absolute truth. His heated gaze slid over her, then Aidan paused. "You told me that you felt fine. Do I need to call Gabe back?"

"No! I mean. I am fine. Still a little shaken from the accident." Jenna swallowed hard. The change in Aidan's behavior toward her had her head spinning. Things were suddenly moving too fast.

Jenna wasn't oblivious. She'd noticed there was sexual tension between them, albeit muted. There was nothing dampening it now. It was like the accident had removed a barrier. She could now see the full brunt of his desire.

Aidan's intense focus thrilled her and frightened her. Jenna wasn't convinced she could handle the heat without being consumed, which was why she found herself trying to bow out.

"Doubt I'd be very good company tonight," she said.

Aidan was giving her the perfect opportunity to interview him, but the offer came with strings. Strings that threatened to bind her, making escape impossible.

Part of Jenna ached to give in. It had been so long since she'd *touched* another human being, or been held all night in someone's arms. Her skin prickled. If she concentrated, she could almost feel the warmth of his hands on her body. But there were other things to consider beyond primal needs.

Carl's pugnacious face flashed in her mind.

The thought of running into him drove the heat from her body, sobering her. She had no idea what Carl would do. Would he start a fight? Try to drag her into his car like the last time?

Jenna didn't want Aidan in the line of fire. Better to drive a wedge between them now, than to have harm come to him. This wasn't his fight. It was hers.

"It's just a casual dinner. I'm not looking to be entertained." Aidan seemed unnaturally calm. Like accidents, house calls, and strangers disrupting his life were the norm around this place.

She took a different tack. One Jenna was sure would hit its mark. "Wouldn't you prefer one of your women to go with you? No doubt any one of them would jump at the chance." The snap in her voice surprised her. All she'd wanted to do was douse the rising flames, but somehow her tone had had the opposite effect.

Aidan's amber eyes appeared to glow and he looked unduly pleased. He didn't dispute her claim. How could he? She'd seen the models with her own eyes. He also didn't gloat, but then again, he didn't need to. He was well aware of how appealing he was to the opposite sex. The only thing that had changed was now he knew she wasn't immune to his charm.

"I want you," Aidan paused, "to join me tonight."

His words seared her flesh, exposing her vulnerability. She wasn't clueless. She hadn't missed the double-entendre. In desperation, Jenna tried one last time to dissuade him.

"If you're looking to add to your harem, then you'd better look elsewhere."

A nerve in Aidan's jaw started to tic. "I do not have nor have I ever had a harem. They're not culturally relevant for me and the concept is outdated. Don't you think?" he continued. "What I do have is a lot of responsibility. More responsibility than you could ever imagine."

Jenna massaged her temple. This wasn't working like she'd hoped. The barb had hit too close and clearly wounded him. She hadn't meant to hurt him. She only wanted to prevent him from making a mistake. And perhaps stop herself at the same time.

"I'm sorry," she said. "I didn't mean it like that." She had, but said aloud it sounded mega-bitchy. Not at all like she'd intended. "I have a bit of a headache."

Aidan's gaze bored through her. "Perhaps we should dine some other time, when you're feeling more up to it." He turned to leave.

"No." Jenna stopped him.

This was her last chance to get that interview, and the last opportunity to be held in his arms. There wouldn't be another. She stared at him. Saw the heat. Saw the offer in his eyes. If she wanted more, Aidan made it clear he'd oblige. Did she dare accept?

"I'll get cleaned up and be out in thirty," she said.

Aidan arched a brow.

"It won't take me long." Jenna planned to pack once she showered. After dinner, Aidan might very well toss her out of his house. She wanted to be ready for every contingency.

And just where do you think you'll go without a car? You wrecked the one he gave you to drive. It's not like he's going to loan you another.

Her shoulders slumped. She'd forgotten all about the Bug. "Maybe I should go check on my car before we leave." Could she somehow rig it to run? Doubtful. All she had to do was make it to the next town. Jenna supposed she could hitchhike again, but that was a last resort.

Aidan shook his head. "Not necessary. I had your vehicle repaired. I'd planned to surprise you, when you got home from work."

Jenna's heart sank. He was killing her with kindness, one act at a time. She didn't think she'd survive another good deed. Aidan was making it so hard to betray him.

"When did you find the time?" she asked.

"Nic looked it over the night it was towed in. After he met you, he sent Josh into the city for parts."

"So that's the errand he was running?" She shook her head.

Aidan nodded. "Don't be upset. Nic took care of the repairs personally as a favor to me," he said.

There was something about his tone that gave Jenna pause. Why would Nic owe Aidan a favor? The guy worked for him.

"I should probably go out and thank him," she said. "Is he still in the garage?"

Aidan caught her arm, his thumb brushing gently over her skin. "There's no need. He was honored to help."

"Honored?" She let her incredulity show.

"When you speak to him later, you'll see. For now, get ready. My hunger is growing by the second. Soon I'll be ravenous and we might not make it to the restaurant." Heat poured off his body, causing his wild scent to deepen. The woodsy spice perfumed the air, making her feel giddy.

Thoughts of food deserted her. Despite a slight headache, something inside Jenna flared to life, answering the unspoken question she saw in his eyes. Was she prepared to meet the inferno head on? If not now, when would she get another chance?

"I better hurry." She hiked her thumb over her shoulder toward her room.

"You do that." Aidan's feral grin curled her toes and sent a thrill tripping down her spine. He glanced at his watch, then leaned in next to her ear. His warm breath brushed the skin, then he inhaled. "If you're not out in twenty-five minutes, I'm coming in after you." Threat. And a promise.

12

The drive into town was a strange combination of tension and heightened awareness. The knot in Jenna's stomach grew the closer they got.

Was she going to go through with this? Could she really betray Aidan after all he'd done for her? If she did, that would make her no better than Ethan. The thought made her skin crawl.

She scanned the streets searching for Carl. Ethan's lackey had to be here somewhere, lurking in the darkness like a troll.

"One problem at a time," Jenna muttered to herself.

Aidan looked at her, but said nothing.

A spot opened up like it had been waiting for them. Aidan pulled the luxury sedan into the spot and parked. Jenna reached for the door handle.

"Sit tight." He got out and walked around the front of the car to open her door.

No one could fault him on his manners.

"This really isn't necessary." Jenna glanced up and down the sidewalk. Where was he? There was no sign of Carl, but she was determined to remain vigilant.

Aidan smiled. "We're celebrating the repair of your vehicle, remember?"

Jenna stopped. "About that, I know I keep saying this, but I will pay you back for parts and labor. It might take me a while, but I am good for it."

He rested his hand on the small of her back and led her into a cozy restaurant that only had ten tables. Candles fluttered as he opened the door and stepped aside for her to enter.

"Mr. Fortier, how lovely to see you." An older man rushed forward to greet them. "It's been a long time."

Aidan shook his hand. "Too long, Francis. Do you have my table?"

The man's brown eyes crinkled. "But of course." He led them toward the back of the room into the corner. Francis snapped his fingers and one of the bus boys rushed out carrying a table. He set it down and moved back as another one brought out two chairs. Within seconds the table was set and ready for them to dine.

Aidan signaled Francis to back away. "Allow me." He held Jenna's chair out and waited for her to take a seat.

Jenna gave him a small smile and sat. Could she feel any worse? She didn't think so. How could she have ever believed that Aidan was anything like Ethan?

He took his seat across from her, angling the chair until his back was against the wall, then perused the wine list. "Do you have a preference?"

"Red."

"Red it is." Aidan closed the menu and ordered a bottle.

Jenna waited until the waiter poured the wine, then asked her first question. "Are you originally from Breakbend?"

"No, I just like the area. There are a lot of woods to get lost in," he said.

"You like getting lost in the woods?"

He smiled. "On occasion. Keeps my instincts sharp. What about you? Where are you from?"

"I grew up all over," she deflected.

People like Aidan wouldn't understand how she grew up. Wouldn't understand what it was like to go without, to be neglected, to have to lock your door at night to prevent one of your many 'fathers' from coming in.

Jenna lifted the glass of wine to her lips and took a deep swallow to keep from choking on the memories.

"So what made you want to keep wolves?" she asked.

He stared at her, his expression inscrutable. "They're not bees. I don't so much keep them as allow them to roam on my land."

"If that's the case, how did you tame them?" she asked.

"I didn't." Aidan paused their conversation while the waiter took their order. When that was finished, he continued. "Wolves sense things on a deeper level than people. They can smell your fear, your intentions, and especially your pain." He gave the last word added emphasis.

Jenna shifted in her seat. "Do you have family nearby?"

Aidan shook his head and laughed to himself. "I *always* have family around. It's difficult to find a moment to myself. What about you?"

"No, no family."

The answer surprised him.

Jenna opened her mouth to ask her next 'interview' question.

Aidan held up his hand to stop her. "Don't you want to write this down for accuracy's sake?" He sat back. "I'll wait until you get your notebook out of your purse."

Blood rushed to her face until the pressure threatened to pop her ears off. How was it possible to feel so hot and so cold at the same time?

Jenna considered denying his assertion, but she couldn't. What was the point? She'd never been the type of person to betray another. It just wasn't in her nature.

Jenna thought she could get the interview without him knowing, but she had a feeling she would've confessed even if Aidan hadn't seen through her deception.

The wine in her stomach turned to vinegar. "I'm sorry." Jenna placed her napkin on the table and rose to her feet.

"Where do you think you're going?" Aidan kept his seat and casually swirled the wine around in his glass.

"I thought now that you caught me, you'd want to..." The words died on her lips.

"Please sit down, Jenna. We need to talk." Aidan waited for her to take her seat. "But first tell me why you were trying to get an interview."

Jenna's chin dropped. "I needed the money." She sighed. "I have some legal issues that I have to take care of. The situation is embarrassing and I'd rather not go into detail. Suffice to say, landing an interview with you would go a long way toward hiring the experts that I need."

"So you're not just trying to further your journalism career?"

She scoffed and glanced around to make sure no one had heard her. "I'm a mechanic, Aidan, not a journalist. This is just a job to pay the bills. My passion is cars. Running into you was a coincidence."

Aidan took a sip of wine. "Why didn't you just say so?"

Jenna sat up. While she spoke, she straightened the silverware in front of her. "I didn't know how. You were being so nice. At first I was suspicious. People like you aren't normally—"

"People like me?" He cut her off with an arched brow.

"You know what I mean." She sighed. "People in your income bracket aren't normally philanthropic toward individuals."

"True," he said. "So what changed?"

My feelings for you, she wanted to say, but didn't dare.

Cars drifted by the window down the darkened street. People strolled along the sidewalks. Still no sign of Carl, but he was out there somewhere. He wasn't about to stop pursuing her.

"I ran out of time," Jenna said.

Their food arrived. The aroma of rich tomato meat sauce filled the air. The waiter placed a basket of fresh baked breadsticks in the center of the table. The food looked great. Smelled great. But Jenna was no longer hungry.

Aidan picked up his fork and stared at her expectantly. "The food here is fabulous. Don't let it go to waste."

Jenna blew out a heavy breath and picked up her fork. "When we get back, I'll get my things and leave."

He took a bite and chewed his pasta slowly, seeming to mull over her words. Once he swallowed, he asked, "Why would you do that?"

"I know you have something going on over the weekend and honestly, I feel awful for betraying your trust. I think it's best if I just pack up and move on."

"Best for whom?" Before she could respond, he said, "Eat, we'll discuss trust later."

13

Someone was watching them.

Aidan had been distracted by Jenna's ripe and ever-changing scent. The sensual aromas made him want to push his plate of pasta aside and eat her instead. That overwhelming desire was why he hadn't immediately heard the soft clicks. Now the noise had his full attention.

It took him a moment to locate the source of the sound. Once he did, his anger surfaced.

Was photographic evidence also part of her 'plan'? He kept calm, even though all he wanted to do was run outside and confront the enemy.

"Did the interview I gave you include a photo spread?" He'd know the second she lied.

Jenna's brow furrowed. "Don't think so." She picked up her napkin and dabbed the side of her mouth. "If it did, then the editor didn't let me know about it. I could ask the paper to cover the cost of a photographer, if you'd like. Why do you ask?"

"Because I'm not fond of having my picture taken." It was dangerous for Lycans given their slow aging process and long lives.

"Okay, I understand. I'll let Paul Welling know," Jenna replied, undisturbed by his response. She picked up her fork and took another bite. Her scent never wavered.

She was telling the truth.

So who was watching them? And why take the pictures? And did this have anything to do with why Jenna was so scared?

Aidan spotted movement in the alley across the street. The man hadn't concealed himself well enough. If he had, Aidan might not have detected him, which meant he wasn't dealing with someone used to hunting Lycans.

The lighting in the restaurant made it difficult to make out the man's features, but Aidan could see he was a burly man. He needed to get the man's scent before it faded, then there wouldn't be anyplace for him to hide.

Their spy was gone by the time dinner drew to a close. Aidan waited for Jenna to finish her coffee. She'd gotten her interview, but hadn't spilled all her secrets yet.

Aidan needed a better setting, a more private one, before they continued their conversation. Fortunately for him, there were other ways, more pleasurable ways to obtain the information. Once he had her safely sequestered, he'd get his answers. Aidan would find out who the man across the street was and how he factored into the picture.

"Ready?" he asked.

Jenna nodded. "Thank you again for the interview. You've saved my life."

Did she mean that figuratively or literally?

"It's still early. How about we go for a stroll once we get back to the compound?" he asked.

"I could stand to work off some of these calories." Jenna glanced at her watch. "But are you sure it's safe?"

"Safe?"

"With the wolves in the woods?"

"Ah," he said. "They won't bother us."

"Wouldn't be too sure. The black one and I have bonded. He doesn't like it when other people are near me."

Aidan bit back a grin. "Wolves are very territorial, but then again, so am I." He allowed his gaze to roam over her body. He planned to help her work off every calorie she ingested—after their walk.

Jenna blushed.

Aidan quickly paid for the meal, then walked around the table. His hands rested lightly on her shoulders before sliding to the back of the chair. He gently pulled it out. "I can't wait to see you in the moonlight." And neither could his wolf.

He made it sound like he couldn't wait to see her naked. Jenna could think of a lot of reasons taking a walk was a bad idea. The biggest of all was Aidan himself.

For the first twenty minutes of the dinner, she'd been riddled with guilt and terrified that Carl would show up. Sometime during the meal, she'd relaxed. Her guilt had abated and the sexual tension had returned. The heat had continued to build until Jenna half expected to see smoke rising from her skin.

She didn't think she'd make it through a walk without jumping him. Heck, Jenna wasn't convinced she'd make it to the car.

She stood, doing her level best to avoid eye contact. It had been the eye contact that had sucked her in, in the first place.

Aidan's amber gaze trapped her, immobilizing her as effectively as the real thick substance. He had a way of staring that made her believe she was the most important person on the planet. Jenna could see how a woman could easily become addicted.

He flashed her a devastating grin that sent butterflies aloft in her stomach. "Let's go."

Jenna scanned the sidewalks before she stepped outside.

"Looking for someone?" he asked.

She shook her head. "No, it's habit. I like to be aware of my surroundings."

"Smart woman." Aidan opened the car door for her and waited for Jenna to climb inside. Before he shut the door, he said, "Excuse me for a moment."

Jenna watched him dart across the street and slip between two buildings. Where was he going? What was he doing?

Aidan didn't strike her as the kind of guy who urinated in public, not when there was a perfectly good restroom in the restaurant. He was back before she could ponder it further.

He opened the car door and climbed in. "All set?"

"What were you doing in the alley?" she asked.

"I needed to check something really quick."

"What?" she asked.

"Nic thought he lost his wallet over there," he said.

Jenna glanced at the dark alley. "You probably need a flashlight to find it, unless it glows in the dark."

"True." Aidan's amber eyes glittered with amusement. "Fortunately, I discovered everything I needed to know."

Aidan had hoped that the house would be quiet by the time they returned from dinner. He should've known better. The estate bustled with activity as everyone prepared for the moon run.

He pulled the car in front of the house, then opened the door for Jenna. Once he helped her out, Aidan popped the trunk and grabbed a blanket that had been tucked in the back. "I think we picked a good night to go for a walk."

Jenna raised a brow at the blanket, but didn't comment. She glanced at the house. "What's going on?"

"Prep for the weekend festivities," he replied. "Come." Aidan shoved the blanket under his arm and took her hand. He led her around the back of the house and across the yard. "I'd like to show you one of my favorite spots."

She smiled.

"You warm enough?" He examined her sweater, then checked her feet. The shoes she had on were practical like the woman. No need to go in and change, but he wanted her to be comfortable.

"It's a mild night. I should be fine. The walk will get the blood pumping," she said. "And if it doesn't, I could always use the blanket under your arm. That is why you brought it, isn't it?" Her green eyes sparkled with mirth.

Aidan thought it best to keep his mouth shut. Any answer he gave would either incur her wrath or reveal his intentions. He walked them into the woods.

"Don't we need a flashlight?" Jenna asked.

"Not with the moon so full above us. Give your eyes time to adjust." Aidan guided them down a rarely used path that wound its way through the woods, eventually buffeting a small creek.

"This is beautiful. You were right. I can see just fine." She tripped. "Well, good enough anyway."

Aidan navigated around stones and toppled limbs, making sure that Jenna didn't stumble again. "It's not far now."

The sound of rushing water grew louder. The damp scent of moist leaves mingled with the forest around them. The trees parted and they stepped into a small clearing.

Moonlight glistened off the rippling pool, its pale light shimmering like diamonds tossed onto a velvet screen.

Jenna gasped.

The pristine scene didn't look real. "Is this man-made?"

Aidan shook his head. "No, that's why I love it."

"It's beautiful," she said. "I've never seen anything like it. How did you find it?"

Aidan glanced at her, then tilted his chin up until he was staring at the moon. "I spend a lot of time in the woods. Every chance I get. I found it on one of my many outings."

She looked around, drinking in the primeval beauty of the place. "Does anyone else know about it?"

"Probably, but they don't come here," he said.

"Why?" she asked, unable to tear her gaze away from his upturned face. The man was truly stunning. In the moonlight, with shadows delineating his features, he looked wild, untamed, barely human, as he basked in the pale light.

"Because this is my special spot. My favorite spot," he said, as if that should explain everything. He spread the blanket out on the ground.

Jenna shook her head, surprised that his arrogance only added to his attraction. "Do you ever go swimming here?"

Aidan's chin dropped and their eyes met. "Are you offering?"

"It would probably be a little cold for me." Though the idea was tempting, since neither of them had a swimsuit.

"I could keep you warm," he whispered.

And just like that, the temperature around them shot up. At least it felt like it to Jenna. Her mind immediately recalled his naked body, standing by the woods. She bit her lip and looked away, afraid that if she met his amber gaze, she'd be lost.

Aidan's finger hooked her chin and gently brought it around, until she had no choice but to look at him. "We won't do anything you don't want to do," he said.

That was the problem. Right now, her good judgment had its fingers stuck in its ears and was yelling, 'la, la, la, I don't hear you'.

When she didn't respond, Aidan dipped his head. Their mouths were now but a breath apart. The heat between them radiated with the fires of a thousand suns. Jenna couldn't focus. Her mind fogged as she stared at his sensual lips.

"You expect too much of me." Aidan groaned and closed the distance between them. Their lips met, then fused together.

Jenna's world tilted and began to spin. He slid his tongue along the seam of her mouth, silently begging for entrance.

He didn't have to ask twice.

Fire exploded inside of Jenna. Months of avoiding human contact came rushing to the forefront. She opened her mouth and let Aidan explore. Her fingers flitted against his arms, then tightened.

Jenna clamped onto Aidan's biceps and pulled him closer. The tone of the kiss changed as she let her passions loose to take over. Growling reached her ears, but Jenna couldn't tell if it was coming from her throat or Aidan's.

He tightened his grip on her and eased her onto the ground. The ferns and grass beneath the blanket cushioned Jenna, as Aidan deepened their embrace. His hand moved from her waist up her ribcage, stopping short of the soft swell of her breast.

Jenna ached for him to touch her. A tactile creature deprived for too long, she was greedy for every touch, every taste. Aidan continued to tease her flesh, while he fed from her mouth. Jenna arched beneath him, her grip tightened as fire streaked through her, leaving her breathless.

She gasped. "Aidan, please."

His big palm cupped her and squeezed.

Jenna jolted, feeling the sensation all the way to her toes. Aidan kneaded her breast, while he plucked at her nipple. He tore his mouth away from hers and shoved his hands up her shirt, lifting the material as he did so, exposing her to the night air.

Aidan lowered his head and kissed her stomach, his tongue making lazy circles over her skin. The moisture caused gooseflesh to rise, but Jenna wasn't cold. She was spontaneously combusting, burning from the inside out.

He continued to feast on her flesh, nibbling and licking his way around her nipples, never removing her bra. Jenna couldn't stay still. She writhed, trying to get closer. She needed him to touch her. All of her.

Eventually his teasing was too much. Jenna grasped his head, sinking her fingers into his hair, and yanked his face forward.

Aidan's nose sank into the crevice between her breasts. Jenna thought she felt him smile, but she was too far gone to look down and see. Aidan bit down on the clasp, holding her bra together. The material parted and her breasts spilled out.

He inhaled, his big body shaking as he did so. "You are magnificent," he murmured, then ran his tongue over her bare skin.

Jenna quivered.

Aidan sucked on one nipple, while he palmed the other, making happy noises in the back of his throat. Each lick, each swirl, each tug of his mouth made the sensitive spot between her legs throb.

He hadn't even touched her there yet. Jenna was afraid she'd explode before he did.

"Aidan," she gasped.

Aidan shivered as his name fell from Jenna's lips. How many hours had he imagined this moment? This woman naked beneath him? His fantasies failed by comparison to the reality. Jenna's skin was like silk under his mouth.

He sucked in, swirling his tongue around the kernelled flesh. It hardened even more. Aidan closed his eyes in ecstasy. He could feast on her for hours.

The hotter she got, the more musky and delicious she smelled to him. He couldn't wait to bury his face between her legs and taste her essence.

He shuddered again, trying to keep his wolf in check. He'd promised him that he'd let him take her, but his control was hanging on by a hair.

Aidan reluctantly released her and quickly slipped his jacket off and tugged his shirt over his head. Jenna's eyes widened as she watched, then she smiled.

Her fingers brushed his chest. "You are amazing. Almost unreal in the moonlight."

He grinned. "Glad you think so."

"I do." She ran her hands along the ridges of muscle that covered his abdomen.

"Your turn." Aidan helped her sit up, so he could finish taking her shirt off.

Jenna's gaze met his. "Are we really going to do this?"

Goddess, he hoped so. Aidan didn't think he'd survive, if she stopped things now. But he wouldn't pressure her. He needed her to come willingly to him. To his wolf. He had to prove to it that she wasn't his bondmate.

If you do this there will be no turning back, a little voice whispered in his head. *There will be consequences.*

Aidan knew it was the truth, but right now he didn't care. He was tired of always doing the right thing. Just this once, Aidan wanted something for himself—for his wolf.

He rested his forehead against hers. "We can stop whenever you like." He hesitated. "Do you want to stop?"

Jenna shook her head. "Do you?"

"Hell no!"

She giggled.

Aidan latched onto her mouth and didn't stop kissing her until she was breathless. His body couldn't get much harder. Even his shaft was straining to be free.

Don't fail me. It was a plea and a prayer.

Soft breasts brushed his hard chest, causing Aidan to quake.

Every sensation felt new, fresh, and unique.

His hands trembled as he reached for the zipper on her pants. "Last chance," he murmured. It was the truth. Aidan had a feeling that once he claimed her body, there'd be no escape for either one of them.

Words evaded Jenna. She existed in a world of sensation. Aidan's hard chest abraded hers, making her nipples throb. His hands seemed to be everywhere at once, coaxing, inflaming, and enticing. The firm ridge of his shaft, brushed her stomach, leaving her aquiver.

She reached between their bodies and grasped him through his jeans, giving him the answer to his question. Aidan moaned and his hips rocked forward.

"Do that again," he hissed.

Jenna did, relishing in the power she held over him, over his beautiful granite-hard body. She released the button on his pants and slid the zipper down. He did the same to her. Jenna wiggled out of her denims, then hooked her foot in his waistband.

Aidan snagged a condom out of his pocket, before Jenna pushed his pants down, then kicked his clothes away. They were both sprawled on the ground in their underwear. There was a sharp rip and Jenna saw Aidan toss her black panties aside.

"That's not fair." She laughed.

"True, but it's effective," he said.

"What about yours?" she asked.

"In a minute." His eyes shimmered like molten gold in the moonlight. "First I want to feast." Aidan slid down her body. He used his broad shoulders to part her thighs, then he looked at her and gave her a feral grin.

Jenna's eyes rolled back in her head at the first swipe of his tongue and her whole body trembled. The look of sheer concentration on his face as he devoured her was enough to undo her.

Add to that his innate oral skills and you had a deadly combination. Jenna's thighs shook as he flicked and swirled, then plunged inside her only to return after a moment to repeat the whole process again.

She clawed at the ground. Her body quaked with the need for release, but Aidan wouldn't give it to her. He continued to tongue, taste, and tease her hidden folds, savoring her.

"Aidan!" she cried out, both in warning and desperation.

Her hips rocked as she sought that final connection, the final piece that would send her sailing into oblivion. Just when release was within reach, he stopped.

Jenna growled and slammed her fists onto the ground. "Don't you dare."

Aidan wiped his mouth with his discarded shirt and rose above her. "I'm not going to leave you hanging." He removed his underwear. His large shaft bowed under the weight of his erection, as he rolled a condom on. "I want you to take me with you."

He positioned his flushed crown at her soaking entrance, then scraped his thumb over the throbbing bundle of nerves at her apex.

Jenna screamed as her orgasm ripped through her body. The sound was followed by a deep moan as Aidan thrust, burying himself to the hilt inside of her. The conflicting sensations prolonged her release and sent another one rippling through her.

She'd never felt so full, so stuffed in her life. Aidan had looked big from a distance, but up close the man was massive in every way possible. Jenna gulped in air, as her body struggled to adjust.

Aidan squeezed his eyes closed and tried valiantly to breathe. Jenna's body gripped his shaft like a vise. It was heaven and hell at the same time. She was tight, so blissfully tight. Nothing had ever felt better.

Relief flooded him. He was whole. Healed from his *affliction*. His body was working. He'd been so afraid that it wouldn't. That it would fail him again. Afraid that his wolf would change its mind at the last second and abandon him.

Aidan wasn't sure what he would've done, if his body hadn't responded. He pushed the horrifying thought aside. Everything was okay. Better than okay. It was great! Now he just needed to move. But he couldn't. Not until Jenna was ready.

Aidan grit his teeth. Sweat broke out over his body, while her channel continued to pulse. It took another minute or so for her breathing to return to normal. By then, Aidan was in agony.

"Let me know, if you need me to stop." He rocked his hips back.

Her lashes rose, but her passion-filled gaze remained unfocused. She didn't speak. Instead, Jenna pulled his mouth down to hers and kissed him. Relief overwhelmed him and Aidan let go, allowing her to pull him under.

His hips jerked, sending his shaft burrowing inside of her.

Jenna moaned and deepened the embrace.

Thank Goddess! Aidan thrust again. She felt so perfect, so utterly right. Their bodies fused and melded, coming apart and together in perfect synchronicity. He couldn't tell where he ended and Jenna began.

His wolf struggled to the surface, until it stared out through his eyes. Aidan's mouth began to water and his teeth lengthened.

No! He screamed in his head. *You're wrong!*

His wolf snorted, then snapped at him.

With the moon nearly full, there was no stopping the beast.

Jenna's knees grasped his hips and she locked her feet around him, not realizing the danger she was in. Her hands continued to explore his shoulders and back, while her lips found his earlobe.

Don't bite me. Please don't bite me. Aidan pleaded, but not a word came out of his throat. He was beyond speech.

Jenna latched onto his earlobe and nibbled. Aidan grew even harder and his thrusts became more primal. His lips found the curve of Jenna's neck where it met her shoulder. He licked the spot, numbing it. The salt of her skin exploded on his tongue, yet he couldn't stop.

Aidan's shaft continued to grow and expand, until he burst out of the condom and filled every inch of Jenna's channel. He knew what it meant. It was what his wolf had been telling him all along.

He should've been terrified, but Aidan wasn't. No doubt later he would be. But right now, the only feeling he could muster was *relief.*

Jenna's hips canted and she mewed. Aidan thrust harder, though it was difficult to do so locked so tightly within her body. He shook, rocked by the first of what would be many orgasms tonight.

The movement swept Jenna up and took her with him. She screamed. Her eyes rolled back in her head and her body convulsed with pleasure.

The sound her unrestrained release made Aidan's wolf howl with joy. His baying increased in volume, as Aidan leaned over to nuzzle Jenna's neck. He licked her one more time, then opened his mouth wide.

"I'm sorry," he said, "but the decision is out of my hands."

Aidan bit down, breaking the skin. Her salty sweet blood filled his mouth, drowning his senses. He swallowed, drinking her in. Aidan had never tasted anything so delicious, so powerful. And she was his.

His for all eternity.

He lifted his head and bellowed, announcing the claiming of his bondmate to the moon. Jenna whimpered, but her eyes never opened.

Blood dripped from Aidan's chin onto the ground. He buried his face in her neck and cleaned her. He could remove most of the blood, but his mark would remain for all to see.

He kissed the spot. Jenna sighed, but didn't shy away. It didn't matter. Fate had already sealed all the exits.

14

Jenna snuggled deeper under the covers, relishing the softness of the bedding. A plush pillow cradled her head and her body ached in a deliciously decadent way. Memories of the previous night filled her head.

Aidan had been insatiable. She didn't know anyone past the age of sixteen who could recover so quickly. He'd had her six more times before Jenna had collapsed from exhaustion.

Until last night, she'd never known that a powerful orgasm could make someone faint from pleasure overload. It proved once again that she'd been dating the wrong men.

As if she needed more proof.

Jenna grinned and cracked an eye open. Her smile slowly faded. The room didn't look right.

The familiar dresser that sat against the wall was gone. It had been replaced by a heavy wood piece that stood at least a foot and a half taller. The walls were also a darker color cream.

She glanced over. The spot beside her was empty. The sheets cool to the touch. Her attention was drawn to the massive headboard that resembled a sleigh. Recognition hit and Jenna bolted upright.

How did she get to Aidan's room? For that matter, how did she get back to the house? The last thing she recalled was dawn illuminating the sky and being too exhausted to walk.

A memory of Aidan carrying her through the woods, cradling her against his powerful chest, exploded in her mind.

How humiliating!

Jenna fell back onto the bed. Geez, one night with him and she'd become a swooning heroine from a romance novel. She snorted and shook her head at how pathetic she'd been, then sat up once more. Jenna knew she couldn't stay in Aidan's room, eventually either he'd return or someone else would find her there.

She threw the covers back and slipped off the bed. Jenna listened, but didn't hear the shower running. She glanced toward the patio. The doors to the balcony were closed.

Where was Aidan? And why hadn't he taken her back to her room? Surely it would've been easier than carrying her up the stairs and tucking her into his bed.

Jenna looked around again. Her gaze landed on a piece of paper, sitting on the nightstand. She saw her name written on it and picked it up.

Jenna,

I had a meeting set for early this morning that couldn't be rescheduled. I didn't have the heart to wake you after what I'd put you through last night. There are things I must tell you, but they can wait until you get back from work.

Aidan

Jenna flipped the note over, but there was nothing written on the back. Not exactly the most romantic message, but she hadn't expected it to be. They'd had sex. Amazing sex. Stupendous sex. But sex nonetheless.

Aidan hadn't proposed marriage. He hadn't even suggested that they date. She appreciated the fact that he'd taken the time to drop her a note, but Jenna wasn't going to read too much into the gesture.

She found the pad of paper Aidan had used to scribble the note in the drawer of his bedside table. Jenna composed one of her own and tucked it under the lamp on his side of the bed where he was sure to find it.

Her note wasn't eloquent, but she did tell him how much she'd enjoyed last night. Jenna hoped that when she saw Aidan again that it wouldn't be too awkward, but she couldn't worry about that now because she had to get to work.

Jenna poked her head into the hall to make sure it was clear, then dashed out of Aidan's bedroom. She ran down the stairs, praying the whole time that no one saw her.

She wasn't ashamed of what she and Aidan had done, but she'd rather avoid the embarrassment of being caught wearing the same clothes she'd worn the night before.

It took three tries, but Jenna finally found her bedroom. She showered quickly and put on some makeup. She was about to pull on her shirt, when Jenna noticed an odd mark near the crook of her neck. She leaned in to get a better look.

It was a love bite.

Jenna ran her fingers over the spot, recalling the moment it happened. She and Aidan had been completely out of control, going at each other like savage animals, biting, clawing and grunting. Jenna had never been one for rough sex, but with Aidan it had seemed natural.

She'd matched him move for move, kiss for kiss, and shout for shout. He'd brought out a side of her that she hadn't known existed. Now that she did, Jenna couldn't imagine being any other way.

Jenna pressed down on the spot. The area was tender to the touch. She examined it closely.

Teeth marks.

She should've been appalled that she'd let him *brand* her in such a way. After all, they weren't teenagers exchanging hickeys. But for some inexplicable reason, she felt the opposite.

Jenna *liked* seeing Aidan's mark upon her skin. It seemed intimate, personal—oddly territorial. Which of course was ridiculous, since it was just a hickey.

She glanced at the evidence of their lovemaking one last time, then got dressed. Maybe next time around she'd tell Aidan to lay off the biting.

If there was a next time, an insidious little voice whispered.

Jenna knew she couldn't make too many plans. She had no idea how things would unfold with Ethan and the lawsuit she planned to file against him. Until she found out, there was no sense thinking about a future with Aidan.

She flipped off the light and rushed out of the room. Jenna hurried down the hall. She could see the door to Aidan's office was closed as she drew nearer. She debated whether to knock and say goodbye.

The note had said he was in a meeting. Would it still be going on? She didn't want to interrupt something important, though she was tempted.

Jenna wanted to see him, even if it was only for a moment. In the end, she decided that wasn't a good enough reason to disturb him. They could talk when she got back.

She left the house and jogged down to the garage. Her Bug was waiting outside for her with the keys in it. Jenna squealed in delight and climbed into her car.

"I've missed you." She patted the Bug's dashboard and started the engine.

Bernie came out of the garage. "How does she sound?"

"*He* sounds great." She laughed. "Please thank Nic for me."

"Will do." Bernie reached into the pocket of his coveralls and pulled out a business card. "Give us a call, if you have any problems."

Jenna took the card. "I will. See you later."

He smiled as she cranked the radio and slipped the car into gear.

Jenna waved to him, then drove off. This time when she turned left toward Breakbend, she knew her life had finally taken a turn for the better.

* * *

Robert breathed through his mouth so he wouldn't have to smell her. Jenna's human scent covered Aidan like cheap cologne, making him gag.

How could the Alpha have slept with her without vomiting during the act? The odor was so bad that Robert could almost *taste* her.

He dry-heaved at the thought.

Now that Aidan had slummed it by fucking the human, was it too much to hope that she was finally out of his system and would soon be out of the house?

"Go to my room and grab the file sitting on the dresser," Aidan said.

Robert slipped out of the office and gasped, filling his lungs for the first time in over an hour. He took several deep breaths as he climbed the stairs, trying to get the rank weedy scent of the human out of his lungs.

It wasn't until Robert reached the top of the stairs that he noticed he could still smell her. The scent should've faded.

Robert frowned and searched the hall, but he was alone. He tilted his head and listened. No retreating footsteps. Obviously breathing through his mouth hadn't worked. The human's stench was more powerful than he'd imagined.

He shook his head in disgust and strode down the hall. When he reached Aidan's bedroom door, Jenna's scent became cloying. Robert stared at the door in confusion, then threw it open.

He took one step inside and fell to his knees. Jenna's scent was everywhere and seemed to permeate everything. Robert gagged and staggered to his feet. He stared in disbelief at the rumpled sheets on the bed.

Normally only Aidan's side of the bed was disturbed, not both. He glanced at the pillows. There were two distinct impressions.

No! It couldn't be. He had to be mistaken.

The Alpha never spent the night with any female. That privilege was reserved for his bondmate.

Robert rushed forward, shoved his nose in the bed, and sniffed. One side of the sheets smelled of wolf, while the other...

His stomach churned as the truth hit. Jenna had slept here. In the Alpha's bed. All night. Her scent was too strong for it to be otherwise.

Why would Aidan allow such a thing? The bond was sacred to the

Moonlight Kin. It was said to be a gift from Freki herself.

Robert quickly searched the room, but the human was nowhere to be found. He was about to leave, when he noticed a piece of paper tucked under the lamp. Robert snatched the sheet off the table and scanned the note.

Cold enveloped him as the words and their implications slowly sank in. Robert crushed the paper and tossed it in the wastebasket, then grabbed the folder that Aidan had requested.

Things were worse than he'd imagined. Robert could no longer stand by and watch the pack disintegrate. He had to act now.

As soon as the meeting ended, Robert intended to confront the interloper. If she refused to leave, then he'd have no choice, but to kill her. And he'd do so, knowing that he acted in the best interest of the pack.

* * *

Jenna typed up her interview, while Paul Welling hovered behind her. He'd been acting like a child on Christmas morning, waiting for the go ahead to open the biggest box under the tree.

She finished the last line and hit send, so that it went straight into Paul's inbox. He raced into his office to make sure the email had arrived, then yelled for Jenna to join him. Paul opened his desk drawer and pulled out a stack of twenties.

"This is just something to tide you over until we sell the article to one of the leading magazines. With any luck, we'll be able to get a bidding war going." He handed her the cash. "There should be a thousand dollars there."

The amount was less than Jenna had hoped, but enough to get the legal process started. She shoved the money into her pocket next to the card Bernie had given her. "Thanks!"

"Take the rest of the week off, but I expect to see you here on Monday," he said.

Jenna didn't answer because she wasn't sure she'd be here come Monday. Much depended on what the attorney she was going to hire suggested that she do next. She left Paul's office feeling like a weight had been lifted off her shoulders.

Molly saw her come out. "Did Paul give you the rest of the week off?"

Jenna nodded.

"Did he tell you that we normally don't work on Fridays?" she asked.

Jenna laughed. "No, he failed to mention it." She looked back at his office. The door was closed. He was probably already on the phone, trying to sell the rights.

"He'll be happy now that he has his interview, but I doubt it gets him out of Breakbend," Molly said. "Newspapers aren't what they used to be. Everyone is reading online. Paul's still living in the past."

It didn't matter to Jenna. There was no one right career path these days. Everybody had to get creative.

"What are you going to do now?" Molly asked.

"I have an appointment with an attorney, then I'm going to head back to the Fortier estate," she said.

Molly grinned. "Any special reason you're going back there?"

Jenna looked away. "None that I care to mention."

Molly giggled. "I knew you were holding out on me about Aidan Fortier."

"I don't know what you're talking about," Jenna said.

"That hickey on your neck says otherwise," Molly teased.

Jenna couldn't stop the smile from spreading across her face. "Have a good weekend."

"I will," Molly said. "But I bet yours is better."

She chuckled, hoping Molly was right. Jenna stepped out onto the sidewalk and took a deep breath. She'd parked the Bug down the street, where it would stay while she visited the attorney's office. He was only a few blocks away and she could do with a walk.

Jenna found the office and spent the next hour explaining her situation. She'd been nervous when she first arrived, but Wilson Bennett had quickly put her mind at ease.

By the time she left, the attorney had accepted the job and he'd already started making phone calls on her behalf.

Jenna strolled down the sidewalk with a smile upon her face. It felt good to finally have someone on her side, fighting on her behalf. She could see her Bug peeking out from behind a red truck up ahead.

She dug into her pocket and pulled out her keys. It was only as Jenna drew nearer that she noticed a man leaning against her car. His long legs stuck out, but the truck obscured the rest of his body.

When Jenna was about twenty feet away, the man stood, giving her a clear view of his face. She felt the blood drain from her as her past came crashing down upon her.

"Darling, I've missed you." Ethan opened his arms wide and approached her like he was going to hug her.

Jenna turned to run to the Gazette and slammed into Carl Rich. She bounced off Carl's chest. He captured her wrist and squeezed, until Jenna whimpered in pain and dropped her car keys. He caught them before they hit the ground.

"That's for kicking me in the balls," he spat, then jerked her around to face Ethan. "I believe you have a date in Vancouver that you can't miss."

The bell on the door of the paper chimed. Jenna glanced back and saw Molly step out with a pink sweater in her hands. She waved when she saw Jenna, then her smile slowly faded.

Jenna tried to warn her away with a pointed gaze, but Molly wasn't taking the hint.

"Thought you'd be long gone by now." Molly glanced at her watch. "If I had a sexy beast waiting for me at home, I wouldn't still be here in town."

"I don't know what you're talking about," Jenna said. *Shut up. Please shut up.* There was a chance that Ethan and Carl didn't know about Aidan. Jenna wanted to keep it that way.

Molly's frown deepened.

Ethan pulled Jenna into his arms and stroked her back. "Smile for your little friend," he whispered. "We wouldn't want anything to happen to her."

He was right. It was better to play along, until she could escape. Ethan had already proven that he'd ruin anyone who crossed him. Jenna didn't think he'd blink an eye at dismantling Molly's family's newspaper business.

Jenna gave Molly a strained smile. "As you can see, I have a lot of friends." She indicated to the men. "Too many to keep track of."

"Here in town?" Molly asked, eyeing Carl and Ethan in bewilderment.

"Yes," Ethan said. "If you don't mind, we'd like to continue this reunion in private." He winked at her. "I'm sure you understand."

Molly didn't say anything, but her disapproval was apparent.

"I'll see you on Monday, Molly." Jenna nudged Ethan to distance him from the woman. She had no idea what he'd do, if given half the chance.

"Yeah, see you then." Molly nodded, then walked back the way she came.

Jenna watched her go. Her smile faltered, but did not fade.

Molly looked confused, when she glanced back.

Jenna waved goodbye.

Molly shrugged, then slipped inside the Gazette building.

"It appears Carl was right. You've found yourself a new friend," Ethan said.

"Molly's not my friend. She's just a co-worker." There was a chance he'd leave her alone, if Ethan believed Jenna really didn't know her. He only liked hurting the people she cared about.

"I'm not talking about Molly," he said. "What's his name again, Carl?" Ethan snapped his fingers.

"Aidan Fortier."

Jenna's blood went cold. Molly hadn't mentioned Aidan by name, so how had Carl found out about him? Aidan had only come to town with her one time.

"I knew it," Jenna said. "You've been following me around Breakbend."

"It's my job." Carl smirked.

"For how long?" she asked.

"Long enough," Carl said.

She looked at Ethan. "Leave Aidan out of it. He doesn't have anything to do with us. With this." She waved her hand between them.

Ethan tilted his head and smiled at her.

A long time ago, she would've thought that expression was cute, but now it made Jenna's skin crawl. She'd seen that same smile on Ethan's face right before he'd thrown the legal documents on the table, showing her that he'd swindled her out of her garage.

"I'd love to leave Fortier out it. I really would." He pressed his hand to his chest, feigning sincerity. "But you ran from me Jenna, which proves that I can't trust you. There's no way for me to know for sure that he isn't helping you."

"I told you he's not."

"Once again, I'm only left with your word." Ethan rubbed his jaw thoughtfully. "I suppose there is a way that you could prove to me that you're telling the truth."

She grit her teeth. "How?"

"Return to Vancouver with me willingly as a show of good faith, then I might consider giving your new *friend* a pass." Ethan paused dramatically. "Of course, you'd have to do everything I asked once we got there, but that's only fair considering what you've put me through."

"For how long?" She braced for his answer.

Ethan's smile widened. "Until I finish closing the deal. Shouldn't take more than three months, once the papers are signed."

Three months?

How was she supposed to explain to Aidan that she'd be gone for three months? The separation would destroy their burgeoning relationship before it ever got a chance to start, which was probably the reason Ethan had suggested it. He wanted to see her in pain. He wanted her to lose everything...again.

Jenna's heart thundered in her chest, threatening cardiac arrest. She knew Ethan well. He'd never honor his word. The fact that he'd even brought Aidan's name up meant that he'd been doing research into his background.

What had he found? Heaven help Aidan, if he'd already spoken to the people in town.

She thought about the wolves, Aidan's unusual living arrangements, his odd behavior, and his obsession with privacy.

If Ethan exploited even one of those things, it could destroy Aidan's reputation.

No doubt he'd pursue them all.

Jenna couldn't let that happen. It was her fault Ethan was here. It was up to her to stop him. "I'll do anything you want," she said. "As long as you leave him alone."

"I had no idea you'd grown so attached, so quickly. You've only been here for what, a week?" Ethan touched one of the loose curls hanging near her face. "Carl had suggested that you were sleeping with the man, but I assured him that you were too frigid to be a whore." His gaze lingered on Aidan's love bite, then he looked at the investigator and shrugged. "Guess I was wrong about that too, Carl. She is a slut."

Jenna jerked her shirt over to cover the spot, then glared at Ethan's flunky.

Carl sneered. "I call them like I see them."

Ethan wound her hair around his finger and yanked hard to get her attention. "You know this changes things, don't you?"

Jenna scowled at her ex. "It changes nothing."

"Beg to differ," Ethan said. "When this whole thing started, it was just between you and me. Now that I know you've been sleeping with Fortier, it makes me wonder how much you have told him."

"We never had sex." Jenna's body shook with rage as she lied through her teeth. "I haven't told Aidan anything about you. Not your name. Not where you're from. Nothing. He has no idea who you are. He doesn't even know that we *dated*." She poured her contempt into the last word. "Hell, he doesn't even know that you exist."

Ethan tsked. "I wish I could believe you, but with your history of lying..."

"I never lied," she ground out. "You on the other hand did nothing but."

"Let's agree to disagree." Ethan led her down the street. Jenna had to jog to keep up with his long strides.

"It's important for people like you to understand that it's not okay to screw with people like me. It sets a bad precedence, if these things go unpunished," he said. "That's why I think I'm going to have to make an example out of your friend. You leave me no choice."

"Then I'm not going with you." Jenna struggled to break free. His punishing grip tightened, leaving finger marks on her arm. She cried out, catching the attention of a few people walking down the sidewalk.

He scowled at her, then smiled at the growing crowd, pouring on the charm. "She's had a little too much to drink." Ethan tipped an imaginary bottle to his lips.

The people's reactions to the news varied. Some still looked concerned, while others appeared disgusted by her behavior.

Ethan lowered his voice. "The more you fight, the worse it's going to be for him."

Jenna stopped struggling. What was the use? He'd won. He always won. She thought she could challenge him. Get back what he'd taken. But seeing Ethan today made her realize that she'd been fooling herself. No matter how hard she worked, Jenna would never have enough resources to go toe-to-toe with him.

Ethan looked at Carl. "Let's finish this conversation on the plane." He put his arm around Jenna's shoulders and led her toward a gray SUV. "Come along, darling. We have a lot to discuss."

15

Robert LaBeouf could not believe what he was seeing. A horn beeped and he jerked the wheel, narrowly avoiding a collision. He'd come to town to confront Jenna, but before he got the chance, he'd accidentally uncovered her treacherous secret.

He watched the man pull Jenna into his arms and hold her close. She didn't try to get away. Instead, Jenna smiled and hugged him back, stopping only long enough to chat with a friend.

Once the woman departed, the man put his arm around Jenna's shoulder and led her down the street. Robert seethed on the Moonlight Kin pack's behalf. Aidan had been duped just like he'd suspected.

By a human no less.

Robert turned the car around and cruised by the loving couple once more. He watched Jenna and the men climb into a gray SUV and head out of town. On the way back to the estate, he spotted her car sitting near a coffee shop.

Why hadn't she taken it?

Maybe she was coming back for it? Or maybe she'd gotten everything she wanted from Aidan and the pack and didn't need it anymore. The thought filled him with righteous fury.

The Alpha had insisted that the vehicle be repaired for her. The pack had dropped what they were working on to accommodate his wishes. Josh had even made a special trip into the city to get the parts. And this was how she showed her gratitude.

The only thing that cooled Robert's anger and kept it from becoming a murderous rage was the knowledge that he'd personally get to inform Aidan that his little human pet had run off with another man. He grinned.

Robert couldn't wait to see the look on the Alpha's face when he found out that he'd been deceived.

"Are you certain?" Aidan asked. "Two men, not one?"

His body trembled with barely contained rage. How could Jenna do this to him after what they'd shared last night? After everything he'd done for her?

His wolf couldn't have been wrong about her, could he?

Thank Freki, he hadn't told the pack yet that he'd marked her as his bondmate. Aidan had planned to do so this weekend. Now it was the last thing they needed to hear, especially if she'd run off with two men like Robert said.

What was he going to do? Aidan didn't think he could live without her.

His wolf demanded that he go after her. Find her. Kill the men that she was with and bring her back.

It was tempting, but not the smartest plan, especially if Jenna chose to go with them. The idea that she'd picked another male over him wounded Aidan in a way he'd never experienced before.

The pain seared his soul, leaving him in agony. It was the kind of open wound that wouldn't heal easily...if ever. She'd rejected him. His claws extended. With sheer force of will, Aidan forced them back inside. This situation called for logic, not emotion.

What if the men were the ones Jenna was frightened of? The ones she'd been running from? Fear replaced some of his anger.

But why would she go with them, if that were the case? There'd been people out. Enough witnesses around that she could've escaped had she wanted to. And why would she embrace one of them? It didn't make sense.

"Tell me again exactly what you saw," Aidan said.

Robert started from the beginning, repeating the story verbatim. "If you don't believe me, you could ask the woman she was talking to."

"Woman?" Aidan asked. "What woman? Why didn't you mention her before?"

"I didn't think about it until now. Seeing Ms. Dane in another man's arms made me forget everything else."

Aidan winced. He couldn't get the picture of Jenna being held by another man out of his mind. His wolf struggled to break the tenuous grip he had on it.

Like a good little wolf, Robert kept his gaze trained on the floor. "I believe the woman works at the paper with Ms. Dane. They had a short conversation, then I saw her go into the building."

Aidan had hoped that Robert was wrong. He knew the wolf wasn't lying. That had been the first thing he'd checked, when he'd reported the news. He wouldn't have put it past him since Robert hated all humans, but in this instance he was telling the truth.

He ran a hand through his hair and scrubbed it over his face. Aidan shouldn't have let her out of his bed. He should've found a way to keep her in his room, until they got a chance to talk.

Jenna was his mate. Was his period. His mark proved it. Didn't matter whether a human male could recognize such a thing. He knew the truth. Soon Jenna would, too.

"What do you want me to do?" Robert asked.

"Nothing," Aidan growled. The last thing he needed was for Robert to involve himself any further. Jenna was his responsibility. He'd have to be the one to ferret out the truth. Even if that truth turned out to be something Aidan didn't want to hear.

* * *

"Father, I was using the plane," Ethan whined and gave the phone a petulant pout.

They'd driven to the small airport where Ethan had parked the jet, but it was gone by the time they got there. It was everything Jenna could do not to laugh at his first world problems.

"I realize it's not mine, but I needed it to get back to Vancouver," he said. "I have very important business to attend to. No, it's not more important than yours. I didn't say that."

Jenna watched Ethan pace back and forth like a caged hyena. The dingy room he and Carl had brought her to didn't strike Jenna as the kind of place Ethan would frequent, much less spend the night in. Its faded mauve comforters, cheap worn out furniture, and tissue thin towels did however suit Carl to a 'T'.

"Fly commercial? Are you serious? Why would I do that, when there's a perfectly good corporate jet available?" Ethan stopped walking. "Yes. I understand. When can I have it back?" He squeezed his cell phone until his knuckles cracked. "No chance of getting the plane any sooner?" He paused. "I see."

Carl sat at the table, flipping through a Breakbend visitor's guide. It appeared like he wasn't paying any attention to Ethan, but Jenna knew better. The beefy investigator was like a sponge. He absorbed everything, noted every detail.

"I'll expect it here Saturday morning." Ethan pressed a button to disconnect the call. "I can't believe this. You're sure this is the last room available."

"Yep," Carl said. "There's a fishing tournament in town. We were lucky that I hadn't checked out yet."

Ethan looked around the room and scowled.

What were they going to do until Saturday? Jenna wondered. She didn't relish the idea of staying in this motel room with them for two nights.

"Why didn't you just bring the paperwork with you?" Jenna asked. "It would've saved us both a lot of time and trouble."

Ethan shoved his phone in his pocket and walked over to where she sat on the edge of the bed. "I'm not buying a fast food restaurant from you. This type of land deal requires several attorneys to be present. I can't just pull random people off the street to be witnesses," he snapped.

"I'm surprised you didn't forge my signature," she said.

He looked at her, his expression inscrutable. "I thought about, but again, it wasn't feasible."

She stood and stretched. "What's going to happen now?"

Ethan glared at her. "Now we wait." His gaze swept the room and his lip curled in disgust. "Carl, go out and get us a pizza. Bring back a bottle of disinfectant while you're at it. Jenna and I need some alone time."

Fear slithered down her spine. What did Ethan mean? Surely he wasn't referring to... She shuddered at the thought. If he touched her, she'd kill him. Jenna couldn't imagine having any man's hands on her other than Aidan's.

It didn't make sense given the short time they'd known each other, but it was the truth.

Carl grunted and left the motel.

"Take a seat." Ethan pointed to the chair Carl had vacated.

Jenna walked across the room and sat down.

"I looked up your friend before I left," he said. "Fortier is an interesting man. His resources are comparable to my own. Is that why you slept with him?"

Jenna blanched. "I never said anything about sleeping with him. You're the one with sex on the brain."

"Perhaps, but I'm not the one with the giant hickey." Ethan stared pointedly at the love bite on her neck.

She reached up and covered the spot with her hand. "That's not from Aidan," Jenna said.

Ethan arched a brow. "Carl hasn't seen you with anyone else."

"Yeah, well, Carl wasn't with me 24/7," she said.

"He didn't need to be." Ethan walked over to his briefcase and pulled out a folder. He tossed the contents onto the table.

The photos were of her and Aidan at the restaurant.

"Is that you?" Ethan asked.

Jenna's jaw clenched. "You know it is."

"Good," he said. "We're in agreement. So if that's you, then who is that?" Ethan pointed at Aidan.

Jenna didn't respond.

Ethan sighed. "You might as well answer me. I already know who it is."

"It's Aidan," she said quietly. "But it's not what it looks like," Jenna added quickly.

"Really?" He sat back in his chair and crossed his arms over his chest. "It looks like a romantic dinner for two."

Jenna shook her head. "It wasn't." She pointed to the small notepad on the table in one of the photos. "That was the night he gave me an exclusive interview for the paper."

Ethan's brows rose to his hairline. "I didn't realize wine was a necessary part of the interview process."

Jenna's mouth snapped shut.

He laughed mirthlessly. "So how long have you been fucking him? And don't lie to me. You never could lie worth a damn."

Jenna shot to her feet. "It's none of your business."

Ethan rose from his seat. He stood so close that they nearly touched noses. "Anything that could possibly jeopardize this land deal *is* my business." He pointed to the photos. "I didn't bring Fortier into this mess. You did. Whatever happens to him is all on you."

Tears prickled Jenna's eyes, but she refused to let Ethan see her cry. She'd already wasted too many tears on the bastard. He was right though. If anything happened to Aidan, it would be her fault.

"I need something to drink." She turned away from his knowing gaze.

"There's water in the tap," he said.

Jenna pulled a face. "I was thinking more like a soda. I'm pretty sure that I saw a vending machine tucked between the buildings."

Ethan stared at her. "You run and I'll make it my personal mission in life to destroy him. You understand?"

She nodded, then walked to the door.

"You have five minutes," he said. "If you're not back by then, I'll make a phone call."

Jenna put her hand on the doorknob.

"And Jenna," he said.

She froze.

"Pick me up a Coke while you're at it." Ethan grinned and tossed her some change.

Jenna picked the change up off the carpet and slipped out the room. He was going to try to destroy Aidan no matter what she said or did. She could see the intent in his eyes. All she'd done was delay the inevitable. She just needed to figure out how to delay it a little longer, so she could warn Aidan.

The motel was laid out in a typical V-shape with all the doors facing the parking lot. There were several cars parked in the lot, mostly pickups that held fishing rods in their back windows.

Light blue paint covered the walls, but did little to hide the age of the building. Jenna wasn't thirsty. She'd just needed to get away from Ethan, so she could think. Warning Aidan was priority number one. Nothing else mattered.

She reached the vending machine and dug into her pocket to retrieve the change Ethan had given her. Jenna bought a couple of sodas, then slowly walked back toward the room. A door opened to her right and an elderly man stepped in front of her, wearing a fishing hat.

"Excuse me," he said. "I didn't see you there."

Jenna smiled. "No problem." She started to walk off, then stopped abruptly. "Sir, could I use your phone?"

His bushy white brows rose and fell like caterpillars inching across a cracked sidewalk. "What's wrong with the phone in your room?"

"It's out of order," she said. "I don't own one of those fancy cell phones."

He snorted. "Me neither. Though the wife keeps badgering me to pick one up." He swept his hat off and scratched his head. "I suppose it would be okay, but don't stay on long. It's a local call, isn't it?"

Jenna nodded.

"Okay, then." He stepped aside.

Jenna hurried into the room and fished out the card Bernie had given her. She tapped her foot impatiently as she waited for the call to connect. She didn't have much time. Two minutes at the most. "Pick up. Pick up. Come on, Aidan."

"Fortier residence," a voice said.

She recognized Robert's nasal tone immediately. "May I please speak with Aidan?"

"May I ask who's calling?" he asked.

Jenna growled in frustration. He knew who it was. He was just messing with her. "I don't have time for games, Robert," she hissed. "I need to talk to Aidan. It's important."

Silence greeted her.

"Are you still there?" What if he'd hung up on her? What would she do then?

"I'm sorry, but Mr. Fortier is unavailable. He's made it clear that he has nothing more to say to you," he said.

Jenna recoiled. "What? Why?"

Was that what Aidan planned to tell her tonight? Had he decided sleeping with her was a mistake? It hurt to breathe, but Jenna shoved the pain aside. It didn't matter.

She was a big girl. She had entered that clearing with her eyes wide open. No expectations. No demands. They were both consenting adults.

Jenna had known going in what Aidan wanted, because she'd wanted the same thing. If Aidan had misgivings about last night, then so be it. None of that changed what she needed to do.

"Please, Robert."

"I saw you in town with your *friends*," he said. "You couldn't keep your hands off each other. It was disgusting. If you cared at all about Mr. Fortier, you wouldn't have humiliated him in such a public manner."

Jenna's stomach churned. "You don't know what you're talking about." How could he think that Ethan and Carl were her friends?

"Don't I?" he asked. "Your true colors are showing. Not a surprise, considering you got everything you wanted."

All Jenna wanted was to end this. "Robert, please. I'm begging you. This is an emergency. I need to warn Aidan. It won't take long. I promise."

He snorted. "Your assurances are worthless. I'll relay your concerns to Mr. Fortier. Please do not phone again." Robert disconnected the call.

Jenna stared at the handset in disbelief. She could only imagine what Robert had told Aidan. What he would tell him once he saw him again. Would he even bother to let him know that she'd phoned?

This could not be happening. Jenna put the phone down and walked out of the room.

The elderly man had been quietly waiting outside the door to give her some privacy. "Is everything okay?" Concern softened his aged brown eyes and mellowed his tone.

Jenna shook her head. Nothing was okay. Nothing would ever be okay again. She'd lost Aidan before she'd ever really had him.

Once again, Ethan had cost her what she held dear. And thanks to Robert LaBeouf, she couldn't even warn him that trouble was coming.

"Thank you for allowing me to use your phone."

"Anytime," he said.

Jenna walked back to the motel room and opened the door.

Ethan glanced at his watch. "Cutting it close." He held out his hand.

Jenna placed the sodas on the table, then walked into the bathroom and shut the door. The mark on her neck throbbed. She put her hand over the spot and held it there, as if covering it would somehow keep the memory of Aidan's lips burned into her skin.

The tears she'd been holding back welled in Jenna's eyes. She turned on the water, so Ethan wouldn't hear her cry.

16

Aidan lay in his bed surrounded by Jenna's scent. He hadn't allowed the cleaners to change the sheets. Partly as penance for stupidly marking a human and partly because he couldn't stand the thought of losing any part of her.

He'd declined Robert's offer to send a Werewoman to his room. The idea of touching another female was repulsive to him. Aidan knew he couldn't continue to hide. Eventually, he'd have to tell the pack the truth.

Tomorrow the moon run would begin. He'd planned to formally introduce Jenna to the pack once he'd revealed his secret. Thank Freki he'd intended to tell her in person. It would've been disastrous had he put it in writing, since Jenna had taken the note with her.

Should he have worded the message differently? What could he have said or done to get her to stay? Aidan had been asking himself those questions and many others for the past few hours.

He wasn't one for pretty words. Aidan didn't know how to be anything but direct with people. That included members of the female persuasion.

Perhaps he should've told Jenna how he felt? But how could he, when Aidan had only recently discovered what she meant to him?

The emotions were too fresh, too raw. He was still trying to come to grips with the fact that a human female had turned his life upside down in less than a week.

Aidan had assumed that Jenna had been equally affected by their sudden joining, but her actions said otherwise.

No matter how many ways he examined the situation, Aidan couldn't understand what made Jenna leave suddenly without saying goodbye. When she'd told him that she planned to betray him, Aidan thought she'd been referring to the interview.

What if she hadn't? What if there'd been more to her story? What if Jenna had been trying to tell him about the men and he'd been too caught up in her scent to listen?

Aidan knew she'd enjoyed their time together. You couldn't fake that kind of passion. He would've known. *His wolf would've known.*

He rolled over and stared at the wall. There were no answers written on it. No advice for what he should do next. His gaze dropped to the wastebasket near his bedside table.

There was a crumpled piece of paper in it. Aidan instantly recognized his personal stationary. Maybe Jenna hadn't taken his note with her after all.

If that were the case, then Aidan would finally have the answer he sought.

With trepidation, he climbed out of bed and picked up the wad of paper. Aidan slowly unfolded the sheet and straightened it. His heart tripped in his chest, when he saw his name written at the top of the page. He flipped the paper over, but there was nothing written on the back. It wasn't the note he'd left for her. This was a new one.

So how did the note end up in the trash? Had Jenna changed her mind after she'd written it?

Aidan brought the note to his nose and sniffed. Fur rippled down his arm and his vision blurred, as a familiar odor greeted him. He crumpled the note in his fist and rushed out of the room.

He grabbed the first wolf he saw by the scruff of the neck and slammed him into the nearest wall. "Where is Robert LaBeouf?" Aidan shook Nic hard enough to rattle his teeth.

"N-not sure, Alpha. I think he's running with the pack tonight."

Robert only attended formal pack gatherings. He never ran with the pack for the sheer joy of it. He considered that kind of thing beneath him. Why the sudden change? "Are you sure?"

"Bernie said that Robert was in a good mood. So good that he felt like going for a run," Nic said. "He only mentioned it to me because it was so unusual and thought I'd get a laugh out of it."

Aidan shoved Nic away. "I want you to find Robert and bring him to me."

Nic hesitated.

"Did I stutter?" Aidan bellowed.

"No, Alpha." Nic stiffened.

"Then go! Now!"

Robert yipped excitedly as he ran through the woods. The pack shouldered past him, but tonight he didn't care. He'd saved his fellow Moonlight Kin from what would surely have been a disaster.

The pack raced on, chasing a small herd of deer. The old and the weak had fallen behind. Soon the wolves would catch them and they'd feast. He leapt over a fallen tree trunk and plowed on.

Robert had no idea why Jenna thought she needed to warn Aidan, but he had no doubt that the Alpha could take care of himself.

The lead wolf caught sight of the deer. It barked once and the pack split in half, circling around the side of the herd to cut the older and weaker deer off before they could escape. Once a couple of deer were separated from the others, the pack formed a loose circle around them and closed in.

The lead wolf lunged for the deer's back leg and got kicked for his efforts. The wolf whimpered, but dove right back in. This time his firm grip on the deer's shank couldn't be broken. Another wolf leapt, latching onto the animal's neck, ripping its throat out.

The first deer fell, then the other was quickly taken down. Blood flowed, filling the air with its sweet coppery aroma. The wolves moved in to feast. Robert threw his head back and howled. He couldn't remember the last time he'd been this happy.

The pack added their voices, then the wolves each took turns tearing off chunks of flesh. Robert stepped forward after the others finished, his mouth watering in anticipation. He could almost taste the prey's sweet blood. He opened his jaw to take a bite.

Something hard hit him from the side, knocking him away from the carcass. Robert rolled snout over tail, then stumbled to his feet. He growled at his attacker.

Nic snarled back, then bones cracked and reshaped as he shifted to his human form.

Robert watched in confusion, then slowly followed suit. "I waited the appropriate amount of time. It was my turn to eat," he barked.

Nic glanced at the two deer like he'd just noticed them. "This has nothing to do with the hunt. Alpha has sent me to get you. He wants you at the house now."

Robert staggered back. "Why? What's happened?"

Nic shook his head. "It wasn't my place to ask."

Stupid wolf, Robert thought. He would've asked.

"You can go." Robert dismissed the wolf, not bothering to hide his disdain.

Nic didn't move. "He told me to bring you to him."

Robert frowned. "I know where the house is. I don't need an escort."

Nic glared at him. "Let's go." He nodded toward a path in the woods.

Robert's gaze strayed to the wolves around them. They'd all stopped feeding and were now staring at him. "Is this really necessary?" he hissed.

"You'll have to ask the Alpha," Nic said. "I'm just the messenger."

Robert chewed his nails as they walked back to the estate. What in the world could have Aidan so wound up that it couldn't wait until he got back?

Had Jenna phoned again, while he was out? Fear settled in Robert's gut, loosening his bowels. He hadn't done anything wrong. He was only protecting the pack from a bad influence. Surely Aidan knew that and would understand his reasoning.

Dread set in when he saw the lights blazing in the windows and a shadowy figure pacing on the patio. "Alpha," Robert said. "You wanted to see me?"

Aidan growled.

A drop of urine slid down Robert's leg.

"Get in the house," he said, then turned to Nic. "You may go."

Once Robert was safely ensconced in his office, Aidan rounded on him.

"I would've told you that she called," Robert blurted, before Aidan said a single word.

"What?" he asked. Jenna had phoned? When? And where was he?

"That's why you summoned me. Wasn't it?" Robert asked, sounding as confused as Aidan felt.

"No," Aidan said. "I had Nic fetch you for another reason." He walked over to his desk and picked up the crumpled piece of paper he'd found in his room. Aidan held it out for Robert to see. "Explain," he said through clenched teeth. "Then we'll get to Jenna's phone call."

Robert stared at the wad of paper, showing no sign of recognition.

Aidan tossed it at him. The paper bounced off Robert's chest and landed at his feet. He picked it up and opened it. His color drained as he read the note.

"Can you tell me how that note ended up in my wastepaper basket?" Aidan asked. "I know I didn't put it there."

Robert smoothed the crumpled paper in his hands. "I-I have no idea, Alpha."

"Lie!" Aidan roared. "Your scent was all over it. The only other scents on the sheet were mine and Jenna's."

Robert gulped. "I knew the human was going to betray you. I thought it best to lessen the blow."

Aidan's hands curled into fists. "You had no right to interfere."

Robert trembled under Aidan's fierce gaze. "You slept with her. I smelled her on your sheets." His voice cracked. "She spent the night in your room. That privilege was reserved for your bondmate."

Aidan approached him and slowly circled Robert. "I am aware of the social mores."

Robert looked up, his wolf showing in his eyes. "Then why? Why would you dishonor your future mate?"

Aidan stopped directly in front of him. "I haven't. My future mate was right where she needed to be. In my bed, beside me."

Robert stumbled back, a look of horror upon his face. "You didn't. You couldn't. You're...you're an Elder. She's..."

"My bondmate," Aidan supplied.

"But I saw her in the arms of another," Robert said. "If she were truly bonded to you, she wouldn't have been able to stand the contact."

Aidan's vision faded to red. Claws slipped from his fingertips and his teeth sharpened into vicious points. "This note and the call you failed to mention, tells me there's more to this story. Where's Jenna now?"

"I don't know." He cowered.

"Where is she?" Aidan stormed. His clawed hand rose, preparing to strike a fatal blow.

Urine flowed down Robert's leg, then spread across the floor, forming a puddle. "I swear. I don't know where she is." Robert's hands trembled as he held them up to ward off an attack. He slowly backed away, splashing urine with each step he took.

Aidan looked down in disgust, then back at his *former* assistant.

Robert stopped. "The last time I saw her, she was leaving town with the men. They could be anywhere by now."

Aidan growled. "You didn't note the number she was calling from?"

He shook his head. "No, I didn't think it was important."

Aidan barked out a laugh. "You didn't think it was important."

"I was only doing what I thought was best—"

"Don't!" Aidan warned. He was sick of hearing Robert's excuses. "You should've followed her and found out who those men were before you passed judgment on her."

What if Jenna was forced to leave? What if she were in trouble? The thought nearly brought Aidan to his knees. He'd promised to protect her, even if that meant protecting her from herself.

Why didn't you come to me?

Robert whimpered, his gaze bobbing from the floor to Aidan and back down again. "She had her hands all over that male, rubbing him. She was betraying you. It was only a matter of time before she betrayed the pack," he said.

"The only person who has betrayed me at every turn is you." Aidan snarled. "Now get out of my sight! I want you off the property by the end of the moon run."

His wolf struggled to break his hold. It wanted to tear Robert to pieces and gnaw on his bones. He should just kill him and get it over with, then he wouldn't have to worry about Robert trying to slip a knife into his back.

"For your sake, you'd better hope that nothing happens to her," Aidan said.

Robert rushed for the door. He hesitated when he reached it and looked back at Aidan. "Alpha, I swear—"

"Leave now, while you still can," Aidan said. His control was hanging by a pin. One tug and his beast would be unleashed. "I've made my decision." Now he had to find Jenna.

17

Jenna spent a fitful night crammed into the small bathtub. Ethan and Carl had taken the beds. Her only options had been to sleep on the floor or in the tub.

After staring at the cigarette burns and mystery spots, she'd decided the tub gave her the best chance of avoiding a future tetanus shot.

The men had checked on her periodically throughout the night to make sure she hadn't escaped. Unlike Ethan, when Jenna gave her word, she meant it. As long as he left Aidan alone, she'd go with him.

That didn't mean that Jenna wasn't planning on sneaking out and trying to phone him again. She was determined to get a message to Aidan, even if she had to send it via pigeon.

Once the men had showered, Ethan had Carl check the area to make sure no one had raised any alarms. The private investigator returned to the motel in late afternoon to let him know everything was fine. No one was looking for Jenna and her Bug was still parked where she'd left it the day before.

Carl had barely settled into the chair, when Ethan sent him out again. This time for food. Carl grumbled something about 'delivery' under his breath, but did as he was told. Jenna would've found the situation amusing, if it weren't so depressingly serious.

Ethan's cell phone rang. He glanced at the number and smiled. "Manning," he said in lieu of hello.

Jenna wasn't trying to eavesdrop, but the room wasn't big enough to avoid doing so.

"Yes," Ethan said. "She's here with me now." He pulled the phone away from his ear and looked at it, then brought it back. "Can you hang on a minute?"

She sat on the bed, watching and waiting.

Ethan pressed a button. "Dad?" He paced toward the door and back. "That's fantastic! What time will it arrive? Seven?" He nodded. "We'll be there."

Jenna's heart sank. The plane was going to arrive sooner than anticipated. She was running out of time. She had to make a move now because she might not get another chance later.

Ethan clicked over to his other call. "Good news," he said. "Our flight will land around nine-thirty tonight. No sense in waiting. Meet me at my office at ten-thirty and we'll get everything signed and notarized." He hung up and smiled at her.

"I take it we're leaving early?" she asked.

"Yep, we're getting out of this dump," Ethan said.

"What about Carl?" she asked.

Ethan shrugged. "He has a car. He can drive back."

"I'm going to catch a shower before he returns with the food," she said.

With any luck, she could shimmy out of the bathroom window and go use the elderly man's phone again. Jenna would be back before anyone knew she was gone.

Ethan's eyes hardened. "I thought you showered earlier."

Jenna shook her head. "No hot water. You guys used it all."

"Well hurry up," he said. "Carl will be back any minute."

She walked into the bathroom and locked the door. Jenna was about to turn the water on, when she heard Ethan talking. Had Carl returned already? Jenna leaned her head against the door and listened.

"Were you able to get me a list of Aidan Fortier's enemies and private holdings? What do you mean he doesn't have any? That's not possible," he said. "You need to look again. I want the information waiting for me when I return tonight."

Jenna cursed under her breath. She thought Ethan would at least wait until they got back to Vancouver, before he made good on his promise.

What was she going to do?

She glanced at the shower. Jenna needed to use the phone, but there was no way Ethan would let her. His cell rang again. She heard him answer, but this time Jenna didn't listen to his conversation. She'd already heard enough.

Jenna turned the water on and maneuvered the curtain around the spray, then wadded up a towel and dropped it into the tub to make it sound like someone was showering.

She stepped on the side of the tub and examined the window. Thick coats of white paint covered the window ledge, but couldn't disguise the pockmarked, rotting wood beneath. The size of the window made it clear it had been added for ventilation only.

This was going to be tight.

Jenna slipped the lock, then put both hands on the frame. The window creaked loudly, as she pushed and shoved forcing it to open. She heard Ethan say 'hang on a minute', then he was outside the door.

"What are you doing in there?" he asked. The doorknob twisted, but the lock held.

Jenna manufactured a coughing fit, then flushed the toilet with her foot.

"Are you okay?" Ethan called out.

"I'm fine," she said. "Just had a tickle in the back of my throat. Now can I please have some privacy?"

There was a pause, then Ethan said, "Hurry up. Carl's on the phone. He'll be here in five."

"I'll be out in ten minutes." Jenna looked at the closed door, listening for the sound of retreating footsteps.

The second she was sure that Ethan wasn't hovering outside the bathroom door, she leveraged herself onto the small windowsill.

Broken bottles and discarded cigarette butts littered the ground. It wasn't a far drop, but she doubted that she could land silently. It wasn't like she was a frickin' ninja.

Jenna glanced at the tub. An inch of water sat in the bottom of it. She had to go now. There wasn't much time.

She swung one leg out the window, then squeezed the other through. So far so good. She slid a little further. Her hips caught on the frame, stopping her progress. Jenna wiggled and shimmied, scraping her sides as she contorted her body.

The rotting wood cracked under her weight and crumbled to the ground. She held her breath, expecting to hear Ethan at the door. Jenna coughed again, which was hard to do while balancing on her belly.

"Get your ass out here," Ethan said.

"Can I finish going to the toilet first?" Jenna snapped. "It's that time of the month."

The conversation died instantly like she'd anticipated. No guy liked to discuss that particular subject.

Jenna dropped onto the ground, somehow missing all the glass. The gravel crunched beneath her feet, but she doubted that Ethan could hear her over the shower spray.

She sprinted down the back of the building and around the corner. Jenna came to a halt a few feet from the soda machine.

She peeked around the corner. Carl was coming down the sidewalk toward her. Crap! That was quick. She thought she'd have more time before they discovered that she was missing.

Jenna ducked behind the building and searched for a place to hide. There was none. Her heart trampled her ribs, as she waited for Carl to come around the corner and find her.

She heard change jingle, then drop into the soda machine. A second later there was a loud thud as a soda fell into the tray. Carl repeated the process one more time. Jenna listened to his footsteps fade and heard a door close.

She waited a breath, then glanced around the corner again. Carl was gone. Jenna hurried to the old man's room and knocked on the door. It seemed like it took forever for him to answer. When he did, Jenna rushed inside.

"I'm sorry. I don't mean to be rude, but can I please use your phone again?"

The old man frowned. "You want to tell me what's really going on here?"

Jenna gave him a pleading look. "I can't. The less you know, the better."

"If you're in trouble," he said, "we could call the police."

Jenna held up her hands. "No! No police. They wouldn't be able to help." She dropped her arms. "I just need to use your phone again."

"Be my guest." He pointed to the table.

"Thank you." Jenna picked up the receiver. There wasn't a dial tone. She pressed a couple of buttons, but nothing happened. "Was it working earlier?"

The man shrugged. "Don't rightly know. I haven't tried to use it."

Jenna slumped into the chair by the window and scrubbed a hand over her face. This couldn't be happening. No one had this bad of luck. *No one but her.*

Ethan had won. He'd get the land, ruin her, and take Aidan down while he was at it. The thought of Aidan getting hurt sent a fresh wave of pain crashing down upon her.

He doesn't want to speak to you. Robert had made that clear. There'd been no room for misinterpretation.

The elderly man put his hand on her shoulder and gently squeezed. "Are you sure there isn't anything I can do for you?"

Jenna looked up. She was out of options. Well all but one. And she didn't hold out a lot of hope that it would work. She stood.

"Is there any way that you can give me a ride into town?"

The man nodded. "I could do that."

"We'd have to go now." She glanced out the window. "Right now."

Ethan had her keys, but she was a mechanic. Any mechanic worth their salt could hotwire a car, if they had the right tools.

"Where's your vehicle?" she asked.

He pointed to a faded blue Chevy truck parked outside the door.

"Ready?"

He nodded.

Jenna checked one more time to make sure the coast was clear, then ran for the man's truck. She climbed in a second before the door to Carl's room flew open.

Ethan and Carl rushed out, their heads swiveling left and right as they searched for her.

Jenna dove for the floor of the truck. Had they seen her? Were they coming?

The old man climbed into the driver's seat and looked at her. "I take it you're hiding from those men?"

She nodded.

His brown eyes narrowed. "You haven't done anything illegal have you?"

Jenna laughed. She couldn't help it. The stress was too much. "No. Nothing illegal. Cross my heart." She made the sign of an 'X' over her chest.

The old man chuckled. "I believe you." He reversed out of the parking space, then threw the truck into gear. He gave Ethan and Carl a friendly wave as he drove by.

"What are they doing?" Jenna asked, afraid to move from her spot.

"They just ran behind the building. No doubt they'll be climbing into their vehicle in no time to look for you." His gaze focused on the road. "Where to now?"

Jenna inched up until she could peek out the window. There was no sign of Carl or Ethan, but he was right, they would be coming. "I need to get to Main Street, before they do."

"You got it." The old man put his foot on the gas and the truck shot down the road.

She smiled at him. "Thanks," she said, then added, "I'm Jenna."

"Pete." He shook her hand. "Nice to meet you."

"Pete, you wouldn't happen to have a pair of pliers I could borrow, would you?"

He pointed to the glove box. Jenna reached in and grabbed them. "Perfect," she said. "Thanks!"

Pete dropped Jenna off near her car. She'd spent most of the ride into town constantly looking over her shoulder. She knew she didn't have long. Jenna broke the driver's side window out, not caring that people were watching her.

"It's my car," she said, when someone reached for their cell phone.

They scowled at her and walked on.

Jenna quickly hotwired the Bug and threw it into gear. She pulled a U-turn, cutting off several vehicles. They honked at her, but Jenna didn't care. She hit the gas and the Bug raced out of town. She had to get to Aidan before Ethan did.

* * *

"I told you that she was wily," Carl said. "The girl must be some kind of contortionist. You sure she wasn't in the circus before you met her?"

"Positive." Ethan glared at him. "We cannot let her get away."

Carl met his gaze.

"She couldn't have gone far." Ethan pulled a set of keys out of his briefcase and jangled them in front of Carl's face. "I still have these. Even if she hitchhikes back to town, she isn't going to go anywhere."

Carl scratched his head. "What if she went in the opposite direction to throw us off?"

Ethan shook his head. "No, she's heading to Fortier's house. I know it. Jenna thinks she'll be safe there." He rolled down the window and scanned the sides of the road to make sure she wasn't hiding in the tree-line. "I'm sure that Fortier will see it my way, once we have a man-to-man chat. He'll understand why harboring her is a bad idea."

Carl looked in the rearview mirror. "I wouldn't be too sure," he muttered. "He seemed awful possessive, when I saw them together."

Ethan waved his concern away. "I'm sure we'll be able to reach a mutually beneficial financial arrangement."

"Money can't buy everything." Carl glanced in the side mirror, then changed lanes.

Ethan looked at him. "Yes, it can. You just need to have enough of it."

18

Jenna spotted the headlights in the distance, when she was a few hundred yards from Aidan's driveway. The Bug was going as fast as it could, but it was no match for the turbo-charged SUV following her.

She slowed just enough to make the turn, then floored the vehicle once more. The massive metal gate came into view. Jenna leaned out of her car and hit the buzzer.

No one answered.

She could hear the roar of the SUV's engine as it drew closer. Jenna hit the buzzer again and again. Where was Aidan? It occurred to her that he might not open the gate because she was the one trying to gain entrance.

Jenna slammed her palm onto the buttons and ran it across them all. In her rearview mirror, she saw headlights go by the entrance to the drive, then heard a screech of breaks.

"Please, Aidan. Let me in," Jenna cried. The SUV backed up and stopped, then turned down the driveway.

The speaker crackled. "I told you that Mr. Fortier doesn't want to speak with you," Robert said.

"Damn it, Robert! They're right behind me," she shouted.

There was a growl and a loud squeak, then Jenna heard Aidan's voice come over the intercom system.

"Open the gate."

The gate slid open. Jenna didn't wait for it to open all the way. The second it was wide enough for the Bug to squeeze through, she drove in.

Gravel crunched under the SUV's wide tires as the vehicle bore down upon her. The high-beam headlights illuminated the woods around Jenna, temporarily blinding her.

The gate reversed direction. Jenna gripped the wheel tight, her gaze locked on the SUV. There was no way she could outrun the vehicle, if it made it past the gate.

"Shut. Shut. Shut," she chanted under her breath.

It was going to be close. Jenna's heart leapt into her throat, as the vehicle barreled toward her.

The distance between the gate and the wall narrowed. It wasn't going to fit. The SUV fishtailed and skidded to a halt. The gate wouldn't hold Ethan off for long, but at least it bought her a few minutes. Jenna exhaled, then hurried the rest of the way down the driveway.

"What the hell are you doing?" Ethan shouted. "Why didn't you follow her?"

Carl stared at the closed gate. "Not sure if you noticed, but that gate is over a foot thick. It would've crushed our vehicle had I tried to drive through."

Ethan slammed his fists onto the dashboard, then jumped out of the SUV. He could hear the puttering of Jenna's car as she drove away.

He pressed the intercom button and waited for someone to answer. No one did. Ethan pressed all the buttons, then walked over and honked the horn.

A voice came on the line. "May I help you?"

"Yes, I need to speak with Aidan Fortier," he said.

"I'm sorry, but Mr. Fortier is unavailable tonight. You'll have to come back some other time."

Ethan growled. "I can't come back. I have a flight waiting. It's imperative that I speak with him tonight. It's about the woman that you just let in. She's not who you think she is."

There was a pause.

"Name please?"

"Ethan Manning."

"One moment."

Now they were getting somewhere. Ethan waited impatiently. Jenna thought she'd found safety. Thought she could hide from him. She was about to find out that no place was out of his reach.

The intercom crackled. "Are you still there?"

"Yes," Ethan said.

"Mr. Fortier apologizes for the inconvenience, but he will not be able to see you tonight. He's otherwise engaged."

Ethan gripped the sides of the console. "Did you tell him who I was?"

"Yes, sir."

"I demand to speak to him," he shouted.

The connection cut off.

Ethan spun around and jumped back into the SUV, then turned to Carl. "Find me another way in."

Aidan was waiting for her, when she got to the house. His arms were crossed over his chest and his sensual lips were pressed into firm line.

Jenna threw the Bug into park and jumped out. She rushed toward Aidan, stopping a few feet in front of him. "I don't have much time. I came here to warn you." She glanced over her shoulder toward the dark driveway.

Aidan's nostrils flared, but he said nothing.

"The man outside that gate is after me." She hesitated. "And because you helped me, he's after you, too."

He stared at her, his expression unreadable.

Jenna wrung her hands. "I know you said that you didn't want to speak to me. I won't bother you after this, but I had to warn you."

"Who is he to you?" Aidan asked softly.

Jenna sighed and her chin dropped. "My ex."

"Ex what?" he asked. "Husband?"

Her eyes goggled. "No! God no! He's my ex-boyfriend."

His body seemed to ripple in response to her answer.

Jenna wanted to run to him. Throw herself in his arms. It hurt to see Aidan keep his distance from her, but she'd respect his wishes.

"Listen," she said. "There isn't time to explain everything. Suffice to say, Ethan Manning is a very powerful man. He has the resources to hurt you."

There was a spark in his eyes at the mention of Ethan's name.

"I thought I could protect you, if I stayed away," she said. "We had a bargain, but he reneged on our agreement."

"You ran from me." The pain in his voice shredded her composure.

Jenna closed her eyes and took a deep breath. "I didn't run," she said. "I led him away."

Aidan arched a brow. "It looks more like you led him straight to me."

She flinched. "I had no choice, when I couldn't reach you by phone."

"I thought you'd left me," he said.

Jenna blinked in surprise. "I would never...I tried calling to let you know that I had to leave town, but I couldn't get through."

Aidan's jaw hardened. "You were going to leave with him?"

"Temporarily," she said. "The bargain was that I'd go with him as long as he left you alone." Jenna shoved her hands in her pockets. "I know you think I'm stupid for going with him, but you don't understand what type of man Ethan is."

Aidan stepped closer. "No." He shook his head. "You don't understand what type of man *I am*. And neither does he."

Jenna growled in frustration. "You don't get it. Ethan is going to dig into your life and uncover all your secrets." She held up her hand, when Aidan opened his mouth to speak. "Even if all he finds is what I discovered, it will be enough to discredit you and ruin your business relationships. He can take the smallest thing and completely destroy your life. He did it to me. He did it to my friend. He can do it to anyone."

Aidan was powerful, but so was Ethan. He could use his many contacts to bring down Aidan's little empire, even if Aidan didn't think so.

He stared at her.

"Aren't you going to say anything?" Jenna needed him to tell her that everything was going to be all right. That he forgave her for leaving. Anything!

Aidan inhaled and slowly circled her. "You smell like him."

Of all the things he could've said, that was what he went with?

Jenna frowned and sniffed her clothes. "I left my things here. I didn't have any clean clothes with me."

"I don't like that smell on you," Aidan said.

Jenna didn't think she stunk that bad. She had showered last night. Sure, she'd had to put on the same clothes, but it was either that or go naked.

"I think we have a bigger problem right now than my body odor. Ethan has a plane standing by to take us to Vancouver," she said. "He's having someone do an in-depth background check on you as we speak. He's searching for your enemies, so he can turn them into his allies. Now that you know, you can prepare for his next move."

"He won't find any," Aidan said. "None living anyway."

"Yes, well, give him time. He's incredibly persistent." She paused. "Listen, Aidan, I'm really sorry I got you into this mess. It was not my intention."

His sharp gaze searched her face.

"I'll get my things and get out of here." Jenna moved to go around him, but was stopped by Aidan's outstretched hand.

"I'm afraid it's too late for that now," he said.

"Too late for what? Just let me grab my clothes. I know Ethan will leave once I do."

Aidan shook his head. "No one is leaving. The estate is on lockdown."

Jenna stared at him. "Lockdown? Why?"

"The wolves. They're hunting tonight." He pointed to the moon. "It's full."

Okay...

"I'll be safe enough in the car. I'm pretty sure wolves can't open doors," she said, not bothering to hide her exasperation. "Now I need to hurry. There's no way Ethan will leave here without me."

Aidan stepped into her personal space. "There's no way he'll leave here with you."

Before Jenna could respond, he grabbed her and tossed her over his shoulder. She struggled to raise her head. "Aidan, what are you doing? Have you lost your mind?"

He didn't answer. Instead, Aidan carried her into the house.

"You need to put me down. This will only make matters worse."

Aidan climbed the stairs two at a time. He didn't put Jenna down until they reached his bedroom. The second he did, she backed away. "I have to go. If I leave now, I can try to salvage this situation."

He stalked toward her, his amber eyes glowing in the low lighting.

Jenna held up one hand. "Aidan, think about this logically."

"Oh, I am." The words had barely left his lips, when his mouth came down upon hers in a punishing kiss.

Large hands cradled her jaw as he tilted her chin to deepen the embrace. Jenna's head spun, as his lips pulled her under. Aidan's tongue darted into her mouth, igniting an inferno inside of her.

With the last of her strength, she wrenched her head away. "There's no time for this."

"There's *always* time for this." Aidan resumed his sensual assault. He devoured her with his teeth, his tongue, his lips. It was as if he couldn't get enough of her. He came up for air long enough to issue one final order. "Take your clothes off."

In that moment, Jenna knew she was lost.

Aidan's beast rode him hard. He couldn't stand the smell of the men on Jenna's clothes. The only scent that should be upon her was his.

He slowly backed her against the bathroom wall, kissing, tasting, and exploring every inch of her mouth along the way. She was protecting him.

Of all the things she could've confessed that was the last thing he had expected. Her confession sealed Jenna's fate, though she didn't quite know it yet.

Aidan didn't need protecting. All he needed was her.

When her shoulders touched the wall, Aidan lifted her by the waist. Jenna's thighs spread the second her toes left the ground. She automatically wrapped her legs around his hips. Aidan growled and his grip on her tightened.

She was his. *Theirs.* They'd marked her. No man could take her away from them.

A rending sound filled the silence as Aidan ripped the last of her clothes off and dropped them onto the tile floor. Within seconds, Jenna was naked. Her firm breasts quivered as they were crushed against his chest. Her heat seared his flesh.

"I want you," Aidan murmured. "I thought I lost you." He ground his hips into her soft folds and she whimpered.

"Aidan, we have to stop. Ethan isn't going to wait out there forever. He's desperate. He'll do anything to get to me." Her plea ended on a sigh as he slipped two fingers inside her moist channel.

"He'll have to go through me first." Aidan pulled his fingers out and brought them to his nose. He inhaled.

Jenna smelled of hot-spiced woman mixed with a hint of *wolf.* Aidan smiled to himself, licked the juices off, then plunged his fingers back inside of her.

Her body wept as Aidan drove Jenna higher and higher. "Don't ever leave me again." His voice was barely recognizable.

Aidan held her with one arm and shucked his clothes with the other, then he carried Jenna into the shower. Blindly, he turned the water on, needing to remove the other male's scent and replace it with his own.

The moon called to his beast to reveal himself. Aidan clenched his jaw and hung on to his humanity. He had to keep it together for a little while longer.

His hands were thorough as he lathered her up and rinsed her off. Aidan kissed her the whole time, not wanting to be separated.

The second she smelled like Jenna again, he lifted her up and shoved her back against the tile wall, bracing her with his big body. Without preamble, Aidan entered her.

"Mine!" he shouted, driving himself to the hilt.

Jenna cried out as his hard shaft slid home. Her body bowed, bringing her luscious breasts into view. Aidan leaned down and latched onto her nipple.

He sucked hard, drawing the tender flesh deep, then raked it with his teeth. Jenna sobbed. Her blunt nails dug into this back and she pulled him closer.

He'd almost lost her. Aidan was half out of his mind with rage and relief. His beast demanded that he take, he claim—he mark once more. His body shuddered as the moon commanded that he shift.

"Not yet!" he grit out.

Aidan rocked his hips and thrust hard, lifting her higher. His mouth came down upon hers, swallowing her cries. Jenna writhed against him, then her body convulsed.

She tore her mouth away and gasped. "Yes!" she shouted.

Aidan felt his shaft expand, locked in a velvet vise that he had no wish to escape. His body stiffened, then jerked. He felt his essence spill into her. This was where he belonged. Where Jenna belonged.

His gaze strayed to the mark on her neck. His mark. Aidan felt his teeth lengthen to sharp points. Blood roared in his ears as he licked the spot once, twice, then bit down.

Just like the first time, blood rushed into his mouth, firing his senses. Unlike their first night together, this time Jenna was totally aware of what was happening. Her breath hissed out of her lungs, as his sharp teeth held her in place.

Aidan expected her to fight him, shove his head away, or at least try to resist. Instead, Jenna did something that shocked and humbled him. She reached out and cradled his head, holding him to her body.

Overwhelmed with a tidal wave of emotion, Aidan's knees quivered, threatening to give out. He licked the wound, letting the water wash the blood away.

Jenna had given him the gift of trust. "Thank you," he murmured, nuzzling her neck. Aidan would remember this moment for the rest of his life.

Someone pounded on the door to the bedroom. Whoever it was didn't wait for Aidan to answer. Three of his men rushed into the room. Aidan slipped out of Jenna and pushed her behind him, ready to fight to protect her.

He turned the water off. "What is the meaning of this?" he snarled.

Bernie stepped forward. "The humans have breached the walls. They're inside the compound."

"Find them!" Aidan waited for the men to leave, then turned to Jenna. Her flushed face was now pale with fear. "I need you to wait here. Don't come outside no matter what you see or hear. It's not safe. The wolves will be out in force. When they are hunting, everything in the woods looks like prey."

"I'm not afraid of my wolf," she said.

He gazed down upon her, letting the emotions show that he did not dare speak aloud. "You should be. He's more dangerous now than he's ever been." Aidan kissed her hard, then rushed out the door...naked.

19

Wait inside while he goes off to face Ethan on his own. Naked. Not gonna happen.

Jenna wasn't stupid and she wasn't blind. She knew something seriously weird was going on with Aidan. She had no idea what it was, but she was determined to get to the bottom of the mystery just as soon as she saved him and her wolf.

Aidan had implied that he was just as dangerous as Ethan, but she didn't believe him. He'd gone out of his way to protect her. Now it was her turn to protect him.

Jenna quickly gathered her clothes and was about to get dressed, when she caught a glimpse of herself in the mirror.

So that's what it looked like to be ravished. Her gaze was drawn to the mark Aidan had left. The spot was more distinct now that he'd bitten her again. Deep enough to leave a scar.

She'd worry about Aidan's biting fetish later.

Jenna dressed quickly and opened the door. She took one step out the room and walked straight into Nic. She stumbled back.

"Nic?" Flustered by his sudden appearance, she asked, "What are you doing here?"

He glanced at the love bite on her neck. Nic's eyes widened in surprise, then his gaze dropped to the carpet. "Aidan asked me to look after you."

Jenna's eyes narrowed. "Really? Then why does it look like you're standing guard?"

Nic had the good grace to blush. "Standing guard is a form of looking after you."

"Funny," she deadpanned. "Now get out of the way. I have to stop Aidan."

Nic didn't budge.

"Seriously, big guy, I need you to move. Carl is armed." The words had no sooner left her mouth, when four shots rang out.

Nic jolted.

Jenna gasped, then shoved him out of the way.

"Wait!" he shouted. "Jenna, come back!"

She didn't look to see if he was following. Jenna kept running. She ran to the front door, then switched course at the last second. Nic cursed and slammed into the door, his size preventing him from easily changing direction.

Jenna sprinted for her room. She made it inside and locked the door. Nic pounded on the wood, demanding entrance.

She had no time to waste. Jenna bolted across the room and threw open the patio door. She could hear the wolves howling, the mournful sound ripping at her heart.

Had Carl shot at Aidan and his men or had he fired at the pack? What if they were hurt? Cold seeped into her bones until they ached. They had to be okay. For her there was no other option.

Jenna ran into the woods, stumbling over fallen tree limbs and crashing through bushes. She heard Nic behind her. He was gaining ground. He should've caught her by now, but for some reason he'd let her escape.

The sound of the howling grew louder. Jenna's eyes finally adjusted to the full moon's glow. She could see a clearing up ahead and shadows moving.

Jenna broke through the tree-line. There were two wolves lying on the ground, whimpering and crying. A dark stain spread rapidly beneath their bodies.

Carl brandished his pistol, swinging the gun wildly, threatening to shoot the next animal that moved. He aimed at a big, black wolf, standing in the middle of the pack.

Jenna recognized the animal instantly.

It was *her wolf.*

"No!" Jenna screamed and raced forward. She jumped in front of the wolf, before Carl could fire. "Don't shoot." She held up her hands, knowing that wouldn't stop a bullet.

Carl's hand shook. "Get out of the way. These aren't wolves. They're monsters."

Ethan's pale face registered shock and something else. His gaze darted frantically from wolf to wolf, as if he were waiting for something to happen.

The wolves continued to howl and snarl, baring their fangs. They slowly circled the men, searching for a weakness so they could attack.

"You shouldn't have shot them," Jenna said. "They weren't bothering anyone."

"Move aside," Carl said. "I can't get a clean shot."

Jenna stepped every time her wolf did, resting her hand on its head, so that Carl would never have a clear line of sight. "Just go!" she pleaded.

"You don't understand." Carl checked his ammunition.

No, she didn't understand what was happening, but right now Jenna didn't care. She just needed to protect her wolf. "Leave now and I'll come with you," she said.

The suggestion seemed to jerk Ethan out of his stupor. He held out his arm and gestured for her to come to him.

Jenna shook her head. "Not until Carl lowers his weapon."

"Do it!" Ethan shouted.

"But, boss," Carl said.

"I said do it!"

Carl lowered the gun barrel.

"He's put it down. Now come here," Ethan said.

Jenna took one step and Ethan lunged for her. He grabbed her around the throat and pulled her against his chest.

"What are you doing?" Jenna gasped. She tried to wiggle out of his hold, but it was impossible. He had a death grip on her.

Ethan's gaze remained locked on her wolf. "I'm not leaving here without her." He tightened his grip until she could barely breathe.

Jenna choked. "Who are you talking to?"

"Him." He pointed to her wolf.

"Are you insane? That's an animal," she said.

He shook his head vehemently. "No, it's not."

The black wolf's form shimmered like waves of heat rising from asphalt. Fur receded and disappeared. The process only took a few seconds. When it was over, Aidan stood naked in the clearing.

Jenna couldn't believe what her mind was telling her. It was like the film had snapped inside her brain. She knew what she'd seen, but the knowledge did not compute.

Magic wasn't real and werewolves didn't exist. Everyone knew that, even children, but she was all out of rational explanations.

"Jenna's not going anywhere," Aidan said. "Not with you. Not with him." His amber eyes glowed in the dark, reflecting the moonlight. "She's mine."

"It was you," she whispered. "All along."

He nodded, but his gaze never left the men.

"How?" she asked. "How is any of this possible?" It couldn't be. Jenna had to be suffering from a head injury. She was probably lying in a hospital right now. That was the only thing that made sense. Or it would, if Ethan's hand around her throat didn't feel so real.

Aidan didn't answer.

"Jenna's coming with me," Ethan said. "We have business that doesn't involve you."

Aidan stepped forward and the wolves fanned out. "If it involves her, then it involves me."

She shook her head. "Aidan, back away. I don't want anyone else to get hurt because of me."

"Not going to happen," he said. "You don't understand what you mean to me. What you mean to my people." His tone told her that he wasn't bluffing.

Jenna watched the wolves as they prepared to attack. "Ethan, let me go or you're going to die."

He shook his head and held her tighter. "Uh-uh, I'm going to expose your freak boyfriend and his friends." He indicated to the pack.

"That's unlikely given who your family is," Aidan said. "Their reputation has been carefully cultivated over the years. They're not about to let you or anyone else destroy what they've worked so hard to obtain."

"Carl's my witness," Ethan said.

Aidan gave him a sad smile. "It's my job to protect the pack from any and all threats."

"I knew you were a piece of trash, Jenna, but I didn't think you would sink so low that you'd actually fuck an animal." Ethan gestured to Aidan.

Aidan flinched and couldn't meet her gaze.

"Now we're getting out of here." Ethan took a step back. "Shoot him if he moves."

"No!" Jenna cried.

"I'm invoking Lycanian law," Aidan said. "Acknowledge if you accept my ruling."

The wolves began to howl.

Aidan's gaze moved from Ethan to Carl. He seemed unnaturally calm. "You are both a threat to the pack. This cannot be allowed."

Carl inched back, glancing over his shoulder, searching for a means of escape.

"Shoot him, damn it!" Ethan bellowed.

Carl raised the pistol and took aim.

Aidan gave an almost imperceptible nod.

Wolves leapt from the shadows, landing on Carl, ripping his gun out of his hand. They tore into his flesh, shredding skin and breaking bone in seconds. By the time they were finished, all that was left of the private detective was a pile of bloody clothes and a gold ring that had been on his pinky.

Aidan stared dispassionately at the macabre scene, then slowly looked at Ethan. "You now have a choice to make. You can let her go and leave this place never to return or you can join your friend in death."

"P-people are going to know what you've done," Ethan stammered.

Aidan took a step closer. "And what exactly are you going to tell them? That werewolves ate your hired hand?"

Ethan's mouth opened and closed as the reality of the situation hit him. His gaze pleaded with hers.

Jenna almost felt sorry for him. Almost. Her stomach churned as she stared at Carl's remains. It didn't have to end like this. They could've just left.

The nausea soon gave way to...*hunger*. Jenna's eyes widened, when her mouth started to water. She clutched her stomach.

"It's okay," Aidan said, looking directly at her for the first time.

But it wasn't okay. There was something seriously wrong with her.

"Make your decision, but know this before you do," Aidan said. "My wolves are everywhere—that includes your precious Vancouver. If you do anything to harm the pack or if you come after Jenna again, they will find you and they will do the same thing to you that they just did to that man."

The wolves snapped at his heels. Ethan tried to use Jenna as a human shield, but there were too many of them.

"I'll have your answer now, human."

Ethan looked at Jenna one last time, then shoved her away. Aidan caught her before she fell. Ethan didn't hesitate. He turned and ran into the woods.

"Follow him," Aidan said.

Several wolves peeled off from the pack and ran into the woods after him.

"Summon Gabe to tend to the injured."

Aidan was afraid to look at Jenna. Her green eyes had been so wide, she'd looked like a Manga character. He'd smelled her fear, but he couldn't do anything about it. She had to know the truth. The whole truth. In his gut, Aidan believed she was strong enough to handle it and what was to come.

He guided her through the woods back to the house. Aidan didn't touch her. She looked like she'd shatter if he did. Her teeth were chattering and sweat covered her skin.

"What's happening to me?" she asked without looking at him.

Aidan didn't answer. Instead, he walked her into the house and back to his bedroom. The second he closed the door Jenna began to pace.

"I'm the same man you had dinner with," he said. "The same one you made love to. I'm not an animal. Not in the way that he implied."

She glanced at him, but didn't stop moving. "My skin itches. It feels like bugs are crawling beneath it."

Aidan moved away from her, giving her some space. "I know this is a lot to take in."

Jenna stopped and glared at him. "You think? I just saw a man ripped into pieces by...by... What are you exactly?"

He sighed. "My people have had many names throughout the centuries, but we are called the Moonlight Kin." Aidan shrugged. "Humans have another name for us."

"Werewolves," she whispered. "The people in town were right."

Aidan nodded.

"But how? Werewolves don't exist." She started pacing again. "How could you have remained hidden without anyone finding out?"

"It's getting harder and harder to do with the technological changes, but we manage."

"I know you're telling the truth because I saw it with my own eyes, but the whole thing is preposterous. Are you sure I'm not lying in a hospital somewhere hooked up to tubes?"

"I assure you this is real," he said.

She stopped walking and stared at him again. "You bit me." Jenna placed her hand over his mark. "I thought it was just a weird fetish, but it's not. Is it?"

Aidan wasn't ready to discuss what the bite meant yet. Not until he had a better idea of how she was going to react. "Do you plan to return to Vancouver?"

The change of subject surprised her. She seemed to think about it a moment. "Getting my garage back was all I've been dreaming about for the last few months. Now, I'm not sure I want it anymore." Jenna crossed her arms over her chest. "Vancouver holds too many bad memories for me. Besides, what I've seen tonight isn't exactly something I can ever forget."

"No," he said. "This night will stay with you for the rest of your life."

She shivered. "What happens now?"

Aidan arched a brow. "That's entirely up to you."

"Would you really let me leave?" she asked. "I know your secret."

He stared at her a long time, trying to figure out how to answer. She did know his secret, but not all the secrets he'd kept. "You are not a prisoner, Jenna. I won't force you to stay." He might beg her to, but only as a last resort.

She bit her lip. "Good to know." Jenna started moving again. "Hypothetically, what would happen if I stayed?" she asked, then added, "Do you even want me to stay?"

"You already know the answer to that question," he said, feeling a glimmer of hope.

She took a tentative step closer. "Okay, then answer my other question."

"What do you want me to say?" he asked.

"I'm not like you, so how would it work?" She ran her hand along her arm to ward off a chill.

Aidan closed the distance between them. "Would you like to be?"

Jenna balked. "What are you going to do, raise a magic wand and presto-chango I'm instantly like you?"

"You watch too many movies." Aidan shook his head.

She sighed. "Maybe, but that doesn't change the facts of the situation. I'm not like you."

He brushed his fingertips along her jaw. "You could be, but once the process is done, it cannot be reversed."

"Would I be like you then? Like the others?" Her sharp teeth latched onto his thumb.

"Yes." Aidan smiled encouragingly. "You'd be part of the pack, part of the family—a very important part."

Everything was happening too quickly for her. Jenna knew she should slow down, but it felt like her blood was boiling in her veins and for once it wasn't because she was standing close to Aidan.

This was crazy. Insane. Any normal human being would run screaming from the house, but Jenna had never been typical. Nothing about her life had ever been normal. Aidan was offering her a chance to have a family. A real family for once in her life. Could she really pass that up?

She couldn't deny her feelings for the man. If she'd been in doubt, that ended when she thought Carl was about to shoot her wolf. Panic had overcome her.

In that moment, Jenna had felt such a profound sense of loss. It hadn't made sense at the time, but now she knew why. When she'd seen Aidan shift for the first time, all she'd known was relief.

"What would I have to do?" she asked nervously.

"Nothing." He shook his head and kissed her. "It's already begun."

Jenna's eyes widened. "The bite."

He nodded. "The bite."

"I thought that was a myth," she said.

He shrugged. "Some things have a grain of truth."

"You could've asked before you made that call, since it's my life we're talking about. I would've liked to have been consulted first," she said.

"I understand," Aidan said. "But it was out of my hands. The wolf had chosen its mate."

"My wolf?"

He smiled. "Your wolf."

"Will it hurt?" Jenna swallowed hard.

"A little," Aidan said. "But I'll make sure that all you remember from the change is the pleasure." He pulled her into his arms and kissed her, then made good on his promise.

EPILOGUE

Two months later…

Jenna took off through the woods, jumping over tree roots and racing around bushes. She could hear Aidan behind her, his panting breaths getting closer. He jumped out from behind a tree trunk.

She yipped and dodged right, slipping easily under a downed limb. Aidan barked and followed her. They raced through the woods, enjoying the pleasure of the night.

It had taken Jenna a while to get the hang of the change. She hadn't quite gotten to the point where she could control it, but she'd finally recognized when it was about to happen.

Aidan herded her toward his favorite spot. Jenna let him. It was a game they played that they both enjoyed. He shifted when he reached the small pool of water. Jenna did the same.

"That was fun. Let's do it again." She grinned at him.

"Soon." He brushed his lips over hers, stealing a kiss. His big hands slid down her body, resting on her shoulders.

Jenna sunk into the embrace, enjoying the sensual exchange.

Aidan's grip firmed and he…pushed her into the pool. Jenna came up sputtering and gasping. Gooseflesh rose over her skin from the cold water.

"Oh, you're in trouble now, mister." Her teeth started to chatter. "I can't believe you did that."

Aidan laughed. "I told you I'd pay you back when you least expected it."

Jenna bit her lip to keep from smiling. "Are you going to help me out of here?"

"And have you pull me in? I think not."

"Spoilsport." She laughed.

Aidan's head jerked to the right. "Don't move!" He growled and his body started to shimmer and shift.

The foliage parted and a huge behemoth of a man stepped into the small clearing. He stood a good four inches taller than Aidan and his shoulders were nearly a foot wider. His face was *Elfishly* pretty, but he had the body of a professional wrestler.

If you could get past the fear factor, he might be kind of cute. Though Jenna would never say so in front of Aidan.

The man had long white hair and silver eyes that moved like mercury. Jenna ducked down, until her head and chin were the only things visible.

Aidan stopped mid-shift. "Tristan? What are you doing here?"

"I've been sent by the Lycanian Elders to check on you and your new mate. A complaint has been filed." His shimmering gaze flowed from Aidan to Jenna.

"Let me guess, Robert LaBeouf?"

Tristan flashed teeth, but he didn't smile. Jenna had a feeling he rarely smiled.

"You know I cannot tell you who has filed the complaint," Tristan said. "Not until I've finished with my investigation." He took a step toward the pool, but Aidan cut him off with a deep growl.

"What exactly are you investigating?" His voice remained calm, but his body was tense.

"You are the second among us in the last several months who has chosen a human for a mate," Tristan said. "It has raised some concerns. We need to determine whether the anomaly is contained within your bloodline or if outside forces are at work."

Aidan stiffened. "Those concerns have not been brought to me. Odd, since I am still an Elder."

Tristan arched a snowy white brow. "For now."

"And if it's not my bloodline?" Aidan asked.

"There are others who do not care for our kind," Tristan said. "As an Elder, you know this."

Aidan paled. "The *Darkling* have not entered this realm for centuries."

"Yet, I've found signs that indicate otherwise." Tristan moved to go around Aidan, but he stopped him again.

"I will not harm her," Tristan said. "I swear on my family honor."

This time when he stepped to the side, Aidan didn't try to hinder his progress.

"I am Tristan Chevalier." He crouched down next to the pool.

Jenna ducked down even further. "Nice to meet you." She didn't extend her hand for fear she'd flash him. She hadn't gotten used to how at ease the wolves were with their nakedness.

Tristan smiled. "She smells like you." He sniffed. "So does the pup she's carrying."

Jenna's eyes widened. They hadn't told anyone yet. They were waiting, enjoying the moment for themselves.

"What are the *Darkling*?" Jenna asked.

"They are the stuff of nightmares." Tristan rose. "I will let the Elders know that your bond is intact and that you've bred true."

Aidan stared at him. "You do that." Sarcasm dripped from his words.

"Keep your eyes open," Tristan said. "If the *Darkling* are back, then we'll need all the strength we can muster."

"I will," Aidan said, glancing at Jenna with concern. "If they have returned, they will seek the Sighted Ones."

"I know." Tristan stepped into the woods. "It's why I intend to find them first."

Before he could disappear, Aidan stopped him. "Once the wolf makes its decision, there's nothing you can do to change its mind."

Tristan looked at him, his expression solemn. "I won't have to worry about that."

Aidan grinned. "Funny," he said. "I thought the same thing."

Tristan trembled like someone had walked over his grave, then his image wavered. A second later, a white wolf the size of a polar bear stood in his place.

He stared at Aidan with those fathomless silvery eyes for a moment longer, then silently raced into the woods.

Jenna struggled out of the pool of water. Gooseflesh covered her skin. Shivering, she asked, "Should I be worried?"

Aidan pulled her into his arms and held her close, then kissed her forehead. "No, Tristan's just being cautious. It's his nature. *Our nature.*"

She snuggled against his chest. "I get that, but what about the rest of it? The whole human-wolf, wolf-human thing?"

"Ah, that." Aidan laughed. "Tristan thinks he can outrun fate."

"If that were the case, then I wouldn't be the Alpha's mate." Jenna playfully nudged him in the ribs.

"No." He nuzzled her ear. "But you'd still be Aidan's mate."

# # #

THANK YOU NOTE

Thank you for taking the time to read *Moonlight Kin Vol. 1*! If you enjoyed Damon and Aidan's stories, then please consider leaving a **REVIEW** to let other readers know. If you've already left a good review somewhere, drop me an email to let me know, so I can thank you personally. For more information about upcoming books—including *Moonlight Kin 5: Lucien*, access to free reads, and surprise giveaways, sign up now for my newsletter at: www.jordansummers.com.

Moonlight Kin 3: NIC-Excerpt

A shadow of ash spread across the highway, staining the asphalt a deeper shade of gray. Fissure cracks appeared, threading their boney fingers wide until the earth bucked beneath Jerry Seaver's semi-truck. He clenched the wheel and fought to keep the heavy load from jackknifing on the road.

"Damn earthquakes," he muttered under his breath, but his heart continued to pound.

Thunder cracked in a cloudless blue sky. Jerry poked his head out the window. He squinted against the sunlight and looked around, but the only thing he could see was a green ocean of trees rocking gently in the breeze.

The fine hairs on his arms rose, along with the pressurization in the cab of his truck. Jerry's ears popped. His unease increased despite the natural beauty around him.

He wiped his hand across his grit-covered face and it came away moist. The highway stretched out in front of him with no cars in sight. There wasn't a town around for miles. Jerry was alone. The sudden change in the air reminded him just how isolated he was on this back road. Suddenly the shortcut he'd taken wasn't such a good idea.

He shifted gears and pressed his foot down. Smoke billowed out the semi's exhaust pipes as the engine strained to pick up speed. Jerry didn't want to be out here surrounded by oppressive woods any longer than necessary.

A half a mile in front of him the air shimmered like waves on a pond. It was too cool for the mirage to be heat rising from the asphalt. Jerry's foot eased off the accelerator and the truck slowed, but he wasn't about to stop. The glistening increased and the air yawned, opening wide to reveal its gaping black mouth.

"What the hell?" Jerry leaned forward to get a better look at…at…he had no idea what he was seeing. The sun gleamed off his red hood, but didn't penetrate the dark entrance ahead.

It wasn't real. It couldn't be.

"You're just tired," he muttered aloud.

Jerry rubbed his eyes and shook his head. He'd been driving for ten hours and hadn't gotten much sleep the previous night. He was determined to get to Vancouver today.

The crisp air worked to keep him awake, but wouldn't prevent hallucinations. This had to be one, because what he was witnessing didn't make sense.

He reached for his Red Bull and took the last sip. Moisture dribbled down his chin onto his shaggy beard. Jerry wiped his mouth with the back of his hand, then crushed the can and tossed it over his shoulder before grabbing another out of his cooler.

Jerry pressed the cold can to his forehead, then popped it open. He took a deep swallow, then checked to see if the *hallucination* still hovered above the road.

The tear had widened, revealing more of the gloom. If it got any bigger, it would swallow his truck. Something moved in the shadows. Fear plunged its icy fingers into him, locking on to his spine.

The gap expanded and someone—no, *something*—fell out, then the opening snapped shut.

Jerry was too close to stop and too scared to react. His truck barreled down upon the…he squinted…*creature*, striking the black mass. A loud bang filled the cab as the shadowy thing smacked the grille and flew through the air, landing on the side of the road.

He glanced into his side mirror to see where it had gone. The black creature rose, took a few steps, then collapsed in the lane.

Jerry crossed himself and prayed that it was dead. Whatever he'd struck wasn't human, wasn't of this world. He had seen where it had come from with his own eyes and he wasn't about to stick around to find out if it was okay. With his heart in his throat, Jerry shifted gears and tore down the road.

An hour later, he pulled his rig into the truck stop and washed the blood off the grill. By the time Jerry Seaver reached Vancouver, he had convinced himself that he'd imagined the whole incident.

1

Mindy MacDougal stopped her car next to the curb. Celina Gibson opened the passenger door and handed her the pepperoni pizza, then climbed in.

The aroma of tomato sauce, oregano, and sausage filled the small cab, making Mindy's stomach growl.

"I don't know if I can wait until we get to the house to have a slice," Mindy said.

Celina buckled her seatbelt, then reached for the warm box. "If I can wait, you can wait." She glanced at Mindy. "Isn't that Izzy's shirt?"

Mindy grinned. "Yep!"

"Can't believe she let you wear it. I tried to borrow it one time and she threatened to break my fingers."

"Yeah, Izzy is weird about sharing things. She never wants anyone to wear her clothes or use her stuff. Said it made them smell funny." Mindy laughed and put her blinker on, then pulled away from the curb. "If she didn't want me to wear her clothes then she shouldn't have left them in the closet when she moved out."

"I still can't believe she's gone," Celina said.

Mindy squeezed her hand. "I know you miss her, too."

Celina and Isabel had been best friends for a few years, then this last year Izzy pulled away. It was a pattern she repeated when anyone got too close. To soothe Celina's hurt feelings, Mindy had stepped in as a surrogate for her sister. She wasn't as good company as Izzy, but she did her best.

"She was always threatening to move. I just didn't think she'd go through with it. I mean, where else is she going to get such a sweet setup?" Celina asked.

"What do you mean?" Mindy glanced at her.

"You paid her rent. You did her laundry. You bought all the food. Isabel never had to do anything while you were around." Bitterness tinged her tone.

Mindy's face heated. "It was my choice. She never asked me to do any of those things."

"She never had to," Celina retorted. "Wish I had a younger sister like you."

Mindy sighed. How could she explain in a way that Celina would understand?

She hadn't always been the responsible one. There was a time when she and Izzy had been footloose and carefree. That was before Izzy's penchant for outlandish storytelling took a dark turn, before the expensive psychiatrists, before the psych meds, before all the experimental treatments.

Nothing their parents tried could eliminate Izzy's "visions" or quell her talk of monsters. To this day, her sister was utterly convinced of their existence.

The treatments did succeed in one area. They successfully changed Mindy and Izzy's relationship. Her role in the family dynamic evolved from close ally to her sister's keeper.

The change hadn't been easy for Mindy. At first, she'd chafed at carrying so much responsibility. She missed her freedom. She missed having fun. But there was only room for one bad girl at the table and Izzy had claimed the spot.

Now that Izzy was gone and Mindy was finally free, she didn't know quite what to do with herself.

Celina chewed on her bottom lip. "Did she at least say goodbye before she left?"

She did her best to hide her pain, but Mindy didn't think she was successful. "You know my sister. Goodbyes are so...responsible. She called you, though, didn't she?"

"Yeah, but she didn't tell me that she'd moved out," Celina said.

"Then what did she say?" Mindy asked.

"She told me to watch out for the monsters," she said.

Mindy rolled her eyes. "What's that supposed to mean?"

Celina shrugged and looked away, but not before Mindy saw fear in her eyes.

"Don't let her freak you out," she said.

"You know, this might turn out to be a good thing in disguise," Celina said. "You've been taking care of your sister for years. Izzy could do with a serious dose of reality."

Mindy knew she was right, but it would take some time to adjust to all the changes.

"She's your big sister. It's past time that she acts like it," Celina said.

"We're only a year apart," Mindy said. "Not exactly a huge gap."

"Doesn't matter. She's still older," Celina said. "Have you heard from her since she left?"

"She called Wednesday night, but I was at school," Mindy said.

"Did she at least leave a message?"

Mindy hesitated. "Yeah, sort of."

"Uh-oh. What did she say?" Celina asked.

Mindy sighed. "Maybe you can make sense of her message. She said the winds told her it was time to move on. That there was darkness coming."

Celina's perfectly shaped brow shot up. "The winds? Darkness? Last time I checked, wind didn't talk. And darkness"—she looked out the window—"comes every night. Did she tell you anything useful? Like where she was going?"

The question surprised Mindy. She thought for sure Izzy would've told her best friend where she was going. But one look at Celina's face made it clear that she hadn't. Weird. Should she tell her? She couldn't see any harm in letting her know.

"Apparently, the winds gave my sister directions to New Orleans." She laughed.

Celina gasped.

"What is it?" Mindy asked.

"Nothing," Celina said.

"Tell me."

"I just always wanted to go there. Izzy and I talked about it a lot. She said we'd run away there one day." Celina grew quiet. "Guess that won't be happening now. She'll fit right in down there."

That was what worried Mindy. What if Izzy didn't come back? What if there was no room in her 'new' life for her sister?

"I hope she's okay," Mindy said.

"You need to stop worrying about her," Celina said. There was sternness in her voice that hadn't been there a moment ago.

She was right, but the saying about old habits dying hard was true. "It's what sisters do," Mindy said quietly. She was surprised Celina wasn't more concerned given how much she knew about Izzy, but maybe she was in shock about New Orleans.

"I know you love her, but your sister is a flake. You have to live your own life now," Celina said. "It's past time Izzy learns to stand on her own two feet."

Mindy didn't want to think about Izzy anymore. It would mean examining her own sorry life. "So what's on the agenda tonight?" she asked.

"I thought we'd go for a Ryan double feature." Celina reached into her purse and pulled out two DVDs. "Dibs on Gosling."

"Man," Mindy said. "That's not fair."

Celina laughed. "Like settling for Reynolds is such a hardship."

Mindy glanced at her and smiled. "True. I wouldn't exactly kick him out of my bed."

"No woman with a brain in her head would."

Lights faded away as they drove out of town and made a right onto a back road that would eventually lead to Mindy's home.

Thick woods on both sides of the road swallowed what little light came from the headlights. Mindy cranked the radio and pressed on the accelerator. The miles rolled by.

Celina was doing her best pop princess impersonation when Mindy spotted the entrance to a long drive.

"Hey." She nudged Celina. "Is that the road you take to get to that club you're always talking about? Pits or something."

Celina stopped singing and looked out the window. "Yeah, that's it," she said reluctantly. "The place is called Sticks." She crossed her arms over her chest and sank down in her seat. "Izzy never really liked it. She said the place made her feel uncomfortable. She only went there a few times."

"Really?" Mindy asked. "I was always under the impression that Izzy liked it. Well, as much as she liked anyplace."

"No!" Celina said. "The only time she ever wanted to go there was when she had the urge to dance."

Dancing was one of the few passions she and her sister shared these days, but they rarely indulged in the activity at the same time.

"Can't believe that I've driven by the entrance so many times and never noticed it before," Mindy said. "For some reason, I could've sworn that you and Izzy told me it was on the east side." She was positive they had.

Celina laughed off her comment, then shifted in her seat. "You aren't exactly Ms. Observant," she remarked.

It was common knowledge around the animal clinic that Mindy was driven and focused, but only on work and school. What little time remained had gone toward caring for Izzy and protecting her.

Mindy stared at the entrance through her side mirror until it faded into the night. "Now that I know where it is I'll have to go," she said.

Celina cleared her throat and picked at the edge of the pizza box. "I'm not sure Sticks is your kind of place." She stared out the window as she spoke.

Mindy frowned. "What do you mean? You said it was fun. You told me there were tons of good-looking men. I know you've been going there just about every weekend with your friend Erin. Izzy went with you last week." She took a breath. "In fact, you've gone there with everyone but me."

"Isabel didn't have a good time," Celina said softly. "She hated it so much that she made me promise not to take you there."

Why would her sister do that? Mindy vaguely remembered Izzy coming home freaked out, but since that wasn't unusual, she hadn't been concerned at the time. Now she was.

Though she'd never shown it, Mindy's feelings had been hurt that Celina had never invited her to go with them to the bar. Had she asked, Mindy may have very well declined the invitation, but Celina had never bothered.

"Why would Izzy ask you to make that promise?"

"Why does Izzy say or do anything?" Celina asked, smoothly deflecting the question. "To find out the answer, you'd have to ask your sister."

They both knew that would never happen.

"Did anything unusual happen the last night you guys were there?" Mindy asked.

Celina readjusted the pizza box on her lap. "Not that I recall. It was a blast like always."

"Then I don't get why you and Izzy think I should avoid it," Mindy said.

"I can't speak for your crazy sister," Celina said. "But knowing you and knowing Sticks the way I do, I can honestly tell you it's not your type of place."

Why is Sticks great for Celina, but not for me?

Appearance-wise, they were polar opposites. Celina was tall, had long, dark hair, sun-kissed skin, a stunning face, and a trim figure that models would kill for.

Mindy had learned to live with being vertically challenged. Her curvy body was made for a different era—an era that didn't give side-eye to a woman who enjoyed eating a whole sandwich and a side of chips.

"Don't think you're going to get away with that answer without explaining yourself," Mindy said.

"You know what I mean," Celina said.

Mindy shook her head. "No, I don't. What exactly is *my* type of place?" She immediately pictured a library and rolled her eyes. How long had Celina and her sister been conspiring behind her back? It made her angry that between them they'd decided what was and wasn't good for her. How dare they after everything she'd done! She was the poster child for responsible behavior.

Celina's face pinched.

"Spill it!" Mindy wasn't about to let her off the hook.

Celina sighed. "You're more of a coffee bar kind of girl. Sticks is wild. Most nights it's a free-for-all."

Mindy's heart sank. "Are you saying I'm not any fun?" Celina wouldn't be the first one of her friends to imply she didn't know how to have a good time. Being her sister's keeper had left little time for a social life. The added responsibility had cost Mindy a lot of friendships over the years.

There were times, though—in the dead of night—that Mindy wondered if her sacrifice had been worth it. Wondered what would've happened if, just once, she had shrugged off her responsibilities and kicked up her heels.

Celina's brown eyes widened. "I didn't say you weren't fun," she insisted.

"No, you implied it." Mindy frowned as childhood taunts of "Monotonous Mindy" echoed in her head. She wasn't monotonous. Not anymore. She could have fun. There was no one to hold her back now. Tears unexpectedly made her eyes burn. She blinked them away before Celina noticed.

"I'm sorry. I didn't mean to hurt your feelings," Celina said. "It's just that Sticks isn't your typical bar. It's really rowdy. Fights are common.

Most of the guys that go there are...*different*. You're used to hipsters, not the kind of chest-beating, blue-collar he-men that frequent Sticks."

Mindy glowered. "I like he-men. I just haven't met many in real life." Try never.

She wasn't lying about being attracted to those types of guys. Or *any* type of guy, for that matter. It had been a long time since Mindy had dated. Her dry spell now resembled the Mohave. She was willing to try anything at this point.

"And I enjoy going to wild places on occasion," she said.

Celina snorted. "Name one wild place you've gone to. Seriously, just one. Before you answer, I want the dates, too, because I can't remember the last time you went to a rowdy bar," she said. "For as long as I've known you, you've planned your 'impulsive' moments."

"That's not true."

"Yes, it is," Celina said.

Heat spread up Mindy's neck and into her face. She took her eyes off the road. "Perhaps if you'd invited me to go along with you just once, we wouldn't be having this argument." Her voice cracked.

Celina patted her arm. "I told you that Izzy didn't want me to. She made me promise."

"Well, Izzy isn't here anymore. This isn't about her. This is *my* life we're talking about, not my sister's," Mindy grumbled.

Maybe Celina and Izzy were right. Maybe she wasn't any fun. Maybe her sister had inherited all the fun genes in the family. That would explain why Celina always took her other friends to Sticks and left her at home.

Celina glanced out the windshield and slammed her hands against the dashboard. "Mindy, look out!"

#

RELATED TITLES

Moonlight Kin 3: Nic
Moonlight Kin 4: Tristan
Moonlight Kin 5: Lucien (coming soon)

OTHER PARANORMAL TITLES

Phantom Warriors 1: Bacchus
Phantom Warriors 2: Saber-tooth
Phantom Warriors 3: Talon
Phantom Warriors 4: Arctos
Phantom Warriors 5: Linx
Phantom Warriors 6: Riot
Phantom Warriors 7: The Dark King
Phantom Warriors: Hawk's Slave
Phantom Warriors: Pit Fighters: Cage,
Atlantean's Quest 1: The Arrival
Atlantean's Quest 2: Exodus
Atlantean's Quest 3: Redemption
Atlantean's Quest 3.5: Atlantean Heat (Novella)
Atlantean's Quest 4: The Return, Paris After Dark

About the Author

Jordan Summers is a New York published author. She has thirty-two books to her credit and has sold over 155,000 ebooks. She's a member of the Horror Writer's Association, International Thriller Writers, and Novelist Inc. To learn more about the author's upcoming work and to get access to exclusive content, sign up for her newsletter at: www.jordansummers.com

www.ingramcontent.com/pod-product-compliance
Lightning Source LLC
Chambersburg PA
CBHW061618210726
48287CB00001B/193